The Absent Activist

A Norfolk Mystery

Copyright © 2019

All Rights Reserved

This is a work of fiction. Names, characters, businesses, places, events and incidents are either the products of the author's imagination or used in a fictitious manner. Any resemblance to actual persons, living or dead, or actual events is purely coincidental.

For more information on the author and more books, visit

http://www.markmckayauthor.com

Contents

PROLOGUE	1
CHAPTER 1	11
CHAPTER 2	24
CHAPTER 3	34
CHAPTER 4	48
CHAPTER 5	65
CHAPTER 6	82
CHAPTER 7	97
CHAPTER 8	110
CHAPTER 9	125
CHAPTER 10	142
CHAPTER 11	155
CHAPTER 12	173
CHAPTER 13	184
CHAPTER 14	200
CHAPTER 15	214
CHAPTER 16	229
CHAPTER 17	243
CHAPTER 18	255
CHAPTER 19	273
CHAPTER 20	289
CHAPTER 21	306
CHAPTER 22	323
CHAPTER 23	338
CHAPTER 24	354
CHAPTER 25	369
CHAPTER 26	386

Prologue

Norfolk, United Kingdom. 2018.

Sarah de Malmanche, a confirmed city dweller in her mid-thirties, had been living in a tree house in rural Norfolk for the last six months. Not exactly on a permanent basis. There were times when she'd leave the forest that she and twelve other environmental activists were occupying, so she could go back to her flat in Norwich, just for the luxury of a hot bath if nothing else. And she was working, of course, which meant she had clients to see quite regularly. She worked in alternative medicine as an Ayurvedic lifestyle consultant.

They called it a forest, but technically it was ancient woodland, and 100 hectares of it were due to be razed to the ground to make way for a new housing development. The rest of the development was made up of 500 hectares of agricultural land bordering the forest, where construction was already underway. When that first phase was done, the woodland would be cleared.

But not long after work began on phase one, a small group of young people moved into the forest and began building tree houses in the big oak trees. They draped banners across the branches announcing that 'Foxdown Wood stays!' and they built walkways between the trees, so they could get around without being caught out by anyone in authority on the ground.

Nobody bothered them at first, because nobody knew they were there. That changed when the local press got wind of what was happening, and sent a reporter out to get the story. Once the news broke, a somewhat astonished representative from the building firm that had been appointed to start construction showed up. He told the six people in the trees that they were trespassing and if they didn't leave, they would be evicted. A month later they were still there, and no effort had been made to remove them. But they knew that one day in the not too distant future, that would all change.

Sarah never read the newspapers, but she went online occasionally to check the news, which is how she found out about the 'forest sitters', as the *Eastern Daily Press* had dubbed them. She had no track record as an activist of any kind, but she was a paid up member of Greenpeace, and she supported their work and signed the online petitions that landed in her inbox on a regular basis. She was content to be an armchair activist who wanted to see the Arctic saved from reckless oil exploration, and the orangutans rescued from the palm oil producers of Indonesia. All done with the click of a mouse and a monthly payment to help bring it all to fruition. She couldn't get any more committed than that, though.

But when she read about the forest sitters, she got curious. It was close to home and she thought she would visit them. It was a half-hour drive to Foxdown Wood from her flat in Newmarket Road, so, one sunny spring morning, she got in her ancient Peugeot and set off. When she arrived at the car park on the outskirts of the wood, she was surprised to find that there were only a few other cars already there. She'd expected there to be more interest in the new residents. Undeterred, she locked up the car and set off along the main path into the forest.

It took her a while to find them, but eventually she heard signs of life off the main path, and she wound her way through the trees until she came to a small clearing. There were voices coming from above, and when she looked up she could see two tree houses, each one nestled 25 feet up between the branches of two tall oaks. Even from where she was standing they looked like well made, sturdy dwelling places. She was wondering just how you actually got up there when a rope ladder unfurled from above, and someone started descending. A minute later, she was face to face with him. He was tall and slim with blond hair and blue eyes, and she thought he was probably ten years younger than her.

'I saw you,' he said, in an accent she knew straight away was German. 'Are you friend or foe?'

'Friend, I think. I just wondered if you wanted some support.'

Which is how it all started. His name was Karl and he was there with his girlfriend, Bettina. It turned out that they were the ones with the tree house building expertise; they were veterans of a similar forest sit that they'd been involved with in north-west Germany. They had been trying to save an even more ancient forest from being cleared so the ground could be mined for lignite, or brown coal. The dirtiest fuel in Europe, as Karl described it. There had been protestors in the German forest for almost six years, before they were finally evicted on the orders of the mining corporation.

Now Karl and Bettina were passing on their knowledge to their English counterparts, who consisted of three men and one woman, all in their twenties. Only two of the men were local, the other man and woman came from Taunton in Somerset and they were members of Earth First!, an environmental group known for its radical approach to direct action. They weren't at all militant, though, and once they realised Sarah wanted to help, they invited her up to have a look around.

Now, six months later, she was a semi-permanent resident. There were four tree houses by this time, the latest two had been built in oak trees standing next to each other about 50 yards away from the original dwellings. Six more people from London and Norfolk occupied those; three men and three women.

It was August and it was hot; the summer had been sweltering this year. The tree sitters had got more publicity and visitors, and in the time since Sarah's arrival there had been three demonstrations organised, with people turning up from all over the country to stand on the edge of the wood, where it adjoined the agricultural land. They marched up and down and waved placards, and when they weren't doing that they sang and chanted 'Foxdown First!' for the TV cameras. By the time of the third demo, there were hundreds of them on site. So were the police, and so were the grim-faced people from the building company, and the development consultancy who had hired them. And during that third demo, people waving placards started running through the building site and occupying bulldozers, which is when the arrests started. For the first time, peaceful protest got bent out of shape. Some machinery was damaged, which made certain people very unhappy. And the atmosphere soured.

That had been a week ago. Over the months, Sarah had got into the habit of driving into Norwich to do her treatments and consultations during the day, and then coming back in the late afternoon. Occasionally she and Karl and Bettina would decamp to her flat for an evening so they could go out for a drink, or just chill out in relative luxury. Not that the tree houses weren't comfortable; they had beds and little stoves, and in this weather they were warm enough. The toilet facilities left a little to be desired; you had to come down to ground level and use an outdoor construction that was built over a deep hole in the ground. If you wanted a wash, you walked to a nearby stream and stripped off. All fine in the summer months, but in winter? Sarah wasn't so sure.

It wasn't a question that occupied her mind on that hot August evening. She had come out to the forest after a day's work in Norwich, to be told that everyone was going to the pub to celebrate a group member's birthday. She was tired and didn't really fancy drinking, so she said she'd stay and keep an eye on things. Karl and Bettina said they'd stay too, and keep her company. By 9 p.m., it was just the three of them. The others had set off on the walk to the Foxdown Village pub, and weren't expected back until the small hours.

The sun had gone down an hour earlier, and dusk was turning to night. The bird song dropped a notch, and the chattering of squirrels ceased. Soon, the wood would belong to the owls and badgers, denizens of the night. There was a full moon rising, and on nights like this the place took on an elemental, almost magical aspect. It became still, and the only sound was the rustle of the leaves moving with the night breeze, and an occasional shuffling in the undergrowth to betray the presence of some animal down below. It was spooky and calming all at the same time. Or that's how it struck Sarah. Spooky or not, it never stopped her from sleeping. She was in a tree house with Karl and Bettina, and the rest of the gang were still not back when they turned in for the night at 11 p.m. By midnight, they were all asleep. So, when something out of the ordinary happened then, they were taken by surprise. They were woken by a gruff male voice, coming through a megaphone.

'Come down now. Or the tree comes down. With you in it.'

The sound of chainsaws starting up stirred them into action. Karl rolled up the curtain covering the gap in one wall that served as a window, and leaned out.

'This is a peaceful protest,' he shouted. 'No violence! Leave us alone.'

Sarah joined Karl by the window. There was enough light from the moon to make out at least four men down below, all gathered around their tree. They were wearing overalls, and their faces were covered with scarves. If there were others out there as well, she couldn't see them.

'You have two minutes,' came the voice from the megaphone.

'Shit, what do we do?' said Sarah, her pulse suddenly racing.

'They won't do anything,' said Karl.

The chainsaws kept buzzing and the minutes passed. Then they started cutting into the tree. Karl looked down again.

'I don't believe it,' he said. 'I'll go down and talk to them.'

The rope ladder had been replaced by a system of cables and pulleys. You got yourself into a harness, and hoisted yourself up and down as and when you needed to. But there was only one harness for their house, so it was one person at a time. Karl pulled on his jeans and a shirt, and went outside onto the platform where it was all set up. A few seconds later, he was on his way down. Whatever he said when he got to the ground didn't stop the chainsaws. The oak tree had a thick trunk, and Sarah thought that even if it toppled it would only end up leaning against another tree, but that didn't give her much reassurance. The best thing to do was get the hell out.

'Bettina, it's just this tree they're working on. Go across the walkway to the other one.'

They were both dressed by now. Bettina was a pretty, dark-haired woman with serious brown eyes, which she turned on Sarah.

'You follow me straight after, yes?'

Sarah nodded. 'Yes, yes. Go!'

The walkway was a series of boards, secured on either side by ropes. There were additional ropes at waist height strung taut between the two trees, to help with balance. It was safe enough, but it required a certain amount of concentration when making the crossing. Bettina didn't hang around, she went out onto the platform recently vacated by Karl and stepped onto the walkway. Sarah watched her as she clutched the ropes on either side and walked the thirty feet it took to reach the platform on the other side. She made it without incident. Now it was Sarah's turn. She stepped out and began to walk.

She was halfway across when she heard a sharp, cracking sound. The tree she'd just left was moving, it had listed inwards and was bearing down on her. The walkway began to sway, and then the ropes holding the boards to the tree ripped apart. The walkway collapsed and Sarah had nothing left to step on but empty air. She screamed, and fell 25 feet to the unyielding forest floor below. When she didn't move, nobody knew if she was alive or dead. The chainsaws stopped and before Karl could intervene, Sarah was surrounded by the four men who had caused the fall.

'You bloody dickheads,' said one of them. 'This wasn't supposed to happen.'

He stooped over her to check for signs of life.

'She's breathing,' he said.

'Anything broken?' asked another.

'How do I know? She's unconscious. We need to move her, carefully.'

'Get an ambulance,' said Bettina, who was now on the ground. The men were so clustered around Sarah that she couldn't get a good look.

'I'm a doctor,' said the one doing the examination. 'I know what I'm doing. We will take care of it. Get the tarpaulin from the van, Dave.'

Dave wasn't away for long. When he returned, Sarah was lifted on to the tarpaulin and each of the four men took a corner. They carried her away, while Karl and Bettina watched in uncertain silence. Dave came back for the chainsaws.

'She's coming around,' he said. 'We're taking her to accident and emergency at the Norfolk and Norwich hospital.'

'I'm coming, too,' said Bettina.

'No, sweetheart, you're staying right here.'

They stared at each other. Dave's face was still covered by a scarf, right up to the eyes. They bored into Bettina, and she was the one who looked away first. Then Dave left.

And that was the last time Karl and Bettina saw Sarah.

Chapter 1

That same night around midnight, Sarah's twin brother Ralph sat bolt upright in his bed in London. He came out of a deep sleep into a state of full awareness. His sudden movement woke up the woman next to him.

'What are you doing?' she mumbled, in sleepy irritation.

He didn't answer. He stared straight ahead into the darkness as if he hadn't heard the question.

'Ralph?'

He shuddered. Then he wondered why. It was hot tonight, and the bedroom window was wide open. He could hardly be cold.

'Sorry,' he said. 'Something just happened.'

'What?' She sat up. 'Is someone here?'

'No, Holly. Nothing like that.'

She was still not quite with it. She leaned her naked body against his and put her arm around him. They'd been sleeping under just a sheet, which now managed to float away down the bed somewhere and disappear. The heat made nightwear redundant, and the sheet wasn't really needed either. Two bodies in close proximity generated more than enough warmth on a night like this.

'What is it, then?' she said. 'Did you hear something?'

He shook his head. 'No. I don't know what it is. I must have had a dream, but I don't remember anything.'

'So, what happened, then?'

He had a feeling. It was like he'd mislaid something and its whereabouts was making him a little anxious. He sighed.

'Beats me.'

She nibbled his neck. 'Idiot. Lie down. It's the middle of the night and I have to work in the morning.' She reached out for the sheet and couldn't find it. 'Never mind,' she said, and curled up on her side. Ten seconds later, she was fast asleep.

Ralph retrieved the sheet and covered them both. He lay on his back and stared at the ceiling. What was that all about? he asked himself. Probably nothing. But that anxious feeling was still there, hovering in the background. Must have been an unpleasant dream, he thought. Strange that I can't remember it. He closed his eyes, but unlike Holly, it took quite a while before sleep claimed him again.

When he woke up it was 8 a.m. and Holly was dressed, ready for work. She sat down on the bed next to him.

'You should have got me up,' he said.

'You were dead to the world. Besides, what have you got to do today?'

He looked at her. She had on her management uniform; a smart black jacket and matching skirt.

'Actually, Gerald said he had a job for me. Told me to come in about ten.'

She sighed. 'What, another surveillance job? Tailing cheating spouses?'

'Probably.'

She stood up. 'I wish you hadn't lost your real job. Well, whatever. I've got to go. See you tonight.'

She kissed him and walked out. A minute later, he heard the sound of the door closing. He yawned. Holly was five years younger than him and she was a career woman, a real go-getter. She worked in hotel management, and she had her trajectory to the top all mapped out. In a year or two she'd move from junior into senior management, and from there she intended to make her way right up to a seat on the board. Her life revolved around that aspiration. She was blonde, blue-eyed and attractive, and she had no qualms about using her appeal to get where she wanted to go. From his perspective she was feisty and fun, and made good money. Which was fortunate, because he didn't just now. He was lucky to have her as a partner, or at least that's what he told himself most of the time.

Until six months ago, he'd been a software developer at a start-up company in east London. They were developing virtual reality apps in the area of guided meditation, and Ralph had joined on the promise of stock options and instant riches once the company went public. Guided meditation, using a VR headset to enter a beautiful virtual setting, was taking off in the US and he'd been assured by the guys hiring him that they had a head start on the competition over there.

But it didn't quite work out that way. Instead, the venture capitalist backing the endeavour decided not to inject the next instalment of funds as promised, and the company collapsed. Twenty people found themselves unemployed, without a stock option in sight. He'd been working on what was considered a low salary in the tech sector, because he was going to reap the rewards later. Initially, he was sanguine about being laid off because he thought he'd find another job easily enough, but it hadn't materialised as yet. And to tell the truth, he wasn't looking as hard as he should. Writing code was OK, but it didn't exactly set his world on fire. He had some money saved, but Holly was picking up two thirds of the rent on their one bedroom flat in Greenwich right now. At first it hadn't bothered her, but after six months her generosity was wearing thin. And it was showing.

He might no longer have a 'real' job, as she put it, but in the meantime he'd got a part-time one through a friend. And it was about as far removed from programming as you could get; surveillance work with a private detective agency in Catford, south London. The Catford Investigation Agency, no less. South London's answer to the CIA, as he liked to think of it. And now it was time to get up, get showered, and turn up for work at that establishment.

But he couldn't bring himself to get out of bed. Whatever it was that had woken him in the night was still preying on his mind. Something wasn't right, and a split second later he thought of Sarah. Had something happened to her? There was no logical reason to think so, but once the thought entered his mind it refused to go away. Easy enough to find out, of course. All he had to do was call her.

He made himself get up. Shit, where was his phone? He put on a pair of shorts and went into the lounge, all the time conducting an internal monologue with himself. Why hadn't it occurred to him last night that something might have happened to Sarah? Because he didn't want to know, that was why. The last time they'd spoken they'd had a fight, and he was still pissed off with her. He was expunging her from his memory, as if such a thing were even remotely feasible. They'd been in each other's heads since birth; they thought the same thoughts and felt the same feelings. It had its advantages, but at times it felt claustrophobic. If one of them did something the other didn't approve of …

He found the phone on the kitchen table. It had been a month since they'd spoken on the phone, and on that occasion he learned that the something Sarah didn't approve of was Holly. Never had, apparently. The annoying thing about it was that he hadn't known Sarah felt that way. For Christ's sake, he thought, she waited two years to tell me that? If she'd said something right at the beginning

… He found Sarah's number and hit the dial key. It rang twice and then went to voicemail. He left a message.

'Hi, it's me. Call me when you get this.'

She's probably fine, he thought. But he was still worried. Who else could he call? No point in calling his parents, they were in France and neither he nor Sarah ever visited them anyway. Too much bad blood. There was Sarah's friend Chloe, of course, but he didn't have her number. He had some photos of the three of them together on his phone, on a night out in Norwich. He brought up his photos and swiped through until he found the one he wanted. Yes, out on the lash in one of Norwich's many pubs. The Unthank Arms, if he remembered it right. They were standing together at the bar and he was in the centre, with a girl on each arm. There was no mistaking the similarity between Sarah and himself. They both had dark hair and brown eyes, and they were both tall and slim, with narrow faces. Their cheekbones were identical. In repose, Sarah's face had a touch of melancholy, while he had a slightly closed, impenetrable aspect to his expression. On this occasion they were both smiling, and Chloe, who Ralph actually fancied more than he should given his attached status, was grinning. She was black-haired and blue eyed and she had a sensual mouth, not to mention a wicked sense of humour. He liked her. Why didn't he have her number, damn it?

There was nothing to do until Sarah called him back. If that didn't happen in the next few hours, then he'd really be worried. In the meantime, he had to go to work. He left the phone on the table and then went and had a shower. After that he put on a suit, because most of his surveillance jobs involved walking around central London and according to Gerald, who was one of the two senior partners at Catford Investigations, it was the most nondescript if not downright bland form of attire you could wear in a city setting. It helped you blend in.

He took the train to Catford Bridge. It meant changing trains at Lewisham, but if there were no delays it was a twenty-minute journey and it was much less hassle than taking the car. You could never find a parking space. When he got to Catford Bridge station it was only a five-minute walk to the office, and he arrived with time to spare.

The office was actually a house located in a side road off the North Circular, one of London's ring roads. It belonged to Gerald and Sandra Devonshire, the owners of Catford Investigations. The ground floor had been converted into office space and consisted of a reception room, two meeting rooms, and an open plan area with desks and the usual office equipment. Ralph rang the bell, and when the buzzer sounded he pushed the door open and went in. If Sandra wasn't out working then she would normally be the one on reception, but today it was Vivian, a young Afro-Caribbean woman who came in whenever she was wanted. She looked up at his approach.

'He's expecting you,' she said. 'Room two.' She gesticulated in the general direction of room two.

'I know where it is, Viv. You OK?'

She nodded, but her face said otherwise. Vivian had her moods; she was married with two kids and her husband wasn't around much. No one knew exactly why. All Ralph knew was that if Viv was in a bad mood it was usually because her man was at home this week. Driving her and the kids mad, she once told him. He hadn't asked for details.

He knocked on the door of room two and went in. It wasn't a big room, and more than four people would have made it feel crowded. Two landscape prints adorned the white-painted walls and there was a sash window at the far end, in front of which was a wooden desk. Behind it sat Gerald. The desk was rather bare, and in Ralph's opinion it served no purpose other than to separate Gerald from whoever he was talking to. There were two high-back leather office chairs in front of it. Ralph swung one around to face his boss and sat down. He stole a look at one of the prints, which showed a view over the idyllic English countryside of 1800, with an Abbey in the distance.

'You like it?' asked Gerald. He was a grey-haired ex-cop of around 55, with slate-grey eyes to match the hair, and a round, rosy face.

Ralph had always thought he looked too jolly to be a detective inspector, which was his rank when he retired early and then shortly afterwards went into the private detection business. Looks were deceptive, though. Gerald was rarely jolly.

'I guess so,' said Ralph. 'I'm not a great one for landscapes.'

Gerald guffawed. 'Didn't know you were an art critic, Ralph. That's Turner, mate. One of the greats. Gives the place some ambience, and has a calming effect on the clients. But I didn't ask you in for your art expertise. Got something for you.'

'Great, what is it?'

Gerald opened a drawer and took out a brown folder. He pushed it across the desk. Ralph picked it up and opened it. There was a sheet of paper and a photo inside.

'That is Valerie Marshall,' said Gerald. 'Forty-two years of age, works in the City for an insurance firm. Her husband Rodney thinks she's cheating on him. Wants us to follow her and find out if he's right.'

Ralph examined the photo. It was a shot taken on what must have been a night out. Valerie was standing by a window in what looked like a hotel ballroom, he could see a dining table nearby with silver setting and folded napkins. Next to her was a dark-haired man in his mid-forties, in a black tuxedo suit. She wore a long, strapless black dress with a silver necklace and matching earrings, and she had light skin and auburn hair.

'This the husband next to her?'

'Yes. That was taken at some insurance awards thing, last year.'

'What makes him think she's cheating on him?'

Gerald shrugged. 'He told me that she suddenly started working too much. Coming home late when she'd always kept 9-5 hours. Then there were the nights out with the girls, except he knows one of the girls and she didn't remember being out with Valerie on one of the nights in question. Anyway, he ended up searching through her clothes and he found that card.'

The A4 sheet had the address of Valerie's company on it along with some personal details about her. There was a business card clipped to it.

'Poseidon Hotel,' said Ralph. 'What's incriminating about this?'

'It's five minutes' walk away from her office. They do rooms in the afternoon and evenings for two to four hours. You know, *cinq à sept*, as the French like to call it. You must be familiar with the concept.'

'Because I'm half French? I don't need a hotel room by the hour if I want to get laid.'

'I'm sure you don't, Ralph. Anyway, she has lunch at 1 p.m. Put yourself outside her office and see what transpires. If nothing does, try again at 5 p.m. She might go straight after work.'

'And if she doesn't? What else does he want us to do?'

'Nothing, unless he asks us to. Now, grab the surveillance kit with all the camera gear and get going.'

Ralph took the folder with him back to reception. The surveillance kit was ready and waiting for him.

'Sign for it,' said Vivian. She managed a smile this time.

'Give me a pen then.'

He signed and slung the bag over his shoulder. It contained a digital camera that took clear video and still shots from up to 100 yards away, a voice recorder in the shape of a pen, a key fob camera, and two GPS trackers.

'See you tomorrow, Viv.'

It was only 10.15 a.m. He had plenty of time before he had to be outside Valerie's office in the City of London. He decided to walk down to the High Street and find a coffee shop. It was shaping up to be another scorching day, and when he found a Starbucks he went in and ordered an iced coffee. He spied a vacant table in the corner and grabbed it. Then he took off his jacket, which he draped over the back of the chair. Once he'd collected his order and taken a few sips of cold caffeine refreshment, he decided to try Sarah again. This time, the number was answered. But it wasn't his sister.

'I'm looking for Sarah,' he said. 'It's her brother, Ralph.'

'Oh, I'm Bettina,' came the reply.

Then there was a silence. No explanation as to why she was answering Sarah's phone. Ralph was a little confused.

'OK. So, where's Sarah, then?'

'I ... I don't know.'

'What do you mean? What are you doing with her phone?'

'It was in her bag. I have her bag, I brought it with me to the hospital to give to her. I'm at the Norfolk and Norwich with my boyfriend.'

She sounded perturbed, and by now, so was Ralph.

'What's Sarah doing in hospital? Is she alright?'

'Oh, my god, how to explain?'

There were a few words to someone in German, a language he was reasonably familiar with. But he couldn't make out what she was saying. Then she came back to him.

'Ralph, I'm sorry. There was an accident last night in the forest. Sarah fell from a tree and some people said they were bringing her to this hospital. So, we have come here this morning to see how she is.'

'The forest? Oh, yes, she told me about that. There was an accident? How the hell is she?'

'That is the problem, we don't know. They have no record of a Sarah de Malmanche being admitted. She isn't here. She has disappeared.'

Ralph was dumb with shock for a few moments.

'Ralph? Are you there?'

'Bettina, I'm coming up to Norwich. I'll call Sarah's number when I get there. Do you understand?'

'Yes, yes. I will keep the phone with me.'

He disconnected. He sat there trying to process what Bettina had just told him. I knew it, he thought. Shit. He took the straw out of the iced coffee, removed the lid, and drank the lot. A few cubes of ice hit the floor, but he didn't notice. Then he picked up his jacket and walked out. He wasn't sure where he was going at first, and then he realised he was on his way back to the office to return the surveillance kit. There was no way he was going into London now to follow Valerie Marshall. He quickened his pace and by the time he reached the office, he was running.

Chapter 2

Ralph was in a state of mild panic when he got back to the office. Vivian was taken by surprise.

'Ralph, what's wrong?'

He slung the kit bag on her desk.

'Sorry, can't do the job. Just had some bad news and I have to go to Norwich, right now.'

'What's happened? Tell me.'

The door into the main work area opened and Gerald appeared.

'Thought I heard something. Ralph, you don't look too good. What is it?'

Ralph told them what had happened. It all came out rather fast, but they got the gist of it.

'Your sister fell out of a tree? Are you serious?' said Gerald.

'I know it sounds crazy,' replied Ralph. 'She should be in hospital, but it looks like she never got there.'

'Sit down,' said Gerald. 'Tell me again.'

Once he understood, Gerald took control of the situation.

'Alright, mate. I'm sure there's been a mix up. Who took her to hospital?'

'I don't know … "Some people" was all I was told. I need to sort this out.'

'Off you go, then. I'll see if Brett can do Valerie Marshall. Let me know what you find out.'

Brett was the friend who'd got Ralph this job. He was a computer consultant, and he'd installed all the hardware at Catford Investigations. He did the odd surveillance job as well.
'OK, sorry about this. I'm out of here.'
He walked to the station and didn't have to wait long for a train. When he got back to the Greenwich flat, it was 11.30 a.m. The first thing he did was swap the suit for jeans and a T-shirt. Then he threw his laptop and some clothes into a sports bag and checked his wallet. Only £20 in there, but if he needed petrol his credit card would do the job. The last thing he wanted were the keys to Sarah's flat. She'd given him a set ages ago, in case for whatever reason she wasn't around and he needed access. He'd never used them, so it took several minutes of rummaging through drawers until he found them.
He took a last look around. He had everything he needed. He thought about phoning Holly, but she didn't like him calling her at work. She thought that taking personal calls during working hours made her look unprofessional. I'll call her tonight, he decided. On that note, he picked up the bag, grabbed the car keys, and left.
Norwich was about 130 miles north-east of London, and an hour later he was driving his BMW 3 Series up the A11. The trip usually took no more than two-and-a-bit hours, so he'd be there by mid-afternoon at the latest. Ralph knew Norfolk reasonably well, and that was due to previous visits he'd made to see Sarah since

she moved there six years ago. The last time he'd seen her was last Christmas. Holly had been working over Christmas and New Year, much to Ralph's disappointment. Ralph had no family in London, and neither he nor Sarah were keen to go to France to see the parents, so he let Holly get on with it and went to Norwich instead. The photo in the pub had been taken during that visit. Then in the spring, Sarah had called him in London and told him about her move into environmental activism.

'I'll be living in a tree house,' she'd said. 'Not all of the time. We're starting a Facebook group to get support, and you remember Chloe? She's going to help me with it.'

'Living in a what? And what about your work?'

'I can still do that. I'll have my phone, so I can take appointments and manage everything. And it's doing something meaningful, Ralph. It's not like Norfolk needs another housing development. A garden village, they're calling it. It's ridiculous. It's just another bunch of developers out to make money, and to hell with what they destroy in the process …'

He couldn't fault her enthusiasm. He knew she was a supporter of environmental causes, but this kind of active involvement was taking it to a whole new level. Like most other people, he was aware of the issues around global warming and climate change, but it had never occurred to him that he could do anything much to change what he thought of as inevitable. Temperatures would go up along with sea levels, and the whole world would find a way to adapt. They had to. Ralph de Malmanche couldn't change that, and nor could his sister. He couldn't help admiring her effort to try though, even if he thought that saving a little forest in rural England wasn't about to dramatically lower C02 emissions.

He didn't tell her any of that. Instead, the conversation switched to Holly and her insistence on working over Christmas. Sarah was a bit annoyed that Holly hadn't taken time off to celebrate, and be with family. She said that Holly was selfish and had her priorities wrong. And that she was intolerant of other people who didn't share her work ethic.

'And she's unimaginative, Ralph. She doesn't read or like music. She doesn't even like movies. It's all about work and money with her. What on earth do you two talk about?'

He'd been a bit shocked by this unprovoked character assassination, and tried to defend his girlfriend.

'She comes from a poor background. They never had money and so she's terrified of not having it herself. If she's obsessed with being successful, she has a good reason for it. You've only met her a few times, so I don't think you can judge her on such brief acquaintance. What gives you the right to judge her anyway?'

'We don't have money either, Ralph. I'm sorry, I just don't like her. You can do much better.'

It went downhill from there. In the end, he told her to get lost and hung up. He was angry. His sister's opinion mattered to him, and it hurt when she chose to attack the woman he'd spent the last two years with. Perhaps Holly was a little unimaginative at times, but still ...

Echoes of that conversation were in his head as he came up to the Thickthorn roundabout, where the A11 as a motorway ended. From there you could go left towards Kings Lynn, right to Great Yarmouth, or straight ahead into the city of Norwich. When the lights changed to green he went straight ahead, and a minute later he passed the sign telling him he was entering a UNESCO city of literature. It also said he was entering a 'fine city', which never failed to amuse him. Then he was on the Newmarket Road, where Sarah's flat was.

It was a straight road into the heart of town, lined with tall trees on either side. It formed an avenue of greenery on this hot summer's day, and when you looked at some of the rather beautiful old Victorian houses on this road, you might be forgiven for thinking you were entering a very fine city indeed. But Ralph knew that not all of Norwich lived up to this architectural promise.

Sarah lived in one of the beautiful houses, which had been converted into flats in the 1970s. The conversion hadn't spoiled the character of the building, which consisted of eight flats. Sarah's was on the top floor. He was approaching the house, so he indicated and then pulled into the driveway, where he found a parking space on the gravelled forecourt.

He didn't run into anybody when he opened the front door and went up the two flights of stairs to Sarah's flat. They were probably all out at work, he assumed, and he didn't know any of them anyway. He noticed how hot it was up here in comparison to the coolness of the entrance hall downstairs, and when he got inside, the place was stifling. First thing he did was open some windows. He sat down on the big sofa in the living room and got out his phone.

What to do first? Go to the hospital, which was only a five-minute drive away, or go and meet this Bettina woman and get all the details about Sarah's accident? He decided to call Bettina, and she answered straight away.

'I'm in Norwich,' he said. 'Where are you?'

'We are back at Foxdown Wood. We need to start building a new tree house.'

'Did you find anyone at the hospital who knew anything about Sarah?'

'No, we didn't.' She sounded anxious.

'I'm coming to see you. How do I get to Foxdown Wood?'

She gave him the post code of the closest village and he typed it into Google Maps. The directions were easy enough. Before he left, he had a wander around the flat, just to see if anything had changed since his last visit. The place had two bedrooms; Sarah's was at the back. It was tidy enough, apart from a pile of what looked like recently washed dresses and an assortment of tops on the bed. Nothing new or different in here, he decided. He went to the window, which had a good view over the rear garden. He saw a lawn burnt almost to a crisp by the current heat wave, flower borders full of shrubs, and two tall, leafy lime trees. Apart from a few fat pigeons sunning themselves on the lawn, there was no one out there.

Then he checked the second bedroom, which was where he stayed when he was here. Sarah also used it as a treatment room, so it had a massage table and a chest of drawers in there. There were bottles of various oils on the chest, and there was a desk and two chairs in one corner, where she did some of her consultations. Mostly, she worked out of a practice room in the city. There was a mattress leaning up against the wall, which served as his bed when he was here. He'd have to lay it on the floor and find some sheets and covers later.

The living room was the only place that had an anomaly, and that was a guitar. A very nice Martin steel-string, on a stand by the bookcase. It didn't belong to Sarah, unless she'd taken up guitar playing lately. He walked over to the big front window. He could see the BMW down below, but the road he'd turned in from was screened off by a huge red beech tree, which was probably as old as the house. It dominated the view from up here. Finally, he did a quick sweep around kitchen and bathroom. There was a bottle of mineral water in the fridge, which he grabbed, and then he left the flat and went back to the car.

When he arrived at the Foxdown Wood car park some forty minutes later, Bettina was there to meet him. He introduced himself, and then she led him along the paths to the clearing where the tree houses were. He could see that the trunk of one big oak tree was partially cut through, and now the tree was leaning precariously against the branches of the one next to it. There were people up in both trees, and they were dismantling their houses. Others on the ground were picking up boards and mattresses and other belongings as they were lowered or thrown down to them. One of the men involved saw Bettina and Ralph approaching. He came to meet them.

'This is Karl,' said Bettina.

'Ralph de Malmanche.' They shook hands. 'How many of you live out here?'

'Thirteen. Actually, twelve now. There were six of us in this spot, until last night. The others live down the path a bit.'

Ralph took a good look at the people he could see at that moment, which meant those at ground level. There were three of them gathered around the trees, picking things up. Two women and a man. They were all wearing shorts and T-shirts in the heat, and they seemed to him to be quite young. He looked up at the activity going on in the branches, and tried to imagine Sarah living up there. Knowing her, she'd have treated it as some sort of mini-adventure. Until it went wrong.

'Have you reported what happened to the police?' he asked Bettina.

'Not yet. We didn't know what to do when we couldn't find her at the hospital. We just thought it was some kind of mistake.'

'Well, we need to report it. But tell me exactly what happened last night.'

He listened to the story and realised that his sudden waking up in London corresponded pretty much to the time of the attack on the tree. He didn't mention it to Bettina, who was the one doing the talking. There was something he couldn't quite get his head around.

'You just let them take Sarah away?'

They both looked a bit shamefaced. Karl replied.

'It was just the three of us here. Bettina wanted to go with Sarah, but they wouldn't let her. And they had chainsaws. They were prepared for violence, and we are pacifists.'

Ralph looked at them. He was seething inwardly, but there was no point in letting it show. And he knew it was all too easy to criticise them in hindsight. It made no difference now, anyway.

'We're going to the police, right now,' he said. 'You need to tell them what you just told me.'

'Bettina will go with you,' said Karl. 'We have a lot of work to do here. I need to stay.'

'So, what will you do if these guys come back again? You'll just let them finish what they started last night?'

Karl looked grim. 'No, this time we will be organised. We are discussing it now.'

Ralph turned to go, but Bettina was hanging back. She said something to Karl in German. Ralph didn't let on that he understood. He and Sarah had known Germans when they were young, growing up in France. Bettina was saying that she didn't want to go to the police by herself.

'You must go,' replied Karl, still in their native language. 'You need to tell them that Sarah's injured. Maybe even …'

Bettina didn't reply. She spoke to Ralph instead.

'OK, let's go.'

They headed off, back to the car park. Ralph had picked up on Karl's unspoken possibility. He'd seen the height that Sarah must have fallen from and was forced to admit what he'd been suppressing all this time; that Sarah might be dead. Which would account for why she never got to hospital. But he wasn't prepared to accept it as a fact. Not yet.

Chapter 3

The nearest police station was in Reepham, a small market town only ten minutes' drive away. It was on the corner of a residential road, and it looked like someone had just converted the ground floor of a two-storey terraced house into a police station. If there hadn't been a sign above the door telling him that it really was Reepham Police Station, he'd have thought it was a corner newsagent's shop. Perhaps it was, before the police got hold of it. He parked the car, and they went inside and stood at the counter. Nobody around. He was looking for a bell or some way of announcing their presence, when a door opened somewhere and a moment later a woman appeared, wearing the uniform of the Norfolk Constabulary; a hat with a badge and black and white checks around the rim, and a short-sleeved black blouse with matching black trousers.

'I'm PC Whitlock,' she said. 'What can we do for you?' She smiled. She was a pleasant-looking woman in her mid-thirties.

'We've come to report a missing person,' said Ralph. 'My sister.'

The smile vanished. 'Missing since when, sir?'

'Since last night. Tell her what happened, Bettina.'

Bettina repeated the events of last night. As she did so, PC Whitlock's eyebrows rose in either amazement or disbelief, Ralph wasn't sure. When Bettina was done, she had a few comments to make.

'You're one of the protestors in Foxdown Wood, aren't you? Technically, you know, you shouldn't even be there. And you should also know that policing your demonstrations has cost some of my colleagues their weekends.' She sighed. 'But let's concentrate on what you've told me. Four men with covered faces not only tried to cut down a tree, but also carried away this gentleman's sister, a Miss Sarah …?'

'De Malmanche,' said Ralph.

PC Whitlock jotted this down. Ralph wondered if she'd got the spelling right, but she was talking again, so he didn't interrupt her.

'Ms de Malmanche fell from a tree and was on her way to hospital with these men, but never arrived. This all happened less than twenty-four hours ago, is that correct?'

Bettina told her it was correct.

'So, perhaps she went home? Or to a friend's house? Have you tried calling her?'

'She was badly injured,' said Ralph. 'She wasn't in a state to go anywhere. And she didn't go home. I know, I've been there. And she doesn't have her phone with her. We've got it.'

PC Whitlock thought about this for a while.

'Alright,' she said. 'Give me your details and some details about Sarah, Mr de Malmanche. What's your name, Miss?'

'Bettina Kaiser. I'm from Germany.'

'Is that so? OK, I'll get on the phone and someone will come and take some information from all of you who were present last night. It will also help if you can keep everyone away from the scene of the incident. After that, the officer in charge will want to speak to you, Mr de Malmanche. Right now, let's fill in a missing person's report.'

Once Ralph had given PC Whitlock all the relevant details, they left. On the way back, Ralph had a few questions.

'How can you afford to come over from Germany and live for months at a time in the forest?'

The question seemed to startle her a little. 'We … don't need much money. We manage.'

'And that's the same for everyone else, is it? Or are they all on jobseeker's allowance?'

Bettina shrugged. 'I don't really know, Ralph. Is it important?'

'Probably not.'

She changed the subject. 'That police officer didn't like me. I wonder if she knows about the demonstration this weekend.'

'What demonstration?'

'We have invited people to show their support. That's what we usually do. And we get a lot of support at the moment. It's all on the Facebook page. Search for "Save Foxdown Wood" and you'll see for yourself.'

'I will.'

They didn't have much else to say to each other for the rest of the journey back. When they arrived, Ralph walked back to the clearing with Bettina and collected Sarah's things. Apart from her bag and her phone, there was nothing other than a couple of books and a carrier bag with a change of clothes in it, and some toiletries. He deposited it all on the front seat of the BMW and drove back to Norwich.

At the flat, he sat down in the living room again and wondered what the hell he was going to do next. He felt restless. After a bit he got up and just stuck his head in all the rooms, as though he expected something to jump out at him and explain this catastrophe. It didn't, so he went back to the sofa. Then he got up again, retrieved his laptop from his sports bag, and plugged it in. Sarah's wi-fi was up and running and he'd connected to it before, so there was no password to worry about. He brought up the browser and went straight to Facebook.

He found the 'Save Foxdown Wood' group and scrolled down the page. There were photos of the most recent demo, which was only a week ago, he noticed. And more photos of people in their tree houses, drinking tea or just lazing around on their mattresses. The notice for the next demo was at the top of the page, and above that was an option to join the group. He clicked on it. He'd have to wait for an administrator to approve his application to join before he could post anything, not that he really wanted to. He wanted to message Chloe, because he'd remembered Sarah telling him that Chloe helped her run the group.

Then he clapped himself on the head. He had Sarah's phone, and it wasn't password protected. Chloe must be there in her contacts list. He fished Sarah's phone out of her bag and started looking. Yes, there she was; Chloe Miller. Who probably didn't even know Sarah was missing. Chloe was a massage therapist, and she worked out of the same practice rooms as Sarah. He called her but only got voicemail, so he said he was on Sarah's number and could she call him back, it was urgent. She came back to him half an hour later.

'Ralph, how are you? Did you lose your phone? What's so urgent? Sorry I couldn't take your call, I had a client with me.'

He told her what had happened. There was a stunned silence at her end.

'Chloe? You there?'

'That's awful, Ralph. Is it really true?'

'It must be. Sarah has disappeared, I know that much.'

'Did you say Bettina told you all this?'

'Yes, and she told the police as well.'

'Right.' There was silence for a bit. 'I need to speak with her,' she muttered. 'I've got her number somewhere. Once I've done that, I'll post about what happened in the group. Would you mind?'

'Maybe that's not a bad idea. Some of the local members might know something. It's a long shot, but I think you should do it.'

'Might be better than that. Once people are aware of what happened, it might go viral.'

He wasn't sure if that would be a good thing. But if it helped …

'Where are you?' asked Chloe.

'At the flat, you know. Newmarket Road.'

'Do you want me to come around?'

'I don't know what I want at the moment. Actually, I want to talk to you about Sarah. And there's nothing to eat here. Can we meet up? I'll buy you dinner.'

'That would be nice. How about 7 p.m.? At Frank's Bar?'

'Where's that?'

'It's … Actually, meet me outside the Forum. You know where that is, don't you?'

'Sure. I'll see you at seven.'

He had a couple of hours to kill before then. He filled them by searching the web, trying to piece together the history behind the occupation of the forest. The Facebook page had photos of the three previous demonstrations. The first one had happened in March, with only a handful of police in evidence, and not many more protestors. The TV cameras were there, though. The second, in June, had been a lot bigger. More protestors and police, and probably more media coverage, too. People were shown either marching through the wood or standing on the edge of it where it met the farmland, where development was already underway. The last one, only a week ago, seemed peaceful enough. There were a lot more people this time, hundreds of them. All armed with placards and banners, all seemingly relaxed and non-confrontational. It wasn't until he checked some online news reports that he saw the photos of masked protestors running through the construction site, or chaining themselves to bulldozers, and even being restrained by police. The Facebook group hadn't posted any of those.

There was another news article with a photo of the Chief Executive of Kingsley Developments, the company behind the new Garden Village. Mr Fabian Kingsley was quoted as saying that he was in the process of taking legal action against the protestors. He was confident of their removal from the forest very soon, and his only regret was that the process of securing and exercising his writ of possession was taking so long.

Ralph took a good look at Fabian Kingsley. He was in his mid-forties at least, with a broad, handsome face and a piercing, authoritative gaze. Probably adopted just for the camera, Ralph thought. He couldn't help wondering if Kingsley had become frustrated with the legal delays. Frustrated enough to send in four men to scare the protestors away? If anyone had a motive for the attack, it was Kingsley. He made a mental note to ask Chloe about the guy.

He drove into the city to meet her. The Forum was Norwich's Millennium project; a bold, modern building with a 15-metre-high glass facade and an atrium, which ensured plenty of light. It had been conceived as a replacement for the central library, which had burnt down in 1994. It housed TV studios, an auditorium, a new library, and a Pizza Express, among other things. And there was a coffee shop at ground level, called Marzanos. They had an outside area with shaded tables, and he spied Chloe sitting at one of them, sipping a cup of something. He walked over and joined her.
'Hi, Chloe.'
She looked up and then got up. 'Ralph!' She hugged him. 'Are you alright?'
She had on loose, blue cotton trousers and a lighter blue, short-sleeve blouse. Her black hair was up in a chignon.
'I'm OK. You look well.'
She smiled, but still managed to look anxious. 'So do you. Do you want a coffee? Actually, no. Let's get down to Frank's before it starts filling up.'
It was only five minutes away. They walked past the central market, crossed a road, turned left down a side street, and they were there. The sunny weather had brought plenty of people out this evening, and it seemed that quite a few of them had decided to duck into Frank's Bar for some refreshment. There was a little

table free upstairs though, so they grabbed it. Ralph ordered a beer and a glass of white wine for Chloe.

'I feel so helpless,' she said. 'I spoke to Bettina and she told me everything. But she doesn't have a clue who those men were. And Sarah's just vanished. Do you think the police will do anything?'

'I hope so. They said they'd be in touch. If that doesn't happen tomorrow, I'll go back to Reepham and ask them what they're going to do. We can't just do nothing.'

'Bettina sent me some photos. I've posted them in the Facebook group. Take a look.'

She passed him her iPhone. While Chloe scanned the menu, he checked out her post. There was a photo of the tree that had been attacked last night, now leaning at a 45-degree angle against its neighbour. The chainsaw cut was clearly visible. Under that was a photo of Sarah standing in front of the same tree when it was still upright. That was followed by some text:

'We are sad and shocked to report that late last night one of our fellow protesters living with us here in the forest fell from a walkway, when the tree she was occupying was partially cut down by four masked men. Sarah de Malmanche (see photo), who is a local woman, has been an active participant in our efforts to save Foxdown Wood from destruction for the last six months. She was injured but breathing after the fall, and the four attackers must have felt some remorse, because they said they were taking her

straight to the Norwich and Norfolk hospital. But Sarah never arrived and is now MISSING. We don't know where she is or what her condition is. We are praying for her. Please send Sarah your love and good vibes, and please share this post and keep your eye out for her, wherever she may be. And don't forget to come and support us on Saturday, August 18th, at Foxdown Wood. Sarah is missing and we want answers!'

The post was already attracting comments. He skimmed through some of them and saw that the mood was angry. People were shocked and incensed about what had happened. They wanted answers, too.

Their drinks had arrived by this time. Ralph took a swig of cold beer.

'This is going to stir things up,' he said.

'Yes, I know. I'm not going to apologise for that, Ralph. Anyway, it'll put pressure on the police and the authorities to do something, don't you think?'

'I hope so. And where do you fit in?'

'What do you mean?'

'I mean are you an activist, too? Have you been going to these demos? I've seen plenty of pictures online that suggest they're more than just peaceful. What is going on out there?'

She was a bit taken aback by his tone. 'Yes, I've been there and they *were* peaceful until the last one. Some people turned up from

London and it got out of hand. They tried to smash up machinery, and they invaded the site office on the land next door. I asked one of the guys where they were from, but he wouldn't tell me. What he did say, though, was that peaceful protest achieved nothing. Only violent direct action got results, and nothing else mattered.'
'Direct action. You mean destroying property. All that will do is give the developers the green light to get everyone evicted. Or more likely, it encouraged them to send those four guys out there to take some direct action of their own. Shit.'
'Don't get angry with me, Ralph. It wasn't my idea.'
He sighed. 'Sorry, Chloe. You're right. Let's get something to eat.'
They ordered. Ralph had calmed down by the time the food arrived.
'Have you seen much of Sarah since she started this activist thing?' he asked Chloe.
'We share the same practice rooms. I saw her a few times a week. She was fine. Happy. I thought she was seeing someone, actually. She had that look about her.'
'What look?'
'You know. The kind of look you get when you're in a new relationship, and the sex is good. Something was agreeing with her, I know that much.'
'Who was he?'

'She wouldn't say. She just said I was imagining things, so I stopped asking after a bit.'

'That's interesting. She didn't say anything to me, either. Mind you, we haven't spoken for a while …'

They got off the subject of Sarah and talked about what they'd both been doing since he last saw Chloe. She was concerned that he'd lost his job, and thought that with his coding skills he could probably get a new one easily enough in Norfolk, if he wanted to. He tried to find out more about her, and learned that she shared a flat close to the University of East Anglia, with two other women. One of them was doing a degree in Creative Writing, which was something Chloe fancied doing herself. He wondered how much money you could make as a writer, and how much she currently made as a massage therapist, but he didn't know her well enough to just ask. She did mention the fact that she was single, though. Not that it made any difference to him, of course. Then his phone rang. It was Holly.

'Ralph, where on earth are you?'

He abandoned his meal temporarily and went outside to talk. After he'd explained where he was and what he was doing there, Holly was sympathetic.

'That sounds awful,' she said. 'God, I really hope Sarah's alright. Stay as long as you need to and phone me tomorrow. Let me know what's going on, please.'

'I will. Love you.'

'You, too.'

He went back inside. He shared a bottle of wine with Chloe over dinner and, afterwards, drove her home. It wasn't too far from Newmarket Road.

'I could ask you in for a coffee, but my flatmates will probably get the wrong idea,' she said.

'I understand. I'll talk to the police tomorrow and let you know what's happening.'

'Good. And you should come to this demo on Saturday. You will come, won't you?'

'Yes, I'll come. Night, Chloe.'

She kissed him on the cheek, and then she got out of the car and was gone. It was around 10.30 p.m. when he parked back at Newmarket Road and went upstairs to the flat. He decided that instead of making up the bed in the second bedroom, it would be easier just to sleep in Sarah's bed. He hung the dresses she'd left on it in the wardrobe, and draped the tops over a chair. Then he went back to the living room and switched on the TV.

There was some stand-up comedian on channel 4, but he wasn't really into it, and he turned down the sound. It was strange if not downright weird to be here without his sister. Her absence had left an emotional void in him which was only made worse by not knowing how to proceed next. She'd disappeared. It was like she'd never existed.

I'll sleep on it, he decided. Might have some inspiration in the morning. Or the cops might. He turned off the TV and stood up, and that was when he realised something wasn't right. He couldn't figure out what it was. Then he saw it, or more to the point, didn't see it. The guitar on its stand had vanished. Someone had been here while he was out with Chloe and removed it. Someone who had a key.

He had a good look around, and it seemed like the guitar was the only thing the visitor had taken. He went over to the front door after that and pushed up the snib on the lock, so nobody could open it from the outside. Then he turned off all the lights and got into bed. He lay staring at the ceiling until he fell asleep, sometime after midnight.

Chapter 4

The first thing he did the following morning was call Bettina.

'Do you have a key to Sarah's flat?' he said.

'No.'

'Does anybody out there have a key?'

'No! Only Karl and I came to Sarah's place, nobody else. Why do you ask?'

'No reason. Did you have a quiet night?'

'We weren't disturbed. We will finish building the new houses today, I hope.'

'What about the police; did someone come and take a statement?'

'A detective came. We told him what happened.'

Ralph detected a touch of cynicism in her voice.

'Did he say what the next step was?'

'He said nothing about that. I'm not even sure he believed us. He did say he wanted to talk to you. Soon as possible.'

'Well, I'm sure he knows where to find me.'

He left it there, after saying he might drop in later on. He wanted to meet the other people living out at Foxdown Wood, just to get some idea of who Sarah had been hanging out with. One of them might be the mystery guitar thief.

He hadn't had any breakfast, as yet. There was cereal in the flat, but no milk. Or coffee. It was time to visit the supermarket and get stocked up. There was a Waitrose not far away, so he scribbled down a few items on a post-it note and got ready to go. As he pocketed the car keys, the doorbell rang. He went into the little entrance hall and picked up the intercom receiver.

'Hello?'

'Mr de Malmanche?'

'That's right.'

'Detective Constable Derek Ainsworth. I'd like to ask you some questions.'

'Oh, sure. Come up, right to the top.'

He buzzed the man in. That's encouraging, he thought, they aren't wasting any time. A minute later, there was a knock at the door. He opened it to see a man about his own age, wearing a suit. He had short-cropped brown hair and a broad face, with a prominent nose. His hand was extended, so Ralph shook it.

'Come in.' He led the detective through to the living room, where they both sat down. 'I just got off the phone with Bettina, the German girl living out in the wood. She said you'd been to see them.'

Detective Ainsworth had a business-like demeanour about him. He raised his eyebrows.

'What did you think of their story, Mr de Malmanche?'

'Their story? I took it at face value. Why?'

'Couple of things. First, they let those men take your sister away without a murmur. And they didn't see the vehicle she was taken away in.'

'Yeah, I did wonder about that. I asked them why they didn't do anything. They said they were shocked and that they're pacifists.'

Ainsworth grunted. 'If you'd been at the last demonstration, you might have cause to doubt that.'

'I don't know about that. Sarah's missing, that's all I know. And if it happened the way they said it did, she's also badly hurt.'

'Quite.' Ainsworth pursed his lips, deliberating over the next question. He made up his mind. 'Is there some reason you know of why Sarah might want to disappear?'

'Want to disappear … What do you mean?'

'Is there something she's avoiding, for instance?'

Ralph tried not to sound annoyed. 'No, nothing I know of. What are you implying?'

'Nothing. It's not unknown for people to want to disappear, that's all.'

'You think that Bettina made up a story to help Sarah disappear? Really? Why?'

Ainsworth shrugged. 'No idea. But apart from a tree that's nearly fallen down, there's no clear evidence of anything happening the way they describe it. They witnessed this event, and yet they have nothing useful to say about it.'

'Look, detective. I find it hard to believe that Sarah just decided to disappear and then persuaded Bettina to make up some crazy story to cover her tracks. A story that involved cutting down a tree and destroying their accommodation in the process. That would be a lot to ask. Are you telling me you don't believe her?'

Ainsworth held up a calming hand. 'I believe her until I have a reason not to, Mr de Malmanche.'

'What are you going to do, then?'

'We've taped off the scene where Sarah allegedly fell, and the forensics people are looking at it now. But because the protestors have been walking through that area and dismantling tree houses since it happened, a lot of the physical evidence relating to her attackers may have been destroyed.'

That didn't sound encouraging. 'What else can we do while that's going on?' asked Ralph.

'I'd like to add some details to the missing person's report,' said Ainsworth. 'First thing is a risk assessment. Does the continued disappearance of Sarah constitute a risk to her well-being? Assuming things happened as described, then yes, it does. That makes her high risk. She should be in a hospital or at the very least, seeking medical attention. Are there any photos of her I can have?'

'There are some on my phone, I can email them to you. And there's a good one of her on the Facebook page, actually.'

'Thanks, I'll take a look.'

Ainsworth opened a folder he had with him and consulted it for a minute.

'You gave the basic details to my colleague out at Reepham. Description, height, weight … Phone number. You've got her phone, is that correct?'

'Yes.'

'I'll want to look at that. What about a computer?'

'She's got a laptop, but I don't know where it is.'

Ainsworth made a note of that. 'Right, just a few more questions.' He unfolded a sheet of paper and read out the list of questions printed on it. Did Sarah have a medical condition? No. Any financial problems? Not that Ralph was aware of. What about her psychological health, did she suffer from depression? Sometimes, but not clinically. Any family, drug, or alcohol problems? That one made Ralph laugh.

'The family *is* the problem,' he said. 'Both our parents are alcoholics. Sarah isn't.'

Ainsworth raised one eyebrow. 'And drugs?'

'Apart from alcohol? Sarah isn't into drugs.'

'OK. All I need now then, is addresses and contact names for friends and family.'

'We're the only two children. Our parents live in France, and we try to avoid them. She wouldn't go there.'

'Are they aware she's missing?'

'Not yet. I'll contact them, if you don't mind. I'll have to think about the friends. Can I get back to you?'

'Alright. I have enough to start with. Here's my card, it's got my email on it.'

Ralph took the card and said he'd email a few photos straight away.

'We'll start making enquiries at all the Norfolk hospitals,' said Ainsworth. 'Do you live here with your sister, Mr de Malmanche?'

'What? No, I live in London. I'll be staying here from now on, though.'

Ainsworth got up. 'I'll be in touch just as soon as I've got something to tell you.'

Ralph saw him to the door. When Ainsworth was gone, he selected two photos of Sarah and sent them as promised. Then he drove to the supermarket and did some shopping. Once he'd returned to the flat and had breakfast, he drove out to the forest.

He got there to find that work was already well advanced on the new tree houses. Everybody seemed to be involved in the process; there were several people up in the two newly selected trees, all busy erecting walls and a roof over the platform they'd constructed earlier. Helpers on the ground were tying boards of varying lengths and sizes to a rope, which were then hoisted up. The bedding, stoves, lamps, gas canisters, and even a small Persian rug were neatly arranged at the foot of their respective trees, and two people were engaged in repairing the wooden walkway that had broken during the attack the other night.

Bettina was one of them, and as she was the only person he could make any claim to knowing here, he made a beeline straight for her. She was kneeling down and using a hand drill to make a hole in the end of a board, so she didn't notice him until he was right next to her. She looked up at him with a non-committal expression, and then went back to what she was doing.

'A detective visited me this morning,' he said. 'He's going to start checking local hospitals.'

She put down the drill and sat back on the grass. 'What about the men? The ones who took Sarah.'

He sat down opposite her. 'What about them?'

She passed an arm across her forehead to wipe away the perspiration. It was shaded beneath the trees, but today was shaping up to be a replica of the last two weeks; clear sky and hot, burning sunshine. 'It's obvious who sent them,' she said. 'The development company. Fabian Kingsley.'

'Why do you say that?'

The man helping Bettina with the repair job spoke up. 'Who the bloody hell else would do it?'

Ralph looked at him. He was a small, wiry man in his twenties. 'Have you met this Kingsley guy?' asked Ralph.

'He came out here a few times,' said Bettina. 'Told us to get out. He was quite abusive about it, too.'

'He's a prick,' said the wiry one.

'Who are you?' said Ralph.

'Name's Byron. So, now that Sarah's gone, will you be helping us?'

'Helping you? Volunteering to live in the trees, you mean? Sorry, mate. Not my thing.'

'I meant with money. Sarah gave us money.'

'Did she? No, I won't be giving you money.'

Byron shrugged. 'OK. Bettina, I'm off with Karl to get some more rope.'

He turned and walked away. Ralph watched him go, and when he looked back at Bettina again, she looked furious.

'How much money?' he said.

'About £500 a week. She used to turn up with all this cash, but it wasn't her money.'

'Where did it come from?'

Bettina shook her head. 'She just said it was from a well-wisher, and not to ask any more questions. So, we didn't.'

Ralph took a few moments to digest this. 'Did you tell the police this?'

She shook her head. He decided on another line of questioning.

'Was Sarah seeing anyone?'

'I don't think so. If she was, she didn't bring him out here. But it's possible, I guess. Your sister was very secretive, you know.'

'No, I didn't know.'

'That money helped us a lot. Nobody here has a full-time job, so it made a lot of difference. But it doesn't matter, we will manage.'

He asked her about the other people here, and how well they knew Sarah. Bettina said that they were all friends, but it was Karl and herself that Sarah had spent the most time with. And now, apparently, some of those friends were leaving.

'Diana and Steve have decided to go back to Somerset,' she told him. 'They don't feel safe here anymore.'

'What about the rest of you?'

'We are staying, of course. I know what it's like to be intimidated, we experienced it a lot in Germany. You just have to be strong. Anyway, Byron is going to help with protection.'

'Really? How?'

'He lives on a farm near here. I think he's going to get some animal traps. We will set them up at night.'

I bet she didn't tell the police that, either, he thought. He couldn't think of anything else to ask, so he decided to let her get on with her repair job. He stood up to leave, and realised he had one more question after all.

'Do you guys belong to a group? You know, like Greenpeace or something?'

She examined him with her serious brown eyes. 'The guys from Somerset are Earth First! The rest of us are just concerned citizens.'

'Where do you think Sarah is?'

The change of tack took her by surprise. Her eyes widened, but she held his gaze.

'I'm sorry, Ralph, I really don't know. I just hope she is alright.'

'Yeah, me too. Maybe I'll see you on Saturday.'

He left her to it and walked back to the car park. The VW Kombi van with German licence plates that had been parked next to him, was gone. Karl and Bettina's vehicle no doubt, now on its way to find rope and animal traps. Sarah's Peugeot was also there, looking rather sad and dusty. Maybe if he brought Chloe along on his next trip, she could drive it back to Norwich. He sighed. Coming here hadn't shed a great deal of light on Sarah's disappearance, just raised more questions. The kind of questions that someone like Fabian Kingsley or this mysterious well-wisher could answer. Maybe the well-wisher was also Sarah's lover, assuming Chloe was right about that. Or the guitar thief. Or both.

He drove back to the flat, and on the way realised that attending Saturday's demo might give him an opportunity to observe the dynamics of this protest, and find out more about the various interested parties. Kingsley might show up, as might the well-wisher. Yes, talking to people and taking some discreet photos might yield something. He wondered how Gerald at Catford Investigations would feel about lending him some equipment. It was Thursday today, so if Gerald was up for it he could go back to London and pick up a surveillance kit, and still be back for the demo with time to spare. When he phoned, Vivian answered. He told her what he wanted.

'Well, we have spare kits,' she said. 'But that's expensive stuff, Ralph. Hold on a minute and I'll ask.'

Some classical music he didn't recognise filled his ears. Ten seconds later it stopped, and Gerald was on the line. His tone was brusque.

'What are you up to, Ralph?'

'Just want to take some pictures. Discreet pictures.'

'I see. Any news on Sarah?'

Ralph filled him in. Gerald sniffed an opportunity.

'Sounds like a job for a private investigator,' he said. 'You want to hire us?'

'Hardly. I just want to borrow some equipment. And there's a conflict of interest. I already work for you.'

'You're not exactly working for me at the moment, are you?' Gerald thought for a second. 'Some advice. I suggest you let the police do their job before wasting your time with your own personal private investigation. Yes, you can have a surveillance kit, but you'll have to leave a £200 deposit with me before you take it away. I trust that's not a problem?'

Miserable bastard, thought Ralph. Still, as Viv had said, the stuff was expensive. But what exactly did Gerald think he was going to do with it?

'No, that's fine,' he said, hoping he sounded less annoyed than he felt. 'I'll pick it up first thing tomorrow. By the way, how did Brett get on with Valerie Marshall?'

'Valerie? Oh yes. The evening that *you* were supposed to be on her, she left work and visited the Poseidon Hotel. Brett got some good pictures, and even some sound.'

'She was meeting someone?'

'Lots of someones. It turns out she's attending a course on day trading, with about fifty other people. Shares and Forex, apparently. How to make a fortune trading online from home, that sort of thing. Brett said she's a good student, too. Asks a lot of questions.'

'But she's not telling her husband about it. Why not?'

'Maybe she's using his money to place trades. Who knows, but for some reason she wants to keep it to herself. He knows now, of course. Whether that sets his mind at rest or not, I can't say.'

'Doesn't exactly sound marriage threatening,' said Ralph. 'Alright, I'll see you tomorrow morning.'

'I'll be out, but Vivian will be here. Brett was asking after you by the way, so expect a call. And Ralph, I'm sure Sarah will turn up. Try not to worry.'

With that, he rang off. Easy for you to say, thought Ralph. I wonder if you'd be so cool, calm and collected if Sandra disappeared. Still, he had something resembling a plan now, or a partial plan. What came after taking the photos was anyone's guess at the moment. But at least he was doing something, which went some way to offsetting the sense of powerlessness he felt at having no idea where Sarah was, or how to find her.

He thought about what Bettina had said about Fabian Kingsley. She had a point; if anyone wanted to get rid of the protestors, it would probably be him. Would he know where Sarah was? Why not just ask the guy? Time was of the essence, and Ralph didn't know when or even if Detective Constable Ainsworth intended to speak to Kingsley about Sarah. He knew it wasn't really his place to interrogate the man, but not doing it wasn't an option, either. He was Sarah's brother and as far as he was concerned, that was all the reason he needed. He opened up the laptop and googled 'Kingsley Developments'. They had an office in the city; so, he decided to pay them a visit.

Kingsley Developments was on the second floor of a three-storey red brick building near the Anglican Cathedral in Tombland, the more historic part of town. Ralph parked the car up by the Forum where he'd met Chloe, and walked the rest of the way. Ten minutes later, he was pushing open a glass door and entering the reception area. A middle-aged woman sitting behind the reception desk looked up at his approach.

'What can we do for you?' she said, as she tilted her head forward to get a better look at him over the top of her glasses.

'Is Mr Kingsley around?'

'I'll check. Do you have an appointment?'

'No. I just popped in on the off chance.'

'Will he know what it's about, Mr …?'

'De Malmanche. It's a personal matter.'

She assumed a neutral expression and picked up her phone. While he waited, Ralph looked around. Behind the reception desk, there were partitioned areas scattered across the office. They screened most of the occupants from his view, but he could hear the chatter of people behind those partitions, and one guy was visible from here; a man who wasn't Fabian Kingsley. The entire back wall was taken up with four glass partition meeting rooms, only one of which was occupied. The occupant appeared to be talking on a conference phone until he hit a button, looked up briefly, and then started reading something on the table in front of him.

'Mr Kingsley's not available, I'm afraid,' said the receptionist. 'Would you like to leave a message?'

'He looks available to me. I'll just pop in and have a quick word.'

Before she could process that, he'd walked past her desk towards the meeting rooms. Kingsley didn't see him coming until the last second, and by that time Ralph was opening the door and striding in. Kingsley stood up.

'Who are you?'

'My name's Ralph de Malmanche. I want a few minutes of your time.'

Kingsley looked a little wary. 'And why is that?'

'It's about the protestors out at Foxdown Wood. You're doing a development out there.'

'What about them?'

'They were attacked on Tuesday night. My sister was with them, and she had a nasty fall from a tree. She's disappeared.'

Kingsley just stared at Ralph for a moment. His wariness changed to irritation.

'I have no idea what you're on about,' he said. 'It's the first I've heard of it. What do you mean, she's disappeared? She fell from a tree and then just got up and vanished into thin air, is that what you're telling me?'

That got Ralph irritated. 'No, she was taken away by the four men who caused the fall in the first place. Do you know those four men by any chance?'

Kingsley looked astonished for a millisecond, and then lost it.

'Who the hell are you to come in here and make accusations? Are you implying I had something to do with all of this?'

His voice had risen and his face was flushed. Ralph opened his mouth to reply, but Kingsley hadn't finished.

'Until you walked in here, Mr de Malmanche, I knew nothing about this attack you're talking about. Walked in here *uninvited*, I might add.'

He was almost shouting now and the other occupants of the office, some half dozen of them, had come out from behind their partitions, and were watching in astonishment. Kingsley had more to say on the subject.

'I'll have you know that the protestors you're talking about have done nothing but hinder my progress, and frankly, if they fall out of trees and injure themselves, I'm the last person you should come to for sympathy. And you certainly don't come in here with accusations of complicity. Am I making myself clear?'

Ralph was feeling a little angry, too. But he kept his voice down.

'Let's get it crystal clear,' he said. 'You know nothing about the attack in Foxdown Wood, and you also know nothing about the whereabouts of my sister, Sarah. Is that correct?'

They looked each other straight in the eyes for a second.

'No,' said Kingsley. 'Now get out of here, before I have you thrown out.'

'You sure about that?'

'Out! Now!'

'Thanks for your time,' said Ralph.

He turned and strode back across the office, ignoring Kingsley's colleagues. He breezed right past the indignant receptionist with her hands on her hips, and then out through the door and down the stairs to the street.

He set a brisk pace away from Kingsley Developments, and while he walked, he replayed the last five minutes in his head. He hadn't expected Kingsley to admit to any connection with the events in Foxdown Wood, but now he knew one thing for sure. When he'd posed the question and they stared at each other, Kingsley had replied in the negative, while glancing ever so slightly away. You didn't need to be an expert in body language to figure out what that meant. Fabian Kingsley was a liar.

Chapter 5

He drove to Greenwich later that evening. On the way, he had a call from Brett, who didn't waste time with small talk.

'What's this about Sarah going missing?'

Ralph's friendship with Brett Saunders went back to when they met as students, some fifteen years ago. They were both doing Computer Science at Canterbury University in Kent, and they shared a flat together with two girls and another guy.

Brett wasn't a social creature back then. He preferred to spend his free time in his room, honing his hacking skills. He'd been part of a group of hackers who liked to challenge themselves by infiltrating large company IT systems, totally without malice. His hacker moniker was Cybertooth, which Ralph thought was a pretty creative title, given the fact that Brett was such a left-brained, logical nerd most of the time. He was a big, rangy lad then, with a passion for rugby as well as hacking, and a ravenous appetite for junk food, most of which he consumed in front of the computer. He played prop forward for the University team, until he put on too much weight even for that role.

Since then, he'd slimmed down considerably and had been employed as an IT security consultant by a number of companies in and around London. Between jobs, he did 'freelance stuff'. Ralph wasn't sure what 'freelance stuff' was, just that it seemed to involve months of working from home. They'd kept in touch over the years, and often met up for a drink. Brett liked to drag Ralph out to rugby matches at England's Twickenham stadium. In November they'd be back there again for the Autumn International fixtures.

When Brett installed the IT system at Catford Investigations, he told Gerald that he often had spare time on his hands between jobs. Gerald had then persuaded him to do some training in surveillance techniques, so he could use some of that time working for Catford Investigations. Brett had mentioned this to Ralph, and now Gerald had two IT consultants between jobs working for him.

Ralph put the phone on speaker so he wouldn't be caught by police with a phone to his ear while driving, and then told Brett the whole story.

'Really sorry to hear that, mate,' said Brett. 'I was trying to remember the last time I saw Sarah. She came to the England versus Scotland match with us a few years back, I know that much. I just hope she's OK, wherever she is. You reckon this Kingsley bloke might know something about that?'

'Positive.'

'OK, I'll start checking him out. See how security conscious he is.'

'Thanks, I appreciate it. Just be discreet about it, I've already upset the guy and I've only met him the one time.'

'Ralph, please. This is me you're talking to. When am I ever not discreet? Are you staying in Norwich for now?'

'Until Sarah's found. I'm just coming back to London to pick up some surveillance equipment, and then I'll be back for however long it takes.'

'OK, I'll give you a call in a day or two.'

They finished on that note. When Ralph arrived at the flat in Greenwich, it was around 8 p.m. He got in to find that Holly wasn't home. She worked shifts, so that wasn't too unusual, but he thought she'd said she was on earlies this week. He resisted the urge to call her in case she was still working, and raided the fridge instead. There wasn't much to find in there, but he discovered a frozen Chicken Jalfrezi in the freezer, and put it in the microwave. He was washing that down with a glass of Sauvignon blanc when she came in an hour later.

'I wasn't expecting you,' she said. 'Pour me one.'

He did, and she joined him at the dining table. He thought she looked flushed, and her hair was a bit dishevelled.

'I went out for a drink with some people from work,' she said, noticing his curious expression. 'I've had a couple.'

And the rest, he thought. 'Bit unusual for you, isn't it? Going out after work, I mean.'

She shrugged. 'There's always an exception to the rule. Anyway, I thought you'd still be in Norwich. Any news on Sarah?'

'Not yet. The police are on it.'

'How long do you think it will take?'

He got the implications of that question. She wanted him here in London looking for work, and not sitting around in Norfolk, waiting for Sarah to turn up.

'How do I know? If she isn't found in a week or two, then it's plan B. Not that I know what plan B is yet.'

'So, you'll be in Norwich for you don't know how long. I realise that you're worried about Sarah. So am I. But realistically, Ralph, what can you do?'

'I'm in the process of figuring that out, actually.'

She cut to the chase. 'How much have you got left in the bank?'

'Not a lot. Don't worry, Holly. If nothing happens in a couple of weeks, I'll get some contract work. It may mean working away from London, but you'll get my full share of the rent again.'

She looked at him. The look that said she'd heard that statement, or others very much like it, before. But she didn't express her doubts.

'OK. But this time I'm holding you to it. I can't go on supporting you indefinitely.' She got up. 'I need the bathroom.'

That was as close as Holly had come to an ultimatum. Trouble was, he really didn't have much in the bank, and if he was going to put time and energy into his investigation into Sarah's disappearance, he couldn't work at the same time. He was going to have to borrow some money. But not from Holly.

When she returned from the bathroom, the subject was closed. They watched a crime drama on TV for the rest of the evening, which meant they didn't talk too much, and finished the wine while they were doing it. Then Holly said she'd probably had a bit too much to drink and went to bed. An hour later, Ralph did the same.

Once Holly had left for work the next morning, he went out. First to the nearest ATM to get Gerald's £200, and then to Catford to pick up the surveillance equipment. Neither Gerald nor Sandra were around, but Vivian had been advised, and had it ready for him. He'd driven over to Catford so he could just continue straight on to Norwich, but as usual, there was nowhere to park. So he left the BMW on a yellow line and rushed into the office to do the pick-up. He just had time to tell Vivian that nothing had changed before he turned around and headed for the door.

'Let us know when it does,' she said to his retreating back.

'I will, don't worry.'

Then he was back in the car and he'd beaten the traffic wardens. With a sigh of relief, he was on his way. When he got back to Newmarket Road, he had a good look around the flat again, just in case the mystery visitor had dropped in and removed something else. Everything was just as he'd left it. He thought about getting a locksmith in to change the locks on the front door, but decided against it on financial grounds. He'd do it when he had a loan sorted out. Then he sent a text to Chloe to find out if he could pick her up tomorrow morning. They could drive out to the demo together and she could pick up Sarah's car at the same time. He got a reply saying that was fine, and would he pick her up at 7 a.m. She wanted to get there before everyone else did.

He agreed to that and then the rest of his day was free. But he didn't know what to do with it. He ended up in a pub just around the corner from the flat, drinking beer all afternoon and trying to read a book he'd lifted from Sarah's bookcase. It was an attempt to kill his thoughts about her, but it didn't work. He couldn't concentrate on *'The Girl on the Train'* and just got drunk instead. Eventually, he dragged himself out of the pub and went back to the flat, where he managed to cook an evening meal. Not long after that he set the alarm on his phone and went to bed. It was still light outside when his head hit the pillow.

He beat the alarm clock the next morning and woke up around 5 a.m., a little hungover. After a shower and breakfast he felt more like a human being again, and at 7 a.m. he was outside Chloe's place, as arranged. She must have been looking out for him, because as soon as he drew up outside, the front door opened and she was waving at him to come in. When he got inside, he saw that the hallway was jammed up with placards.

'I've been busy,' said Chloe. 'I should warn you, too. Some of today is going to be about Sarah.'

He didn't need much by way of further explanation. The placards had a larger version of Sarah's Facebook photo on them, the one that showed her standing in front of the tree, before the chainsaws got to it. The bottom section had the words 'Where is Sarah?' printed on it, in bold black capitals. Under that was the URL for the Facebook group.

'This should raise awareness,' said Chloe. 'I've been working with the local Greenpeace group on it as well. They've got another hundred of these.' She smiled at the obvious surprise on his face. 'Can we get these in your car?'

'Wow, Chloe,' he said. 'You should have told me. How many have you got here?'

'About fifteen. They should fit across the back seat.'

She was right. The boards were a decent size but the handles were relatively short; the placards were designed for holding above your head and waving around.

'How are the Greenpeace people going to transport their lot?' he asked her, as they drove away from the house.

'They have a bus organised. People are coming from London and all over. I have a feeling that today's going to be the biggest demo yet.'

And it was a perfect day for it; blue sky and sunshine. An hour later, they stopped in at Foxdown Village Hall before going on to the wood. A group of women, most of whom were around retirement age, were busy setting up refreshment tables outside the hall. They seemed to have endless supplies of sandwiches and bottled water to sell. Chloe seemed to know everyone; she wandered around exchanging pleasantries with them all. The main route to the wood passed through the village, so by 11 a.m., if things went according to expectations, there'd be plenty of customers for those sandwiches. Once Chloe had done the rounds, they continued on their way.

'They got fed up with us after the second demo,' she told Ralph. 'But then they decided to capitalise on it. So for the most part, everybody's happy.'

When they got to the wood car park, there was a mobile café there ahead of them. The only other two vehicles to be seen were Karl's van and Sarah's Peugeot. It was only 8.30 a.m., and there was nobody other than the owner of the mobile café in the car park.

'This place will be packed solid in a few hours,' said Chloe. 'Let's get these placards out.'

They couldn't do them all in one trip. The actual site of the demo was on the border of the wood and the farmland, which had no fence or any kind of barrier separating the two. This was the first time Ralph had seen the extent of the housing development. As they dumped the first load of placards, he looked out at the approximately forty partially built houses that were visible on the far side of the site from where he was standing. They were brick shells at the moment, and the rest of the site closer to the border with the wood had bulldozers, diggers, concrete mixers, stacks of building materials, and assorted trucks scattered around, along with a big portakabin that served as the site office. There were two cars parked near the office, but there was nobody to be seen as yet.

'One more thing,' said Chloe, as they made their way back to the car park. 'I've been in touch with the BBC. They want you to do an interview about Sarah by the tree houses, around 1 p.m. I said that shouldn't be a problem. It isn't, is it?'

He looked at her with open admiration. 'You have been busy. Not a problem.'

The tree houses were a few minutes' walk away from where they left the pile of placards. They got there to find that everyone was up and about. A table at the foot of the first two tree houses had appeared from somewhere. It had pamphlets laid out on it proclaiming the aims and objectives of the 'Save Foxdown Wood' protest, and there was a plastic bucket next to them, marked with the word 'Donations'. Bettina was nearby, drinking tea from a mug. She waved at him and while Chloe went over to talk to her, he picked up a pamphlet and glanced through it.

It was a ten-page mini-booklet, and it struck him as more of a manifesto than an explanation of environmental protest, which was what he'd been expecting. The first two pages covered the short history of the protest in Foxdown Wood, and how it had been partly inspired by the German protestors' resistance to the clearing of their ancient forest by the coal mining company. There were some graphs and statistics on rising CO_2 levels, and predictions of higher temperatures and the effects they would have on the human population fifty years on. Then the subject matter changed.

It became a condemnation of industrial society, which was essentially unsustainable. According to whoever had written all this, industrial society was driven by a disregard for basic human values, and was nothing more than a quest for corporate profit. All at the expense of the wildlife it devastated, the consumers it enslaved, the indigenous cultures it callously destroyed, and the planet it was making uninhabitable. The only way to reverse the situation was to de-corporatise, de-industrialise. Civilisation, if that term could be used to describe global society today, had to be destroyed completely and then rebuilt again from the ground up. And if you wanted to participate in this rebuilding? Then you should visit the website of the 'Global Green Garrison', otherwise known as 'Triple G', for more information. Ralph finished reading and then joined Chloe and Bettina. He held up the pamphlet.

'I thought you said you were just concerned citizens,' he said. 'What's all this about?'

Bettina wasn't bothered. 'We *are* concerned citizens. They came here yesterday, and I said they could leave their literature. Don't worry, nobody takes them seriously. They are too extreme to be credible.'

'Was it them who disrupted the last demo?'

She shrugged. 'Yes, some of them.'

'Will they be here today?'

'Yes, I think so. Excuse me, please.'

She walked away. Ralph handed the pamphlet to Chloe.

'I bet the guy who told you nothing but violent direct action worked is a member of this lot,' he said. 'Read it. I have to get something from the car.'

He went back to the car park and got the surveillance kit from the boot. When he re-joined Chloe, she was thoughtful.

'I read it,' she said. 'They mention what they call effective direct action, and I think they have a point, actually.'

'What, we should destroy civilisation? Then what?'

She sighed. 'I don't know. What I do know is that effective direct action gets you noticed. But as far as Foxdown Wood is concerned, we could probably do without it. What's in the bag?'

'Some hi-tech camera equipment. I'm going to take photos.'

'Great! I can post some of them later. I'm going to go back to where we left the placards to wait for people to arrive. Come with me?'

'Sure.'

They returned to the border of the wood and the building site. An hour later, people started trickling in, and an hour after that, the trickle became a flood. They were of all ages and ethnic persuasions. There were long-haired new-agers, and middle-class, clean-cut professional types. Equal numbers of men and women. Many of them had children in tow. Some of them had brought their own placards and banners, and it seemed the message about Sarah had made an impact. The 'Save Foxdown Wood!' slogan was in the majority, but there were others demanding 'Action for Sarah, now!' and 'Find our Heroine of the Wood!' They all had the same photo on them, the one Chloe had posted on Facebook.

A lot of the people now lining up along the length of the dividing line between forest and building site were in good spirits, laughing and joking. Others were less jovial. They were mostly the ones holding the Sarah signs. Ralph felt that there was something more purposeful about them, that they'd come here to make a point. Or perhaps he was imagining it.

He noticed something else. Three transit vans had pulled up outside the portakabin on the building site, and out of them came a dozen large men, wearing the uniform of a private security firm. They all trooped inside, only to emerge five minutes later, when they proceeded to spread out in a line of their own across the site. It looked like this time, if things got out of hand, the construction machinery wasn't about to suffer for it. Not if these guys had anything to do with it.

Fabian Kingsley came out next. He didn't exactly review the troops, but he had a good stroll around and stopped to have a word with each of them. There were some hoots and jeers from the protestors, which Kingsley ignored. Ralph took the camera out and got a few shots of Kingsley and his team, and then the police arrived.

There were about fifty of them, and they proceeded to form their own line between the protestors and the building site. There were big gaps in that line, because the length of the border was at least 200 metres, but then a big truck laden with metal crowd control barriers appeared and drew up next to the portakabin. The police dispersed temporarily to unload and set them all up. When they'd finished, the way into the site was effectively barred. You could, of course, vault one of those barriers, or push it over if you were so inclined. But the message was clear. It was no go beyond that point.

'There were no barriers last time,' said Chloe, as they watched this spectacle unfold.

'It was a peaceful protest, wasn't it?' said Ralph. 'Until your direct action man and his mates started smashing things up. They don't want a repeat performance.'

On the protestors' side, Bettina and two men arrived, with a public address system. They set up speakers as far apart as they could get them, just behind the line of protestors. The amplifier was hooked up to a battery and switched on, and then one of the men did a microphone test.

'One, two, three – where's the BBC?'

The crowd cheered and applauded. Chloe tugged Ralph by the arm, and they got up and made their way through the crowd to where there was some space. They could see Bettina and her friends now, about twenty feet away.

'That's funny,' said Chloe. 'I haven't seen those guys before.'

'Who actually organises these things?' said Ralph. 'Are you involved?'

'Once I know the dates, I liaise with Greenpeace and I post on Facebook. Bettina and the others set the dates and they have contacts with Earth First!, who also spread the word.'

'The Earth First! guys have left. Bettina said they were scared off.'

'Really? She didn't say anything to me about that. But now you mention it, I haven't seen the Earth First! people here today. Steve and Diana lived here, but there were always a few more of them that turned up with the sound equipment on the day. Maybe these are just new people.'

She was distracted by the arrival of the East Anglia division of the British Broadcasting Corporation, who were now setting up cameras. There was another camera crew as well, but Chloe didn't know who they represented. A minute later, it seemed like they were ready to roll. The guy holding the microphone thought so. It was time to get the show started.

'Foxdown Wood! Are you ready to make your voices heard?'

There was a huge cheer from what must have been close to 500 people.

'So, why are we here? What do we want to do?'

'Save Foxdown Wood!'

'Say it again! Louder!'

They did. Several times and for several minutes. When they'd come to a natural break, the master of ceremonies continued.

'I know things got a bit emotional last time. And you can see how the powers that be have responded. All I ask of you today is to consider why we're here. And to consider something else. Just consider what lengths unprincipled people will go to when their interests are threatened. If you don't know yet, I'm talking about Sarah, who lived out here in the forest until last Tuesday. Sarah is a beautiful lady, who stood for something that matters. She wasn't driven by gain at the expense of the environment, or the community. Not at all, she wanted to protect those things. And that's what she was doing, until the tree she'd lived in for the past six months was attacked in the middle of the night. Sarah was injured badly that night, and was taken away by her attackers. That was the price she paid for protecting the environment and the community. Think about that.'

He'd spoken with a passion that had got the crowd's attention. Ralph took a long look at him. He was a good-looking man, in his mid to late forties. He wore jeans and a purple t-shirt and he looked slim and fit, with an air of quiet self-assurance about him. The accent wasn't local, more like posh London. He hadn't finished yet.

'And think of the insult to her dignity, to be taken away by the very people who attacked her. Not to hospital, as they promised, but to who knows where? And think about the callousness of those attackers, not letting anyone know where she is or if she's alright. Who, you might ask, would do such a thing? Who, you might ask, would keep her in hiding against her will? Who, I *do* ask, can tell us where she is? You might like to ask that question too, and you can. Because the people you need to ask are right over there!' He raised his arm and pointed over the crowd's head. 'Where is Sarah?' he yelled.

That was all it took. The placards were raised, the banners unfurled, and the crowd began chanting.

'Where is Sarah? Where is Sarah?'

The mood had changed, just like that. Now, about two-thirds of the 500 people attending were massed together at the front of the crowd, where it faced the police and the barriers, expressing their anger quite openly. Someone had a drum and was beating out a rhythm to match the chant, which soon began to sound more like a tribal war cry than a protest slogan. The less demonstrative members, who had come with small children, were now at the back of the crowd, and their children had picked up on the hostility. Some of them were crying.

Ralph was taking as many photos as he could. Of the man who had stoked this up, of the crowd in its frenzy, and when he finally pushed to the front, of the police and Kingsley's security men. Kingsley himself was nowhere in sight. Some of the crowd was edging forward now, ever closer to the barriers. Ralph was dragged along with them, and just when it looked like a confrontation with the law was inevitable, everything stopped.

In the distance, on the far side of the building site, there was an explosion. Some of the partially completed houses over there were engulfed in a huge ball of flame that rocketed skywards. Bricks and debris shot into the air. A sudden wave of heat, reminiscent of the heat blast you experience when an oven door opens in your face, stopped everyone in their tracks.

The chanting stopped. Jaws dropped. When the reverberations of the explosion died away, and the ringing in everyone's ears subsided, the only noise left was silence.

Chapter 6

The police were the first to react. They moved as one unit towards the protestors, and one of them had a megaphone.
'Clear the area, please. Go back to the car park in an orderly fashion and make your way home. This event is over.'
Nobody needed telling twice. They began to leave. The explosion had deflated their outrage like a popped balloon. A group of around six police then started off in the direction of the blast and as they did so, they pulled back the security men who had started off ahead of them. This was now a police matter. Ralph hadn't moved since the explosion, and from where he was standing, he could see that the far side of the building site was wreathed in smoke. A few flames were visible as well, but they were dying out as he watched. The former brick shells of houses hadn't been roofed as yet, and there wasn't much flammable material for the flames to get hold of, but the fire brigade would need to deal with whatever there was. He looked around for Chloe, but she'd disappeared.
The crowd was slowly dispersing, and they were blocking his view of the man who had been so passionately exhorting the protestors just a minute ago. He made his way back to where he thought the man had been, and once he was able to cut through the queue of people on their way out, he saw Bettina. She was gathering up the speakers from the PA system. A man was helping her, but it wasn't the man who'd done the talking. Then he saw the guy. He was

standing twenty feet away from Bettina, and he was talking and gesticulating furiously at someone. When Ralph got closer, he saw who it was. Fabian Kingsley. Ralph got closer and listened.

'If I find out you're connected to what's just happened here, I'll bloody ruin you,' said Kingsley. 'Personally and professionally. Are we clear?'

The object of this outburst was only mildly less volatile.

'Fuck you, Kingsley. As usual, you're putting two and two together and getting five. Do you think I'd do something like this just to derail your corrupt bloody development? You're quite capable of doing that without my help. But it seems like someone wants to help you anyway. Who have you managed to upset now?'

'If you don't need to do anything then why did you go out of your way to stir up that crowd of morons just now? And don't give me that crap about saving the planet. You're not the type.'

'I'm just concerned about my friend, Sarah. By the way, Fabian, you didn't answer the question.'

'What are you talking about?'

'Sarah. Where's Sarah?'

Kingsley snorted and threw up his hands. 'Jesus, how should I know?'

They stared at each other for a few seconds, and then Kingsley decided to leave. He had a parting shot to deliver first.

'If I find you within 100 metres of any development of mine, or my house, I'll not be responsible for the consequences. Got it?' He looked like his last shred of self-control was about to snap. Then he saw Ralph. 'What the …?' he began. He made an effort to pull himself together, which he achieved by turning his ire on Ralph. 'Find your sister yet?' he snarled.

'Not yet.'

'Sorry to hear it.' He turned away and strode off.

The man he'd just been abusing was looking at Ralph with a curious expression.

'You've lost your sister?' he said.

'I'm Sarah's brother.'

'Her brother? That's news.' He looked confused for a moment or two. Then he put it to one side and introduced himself. 'I'm Benedict Ramsey. I was a client of Sarah's. Call me Ben.'

'Ralph de Malmanche.' They shook hands. 'That was a nice speech you made Ben, though I don't think Mr Kingsley would agree with me. You two know each other well?'

Ben laughed, in a derogatory way. 'Well enough.'

'Well, thanks for your support today. When did you see Sarah last?'

'I guess it was maybe a week or two. I went to see her at her practice in the city. Next thing I know, she's disappeared.'

'If it's not too personal a question, what was she treating you for?'

'I had a back problem. My hips were out of alignment and my spine was compensating for it. Bloody painful. But Sarah was a bit of a magician. She would put on some music, some bloke singing a mantra. A bit weird, but I liked it, actually. Then she had me face down on the table, massaging my spine. She gave me a couple of exercises to do at home between visits. Three treatments later and the pain was gone. In six weeks she did what the chiropractor couldn't do in six months. Talented woman, your sister.'

'Where do you think she might be?'

Ben had unreadable dark brown eyes. 'I wish I knew, Ralph. Listen, are you from around here?'

'London. But I'm staying at Sarah's place. For as long as it takes.'

'Let's exchange numbers. If there's anything I think of or anything I can do to help, I'll be in touch.'

They exchanged numbers, and then Ralph saw Chloe heading in his direction.

'Gotta go,' he said. 'Let me know if you hear anything.'

Chloe was beside him now. She looked at Ben curiously, but didn't say anything. She took Ralph by the arm and steered him away.

'The BBC are still here and they want to speak to you. Come on.'

A camera crew and a woman with a microphone were waiting for them on the way back to the car park. Ralph didn't have any time to think about what he was going to say, because once the casually dressed thirty-something blonde with the microphone told the viewers who he was, she launched straight into her questions.

'Any comment on the explosion we just witnessed, Ralph?'

'It's hardly what we were expecting. I'm shocked. Just glad that it happened far enough away that nobody was hurt.'

'And since your sister Sarah disappeared on Tuesday night, has there been any update?'

'No. As far as I know, the police are no further forward.'

'Sarah hasn't contacted you?'

'No.'

'Where do you think she is?'

'Well, if she's hurt, as I think she must be, I hope she'll turn up in a hospital soon. Otherwise, I have no idea.'

The interviewer stopped talking to Ralph at that point and addressed her viewers, telling them to phone the number on screen if they saw Sarah, or knew anything that could lead to pinpointing her whereabouts.

'They're running the number and the Facebook photo of Sarah in the studio right now,' she told Ralph. 'It's the Norfolk police number.'

'Great. Thank you.'

'Good luck in finding your sister, Mr de Malmanche.'

That was that. He and Chloe then joined the crowd of people making their way out.

'Who was that guy?' asked Chloe. 'The one you were talking to.'
He told her about Benedict Ramsey. Chloe didn't recollect seeing him at the practice rooms, but that didn't mean a lot.
'We see each other's clients coming and going, but never all of them,' she said. 'We don't always work the same hours, either.'
They hung around at the car park for another hour, until the crowd had virtually all gone. Then Ralph handed Chloe the keys to Sarah's Peugeot.
'I'll meet you back at the flat,' he said.
They got in their separate vehicles and drove away. Waiting an hour before leaving had been a good idea; the road wasn't too choked up with traffic, and Chloe stayed right behind him. As he drove, he thought about what had just happened. Who the hell had blown up Kingsley's houses? He doubted that Bettina's group was responsible. They didn't strike him as the type of people who would take such extreme action. But he couldn't rule them out, he hardly knew them. It was more likely to be the Global Green Garrison – Triple G. If their deeds matched their rhetoric, then it was just their style.
It had been planned well in advance, had to be. The building site on the farmland side was fenced in; a high fence, but scaleable. The fence was there to stop thieves getting in and stealing construction equipment; bulldozers and diggers. Stealing that kind of equipment meant having a suitable vehicle to load it on to; a low

loader or something similar, which you couldn't bring in via the wood. But if you were on foot, there would be no problem gaining access from the wood side, because there was no barrier there to stop you. Even if Kingsley had a night watchman on site, it would still be relatively easy to stay out of his way.

The mechanics of how it had been done were hardly his concern. The police would open an investigation, and then it would be their problem. Ralph wondered if the explosion might end up being labelled as an act of environmental terrorism. However you spun it, it wasn't good publicity for the Foxdown Wood protestors. And none of it was helping him find Sarah.

They reached the flat. Chloe drove in behind him and parked next to him.

'Come up and have a coffee,' he said to her.

'Thanks, I will. Look what I found in the glove box.'

She handed it to him. It was one of the pamphlets he'd been reading earlier.

'Where did she get hold of this?' he said.

Chloe shook her head. 'I don't know. I never saw one before today.'

They went upstairs and while Ralph made the coffee, Chloe asked if she could use his laptop. She turned it on and went straight to the Facebook page.

'Lots of comments already,' she said. 'Not good ones, either. A lot of people are putting the blame for the explosion on the tree sitters.'

He came and looked over her shoulder. 'Not exactly fair,' he said. 'But whoever's behind it, I think Bettina's days in the wood are numbered.'

Chloe looked a bit crestfallen. 'Yes, such a shame. The truth is, Kingsley Developments owns the wood and it doesn't matter how much public opinion we raise against him, the bastard will never change his mind. He'll just chop it all down.'

'What if someone made him an offer for it? Some organisation like the National Trust.'

'Someone did make an offer, a Hi-Tech firm in London who put a percentage of their profits into environmental projects. Kingsley wasn't interested.'

She was in a dour mood and so after the coffee, Ralph drove her home. When he got back to the flat, he picked up the pamphlet that she had given him and flicked through the pages, wondering what connection, if any, Sarah had with the Global Green Garrison. If anyone knew, it would be Bettina. He'd talk to her about it tomorrow. He'd go back to the wood and find out if Bettina, Karl, and the rest of them were really just the concerned citizens they claimed to be.

It was only mid-afternoon, but he felt stressed out. Sarah had been gone four days now, and his inability to do anything about it was preying on his mind. They were twins, but since childhood it had been him who'd assumed the role of protector. Since the age of five, and for more years after that than he cared to remember, it was Ralph who had stood up and taken the abuse, and sometimes a beating, from their father Lucien, when he'd had too much to drink.

Lucien de Malmanche had been hailed as the next great French existentialist writer when he published his first novel about a soldier returning from the 1954 French defeat at Dien Bien Phu, in Vietnam. The book was a treatise on the meaninglessness of war and the lives it destroyed, both casualties and survivors. He'd written a follow-up which didn't achieve the same critical success, and was struggling with a third novel when the drinking and the beatings started. Lucien had been a depressive drunk, and nasty with it.

And still is, thought Ralph. And although that abuse had stopped years ago, when his mother Daisy took the children and fled to England, the responsibility he felt for Sarah's safety had never left him. They'd grown up and made their separate ways in life, and of course Sarah was perfectly capable of looking after herself as an adult, but his obligation to protect her was simply hard-wired into him. They both knew it, and it was just an accepted facet of their relationship. If Sarah ever needed her brother, he'd be there for her. Fact. But this time, thought Ralph, I'm here, she isn't, and I'm doing absolutely nothing to find her. Because I have no idea where to look.

His remedy for that was to adjourn to the pub and drink more beer. He thought that at some point he should call his mother and tell her what had happened. Daisy, once the children were at school in England and she'd had her fill of casual affairs, had gone back to Lucien. Now they lived quietly together in Bergerac, in a perpetual alcoholic haze. And as far as Ralph knew, Lucien was still struggling to write that third book. He hadn't been to Bergerac in years, and had no intention of going there anytime soon. Would they even know him? He wasn't at all convinced that his parents even thought about their children anymore.

He dulled his memories and his anxiety with alcohol, and had a nasty moment when he wondered if this excessive consumption meant he was turning into his father, a thought so alarming that he had no choice but to order another pint. After that he played pool with a couple of the regulars, and got back to the flat at 10.30 p.m. He'd stuck to beer, so he was only a little bit drunk.

He opened up the laptop and took another look at the Facebook page, which now had several photos of the smoke rising from the explosion, and lots of new comments. They were mostly comments accusing the tree sitters of causing it, but he noticed several in their defence, too. He had a few photos of his own to go through, but right now he couldn't see how that was going to help him. He'd do it in the morning. He turned the laptop off and went to bed.

He hadn't been up long the next morning when the doorbell rang. It was Detective Constable Ainsworth. He buzzed the detective in and, shortly afterwards, Ainsworth was sitting on the sofa, while Ralph did coffee.

'You missed the explosion yesterday,' said Ralph, handing Ainsworth a mug. 'Any news on that?'

'Not so far. And nothing on Sarah. Well, I say nothing. She isn't in any of the Norfolk or Suffolk hospitals.'

Ralph detected the undertone. 'Is there something else, then?'

'Yes, maybe. Something happened last night at one of Fabian Kingsley's other developments, just outside Aylsham. Do you recognise this, Mr de Malmanche?'

He held up a plastic bag. Inside it was a silver ring. 'I see you're wearing one just like it,' said Ainsworth. 'I noticed it last time I was here.'

'Can I see it?'

'Yes, but don't take it out of the bag.'

Ralph held the bag up to the light. It was a plain silver ring, clearly visible through the plastic. It was identical to the one he wore on his right ring finger, but that didn't mean a lot. There were plenty of silver rings out there that looked just like his. He took off his ring and checked the hallmark.

'I really need a magnifying glass for this,' he said.

'Are your initials on your ring?' asked Ainsworth.

'Yes, "RDM", on the inside. Someone made this ring for me years ago. Sarah had one done at the same time. We gave them to each other as birthday presents.'

'Check the ring in the bag.'

Ralph put a thumb and forefinger around the ring in the bag and turned it so he could see the inside of the band. The initials "SDM" were engraved on it.

'Where did you find this?'

'As I said, something happened at another development that Mr Kingsley has just completed. It's outside the town of Aylsham, and while it's not exactly isolated, it's private enough. A small development of twenty houses, just four of which are occupied at the moment. Anyway, last night, one of the empty houses caught fire. A resident not far away saw the blaze before it got out of hand and called the fire brigade. They got it under control quite quickly. The inside was pretty much gutted, though.'

'You found the ring in the house?'

'Yes. An investigation team went through the place and they found this on the bathroom wash basin. Can I see your ring?'

Ralph gave it to him. Ainsworth had come prepared, he had a magnifying glass in his jacket pocket. He spent the next thirty seconds examining both rings with it.

'The hallmarks match,' he said. 'I'd say with 99% certainty that the ring we recovered belongs to Sarah.'

'So, she was there at some point.' Ralph hesitated, not wanting to voice his next thought. But there was no way around it. 'You didn't find a body in there, did you?'

Ainsworth shook his head. 'No, we didn't. The place was empty, unfurnished. Except for the bedroom. There was what was left of a bed and a couple of chairs in there, and the electricity was switched on in the house. I think someone lived there, or at the very least came and went occasionally.'

Ralph felt a touch of excitement. 'Sarah could have been taken there after her fall. And now she's been taken somewhere else.'

Ainsworth's expression was doubtful. 'It's possible, but I don't think so, Mr de Malmanche. You see, the fire was set deliberately, we know that much. And the resident who reported it saw what she thought was a man and a woman walking away from the scene. It was dark, so she couldn't make out much detail. But it's probable that she saw whoever started the fire.'

'What's that got to do with Sarah?'

'I have a theory about that. Petrol was used as an accelerant. It's possible that whoever was wearing that ring took it off when they washed their hands to get petrol off them. Then for whatever reason, forgot to put it back on again.'

Ralph was thunderstruck. 'That's a hell of a leap you're making. Are you seriously suggesting …?'

'Let's just say it's a line of enquiry. As I said, just a theory.'

'Yes, but what about her fall? A badly injured woman is in no condition to run around starting fires. You're way off base.'

'Sarah is only a badly injured woman if you believe she is, and the only evidence we've got for that is the word of the German couple. Which frankly, I'm not entirely sold on.'

'You don't believe them.'

'As I said to you before, I believe them until there's a reason not to.'

Ralph slipped his ring back on his finger. 'Now you've got a reason, is that it? What does this mean for your investigation?'

Ainsworth shrugged. 'We will be investigating the arson, whatever happens. What I believe is that your sister was in that house at some point. Whether she was held there or started a fire there is up for debate, but it won't stop us looking for her. When we find her, we can ask her.'

'Does Mr Kingsley know about this fire yet?'

'He was informed this morning.'

'You should ask *him* where Sarah is.'

Ainsworth put the plastic bag containing the ring in his pocket and stood up. 'We'll talk to him. I'll be in touch.'

Ralph saw him to the door. Then he sat down, sipped his lukewarm coffee and tried to visualise his sister as an arsonist. It was preposterous, of course. But Ainsworth had sown a nagging seed of doubt in his mind now. Combine that with the pamphlet that Chloe had found in the glove box, and you had just a little mound of soil for that seed to grow in. He told himself it wasn't like her. Sarah was a caring person, and the thought of her carrying out extreme acts of vandalism just didn't ring true. Or had he misjudged her? Maybe he'd have to face up to the truth that he didn't really know his sister the way he thought he did, after all.

Chapter 7

Ralph drove back to the wood the following morning. When he pulled into the car park, he saw three police cars and two police vans. The VW Kombi belonging to Bettina and Karl was there, along with a couple of other cars he didn't recognise. The police vehicles were unoccupied, and he wondered why they were parked there at all. If the cops were investigating yesterday's explosion, then surely they'd have parked on Kingsley's construction site, close to where the bomb had gone off.

That mystery was solved for him when he walked the path to the tree houses. Five minutes in and he saw a line of people coming towards him. They were the tree sitters, accompanied by at least a dozen policemen. He recognised Byron's wiry figure leading them. They all had packs on their backs, and some of them were wheeling suitcases as well. The procession drew level.

'Fuckers are evicting us,' said Byron, as he passed by.

He looked as uptight as he'd been the first time Ralph met him. He realised that not all the tree sitters were with Byron.

'Where are Bettina and Karl?'

'They've already put a load of stuff in the Kombi. They're getting another load.'

'I'll go speak to them.'

He walked on, but he'd only gone a few yards when he was stopped by a policeman.

'What are you doing here, sir?'

'I need to speak to one of the protestors. Is that a problem?'

The policeman had that inscrutable look that policemen are apt to adopt when they're dealing with the public.

'Speak to them about what sir?'

'I'm Sarah de Malmanche's brother.' That produced no discernible reaction. 'You know, the woman who went missing here? I just need to speak to the people who were with her that night.'

'Do you have ID, sir?'

Ralph pulled out his wallet and extracted his driving licence. The policeman scrutinised it, and then turned his gaze on Ralph.

'Alright, but don't hold them up. They're leaving. In fact if you want to be useful, you can help them do that.'

He stepped aside and let Ralph continue on his way. When he got to the tree houses, he found the two Germans busy stuffing their packs. Someone up in the tree was lowering down a cardboard box as he approached. Two policemen stood by, diligently watching it all.

'Want some help?' asked Ralph, as the box made its landing. Bettina and Karl looked up from their packing. 'What are you doing here?' asked Karl.

'I came to talk to you. I want to go over that story you told the cops one more time.'

'Why, don't you believe us either?' said Bettina, with a look that suggested she already felt harassed enough this morning.

Ralph shrugged. 'Suppose I tell you a story, first. About something that happened last night. The cops found Sarah's ring.'

That stopped them both. They looked at each other and then at him.

'Where?' said Bettina.

The two policemen were looking disapprovingly in their direction. Ralph was obviously holding up proceedings, so he picked up the cardboard box, which was heavy with books and a portable gas stove, and told them about Ainsworth's visit while they walked. Karl and Bettina strode next to him, laden with packs and suitcases.

'I told you that detective didn't believe us,' said Bettina to Karl, who merely grunted. 'Now you're saying he thinks Sarah might have set fire to this house? It's ridiculous.'

'Is it? I found a pamphlet just like the ones you had here from that crazy Triple G organisation, in the glove box of Sarah's car. Was she mixed up with them? Are you lot mixed up with them? Just tell me the truth.'

They stopped. Karl put his box on the ground. Bettina put her hands on her hips.

'You really don't believe us, do you?' she said. 'Why would we lie about it? Oh, and we have nothing to do with Triple G, is that clear enough?'

'So, it happened just the way you said it did, end of story. Sarah fell out of a tree and was taken away by four masked men.'

The two Germans looked at each other again. They seemed to make a decision. 'There is something we didn't say to the police,' said Karl.

'What was it?'

Karl picked up the box and they set off again.

'When those men came, they asked for Sarah. When I was on the ground talking to them, they wanted to know if she was up in the tree house.'

'They wanted her, specifically?'

'Yes. They said they'd been in the pub and they knew she wasn't in there with everyone else. They wanted to make her come down, but why, I don't know. They didn't mean for her to fall, I'm sure about that. They just wanted to scare her down from the tree.'

'Why didn't you tell the detective this?'

Bettina answered. 'Because it was so obvious he thought we were making it all up, like a ...' She reverted to German. '*Ein Märchen.*'

'A fairy tale,' said Karl.

No one said anything for a while after that. They reached the car park, and Karl opened up the Kombi. Ralph put down the box he'd been carrying.

'I hope you're not telling *me* a fairy tale,' he said. 'Where are you going now?'

'Back to Germany. It's all over, here. Whoever set that bomb actually ruined it for us. This time tomorrow, we will be back in Berlin.'

'You've got my number, Bettina. If there's anything else I should know, please call me. Have a good trip – *gute Reise*.'

He left them loading up the van. His mind was in a turmoil on the drive back to the city. Why would four men come out to the forest looking for Sarah? What had she done, and to whom? Was it Kingsley who'd sent them? He might even have been one of them. Or perhaps Ralph had it all wrong, and it was somebody else she'd drawn the wrath of. But weighed against that was the fact that Sarah's ring had turned up in one of Kingsley's unsold houses, so if anyone was the prime suspect …

By the time he got back to the flat, he knew what he had to do. Fabian Kingsley had to be thoroughly investigated, and there was a man who could help with that. In fact, he might have done some work on it already. He called Brett.

'Any progress on your investigation into Fabian Kingsley?' he asked.

'I've been poking around the company website. Managed to harvest some email addresses and the site has some vulnerabilities, but that's as far as I've got. Anything your end?'

Ralph told him about the conversation he'd just had with the two Germans. 'I've got more questions than answers,' he said. 'Why did those guys want Sarah? What was her ring doing in a burnt-out house belonging to Fabian Kingsley? And if she was held there, where is she now? Apart from that, I know that someone was seeing Sarah, someone was giving her money, and someone has a key to her flat. Whether they're the same person, I haven't a clue. Right now, I think the best thing we can do is concentrate on Kingsley. Maybe Sarah had something on him, something he didn't want her to share. We need to find out what that is.'

'Won't the cops talk to Kingsley? Ask him about the ring?'

'Sure. But I don't think he will say anything to incriminate himself. And now the detective in charge of the case is implying that Sarah might have left it there by accident when she started the fire. That she disappeared deliberately, and the whole falling from a tree story is bollocks.'

'What? That's crazy.' Brett thought for a while. 'What do you think? Is it possible?'

Ralph wasn't entirely surprised by that question. He was beginning to have his own doubts, but after this morning's revelation, he'd made up his mind.

'Karl and Bettina keep insisting that their story isn't bullshit. I'm going with that.'

'Yeah, I can't really see Sarah deliberately disappearing and then starting a new career as an arsonist. OK, so what we need is Kingsley's personal email and his mobile phone number. When I've got that, I can try a bit of social engineering. If it works, we'll have access to his email. We might find something there that points us in the right direction. Think you can get hold of those for me?'

'I'll try. No idea how right now, but leave it with me. And Brett …'

'What is it, mate?'

'Can't lend me a couple of grand, can you? Just until this is sorted out. I'm low on cash.'

'Umm … No. I'm not exactly rolling in it either at the moment. Sorry.'

'OK. No worries, I'll get a loan or something.'

'Tell you what I *will* do. Once you've got Kingsley's email and phone number, I'll come up to Norwich and assist. With hacking and anything else you need. Is that an option?'

Ralph jumped at it. 'Yes, definitely. You can stay in the spare room. I'll hold you to it.'

They left it at that. Ralph flopped back on the sofa and thought for a bit. First thing to do was get in a locksmith, regardless of the cost. It wasn't going to break the bank. He did a search for local locksmiths, selected one, and made the call. He was assured that someone would turn up later that afternoon and do the business. With that sorted, he then wondered if his bank would consent to lend him anything, given his rather patchy employment record. He couldn't think of anyone else who might be persuaded to tide him over and while he thought about it, the phone rang. The prefix on the incoming number identified it as French, but it still surprised him when he answered and found himself speaking to his mother. She didn't waste time with asking him how he was.

'Ralph, I've just found out that Sarah is missing. Why haven't you called me?'

She sounded suitably irate, and she wasn't slurring her words. The upper class vowels were all intact, but as she was a functioning alcoholic, they rarely suffered unless she'd really overdone it with the booze. He, on the other hand, was a bit lost for words.

'I ... umm ... I've been busy. Who told you?'

'I saw you talking about it on the TV news just now, that's who told me. Have you put on weight? What on earth is going on over there?'

She was using that "I'm about to take control of the situation" tone, which Ralph knew from experience meant the exact opposite. Daisy's way of taking control was to hand over responsibility to someone else, and then get as far away as possible. He had memories of the numerous times she'd done that when he and Sarah were young; leaving them with someone for unspecified periods, or dumping them as boarders at the Steiner Waldorf school in Kent, so she could conduct her latest affair without the inconvenience of attention seeking children. And then having to reappear and sort out the fees she'd forgotten to pay while she was doing it. Daisy's family was minor aristocracy. They had land and money and back in those days, she was the favoured only child. Which meant her father gave her pretty much whatever she wanted, including a trust fund. As a result, she'd never done a day's work in her life. All of that flashed through Ralph's mind and then he sighed.

'I'm at Sarah's place now,' he said.

Then he told her what had happened. She stayed quiet throughout most of it, so he got to the end of the story without too many irrelevant interruptions.

'How awful,' said his mother. It sounded like she meant it, too.

'Will they find her, do you think? I fear the worst …'

'We're doing everything possible. Me, the police.'

'Such a shame. I shall miss her if …'

'What do you mean? You never see either of us! Do you even remember what we look like?'

'Actually, I think it was you who decided never to see *me*. Isn't that right? And you're wrong, by the way. Sarah's been here two or three times in the last year or two. She even managed to have a few civil words with Lucien while she was at it. What do you think of that, then?'

He was shocked. Sarah, visiting the parents? Maybe his mother was suffering from alcoholic hallucinations.

'You sure she's been to see you?'

'Of course I'm bloody sure! I know it might surprise you to learn we're on speaking terms, but things change, Ralph. And while you're on the phone, there are some things you need to know. First, my father died two years ago. Of course, you wouldn't know anything about that.'

She was right, he didn't. He'd hardly known his grandfather, whose name was Wallace.

'Sorry to hear it.'

Daisy huffed. 'Yes, well. He left me everything, including that rambling bloody manor he never did anything to maintain. All sold, now. You say you're at Sarah's flat?'

'Yes.'

'Just so you know, then. It's bought and paid for, by yours truly. If anyone turns up asking for rent, you can tell them to bugger off.'

'You bought this flat for Sarah?' He couldn't keep the disbelief from his voice. Then the obvious occurred to him. 'If you're so flush, can you lend me some money while I'm up here looking for her?'

The indignancy meter ratcheted up a few notches. 'No, Ralph, I can't. And I'd appreciate it if you called me occasionally, just to let me know what's happening in the search for my daughter. I think that's only fair, don't you?'

'Right. OK … I think I can manage that.'

'Good. Oh, and Lucien's quite well, by the way. Finally finished the book, and now all we need is a publisher. It's actually quite a good book. Right, lovely talking to you. Remember to call me, please. Must go. Bye.'

She'd gone. He sat there stupefied for a while, still not believing that Sarah had resumed a relationship with the parents, and even more so by the fact that she hadn't bothered to tell him about it. Which begged the question; what else hadn't she told him?

He decided it was time to turn the place upside down and see if there was something; a document or a note or anything, that might reveal any other secrets she'd kept from him. He'd start in the main bedroom. But before he could do anything, the doorbell rang. It was the locksmith. The next hour was taken up with the selection and fitting of the new lock, and the guy doing the job was chatty, so Ralph felt obliged to make tea and conversation while the work was done. The locksmith had a card machine with him, and after he'd finished and relieved Ralph of £120, he departed.

It was a relief to know that no mysterious callers would sneak in again. They could still get in the main door downstairs, but that was it. If they came in through the main door and then realised that their key to the flat no longer fitted, they wouldn't come back. So, that was one problem out of the way. He went into the bedroom and resumed his search, starting with the wardrobe. Every item of clothing hanging in there was taken out and examined; jacket and blouse pockets were inspected, dresses were shaken and the pockets of jeans and other trousers investigated. Then the doorbell went again.

'Shit,' he murmured. 'Now what?'

He had clothing strewn all over the bed. He thought the locksmith must have forgotten something but when he picked up the intercom, it was DC Ainsworth.

'Can I come up?'

Ralph buzzed him in, wondering if there'd been a breakthrough. Maybe Ainsworth had talked to Kingsley, and he'd learned something that might lead them to Sarah. But it was nothing like that. When he opened the door to Ainsworth, the look on the detective's face was grim.

'I need you to accompany me to the mortuary,' he said.

Ralph's heart sank. 'What?'

Ainsworth realised his lack of tact. 'Sorry. A woman's body was discovered this morning. I can't say it's your sister, so don't assume the worst. Physically and age-wise though, there's a possibility. That's all I'm saying. I just need you to come and look and tell me, either way.'

There was a lump in Ralph's throat, but he managed to speak.

'OK.'

He grabbed his jacket, and they left.

Chapter 8

The mortuary was at the Norfolk and Norwich, which was only five minutes away by car. Ainsworth was driving an unmarked police vehicle, and Ralph sat up front in the passenger seat.
'Can't you identify her from the photos I sent you?' he asked, as they pulled out into the stream of traffic on the Newmarket Road.
'I haven't seen her yet. I'm going on the details the pathologist sent me. He's seen the photos, but he doesn't want to say anything definitive at the moment. She's slim build, tall. Dark hair and brown eyes. Mid-thirties. It's a close match with Sarah, and as nobody has reported anyone else missing recently ...'
They conducted the rest of the journey in silence. When they arrived at the hospital, Ainsworth parked in one of the public car parks and they walked to the West Atrium, where they were met by a mortuary porter, a young woman. She recognised Ainsworth and nodded to Ralph, and then she led them to the mortuary reception room. There were some chairs and a sofa in there, and she motioned for them to sit down while she opened a door to another room, presumably the one with the body. A minute later a man emerged, wearing blue theatre scrubs.
'I'm the senior pathologist, Ryan Dunn,' he said. He was a middle-aged man of medium height, with a round, somewhat solemn face. 'Can I have a word through here, DC Ainsworth?'
'Excuse me,' said Ainsworth.

He disappeared next door with the pathologist. He was gone five minutes, and then he returned.

'Rather than cause you distress by asking you to look, he wants to know if Sarah has any tattoos or distinguishing marks. I thought I asked you the first time I came to see you, but it's not in my notes.'

'Oh. Umm … I don't know about recently, but she's got a tattoo on her right ankle. It's not big. It's a Sanskrit symbol, an Om.'

'A what?'

'It looks a bit like a number three with a kind of circle to the right. I can draw it for you.'

'No, it's easy enough to check. I'll go and see.'

'Wait. There's a little birthmark just above her left hip, a pale white patch.'

'Right.' Ainsworth went back into the other room. He was there for an even shorter period this time and when he emerged, Ryan Dunn came, too.

'You're sure about the birthmark and the tattoo, Mr de Malmanche?' said Dunn.

Ralph nodded.

'They're both present on the woman next door.' He hesitated for a moment. 'Her body is beginning to deteriorate, but the photos you provided, along with those distinguishing marks, are enough. The woman next door is your sister, Sarah.'

'Oh,' said Ralph.

He ran out of words. A feeling of incomprehension, and then numbness, enveloped his whole body. He stared into the middle distance, seeing nothing.

'I'm sorry, Mr de Malmanche. Can I get you something, a glass of water?' asked the pathologist.

Ralph shook his head and forced himself to speak. 'It can't be. I'd know if Sarah was dead. I'd feel it. We're close, I'd just know …'

The water appeared, and he mechanically drank it. He held out the empty glass, which Ainsworth took away.

'Do you feel as though you want to see her?' asked Dunn.

'It can't be her,' said Ralph. He got unsteadily to his feet. 'Show me.'

Dunn led him through to the viewing suite, which was a narrow room with more chairs. A pane of glass separated it from a body covered by a sheet on a trolley, in an adjoining room. Ainsworth came in and stood next to Ralph.

'Look through the glass,' said Dunn. 'I'll go in and uncover her face. Just so you know, it's starting to swell a bit. Are you ready?'

Ralph nodded. Dunn put on his mask and went into the room containing the body. He lifted the sheet to reveal the face. Ralph forced himself to look.

'Do you recognise her?' said Ainsworth.

Dunn was right, the face had swollen a bit, and it was also discoloured. The pale, clear skin that had distinguished it in life was now a light shade of green. But Ralph knew.

'Yes, that's Sarah.'

He turned away and sat down. Ainsworth came and sat next to him, but he hardly noticed. The detective said nothing, and merely waited. Ralph's brain seemed to have been invaded by fog, it didn't seem to want to think at all. Then the young woman who'd brought them in came and sat on Ralph's other side. She took his unresisting hand.

'I'm sorry,' she said. 'I'm Robin. Just breathe for a while, OK? If you want us to go, just say so.'

He didn't want anyone to do anything. They sat for what seemed to him like forever, but was more like a few minutes, and then something occurred to him.

'What happens now?' he said.

'There will be a post-mortem,' said Robin. 'Then we will release the body to a funeral director.'

'OK. I think I'd like to go now.'

Ainsworth led him back to the car and drove him back to the flat. The detective got out and came around to the passenger door, which he opened.

'You going to be OK?' he asked.

'Sure.' The fog had gone, but the numbness remained.

'Call someone if you can, Mr de Malmanche. It helps to talk sometimes.'

Ralph got out and looked at him, rather blankly. 'Where did you find her?'

'Out in the wood at the Blickling Estate. Someone wrapped her in a blanket and dug a shallow grave.'

Blickling was a stately house. It had a large estate with its own wood and parkland, which was open to the public. Ralph had walked the path through the wood with Sarah on a few occasions. It was a beautiful place, once owned by an Earl, and now by the National Trust.

'Who found her?'

'A woman, walking her dogs. Or rather, the dogs did.'

'I see.' Ralph remembered something. 'Did you speak to Fabian Kingsley? About Sarah's ring in his house?'

'Not yet. I have an appointment to see him this evening. Don't worry, Mr de Malmanche. If there's anything to tell you once I've spoken to Mr Kingsley, I'll call. Now that Sarah's body has been found, this is no longer a missing persons investigation. It's become a potential murder enquiry. Oh, and I will have to make a press announcement. Tomorrow morning, I think. If you want to contact relatives before then …'

'OK, I will. Thanks for the ride.'

He found his way back upstairs and into the flat. At first, he didn't know what to do with himself. He went over to the big picture window in the lounge and stared out at the beech tree. It was late afternoon now, and still as hot today as it had been at any time during this sizzling summer. The tree was bursting with leaf, and there were pigeons and doves perched in its branches. The road beyond it was effectively hidden from his view, but not from his hearing; he was aware of the constant hum of traffic passing by. Everything out there was throbbing with heat and life, and yet in the midst of all this vitality, Sarah had simply ceased to exist. Why didn't I know? he kept thinking. Why the hell didn't I know?

He turned away from the window and sat down on the sofa. He picked up the phone and dialled Chloe. He told her what had happened.

'I'm coming around,' she said.

It was only when she arrived and embraced him that he broke down and cried. Chloe was equally upset, but after a while they both managed to pull themselves together enough to sit down and have a conversation.

'I want to post it on the Facebook page,' said Chloe. 'People should know what happened.'

'Wait till tomorrow. I have to make some calls, and Ainsworth needs to make an announcement.'

Chloe dabbed at her eyes. 'It's horrible. Really fucking horrible. Damn it …'

'I know. I could use something to drink. At least I think I could.'

'I can go round to the corner shop and get something. What do you want?'

'Anything.'

They agreed on wine. Chloe went out and while she was gone, Ralph made two calls. The first was to his mother, who was predictably upset. He still found it strange and a little disagreeable to be talking to her, and they didn't speak for long. He said he'd be in touch again with the funeral arrangements, and then he called Brett.

'I'm so sorry, mate,' said Brett. 'You need some company? I can get the train up tomorrow if you want.'

'Yeah. Come up.' He had a thought. 'Actually, no. I'll come down to London instead. I have to return the surveillance equipment. I'll drive down tonight and see Holly, and then I'll pick you up in the morning, once I've dropped it off. Is that OK? Aren't you working at the moment?'

'Not right now. I just finished a job. Penetration test on an insurance company in the City. I need to write up my report on their security flaws, which I can do up at your place. So yes, call me when you're on your way.'

'See you tomorrow, then.'

He couldn't think of anyone else to call at the moment. He could have called Holly, but he was seeing her later, and he'd tell her then. When Chloe returned with two bottles of red, he told her of his plans, and he also shared Ainsworth's revelations about Sarah's ring.

'All that bullshit about Sarah deliberately disappearing and burning down houses was just that,' he said.

'But what was her ring doing in a house belonging to Fabian Kingsley?' asked Chloe, pouring him another glass of wine.

'You'd have to say the ring was there because at some point, so was she.'

'He's the prime suspect, then. What does DC Ainsworth have to say about that?'

'He's going to speak to Kingsley. Now that Sarah's been found, maybe he'll arrest him. I wonder if it will be that easy …'

'It must be him, Ralph.'

Ralph sighed. 'Sure, but why, Chloe? Why would he want to harm her in the first place?'

'Maybe he didn't. It was an accident, her falling. But it doesn't tell us why they were looking for her.'

'No. That's what we have to find out.'

Chloe fixed him with her steady, blue eyes. 'Who's we? Shouldn't you leave all that to the police?'

'Oh, I will. I'll just make some enquiries of my own.'

'I see.' Chloe decided not to pursue the subject. 'Let me know if there's anything I can do. What time are you going to London?'

'About seven, I guess. Actually, I'll download the photos I took at the demo. You can look through them with me now.'

He retrieved the camera from the bedroom and plugged it into his laptop with a USB cable. Ten minutes later, he had everything downloaded. He huddled next to Chloe on the sofa with the laptop on his knees, and they flicked through the images. They were mostly photos of the crowd just before and after the explosion, and there were plenty of faces in focus, but not anyone either of them knew. Not that they knew what they were looking for, anyway. There were several of Ben giving his speech and whipping up a frenzy, with Bettina standing nearby. Otherwise, they were just photos of random people.

'Don't know what I was thinking when I snapped all this,' he said. 'Look at this one. All of Kingsley's security men, just before the police came and put up the barriers.'

'You never know,' said Chloe. 'Don't delete them. One of these people just might just be responsible for the explosion.'

They drank more wine. Ralph would have been happy to drink himself into oblivion, but Chloe read him. Instead of opening the second bottle, she stowed it away in her shoulder bag.

'Will you drive me home?' she said. 'I'll look around our practice rooms tomorrow and see what Sarah left there. Then I'll come and see you after that. OK?'

He didn't argue with her about her confiscation of the wine. He made them both a coffee and once they'd finished that, he took Chloe home. She looked a little worried when he dropped her off. 'Drive carefully,' she said, studying his face. 'Don't drink any more today.' She leaned across and kissed him on the cheek, and then she got out and waved goodbye.

He drove back and only stayed long enough to make himself a sandwich for the journey. Before leaving, he looked around the flat. It had become a kind of ritual, checking the place out and wondering if it would look the same when he came back. He decided to leave Sarah's clothes strewn all over the bed; and then he grabbed the surveillance kit, the sandwich, and a bottle of water. Five minutes later, he was on the road.

On the drive back to London he was held up in a traffic jam on the motorway. The delay cost him an hour, and it was 10 p.m. when he got back to Greenwich. He was a little wound up after being stuck in a car doing nothing for so long, and when he opened the door to the flat, it was with a sense of relief. He could chill out now, or at least try to as much as possible, under the circumstances. He expected Holly to be home and was just about to call out her name, when something stopped him.

It was the sound of a woman moaning. With pleasure. Quiet little cries of pleasure, that were steadily gaining in frequency and volume. And he knew who they belonged to, because he'd heard them before. His whole body went tense. He took a breath, and then stepped his way quietly through the lounge area until he was outside the bedroom door. Stealth wasn't really required, the noise coming from inside the room would have masked the entry of a herd of elephants, as far as he was concerned.

He opened the door and there was Holly, naked and flat on her back on their bed, with her legs wrapped around an equally naked man. The guy had his back to Ralph, and he was plunging into her with great enthusiasm, no doubt spurred on by her cries of encouragement. They weren't aware of him for all of five seconds, and then Holly turned her head to one side and opened her eyes. Her legs tightened around her partner and brought him to an abrupt halt.

'Ralph …' she said.

The man turned. Ralph had never seen him before. He must have been closer to fifty than forty, and his hair was greying at the temples. He was well-built, but he was carrying a little extra weight around the waist. Apart from the loss of enthusiasm evident in his now drooping manhood, he seemed remarkably composed for someone caught *in flagrante*. He glanced at Holly.

'Is this …?'

'The boyfriend,' said Ralph. Holly said nothing. She just looked ashamed.

Ralph had never been in this scenario before. But although he might not know it, he was old school when it came to responding to the situation.

'You arsehole,' he said.

Then he stepped forward, bunched a fist, and lashed out. The punch connected, right on the nose. Its recipient sprawled back onto the bed, and Holly had to twist out of the way to avoid a collision. The man sat up with his hand to his nose, which was bleeding freely.

'Shit,' he said.

'Get the fuck out of here,' said Ralph.

He turned and walked out of the bedroom, slamming the door on the way. He sat down in the living room and held his head in his hands. His heart was racing, and he was finding it hard to hold back the urge to get up and have another pop at Holly's friend. A minute later, the friend and Holly emerged, fully dressed. They ducked into the bathroom together, presumably to do something about the bleeding. When that was done, the man, still holding his nose and avoiding eye contact, walked swiftly through the living room and then out of the front door. Holly went back into the bedroom and stayed there.

There was silence now. Ralph didn't move from his seat. His anger dropped down a notch and he became aware of an aching emptiness, right down in the pit of his stomach. He hadn't seen this one coming, and coming on top of Sarah, it was a little hard to take. His comfortable little world was reeling.

After a while he got up and went to the fridge. There was some white wine in there. He poured himself a large glass, and knocked most of it back in one swig. Then he went over to the living room window, which was partially open. He opened it fully and just stood there, drinking wine and staring at nothing in particular for the next five minutes. When the glass was empty, he went to find Holly. She was sitting cross-legged on the bed, in shorts and a t-shirt, staring blankly at the wall. She snapped out of it when he walked in.

'You didn't have to hit him,' she said.

'And you didn't have to fuck him. Who is he?'

'Nobody you know.'

'I know that, Holly. Why do you think I asked the question? Who is he?'

His voice was rising. Then Holly got angry.

'He's from work, and I have to go in and face him tomorrow. Couldn't you have been a bit more considerate?'

He couldn't quite believe she'd said that. It stopped him for all of two seconds before the sarcasm kicked in.

'I'm so sorry, next time I'll just ask him if I'm interrupting anything, shall I? How old is he anyway? He must be 20 years older than you. What is he, senior management?' Then he laughed. 'Christ, you're sleeping your way to the top, is that what's happening here? Unbelievable.'

'No, that's not what's happening here. What's happening here is that I've met someone who has drive and ambition and sensitivity, and who actually takes the time to notice me! Unlike you. All you've done for the past six months is sit around the place doing god only knows what all day, while I go to work and pay the rent!'

'What are you talking about? I've got work.'

'With that ridiculous private investigation agency? You won't even tell me how much they pay you. They do pay you, don't they?'

'Of course they pay me!'

'Not enough to pay your share of the rent though, is it? Frankly Ralph, you've been using me for the last six months. I don't know what the hell is wrong with you but whatever it is, I'm not prepared to subsidise it. God only knows how many times I've asked you when you're going to get a real job again. Soon, you say. When is soon, by the way?'

'Don't make this about money.' He stared at her, breathing hard. Then, out of nowhere, his rage evaporated. 'The hell with it,' he said.

He turned and walked out. It wasn't until he'd slammed the door behind him and was sitting in the car wondering where to stay tonight, that he remembered he hadn't told Holly about Sarah. As if she'd give a shit, he thought. He found his phone, and called Brett.

'Do you mind if I come over a little earlier than planned?' he asked his friend.

Brett didn't mind. Ralph put the car in gear and drove away.

Chapter 9

Brett lived in a rented flat in Hatfield, just north of London in Hertfordshire. It was an easy train ride from central London to Hatfield, but driving there from Greenwich, on the south side of the river Thames, was a bit of a hike. At that time of night it wasn't too congested, and he arrived around 11.30 p.m.

'Sorry about the time,' he told Brett, when he opened the door.
'Jesus, don't worry about that. Are you OK?'
'Not really.'

They went into Brett's living room. He lived alone and wasn't exactly a stickler for neatness. A pile of assorted books and magazines on one of the two big living room sofas threatened to cascade onto the floor at any moment, and the other sofa had a pile of unironed clothes adorning it. There was a little dining table in the room that had some semblance of order about it – the empty beer bottles on it were placed in a perfectly straight line.

Brett did his paid hacking work from here. There was a big desk against one wall, the top of which housed two laptops and two additional flat screen monitors. Next to it was a sturdy black metal box, a server unit containing lots of storage capacity. Cables connecting this setup coiled their way around and behind it all. On the wall above the desk there was a large framed photograph of a French actress Brett was keen on; a black and white shot of her sitting on a chair in a Paris apartment, the Eiffel tower rising up through the window behind her. She was wearing a black trouser suit, and had one leg crossed elegantly over the other as she regarded the camera with a provocative half-smile. It was a great photo, but Ralph could never remember her name, and he didn't bother trying to now. He sat down next to the pile of clothes instead.

'God, I feel so bloody tired,' he said.

'You look it. Do you want to talk about it? I'll get a beer.'

'You got most of it on the phone. But I'll take the beer.'

He'd been talking to Brett as he drove, so there wasn't much to add to what for Ralph, was a disastrous day. Brett came back from the kitchen and thrust a cold bottle into his hand.

'I haven't even thought about how I'm going to get that email and phone number for you,' said Ralph.

'Leave it to me. But we might not need to go down that road if this Kingsley bloke is arrested.'

'I don't think Sarah's ring will be evidence enough for that. When we get back to Norwich, I'll call Ainsworth and see what the situation is.'

'Let's worry about it later.' Brett raised his bottle of beer. 'Here's to Sarah. One way or another, we'll find out what happened. OK?'

They drank to that. The mood between them was sombre, given the circumstances. Brett had been told about Holly's indiscretion, but he had the sense not to enquire further about it.

'I've made up the spare room,' said Brett. 'We have two choices; I either open the bourbon and we get hammered, or we call it a night right now.'

Ralph grunted. 'I don't think getting pissed will help, and there are things to sort out tomorrow. I want a clear head for that. Let's call it a night.'

They retired shortly afterwards. Ralph lay in the single bed in the tiny spare room and did his best to fall asleep, but it was a long time coming. The bedroom window was open, and there was a breeze wafting through, which tempered the heat a bit. When did English summers get so hot? he wondered, as he tossed from side to side, replaying the day in his mind in what threatened to become an endless loop. But eventually, in the small hours of the morning, he drifted off.

By the time they'd got up and Brett had packed, and then they'd driven to Catford Investigations, it was almost 11 a.m. They grabbed a rare parking space and when they walked into the office, it was to find that news of Sarah's death had preceded them. Not that anyone knew they were coming. Vivian was on the desk as usual, and she was talking to someone on the phone. She looked at Ralph in astonishment.

'Let me call you back,' she said. Then she got up and threw her arms around him. 'We heard,' she said. 'So sorry.'

While they were locked in this embrace, Gerald and Sandra appeared. There were more expressions of condolence before everyone found their seats in the reception area. Sandra was a stocky strawberry-blonde, who was a bit younger than Gerald. She normally projected an aura of no-nonsense efficiency on the world at large, but today, she was all motherly concern.

'How are you feeling, Ralph? We didn't expect to see you so soon. Such a shock. We only saw it on the news an hour ago.'

'A detective in Norwich had a televised press conference,' said Gerald, responding to the look of confusion on Ralph's face.

The penny dropped. 'That was fast. Actually, he said he'd do that today. Did he say anything about an arrest?'

'No, nothing.'

Ralph sighed. 'Right. I'm fine, I guess. I've come to return the surveillance equipment. Then Brett and I are off to Norwich.'

'The what? Oh, right. There was no hurry for that, Ralph.'

'To be honest, I need that £200 I left with you. Bit short right now.'

Sandra turned to Gerald with a disapproving look. 'You charged him to borrow it?'

'It's just normal procedure, Sandra …'

'Pity, really,' chimed in Brett. 'We're launching an investigation of our own. It would be handy if we could hold on to it.'

Sandra took charge. 'Get Ralph his money, Gerald. Of course you can hold on to it, Ralph. For as long as you need it.'

Gerald stood up. 'You're launching your own investigation? Both of you?'

'Assisting the police with their enquiries,' said Brett. 'If you see what I mean.'

Gerald was obviously concerned that two of his freelance employees were about to become suddenly unavailable.

'I do see what you mean. How long do you think these enquiries will take?'

Brett shrugged. 'No idea.'

'Right.' Gerald went off to find the money. He came back with an envelope full of cash.

'There's £500 in there,' he said. 'Your deposit plus a contribution to operating costs from us. If there's anything we can do to help, just shout. Got it?'

'Cheers, Gerald,' replied Brett, taking the envelope. 'We'll take you up on that.'

They stayed for a cup of tea, and Ralph said he'd let them know about the funeral arrangements. Then it was back to the car, and onwards to Norwich. There was plenty of time to discuss their strategy on the way.

'There are three questions I want answered,' said Ralph, as they came off the M25 and onto the A11.

'Which are?'

'Number one; four guys came to the wood looking specifically for Sarah. Why?'

'Good question. But why come out there at all? They could have visited her at home, surely.'

'I don't know, Brett. That's what we have to find out. Number two; someone was giving Sarah money. Who?'

'OK. Next question.'

'Next question is; Chloe thinks Sarah was seeing someone and I think she's right, because someone came into the flat while I was out and removed their guitar. I reckon it was him. Who is he?'

'No idea. But he probably has nothing to do with what happened to her.'

'Even if that's true, he may be able to shed some light on it. And why hasn't he shown up yet? She had some environmental literature in her car, which I think may have come from him. Extremist literature. My hunch is that he isn't showing up because he, or someone he knows, is responsible for the explosion at the demo. So, we have to find him, too.'

'Alright. But given the fact that you say Sarah's ring was at this burnt out house owned by Kingsley, that makes him our main target, right? What motive would anyone else have for trying to scare her or abduct her, or whatever the hell they were trying to do that night?'

Ralph drummed his fingers on the steering wheel while he thought about it.

'I don't know. I thought at first that the whole incident was an attack on the protestors, the group as a whole. I think they came out there with chainsaws to make it look that way, but it wasn't. Maybe it isn't Kingsley, but I'm convinced that the guy knows something. Yes, he's our main target.'

'OK. I'll go to work on him. And who's Chloe?'

'A friend of Sarah's. You'll meet her later.'

They had a clear run up to Norwich, and arrived early afternoon. As they went into the house and up the first flight of stairs Ralph heard a door shutting, and when he got to the landing on the first floor, he met another resident of the house. She was a woman, who he thought was at least 70. Her face was lined, and had a touch of fragility about it, but she had good posture for her age, and an intelligent gleam in her dark eyes. Her hair was short, and almost snow-white. She was surprised to see him, and asked him a question with her eyes.

'I'm Ralph,' he answered. 'Sarah's brother. She has a flat upstairs, do you know her?'

'Is she back?' came the reply. There was nothing fragile about the voice. It was clear and crisp, and the accent was Irish.

Brett appeared behind Ralph, laden with bags containing laptops, and wheeling a suitcase. He stopped and listened.

Ralph answered the question in as level a voice as he could manage. 'No, she's not back. Actually, she died.'

They regarded each other for a second.

'But Sarah's missing,' she said. 'I know that much. She's not dead, surely.'

'No, I identified her body yesterday.'

'Oh, god. I'm so sorry.' She looked upset. 'I'm Eileen. I knew Sarah. I heard you clomping around overhead and I thought it must be her at first, but I saw you out front the other day from my window. Did you come to find her?'

'That's right. How well did you know her?'

'Well, we chatted when we met, and sometimes she brought her massage table down and gave me a treatment. I get pain in my back and shoulders. And we would gossip a little, and drink sherry from time to time. She did mention you.'

'When did you last see her?'

Eileen had to think about that. 'You know, it must have been the day before she had that accident they reported, out in the wood. I was coming in from the shops and I met them on their way out.'

'You met them? Who's them?'

'Sarah and her man, of course.'

Ralph's ears pricked up. 'Really? What man is this? Does he have a name?'

'It's Dominic. Haven't you met him?'

'Never heard of him.'

'That's a surprise. I don't know how long she'd been seeing him, but I do know that they were mad about each other. She told me herself.'

'She never mentioned him to me. What does he look like?'

Eileen looked at her watch. 'I've got a taxi waiting outside. Walk me down.'

They left Brett on the landing and went down the stairs together into the hall.

'He's a bit older than you,' she said, as they reached the front door. 'Good looking. A bit of a hippy, but I'm saying that because of the hair. He's got lots of shoulder-length black hair, a bit wild-looking in my opinion. If he cut it, he'd look quite smart.'

She opened the door. Sure enough, there was a taxi parked outside.

'I don't suppose you'd know if he has a key to Sarah's flat, do you?' asked Ralph.

'I don't know.' She thought for a moment. 'Well, actually, he used to come in and out when Sarah wasn't here, so I imagine he must have. I remember seeing him a few times in the evenings when Sarah was out at the wood. She spent a lot of evenings out there, but she told me he hardly ever went there himself. She never said what he did. Look, I must be going. Will there be a funeral service I can attend?'

'Yes, I'll let you know.'

'Please do. Pop in one evening and we can have a drink. Just knock.'

'Thanks. I will.'

She went out, and the door closed behind her. Ralph ran back upstairs.

'Did you get all that?'

Brett nodded. 'Dominic. They were mad about each other.' He looked around. 'This is a nice house, Ralph.'

'You're right, it is. Come on, you haven't seen Sarah's place yet. One more flight of stairs. Give me those bags.'

They walked up the stairs and went inside. Ralph showed Brett the second bedroom.

'You're sleeping on a mattress on the floor,' he said. 'Don't worry, it's very comfortable.'

Brett raised his eyes. 'Slept on worse. Got anything to eat?'

There was food in the flat, but Ralph's appetite was minimal and he didn't feel like cooking. The Beehive, which was the pub he frequented around the corner, did food, so he suggested that. They went straight there and Ralph managed a ham sandwich. Brett had gammon and eggs. As they returned to the flat, Ralph spotted Chloe walking towards them down the Newmarket Road. She waved, and they waited till she joined them.

'Just coming to see how you are,' she said. She nodded at Brett. 'Hi.'

Ralph introduced them, and then they all went back to the flat. Over coffee, Ralph explained the plan of action to Chloe.

'I would really like to find out who this guy is that Sarah was seeing. I started looking through her stuff to see if there's anything that might give us a clue. We could all do more of that now if you like.'

Chloe was agreeable. Ralph went back to sorting through Sarah's clothes in the main bedroom. Chloe took the second bedroom, which had a desk in it, as yet untouched. Brett said he wanted to unpack a laptop and get set up on the dining room table in the living room. They all got on with their respective tasks.

Ransacking the wardrobe and the chest of drawers in Sarah's bedroom didn't yield anything of interest, so Ralph checked her phone again. The contacts list didn't have a Dominic on it, which was disappointing, so he emptied her bag onto the bed and sorted through the contents. There wasn't a whole lot to look at; a manicure set, lipstick and lip salve, tissues, a box of condoms. Then Chloe appeared.

'I've found her appointments diary,' she said. 'And some other things. Look.'

She handed him a set of business cards encircled with a rubber band. He extracted one.

'Antoinette; Tantric massage,' he said. 'Do you know an Antoinette? What's tantric massage?'

'Read the rest.'

'Sensual full-body massage, performed by attractive and experienced French woman. Call to book or email Tantric_Antoinette@gmail.com. Withheld numbers will not be answered. What's this got to do with Sarah?'

'It's her mobile phone number, Ralph. Look!'

She was right. 'So it is. What is this? Sexual massage? Did you know about this?'

'No, I didn't. I know what tantric massage is, I just didn't know Sarah offered it. And there's more. Here's another card.'

She handed it to him. This one was headed 'Clarissa's Place – private adult venue in Norfolk'. It had a website URL on it, and a phone number.

'Brett, check out this website for me,' called out Ralph. 'Wait, I'll bring you the card.'

'I will, once you give me your wireless password,' came the reply.

'Damn. It's … The router's on the bookcase. It's on a piece of paper under the router.'

They gathered around Brett's laptop, and once he was connected, he typed in the URL. They quickly learned that Clarissa was the mistress of a venue in North Norfolk, offering adult parties by invitation only. The lucky attendees had the option of exploring their sexual fantasies in suitably equipped play rooms, with a variety of sex toys. Active participation wasn't compulsory and if you were shy, it was fine to just watch. But if you were more adventurous, you could ask other attendees you found attractive to explore your fantasies with you. Couples and singles were equally welcome.

'You think Sarah was into this?' asked Brett, as he clicked on the 'Galleries' tab. A number of photos showing bondage gear and restraint tables, among other things, filled the screen.

'There's a massage option,' said Chloe. 'Check it out.'

Brett clicked. There were no photos on this page, just a summary of what was available.

'Tantric massage, to get you in the mood,' read Chloe. 'Treat yourself and your partner to this sensual form of massage as an entrée to the main course. This delicious service is only available at selected parties, and is offered by our beautiful masseuses, Grace and Antoinette. Enjoy a ninety minute massage at a cost of £150. Must be booked in advance.'

'Sounds interesting,' said Brett. 'Bit expensive, isn't it?'

Chloe looked a bit shocked. 'I had no idea,' she said. 'I wonder how often she did this.'

Ralph sat down on the sofa. 'And I wonder who goes to these parties.'

Chloe sat next to him and started flicking through Sarah's appointment book. 'Looks like all of her more normal clients are in here,' she said. 'Dates, names, phone numbers. This is something to work with.'

Chloe started looking through the appointment book. While she did that, Ralph had a request to make.

'Brett, can you find out what I have to do to get an invite to one of those parties?'

'OK. What do you think you're going to find out by going to one?'

'Grace might be interesting to talk to. And I want to see just who goes to these things. We might get a lead.'

'Here's something interesting,' interrupted Chloe. 'There's a Roz Kingsley in here. But this is weird.'

'What do you mean?'

'She came twice in January; once in the clinic and once here, Sarah marked it as a home appointment. But look at February.'

She passed the book to him. 'The 27th,' she said. 'It was a Tuesday.'

He looked. The entry read 'Roz no show. DECEASED!'

'That *is* interesting,' said Ralph. 'Maybe she and Fabian are related. Brett, google Roz Kingsley for me.'

Brett obliged. 'Roz, must be short for Rosalind. OK, here we go.' There were several search results for Rosalind Kingsley in Norfolk, including a news report. It said that Rosalind Kingsley, wife of Fabian, had committed suicide. She was found dead in her car in the car park at Brancaster Beach, a secluded spot on the

Norfolk coast. Two empty bottles were on the passenger seat next to her; one of vodka, and another of sleeping pills.

'The post mortem revealed excess alcohol and a cocktail of drugs in her bloodstream,' said Brett. 'She was 35.'

There was a photo of Roz, taken in someone's garden. She'd been a pretty, willowy blonde.

'Do you know her?' Ralph asked Chloe.

'No, I don't remember seeing her at the clinic.'

'Only a short time since she died, too. Maybe that has something to do with why Kingsley's such a miserable sod.'

Brett interrupted his deliberations this time.

'Did Sarah have a laptop? If I can access it …'

'Yes, but I haven't seen it. It's not in the flat. Was it in her car, Chloe?'

'I didn't see it. Give me the keys and I'll go and check.'

Ralph retrieved the keys and gave them to her. While she was away, Ralph and Brett took a closer look at Clarissa's web page.

'You just have to join the site if you want to attend a party,' said Brett. He switched to the relevant page. 'See? Don't use your real name, but you will have to provide a face photo, so they can identify you. Once you're accepted, you just have to register for a party. And you can book a massage at the same time.'

Ralph had a good look. 'Ah, bit of a problem,' he said.

'What?'

'The massage is for couples only.'

'Yes, but Antoinette isn't going to be there, is she?' said Brett. He saw the look on Ralph's face. 'Sorry, mate.'

'It's OK. I guess that Grace will bring someone else along in her place. Well, I'll join. But I need a partner.'

Just then, Chloe returned.

'Nothing in the car. Not under the seats, or in the boot. Why are you looking at me like that?'

'Chloe, I need to ask you a huge favour,' said Ralph. 'I need you to be my partner. Temporarily, I mean.'

Chloe's eyes opened wide. 'You need what?'

'Just so we can get in and talk to Grace. At the club.'

'But you've got a partner. Holly, isn't it?'

'Not anymore.'

Her astonishment deepened. 'Oh,' was all she managed.

Brett smiled. 'Do you like to party, Chloe?'

He got an ice-melting look in reply. She came across and looked at the screen. She spent a minute taking in the joining and massage requirements.

'And once we're in, do we go through with the massage treatments?'

'I hadn't got that far,' said Ralph.

Chloe decided. 'Alright. I'll be your partner. You can take a photo of me. Who knows, it could be fun.' Her face said she didn't believe it for a moment. 'I'm going to see what else I can find in the bedroom. Let me know when you want that photo.'

She walked away and left them to it.

Chapter 10

After an ambivalent Chloe had allowed Ralph to photograph her, she said she had to get going. She had a client coming to the clinic at 5 p.m.

'Can I drive you?' said Ralph.

'I can walk it. Let me know what happens about this party.'

'OK. Thanks for helping me.'

She picked up her bag. 'If you don't mind me asking, what happened with you and Holly?'

'I walked in on her with another man.'

'What, in bed you mean?'

'Yep.'

'Wow.' She saw the look on his face. 'Sorry I asked.'

He shrugged. 'Shit happens.'

Chloe wasn't fooled by the lacklustre attempt at bravado. 'If you say so. Tell me about it later if you want to, though I probably don't need all the sordid details. Bye, Brett.'

She left. Ralph had everything he needed now, including Chloe's email, to fill in the membership form online for both of them. Brett stood aside while he took over the laptop and did that.

'There's a party on Saturday,' said Brett. 'If they get back to you soon, you could go to that.'

'Maybe you should come along, too. Moral support.'

'Why not? Fill in a form for me as well.'

Once all that was done, Brett wanted to talk about his plan to infiltrate Fabian Kingsley's private life.

'I've done no reconnaissance on him,' he said. 'It can take weeks to plan an attack on someone's cyber life properly, you know that.'

'And you're a white hat hacker. What we're proposing to do is illegal. Grey hat at best.'

Brett nodded. 'Glad you mentioned it. If it gets out that I'm hacking a target without permission, my career as a penetration tester is over. So, we need to be circumspect, but we also need to do something sooner rather than later.'

'Any ideas?'

'You can forget about getting Kingsley's email and phone number. That could take too long, and the little social engineering trick I wanted to try with them is a bit dated. Instead, I want to put a program I wrote onto his machine at work. The anti-virus software won't pick it up because nobody else has ever used it. It will give us a back door into the network, and it has a keylogger as well. Once that's running, we'll get a record of every key stroke he types, including user names and passwords. We'll get into his email account with some of those and start looking for incriminating emails, or whatever.'

'And how do we go about all this, exactly?'

'You've been to his office; how big is the place?'

'I think maybe a dozen people work there.'

'OK. If I can get into the office, I can introduce the program onto any of the computers there, with a USB stick. All I'll need is an open USB port and thirty seconds. Once it's running, I can control everything from here.'

'And if the USB ports are all locked?'

Brett shrugged. 'I'll have to rethink it, won't I?'

'I thought you wanted to be circumspect.'

'I will be. While I'm being circumspect and plugging in the USB, you'll be creating a diversion.'

'What?'

Brett laughed. 'We'll figure out what form this diversion will take later. I've had a look at his website and I know what services Kingsley Developments offer.' He looked at his watch. 'If you drive me into town now, there should be enough time for me to drop in and book an appointment before they shut. Just need to get changed, first.'

He disappeared into the second bedroom and came out ten minutes later, dressed in a suit. 'Right, let's go.'

The drive in didn't take long, because most of the traffic was coming out of town. They parked and walked to Tombland, where Ralph pointed out the red brick building he'd visited once before. 'Second floor. Don't upset the receptionist. I'll be in the Edith Cavell pub when you come out. See it on the corner over there?'

Brett saw it. 'Shouldn't be long.'

He crossed the road and entered the building. He was in there for all of ten minutes and Ralph, who had a good view from the table he was occupying in the pub, saw him emerge. A minute later, Brett joined him.

'How did it go?' asked Ralph.

'Good. I've got an appointment tomorrow morning. Not with Kingsley, with a Mr Jarvis. He's a planning consultant.'

'And what are you going to talk about?'

'I've bought some land and I want to do a site survey and feasibility study, with a view to building a few houses on it. Mr Jarvis is going to help me with that.'

Ralph was amused. 'When did you become a property developer?'

'That's just the thing, mate. I'm not, so I'm seeking professional advice. Makes perfect sense, don't you think?'

'Of course. Want a beer? Actually, best if we go somewhere else. It's a little too close to Kingsley's office here. Did you get a good look around? See Kingsley?'

'Didn't see him. But I got a feel for the place. Come on, isn't this town supposed to have a pub for every day of the year? I reckon we can find one that Fabian Kingsley isn't drinking in just now.'

There were plenty of pubs nearby, but they rejected those. They took the car instead, and a little while later Ralph parked outside the Unthank Arms, which was a particular favourite of his. It wasn't too far from the flat, either. They had a couple of pints in there and then they went home. Brett wanted to do some scans of Kingsley's website with a suite of hacking tools he had installed on his laptop. While he did that, he wanted Ralph to check Kingsley's social media presence, assuming he had one.

'Start with Facebook. If he's there, see if you can find out what interests he has. Who his friends are, what they're saying. Anything that can give us a better picture. You know what to do.'

That took up most of the evening. They also discussed just how Brett's appointment would go the next day, and the timing of the diversion. Then they called it a night.

The appointment was scheduled for 11 a.m. the next day. Brett had put together a document containing photos of a plot of land that he'd ostensibly bought. He'd lifted the photos from a website with lists of property for sale. It would do as a conversation starter, but not much else. Which was fine, because he didn't intend to spend much time with Mr Jarvis before Ralph's diversion cut them short. That was the plan. Brett had adopted the name Bill Stevens for the purpose of the meeting. They arrived outside the offices of Kingsley Developments five minutes early. Brett was suited and booted for the occasion. He took a deep breath and adjusted his tie.

'Right. When you get my text, you know what to do.'

He disappeared inside. Ralph gave him till 11 a.m. exactly, and then followed. He walked up to the third floor, where he stood in the hallway outside a firm of solicitors and tried to be inconspicuous. There was nobody around to ask him what he was doing there, but that could change at any second. Then the text arrived. 'Go!' was all it said.

Ralph was standing right next to a fire alarm. He drew his arm back and whacked the glass with his elbow. As the alarm started blaring through the building, he ran down the stairs and out into the street. From his vantage point by the Edith Cavell, he watched as the occupants spilled out a minute later and began assembling across the road. Then Brett appeared, with a man that Ralph assumed was Mr Jarvis. They shook hands and then Brett walked off. Ralph didn't follow him. Instead he took a different route back to the car park, where they'd arranged to meet. When he got there, Brett was waiting for him.

'How did it go?' said Ralph.

'Worked perfectly.' Brett looked a little flushed, and more than a little pleased with himself. 'Jarvis got up when the alarm went off and said he'd check to see if it was just a drill. While he did that, I plugged in the USB. The program downloads as soon as you do that and nothing came up on his screen to say the USB port was locked, which means we did it!'

'What did you say when he came back?'

'Just that I had another urgent appointment and I'd get back to him.'

'Right. Well done. Now let's get out of here.'

They drove straight back to the flat, so Brett could fire up his laptop and see if the program he'd just infiltrated into the Kingsley Developments network was communicating with his machine.

'We have lift-off,' said Brett, once he'd sat down and logged in. 'I'll need to do some snooping around now. Could take a while, so best if you leave me to it.'

Ralph was happy enough to do that. He opened up his own laptop and checked for mail.

'Our applications for membership of Clarissa's Place have been approved,' he said. 'I'll sign us all up for Saturday's party.'

Brett merely nodded, his attention was fixed elsewhere. Ralph clicked over to Clarissa's web page and registered their attendance. He got an email a minute later, with details of where to go and what to expect. The party was being held at a private house in Burnham Market, a village in North Norfolk. It would start at 10 p.m., and the dress code was either formal or alternative.

Ralph had no idea what 'alternative' meant. He read on, and was informed that newbies were welcome, the dungeon would be open for those who wanted to use it, and one room was reserved as a spanking venue. There was also a link to book the massages. He clicked on it and saw that Antoinette wasn't available but someone called Serena would be there in her place, along with Grace. There was availability for 11 p.m., so he booked in Chloe and himself. He didn't have to pay up front with a card, it was cash on the night.

More money I can't afford, he thought. He was just about to search for loans online, when his phone rang. It was Dr Dunn, the pathologist.

'Mr de Malmanche, I'm calling to let you know that I've done Sarah's post-mortem.'

With the mention of her name, the grief he'd been doing his best to suppress made its presence felt. It was like a needle in the gut.

'Can you tell me how she died?'

'There was definitely a fall. She had a mild to moderate spinal compression. The kind of thing that happens when you fall from a height.'

'It killed her?'

'No. I believe she was alive up to forty-eight hours after the fall. But around that time, she had a brain haemorrhage. Another consequence of the fall, in my opinion. That's what did it, I'm afraid.'

'I see.' Ralph tried to think logically. 'So, she could have been alive somewhere for forty-eight hours. Could she have walked around with that compression you're talking about?'

'Yes, but it would have been painful. The best thing to do in a situation like that is to move as little as possible. Just so you know, I've informed the coroner and now that he has the post-mortem results, he's authorised the release of Sarah's body. Is there a funeral director you'd like to appoint?'

'I don't know any funeral directors. Can you recommend someone?'

'Not officially. But there is someone not far from you. Let me have your email address and I'll send you the details. If you decide to go with him, can you instruct him as soon as possible? Then he can come to the mortuary and collect her.'

'I will, Doctor.'

Ralph gave Dr Dunn his email address and a minute after he'd hung up, he got an email from the mortuary. Brett had stopped what he was doing when he'd heard Sarah's name. He'd picked up on most of the conversation.

'You OK?' he said. 'You look a little pale.'

Ralph lost it, momentarily. 'Course not. What the hell do you expect?' The tone and volume of his own voice took him by surprise. His anger dissipated a split second later. 'Sorry, mate. Don't know where that came from.'

'Don't worry about it.'

Ralph sighed. 'Well, now I have a funeral to organise. I'll call this funeral director and find out how that works.'

He went into Sarah's bedroom to do that. Looking out the window onto the back garden, he noticed that the grass was even more burnt by this relentless heat than the last time he'd stood here and gazed at it. It hadn't rained for three weeks now, and in some parts of the country a drought had been declared. There was a breeze of sorts coming in through the open window, but it did little to relieve the temperature inside the house.

He spoke to a Mr Stansfield of Stansfield and Sons, Funeral Directors. Before the body could be collected, Ralph needed to visit Mr Stansfield with some evidence to prove that he was Sarah's next of kin. Once that was established, he'd need to sign an authorisation to allow Mr Stansfield to collect her body.

'When are you thinking of having the actual funeral?' asked Mr Stansfield.

He sounded altogether too chirpy for someone in his profession, in Ralph's opinion.

'In a week, ten days? I need to notify a few people.'

'Alright. Come and see me this afternoon and we'll talk about it.'

They agreed on 3 p.m. The funeral parlour was just down the road from the supermarket. Ralph could walk it if he wanted to. He said he'd be there, and they concluded the call.

'I'm going out to organise the funeral,' Ralph said, once he'd joined Brett in the living room. 'Later this afternoon. What do you want for lunch?'

'What you got?'

'You can have a mushroom omelette. Even I can cook that.'

Brett thought he could eat a mushroom omelette. Once lunch was out of the way, Ralph washed up and then, allowing himself twenty minutes for the walk, he left Brett to his own devices and set off for the funeral parlour. He arrived with a few minutes to spare.

Mr Stansfield's tone on the phone might have been chirpy, but his appearance didn't quite measure up to it. He was a fifty-something man with a thin, aquiline face. His plentiful grey hair was combed back over the crown of his head and his demeanour was consummately professional; serious, yet sympathetic. Ralph thought the dark suit he was wearing would be stifling in this hot weather, but the funeral director seemed blissfully unaffected. They sat in a comfortably furnished office over a cup of tea, and discussed what had to be done.

It was all a bit overwhelming. There was a death certificate to be obtained from the coroner. Dr Dunn might already have that, thought Mr Stansfield. Then the death had to be registered. Did Ralph want a burial or a cremation? A religious or non-religious service? If he decided on a burial, was a green funeral an option? What about the casket? Open or closed? Would there be a wake after the funeral? And so on. Then of course, there was the cost. When Ralph left an hour later, clutching a booklet outlining it all in detail, his head was spinning. The thought that most occupied his mind though, was how on earth he was going to pay for it all. He'd manage it somehow. They had set a provisional date, subject to receipt of certificates and a deposit, in a week from now, but it could be extended if necessary. Which meant he had a lot of procedures to undertake, and a bunch of people to contact, as soon as possible. Then there was Sarah's estate to think about, such as it was. But he doubted Sarah had written a will. He certainly hadn't written one, and he didn't think it would have crossed Sarah's mind, either.

Over the course of the next three days, he sorted it all out. He had a long conversation with his mother, who surprised him by saying she'd cover the cost of the funeral, and that she and Lucien would be attending. She'd bring a cheque on the day. They disagreed over the service; Daisy was a Roman Catholic and wanted a church service. Ralph knew damn well that if Sarah had any religious tendencies they were more Pagan than Christian, and insisted on a non-denominational service, followed by a green funeral. As she'd given her life in an environmental cause, it seemed only appropriate that she be buried in a forest. Eventually, Daisy gave way. The only thing she wouldn't budge on was the seemingly trivial matter of publishing a short obituary in the local paper, along with a funeral notice.

'And you must write it,' she told him.

'The obituary?' He hesitated over that. How did you condense the life of someone so close to you into just a few choice words? But if anyone was going to do it … 'Yes, I'll write it.'

By Friday night, he'd arranged everything. The funeral would take place the following Wednesday, at the Bluebell Wood Burial Park, in the Norfolk countryside. He didn't expect too many people to turn up. He phoned Benedict Ramsey, as he'd claimed to be a friend of Sarah's, and told him of the arrangements. He emailed DC Ainsworth, in case he wanted to be there. Chloe had said a few people from the clinic and perhaps the odd client, might come along. Otherwise, it was just the parents. Ralph was in two minds about telling Holly; she and Sarah weren't close, and he didn't even know if Holly knew she was dead. Still, he had to go back to the flat and pick up his stuff, not least because the suit he wanted to wear for the funeral was there. If Holly was at home, he'd tell her then.

Meanwhile, Brett had tweaked the program he'd put on Kingsley's computer network and was monitoring traffic. He'd managed to work out which terminal Fabian Kingsley was using by now, and at daily intervals the virus was sending Brett an email, with a report listing all the keys Kingsley had typed. Now all he had to do was work his way laboriously through it all and isolate user names and passwords. Then phase two would kick in. That involved Brett getting into Kingsley's private email and forwarding it all to an address he'd set up to receive it. Whether it would reveal anything incriminating remained to be seen.

But before all that came to fruition, Ralph, Brett, and Chloe had a party to go to.

Chapter 11

They decided on formal dress for the party. As Ralph hadn't had time to go to London and retrieve his own suits, he ended up hiring one for the evening. It was a lightweight blue summer suit, and it fitted perfectly. But at 9 p.m. on a Saturday night, with the temperature outside at 25 degrees Centigrade, he couldn't help feeling a little overdressed. You could lounge around in just a pair of shorts in this weather, and still feel too warm. He said something along those lines to Brett, whose suit was wool and a lot less cool. Brett was pragmatic about it.

'Given where we're going, you probably won't need to wear clothes for long,' he said.

They got into the BMW, wound down the windows, and drove off to collect Chloe. She appeared wearing a figure-hugging, sleeveless, blue silk dress. Brett was relegated to the back seat, while Chloe settled up front in the passenger seat.

'You look very glamorous Mrs de Malmanche,' said Ralph.

She gave him a look somewhere between amusement and admonishment. 'Are we married? You never said anything about being married. We don't have wedding rings.'

'Good point. Let's just say we're in a committed relationship.'

'You mean an open relationship,' said Brett. 'Given the fact we're attending a sex party and all that …'

Chloe laughed, a little nervously. 'Already it's getting complicated. Are we even using our real names?'

'Actually, no,' said Ralph. 'I signed you up as Connie. I'm Rodney, and Brett, you're Bert.'

'Bert! Nobody's called Bert these days, Ralph.'

'Does it matter? It's for one night only. Now, just try and remember who you are, OK?'

It took the best part of an hour to drive to Burnham Market. It was a place well loved by tourists in summer, and was reputed to be a rural retreat for wealthy Londoners with second homes there. The party venue was situated just beyond the village down a long, winding driveway, which culminated in a paved forecourt large enough for a dozen cars or more. It was a big, detached two-storey house made of flint stone, and as far as it was possible to see in the darkness, situated in a completely private setting. The big picture windows were nearly all curtained off but there was light seeping through the gaps, and judging by the number of cars already there, it was probably safe to assume there were plenty of people inside.

'OK, here we go,' said Ralph. 'Be confident, everyone.'

'So speaks the man of experience,' said Brett, somewhat derisively.

They got out and walked up a short flight of steps to the front door. Ralph rang the doorbell. A minute later the door opened to reveal an attractive fifty-something brunette, who had somehow managed to pour herself into a black latex dress with a plunging neckline. It left little to the imagination, and only just managed to contain her bulging breasts, which looked like they might escape at any moment. She seemed blissfully unconcerned by that prospect, and flashed them a smile.

'I'm Clarissa,' she said. 'You must be, let me see …' She found a pair of glasses from somewhere and consulted a sheet of paper. 'Yes, is it Rodney, Bert and Connie? From Norwich?' They nodded as one. 'Come in.'

They went into the entrance hall and stood there while Clarissa gave them the once over.

'You're all new to this, aren't you?' she said. 'I can tell. Do you come as a threesome?'

'No, no,' said Chloe. She put her arm through Ralph's. 'We're together. Bre – I mean Bert, is a free agent.'

'Well, you all look lovely. Right, some ground rules. First, don't feel intimidated. You'll meet people here who you may find attractive, and vice-versa. You can approach and be approached, and the only rule is that a 'No' is final. There's no pressure to do anything you don't want to. In fact, you don't have to do anything other than relax, chat, and have a good time. OK?'

'Sounds fine,' said Brett.

'Connie and I have booked a massage,' said Ralph.

'Oh, good! That's a lovely way to start the evening. What about you, Bert?'

'Umm ... I'm just curious. No massage.'

'Well then,' said Clarissa, taking Brett by the hand, 'Let me introduce you to a few people. But you will save some time for me, won't you darling? Come along.'

She put an arm around Brett and, teetering slightly in her six-inch heels, steered him down the corridor. Ralph and Chloe followed them.

'She doesn't seem like the type to take no for an answer, whatever she says,' whispered Chloe.

She was smiling, which suggested that her earlier nervousness had gone. Ralph also felt a bit less uptight about this whole thing after listening to Clarissa's welcoming speech. There was something no-nonsense and at the same time a little mischievous about Clarissa, a combination which had succeeded in making them feel more comfortable already.

They came out of the hall into a vestibule; a big rectangular space with a marbled floor. A huge vase full of red roses stood on a plinth straight ahead of them, and behind that there were marbled stairs leading up to the first floor. To the left and right of the vestibule there were sliding panels, which were open to allow access between the rooms downstairs. They may have functioned as dining and living rooms in their everyday incarnations, but tonight they contained nothing more than lots of seating, and some glass coffee tables. There was soft jazz music coming from somewhere, and a bar had been set up in the room on the right.

'There are five bedrooms upstairs,' said Clarissa, waving a hand in that direction. 'Just beyond the stairs over there is the entrance to the dungeon. Feel free to look around. If anyone is using it just try not to get in the way, that's all.'

'Where does the massage happen?' asked Ralph.

'I have a couple of rooms set aside upstairs for that. Someone will come and get you when it's time. But please, just get a drink and make yourselves comfortable. I must go upstairs for a minute. Excuse me.'

She released Brett and then he, Ralph, and Chloe ventured into the room on the right. The lighting was low in there, and the decor leaned towards leather. The sofas were big leather Chesterfields and everything else in the room, including wallpaper and carpet, tended towards dark colours. The dozen or more people draped on the sofas seemed friendly enough; they smiled as the new arrivals passed by. They covered the whole age spectrum from 20 to 60 plus, and they exhibited various tastes in sex party fashion.

There was a young, muscular man wearing Doc Martens and leather shorts with braces over his naked torso. Then there was an elderly dominatrix in thigh high boots and a tight black corset. Some of the women, who were predominantly in their thirties or forties, wore either cocktail dresses or designer jeans. Others had opted for sexy lingerie in the agent provocateur style; see-through lacy bras and buttock-revealing panties or thongs. Suspender belts seemed popular, too. The men, by contrast, had less scope. If they weren't into leather shorts or variations thereof, they were in suits. When the trio reached the bar, they were greeted by a young blonde woman wearing a halter neck red dress.

'What can I do for you?' she asked, looking Chloe right in the eye.

'White wine for me,' said Chloe.

She got her white wine, and the men settled for bottled beer. They found an unoccupied sofa and sat down, sipping their drinks and taking in the action around them. It seemed as though most people had come as couples and were either chatting with other couples, or keeping to themselves at this early stage of the evening. There were a few women sitting together who could have been gay or singles. Brett seemed to be the only surplus man in the place.

'There's nothing going on in the other room,' said Chloe. 'Bit odd.'

Two girls sitting together opposite them picked up on her remark. They came over.

'I'm Cheryl and this is Alice,' said one of them. She was a twenty-something redhead, clad in red bra and panties. Alice wore a similar ensemble, in blue.

'That room is set aside for the spanking,' Alice informed them. She had short, spiky blonde hair and a pretty face. 'Will you be joining us?'

Ralph put an arm around Chloe 'We've got a massage soon,' he said. 'Guess we can't.'

'What about you?' said Cheryl to Brett.

Brett raised his eyes. 'Well, I can't see myself on the receiving end, if that's what you're asking.'

'No, we'll be on the receiving end,' she replied.

'Oh, right. Let me think about it.'

They chatted for a while and then the two girls said they'd catch up with Brett later. They left to canvas other prospective spankers. Shortly afterwards, Ralph heard someone calling the name Rodney. She called it twice, and then Chloe nudged him.

'That's you, idiot.'

'Shit, so it is.' He raised a hand. 'Over here!'

A tall, slim, dark-haired woman in a long white dress came over.

'Hi, I'm Serena. You booked a tantric massage for two? You and Connie, yes?'

'That's us.' He stood up and turned to Brett. 'Behave yourself while we're gone.'

Serena led them up the stairs, chatting as she went.

'My colleague's name is Grace. One of you is with her, and the other with me. Separate rooms.'

'Connie's with you,' said Ralph.

'Have you had tantric massage before?' asked Serena. She saw the shake of their heads. 'OK, we'll explain it all in a minute.'

They walked down a hallway, right to the end. There was a door on each side. Serena indicated one of them.

'You're in there with Grace,' she said. 'Enjoy. Did you bring cash, by the way?'

'Sure,' said Ralph. He peeled off £150 in tens and handed it over. Then, clutching the rest, he knocked on Grace's door and went in. It was a smallish room, with enough space for a massage table and a chest of drawers with bottles of oil on it. There was an iPod next to them and some tiny speakers, out of which came some soft new-age melody, setting the mood. Grace was adjusting the volume when he came in. She looked up.

'Hi, I'm Grace. Are you Rodney?'

Like Serena, she had on a long, white dress. She was shorter than Serena though, with shortish blonde hair and a pale, cherubic face. Ralph's face was partly in shadow in this dimly-lit room, but something about it caught her attention.

'Do I know you?' she asked.

He decided he might as well come right out with it. 'No. But you knew Antoinette, didn't you? Or should I say Sarah? I'm Ralph, her brother.'

If she was disturbed by that revelation, it didn't show. 'Yes, you look like her. You're twins, aren't you? She talked about you. I'm sorry for your loss, Sarah was lovely. I didn't know she'd told anyone about her tantric work.'

'She didn't tell me. Truth is, I think there's a lot of things Sarah didn't tell me.'

Grace stood at one end of the massage table and rested her hands on it. 'And what do you want me to tell you that Sarah didn't?'

'Anything. About what she did here, anyone she knew or met here, her relationships. I want to know who killed her.'

'Did you bring my money?'

He put it on the chest of drawers. She walked over and counted it. 'Well, you've paid for a massage. Do you want one? I'll answer any questions I can when we're done.'

'Alright. How does it work?'

'We start with you on your front and then you turn over when I ask. I'm going to give you a complete body massage, and I mean complete. I'll raise your sexual energy right to the brink and when I've done that, you can go and share it with your partner across the hall.'

'Ah, she's not actually my partner.'

Grace laughed. 'Around here, she doesn't have to be. Let's see how you feel about that a bit later. This kind of massage is great for your health, by the way. You'll feel great for days afterwards.

It's a slow process, can't be hurried, and just so you know, I do all the touching. All you have to do is lie back and receive pleasure.'

'And this is what Sarah did?'

'Uh-huh.'

'Right. OK then, let's see how it goes.'

'Good. Take your clothes off and get on the table when you're ready.'

He did as he was told. He hadn't heard anything from across the hallway, such as a door opening and shutting, so he assumed Chloe had opted for the massage as well. Grace put some oil on her hands, told him to just relax and breathe, and then started to work on his back. He closed his eyes, listened to the music, and did his best to receive the pleasure she'd promised him. When they finished ninety minutes later, all the tension of the last few days had melted away.

'So, what did you want to ask me?' said Grace, once he was dressed again.

'Well, for a start, how long did you work together?'

She turned off the music and wiped a little excess oil off her hands with a flannel.

'I've been doing these parties for a couple of years. Sarah came on board about a year ago, I'd say. They have these get-togethers once a month, and sometimes I'd work with her. Either her or Serena.'

'Did Sarah see any clients away from here?'

'I really don't know. We don't tend to mix with most of the people who come to these things. We're just here to offer massage. But actually …'

'Actually what?'

Grace's face was a study in concentration. 'Sarah did socialise with the people downstairs sometimes. She picked up some guy. They had a bit of a fling, and then she dumped him.'

'Do you remember his name?'

'No, she never told me. She kept a lot of things to herself, your sister. The only thing she said about him was that he was a property developer.'

'What? Are you sure?'

She looked a little concerned at the effect she'd produced. 'Yes, I'm sure. Why? Does that mean something?'

Ralph frowned. 'No, it just occurred to me that it might be someone I've met. But that's impossible. When did their relationship end?'

'I guess about six months ago. Sorry I can't tell you more, but I never saw Sarah away from here. Our relationship was professional and that was it, really. Did you enjoy the massage?'

'Yes, I did. I'm buzzing, now.'

'Great. Well, go downstairs and enjoy yourself.'

There was a soft knock on the door and a moment later, Serena popped her head round.

'You done? Ready for the next couple?' she asked Grace.

'Just about.' Grace handed Ralph her business card. 'If you want to know anything else, or if you want another massage, just call. I can come to your place, or you can always come back here.'

Ralph pocketed the card and said goodbye. He stepped out into the hallway, where Chloe stood waiting. They began walking back to the party.

'I really enjoyed that,' said Chloe, taking his arm. 'Think I might have to learn how to do it. Serena said she could teach me if I was interested.'

He smiled. 'Yes, it was nice, no doubt about that.'

'You find out anything?'

He told her what he'd learned. She stopped when he mentioned the property developer and as she had his arm, he stopped with her.

'How long ago?' she said. 'Six months? No, it's not the same person. I mean, if I was right about her seeing someone, it was more recent than that. Surely you don't think it could have been Fabian Kingsley six months ago, do you?'

'That was my first thought, but no. Norfolk must be full of property developers. Could be anyone. Why would she hook up with a creep like him?'

'Exactly.'

When they got back downstairs, there were only a handful of people in the room they'd vacated earlier, and Brett wasn't one of them. The panel of the other room across the vestibule was closed now and there were sounds emanating from the room behind it; mostly laughter. They went up to the bar and asked the blonde girl where everyone had got to.

'Some are in the bedrooms, some in the dungeon, and the rest are through there,' she said, pointing at the closed panel. 'Go and look if you want.'

'I'd like a drink, actually,' said Chloe.

They got drinks and sat down. Chloe slipped her arm through Ralph's again and nestled in to him. It was a natural, un-self-conscious gesture which didn't surprise either of them. They stayed that way without talking for a while, just enjoying the afterglow of the massage experience. Then Brett appeared, still dressed but looking a little dishevelled and quite pleased with himself.

'I told Clarissa we might take off soon,' he said. 'Unless you want to stay. How was it?'

Ralph answered. 'Good, thanks. Where is Clarissa? Better say goodbye.'

'Oh, she's upstairs. She'll be down in a minute, once she gets back into …' Brett checked himself. 'She'll be down.'

Chloe grinned. 'Back into what, Bert? Into that rubber creation, you mean? What have you been up to?'

'I had to do something while you two were upstairs enjoying yourselves. I mean, there was Cheryl and Alice, of course, but then Clarissa just insisted …'

'And you couldn't say no,' said Ralph, laughing. 'Come on then, let's make a move.'

As they got to their feet they saw Clarissa, fully re-latexed, coming down the staircase and looking much cooler and calmer than Brett, all things considered.

'It was lovely to meet you all,' she said, as she saw them out. 'You will come again, I hope.'

'Looking forward to it already,' said Brett.

Clarissa gave him a long kiss on the lips and then let him go. Then they were outside and back in the BMW. Everyone was quiet on the way back to Norwich. Chloe, in the front passenger seat, leaned her head back against the headrest and closed her eyes, and Brett was stretched out across the back seat. It was 1.30 a.m. when they dropped Chloe off, and when they arrived at the house five minutes later, the place was in pitch darkness. With one exception.

'Did we leave the lights on in your place?' said Brett, who was occupying the seat Chloe had just vacated.

Ralph killed the lights on the BMW. 'No, we didn't. What the hell? Come on, if there's someone up there, they probably saw us arriving.'

They didn't waste any time. Ralph had the front door open in a millisecond, and then they were both running through the entrance hall in near total darkness. The lights down here were on a timer, and they'd obviously gone off a while ago. Ralph pulled out his phone and used it as a torch. They were on the landing by Eileen's flat when it happened. The door leading to the next flight of stairs up to Sarah's place opened, and a dark figure rushed out and right at them.

Whoever it was knocked Ralph off his feet, but Brett, whose rugby skills hadn't completely deserted him, tackled the intruder as he went past. The figure, whose build suggested a man, crashed over and rolled down the stairs towards the ground floor. He was laden down with bags slung over both shoulders, and as he rolled, the bags came loose and tumbled down behind him. There was no time to pick them up. Brett was up now, swearing like the prop forward he'd once been and about to give chase. The man ran through the entrance hall, out the front door, and fled into the night.

'What the bloody hell?' said Brett. He didn't go after the intruder. Instead, he picked up what the man had left behind. 'Shit, these are our laptops. He was stealing our computers!'

The noise hadn't gone unnoticed. Eileen's door opened and she appeared in a dressing gown, holding a torch. Someone on the ground floor had been woken up as well, and a minute later they must have found a control switch, because all the lights in the common areas suddenly came on. A man in his forties, with a beard and longish hair, appeared.

'What's going on?'

'We had a break in, it seems,' said Ralph, who was back on his feet and none the worse for the collision. 'He's gone, now. But how did he get in?'

'Side window's broken,' said the man. 'Right at the back of the hallway near my flat. He must have reached in and slid the window up. Shall I call the police?'

'I'll do it,' said Ralph.

'OK, I'm going back to bed.'

Eileen hadn't heard anything. 'Mind you, I was in bed by ten,' she said. 'And I sleep like a log.'

'He won't come back,' said Brett. 'Ralph, we'd better go and see what the damage looks like.'

They got upstairs to find that the door to the flat had been forced open. The wood around the latch, where it fitted into the frame of the door, had been decimated. They found the crowbar that had been used to do it on the floor in the hall.

'Damn it, I just changed the bloody lock,' said Ralph.

'Good thing he didn't come down swinging that crowbar,' said Brett. 'He must have panicked when he saw us arrive.'

'Did you get a good look at him?'

'No, too dark. He was nearly past me when I tackled him, and then he was gone.'

At first glance, it didn't look too bad inside the flat. At least not in the living room. The bookcases had been emptied, but the intruder had stacked books neatly on the floor as he worked. He was obviously a methodical type of burglar. The bag containing Gerald's expensive surveillance gear was intact. The mess was in the bedrooms, where clothes had been thrown haphazardly everywhere and Sarah's consulting desk had all its drawers tipped out, and the contents scattered over the floor. But it seemed that whatever their intruder had been looking for, he hadn't found it.

'Looks like he didn't break anything,' said Brett, as he surveyed the carnage in what was his bedroom at the moment.

'It can all be cleaned up,' said Ralph. 'I'll call Ainsworth later and report it. But what was he looking for?'

'Well, assuming he didn't find anything in writing anywhere, that leaves the computers. I doubt he knew whose they were, so he grabbed all three, hoping one of them was Sarah's. That's what I reckon he was after.'

'You sure your virus hasn't been discovered and traced back to us?'

Brett shrugged. 'Maybe, but unlikely. I'll check in a minute. If the program is still running, then they haven't rumbled it yet.'

They spent the next hour tidying up. None of the laptops had been damaged during the intruder's escape, so when Brett got his up and running again, he was able to check on the virus.

'Still working,' he told Ralph. 'When we've had some sleep, I'll start looking through the reports it's been generating. But we can't assume that this bloke who was just here came from Kingsley Developments.'

'No, but if you're right about Sarah's laptop, then we have to find out where it is. There must be something on it that could incriminate someone. What the hell did she do with it?'

They put that thought on hold for now, because it was almost 3 a.m., and getting some rest was the first priority. And regardless of whatever they could do next to unravel the mystery of tonight's intrusion, there was something else to consider. The time had almost arrived for Ralph to bury his sister.

Chapter 12

Ralph phoned Ainsworth on Monday morning and reported the break in. The detective said someone would come and take a statement, and that he'd see Ralph at the funeral on Wednesday. But Ralph had questions that wouldn't wait.

'Did you speak to Fabian Kingsley about Sarah?'

'I did. He didn't know her, and he didn't know what her ring was doing in a house of his, either.'

'Bit suspicious, don't you think?'

'Whether it is or it isn't, there's no evidence tying it to Mr Kingsley.'

'Do you know any more about the explosion at the demo?'

'A group called Triple G claimed responsibility for that. Don't you read the press, Mr de Malmanche? They're hard-line environmental activists. Extremists. Given that they blow things up, you might even call them terrorists.'

'Do you think they burned down the house as well?'

'If they did, they haven't claimed it yet.'

Ralph thought of the booklet in Sarah's car. 'They had some literature on display out at the wood, you know. But they're not affiliated with the protestors in the tree houses. Or do you think otherwise?'

'I've spoken to a couple of the Norfolk protestors since they were evicted. I don't believe there's a connection.'

'Me neither. When your colleagues arrive to take a statement later, my friend Brett will give it to them. I'm going to London this morning.'

'OK. See you Wednesday, then.'

The locksmith had made an emergency return visit on Sunday to repair the door and install a more secure lock, one that would resist the attention of crowbars and other instruments of leverage. Ralph and Brett had spent most of the day tidying up the flat. As far as they could tell, nothing was missing. But it was hard to know for sure, the burglar could have had papers stuffed in his pockets. Sarah's notebook was still there, with all the names of her clients in it. Brett was going to take a closer look at it today, and also start to make sense of the data he'd got from Kingsley's computer. That would keep him busy for a while.

Ralph, meanwhile, wanted to pick up his belongings from Holly's flat, including something to wear for Wednesday's funeral. Holly would probably be at work, so there was little chance of running into her while he was there. He wasn't sure whether the best thing to do was call her when he got there or just leave her a note. He'd figure that out when he arrived.

He had plenty of other things to think about on the drive to Greenwich. He'd put a notice in the Deaths column of the *Eastern Daily Press*, with details of the funeral at the Bluebell Wood Burial Park. He'd also booked a private room at a pub nearby for the wake afterwards. All of this was costing him money and, after paying up front, he had less than £1,000 left in his bank account. And he still hadn't got a loan sorted out.

His parents were arriving on Tuesday night and they were staying in a hotel near the airport; all he had to do was pick them up the following morning. The only thing he hadn't done was write an obituary. Daisy wouldn't be happy about that, but Ralph thought he could smooth things over by getting a eulogy down on paper and reading it out to however many people turned up on the day. What form that something would take, he had no idea. The Sarah he remembered bore little resemblance to the woman he'd found out about since arriving in Norwich; the one who lived in tree houses, had a relationship with their supposedly estranged parents, and offered sensual massage at sex parties. What else didn't he know about her?

When he got to the flat, he walked into the kitchen and found Holly there, making some coffee. She was obviously surprised to see him and vice-versa, but it didn't stop them from picking up where they'd left off.

'What are you doing here?' she asked, surprise quickly swallowed by indignation.

'I live here, remember?'

'No, Ralph. You don't pay rent and you don't live here anymore. I've got another flatmate now.'

'Mr Senior Management, you mean? Isn't this a bit downmarket for him?'

'Actually, it's another girl. Not that it's any of your business.'

'Shouldn't you be at work?'

'I will be, later. I presume you've come for your things. I've made it easy for you. All your clothes are in two suitcases in the bedroom, and all the books and the rest of it are in cardboard boxes in the hall.'

'Are they? Oh, thanks.'

'You're welcome.'

Suddenly, the animosity between them evaporated. They just stood and looked awkwardly at each other, knowing their relationship was over.

'I'm sorry about Sarah,' said Holly. 'I found out about it on TV. You should have told me …'

'Slipped my mind at the time. Would you make me a coffee? I'll start taking stuff out to the car.'

She made him the coffee. It didn't take Ralph long to move his things, and then they sat together for a while.

'You were right, Holly.'

'About what?'

'I was a jerk. I just let you pay my way.'

'Yes, you did. Are you getting a job?'

'Soon. I'm living at Sarah's place. My mother bought it for her.'

That got a cross between a snigger and a laugh. 'I see. Well, no rent to find there, then.'

'You want to come to the funeral?'

Holly sighed. 'No, I don't think so. We hardly knew each other. She didn't like me, you know.'

So, thought Ralph. The two women knew exactly what they thought of each other, and I didn't have a clue.

'No, I didn't know,' he lied.

'Of course you didn't, Ralph. You're a mere man.'

That seemed like a good note to make an exit on. He took a last look around, handed Holly the keys, and left.

When he got back to Norwich, it was to find that Brett had trawled through all the reports his keylogger had generated and as a result, now had the login name and password to Fabian Kingsley's private email account.

'He logs into it from work,' explained Brett. 'I've logged in and forwarded all his emails to an account I set up. So, if he's been indiscreet about anything, we might find it in one of his emails.'

'How many are there?'

'I don't know. Hundreds. I went back a year and restored all the deleted emails, too. And they'll keep coming, as long as he doesn't realise they're being forwarded.'

'Wouldn't it be better to just settle for what we've got and remove the forwarding instruction? I don't want him to know that someone's accessing his email. And it's totally illegal, Brett.'

Brett grimaced. 'I know that. I'll give it a couple of days. I might be able to get into the folders on his machine and copy the files. Once I've done that, I'll cover my tracks and shut down my program. He'll never know I was there.'

'Let's say forty-eight hours, tops. Last thing I want is for you to be arrested for illegal computer access. OK?'

'Sure, Ralph. Me neither, but we might find gold in those files. Oh, Chloe dropped in while you were out. I told her about the burglary. She said she'd call you later. And she took Sarah's notebook; said she wanted to take another look at it.'

'OK. She's coming with us to the funeral. That's you, me, Chloe and the parents in the BMW. Should be a fun trip.'

'Sounds great. While I'm working on accessing Kingsley's files, will you start looking at the emails?'

'I will. What did the cops say about the burglary?'

Brett raised his eyes to heaven. 'I told them what happened. They weren't overly optimistic about catching the guy, though. They said they'd file a report and take it from there.'

It was pretty much what Ralph had expected them to say. He'd secured the place against a repeat performance, and someone would have to replace the window downstairs, and that was all he could do. He thought it unlikely that the intruder would come back again.

He booted up his laptop, and once Brett had given him the details, accessed the account set up specifically to hold Kingsley's emails. He decided to start at the beginning, as it were, which was in July of 2017, so a bit more than a year ago. Would there be anything in these emails that would tie Kingsley to what happened in Foxdown Wood on the night of Sarah's disappearance? And if there was, would he know it when he saw it?

It was a laborious process. There were work-related emails confirming meetings with various people about Foxdown Wood and other developments Kingsley was undertaking. There was nothing interesting in any of those, unless you found times and dates interesting. There were personal messages between Kingsley and members of an Archery club he belonged to, which were pretty banal. He also had a wine merchant, with whom he'd placed a few orders. Then there were some between Kingsley and his wife, Roz. Ralph learned that Roz had been an interior designer, and she'd done the decor for Kingsley's show homes. They'd exchanged a few emails on that subject and one that was more intimate; a description by Kingsley of what he intended to do to Roz when she got home that evening. She had replied, saying that would be just fine, thank you.

That made Ralph feel like a voyeur. It was an uncomfortable feeling peering into someone's private life like this, but he ploughed on anyway. He got through about fifty emails, and then he'd had enough for one day.

'How are you doing with those files?' he asked Brett.

'I've got them already. They're probably all work files, but you never know. I'm copying them as we speak. You find anything?'

'Not yet. When you've finished copying, let's call it quits for the day. I want to unpack the things I brought back from London.'

When Ralph had done most of his unpacking, they decided to walk into town and have a meal. There was a Pizza Express in the Forum, and they could be there in twenty minutes. Just to be on the safe side, they locked up the laptops and the surveillance kit in the wardrobe, in what was now Ralph's bedroom.

'Are we being paranoid?' said Brett.

'After Saturday night? Not really.'

But they didn't hang around in town for too long. Once they'd finished their pizza, they walked straight home. Ralph finished his unpacking and Brett found some sci-fi series on Netflix he was into, and that was their evening.

The next day, Ralph sat down to write Sarah's eulogy. He allocated the task of email trawling to Brett, who had just deleted his program from the Kingsley Developments computer network and removed all traces of his presence there. Ralph closeted himself in Brett's bedroom with pen and paper and sat at the consulting desk, wondering just how he was going to express his feelings about a lifelong relationship with his twin sister in just a few words. Two hours later, he'd written a whole paragraph. Then a shout from the living room interrupted him.

'Got one! Come and look at this!'

Ralph joined his friend in the living room. Brett was hunched over the laptop on the dining table, grinning like a Cheshire cat.

'What is it?' said Ralph.

'So, I'm up till end of July. And …'

'You've only done one month? We'll be here forever.'

'Never mind that. I've found a connection. Fabian and Roz Kingsley attended a party at Clarissa's Place. At least I assume they did. I've got an email here from Clarissa to Kingsley, saying she's expecting them on Saturday the 29th. See? "Look forward to seeing you again – Clarissa". The Kingsleys are swingers, Ralph.'

Ralph looked over Brett's shoulder. The mail Clarissa had replied to was visible below hers. Kingsley had sent it directly to her. No application for membership for the Kingsleys, it seemed. They'd already gone through that process. They were regulars.

'They *were* swingers,' said Ralph. 'Roz is dead, Brett.'

'Ah, yes. Forgot about that for a moment. But it fits the timescale, Ralph. If Kingsley went every month, he might have met Sarah there. He's the property developer she was seeing, must be.'

Ralph was flabbergasted. He sat down on the sofa, shaking his head. 'No, can't be, mate. It just doesn't make sense. I mean, put aside the fact that the guy's an arsehole for a minute, and just think about it. Sarah was part of a protest that directly opposed Kingsley's development. How could she possibly be having a relationship with him? And he swears he never met her, at least that's what he told Ainsworth.'

'Yes, but your masseuse lady said Sarah dumped the guy well before she got involved with the protest. And if Kingsley is really the arsehole you think he is, why wouldn't he lie about knowing her?'

Ralph tried to find some objectivity. Brett was right of course, but every instinct he possessed told him otherwise. Then he remembered his first meeting with Fabian Kingsley, when he'd asked the man if he knew where Sarah was. Kingsley had said no, and Ralph knew he was lying. But maybe he wasn't lying about where Sarah was, maybe it was a lie about knowing her at all. He tried to apply some logic to the situation.

'OK. So, assuming you're right, the million-dollar question is, why did he lie about her?'

'Maybe he didn't want his private life exposed, Clarissa and so on. That could be embarrassing.'

'Could be. He must have known Sarah was up in that tree house. If they did have a relationship, that would really have pissed him off.

But it doesn't get us any closer to what happened after Sarah's fall, or even if he had anything to do with it.'

'It's a start, Ralph. I'll keep looking. If this is any indicator, there's more to follow.'

'OK, I'll be next door. Just shout.'

Ralph went back to the desk and tried to refocus his brain. But after Brett's discovery, he realised that writing these few lines about Sarah was going to be even more of a challenge now. He put aside all recent revelations and just thought about the woman he'd known and the memories they shared, both good and bad. Eventually, the words came to him.

Chapter 13

The Wednesday morning saw clouds in the sky for the first time Ralph could remember in weeks. They were distant in the sky beyond the city, but they looked black and sombre, matching his mood.

He had a dark-blue suit picked out for the funeral. Brett was similarly attired, and as they left the house to pick up Chloe, few words passed between them. It was hot as usual, but today it felt close and a little stifling.

Chloe had dressed in black; a knee-length dress with fluted sleeves. She had an umbrella with her.

'I think the weather's going to break,' she said, in answer to Brett's enquiring look. 'Maybe this afternoon.'

She sat up front with Ralph and listened as he explained what they'd discovered in Kingsley's emails so far.

'How did you get hold of these emails?'

When she was brought up to speed on that, she merely pursed her lips and shook her head.

'Don't tell anyone, Chloe,' said Ralph.

'Don't worry, I won't. I've found out something of my own. Last night I went to the Foxdown Wood Facebook page and I had a private message. Pretty mysterious, actually.'

'What was it?'

'It was from someone called Hermes. I checked out his profile, but there's nothing much on it, just the minimum information. Whoever set it up seems to have done it just to send me this message.'

'Yes, but what was the message?' said Brett.

'It just said there were two things to help stop Kingsley Developments from clearing the wood. One was that Kingsley bribed members of the planning committee to get approval, and the other was that Roz was no suicide.'

There was dead silence for a while after that. Then Ralph spoke.

'I don't know about the bribery, but if that message is implying that Kingsley killed his wife, I don't buy it. I read an email between them that suggested they were very much in love.'

'That was in July,' said Brett. 'Didn't she die in February? Things can change in a short time.'

'Did you reply to this message?' said Ralph.

'No. I wanted to tell you about it first.'

'Could be a nutter for all we know,' said Brett. 'Someone with a grudge. How seriously can we take it?'

'Good question,' said Ralph. 'Maybe there was an inquest into Roz's death. I'll ask Ainsworth if he knows anything.'

Shortly afterwards, they arrived at the hotel where the parents were staying.

'Time for a family reunion,' said Ralph, as they drove into the car park. 'I'll go in and get them.'

He got out of the car, grim-faced. He hadn't seen his mother for fifteen years and it was even longer for his father. Ralph was ten when Daisy took the children away from Lucien in France to live in England. Twenty-six years ago, he thought to himself. What shape is the miserable old bastard in now?

They were in the reception area, waiting for him. Not that he recognised them at first. He saw them sitting there, Daisy in a long-sleeved black dress befitting the occasion, and Lucien wearing a slightly crumpled, but expensive looking, charcoal-grey suit. They knew him when they saw him, though, and stood up together as he approached the reception desk.

'Ralph, *comment ça va?*' said his mother.

He just looked at them both. Daisy was nearly sixty now. In her youth she'd been something of a beauty, and although the face was somewhat more lined these days, it still bore the qualities that had attracted Lucien and several other men to her when she was in her twenties. It was no mean feat to keep those looks for someone who, as Ralph remembered it, consumed vodka and tonic at regular hourly intervals throughout the day.

'*Maman. Oui, ça va.*'

He wondered why they were speaking French, and then realised it was for Lucien's benefit. Lucien was quite capable of speaking

English, but wouldn't do so unless it was absolutely unavoidable. He had the French version of the English traveller's expectation that everyone should speak his language, no matter what country he happened to be in. Lucien was nine years older than Daisy. The booze hadn't been quite as kind to him as it had to his wife; his face had a few prominent broken veins around the nose, and the jowls were a bit flabby. And he was thinner than Ralph remembered. But he stood up tall in that combative stance that Ralph knew at once, and the expression in those steel-grey eyes was as fierce as ever. He nodded at his son.

'*Bonjour, Ralph.*'

'Hi. Let's go.'

He didn't embrace either of them. Daisy looked a bit put out by the frosty reception she and Lucien were getting; Lucien just glared. They followed him out to the car.

'Shouldn't we be in a limousine?' said Daisy.

'I had to go with a cheap rate funeral,' said Ralph. 'Because I'm broke. So, this is the limousine.'

'Oh. I hope you got Sarah a nice coffin, then. Oak or redwood, or something like that …'

'Actually *Maman*, I thought about just a shroud, they're dead cheap. But she's being buried in a wicker coffin. Cheaper than the traditional model, and fully bio-degradable. She'd like that, if she were here to express an opinion.'

'You're still an insolent bastard,' said Lucien, whose face was reddening slightly at Ralph's bitter tone.

'And you're still ...' Ralph stopped. Why let them bait him? he thought. He knew that Lucien had magnanimously switched to English for the benefit of Chloe and Brett. Why waste an insult in French, if everyone could derive the full benefit of it in English? Brett must have seen the look on Ralph's face; he got out of the car and came around to open the door on the opposite side.

'I'm Brett, and this is Chloe,' he said in his best situation-defusing voice. 'Why don't you hop in the back?'

'Don't worry, *Maman*,' said Ralph. 'She's arriving at the burial park in a hearse. At midday, so let's get moving.'

'You said it was a closed casket,' said Daisy. 'It would have been nice if we could have seen her before she left the funeral home.'

Ralph had been selfish about that. He couldn't bear to look at Sarah in death; once in the morgue was enough. He didn't want anyone else to look at her either.

'Yes, well the funeral director thought it would be best if it was closed,' he said. 'Sorry.'

Daisy didn't reply. She and Lucien got into the car, and Ralph decided that silence might be the best policy for a while. Hostilities were suspended during the drive out to the burial park, even if the silence was less than companionable. A question from Chloe about the flight from France was met with a short 'It was fine, thank you,' from Daisy, and that was the sole content of the conversation for the next hour. It was only when they arrived outside the hall at the burial park where the service would take place, that Ralph thought it might be prudent to advise everyone on what was about to happen.

'Brett, Chloe, and I are pallbearers. The funeral director has arranged the other three, as we're a bit short ...'

'No,' interrupted Lucien. 'I'm also a pallbearer.'

'You should have ...' He cut it short when he felt Chloe's nails digging into his arm. 'OK. Thank you. It won't be too heavy, not like a traditional coffin. We take her into the hall, and then there will be some music and a eulogy, delivered by me. Then we take her out to the Wildflower Wood. That's where she'll be buried. After that, we go to the pub.'

They got out of the car and approached the hall. Ralph had been expecting just a few people, and the whole thing was supposed to be a simple affair. So, when they got inside, he got a big surprise. The place was packed.

'Where did all these people come from?' he said to Chloe. 'And where did all these flowers come from?'

There were some people he recognised, like DC Ainsworth and Benedict Ramsey. Gerald and Sandra had left Vivian holding the fort at Catford Investigations to be there. Even Byron, Sarah's irascible fellow protestor, was there. The others, though, he had no clue about. They were of all ages, and women seemed to predominate.

'I posted on the Facebook group,' said Chloe. 'That's where a lot of them come from. And I set up a Just Giving page for Sarah. Raised nearly £3,000 in two days. That's paying for the flowers, and for the food and drink afterwards.' She smiled, enjoying his reaction.

Ralph was amazed. 'Chloe, you brilliant, brilliant woman.'

'Second that,' said Brett.

The area around where the coffin would be placed was littered with bouquets of roses, lilies, posies, and carnations, to name a few. There were more flowers in vase arrangements, or entwined in heart-shaped wreaths. They filled the space with a kaleidoscopic display of reds, blues, oranges and white. To one side stood a microphone on a stand and a lectern, behind which stood a man who Ralph knew must be the hall facilitator. He introduced himself.

'I think there are more people here than you expected,' said the man, who was tall, grey-haired, and had a dignified look about him. 'I'm Derek. When the music starts, I'll ask everyone to sit. I'll read the order of service, and then you can bring Sarah in. Is it just you who's speaking?'

'Yes, just me.'

Derek did as he'd promised. On the stroke of midday, the first notes of Beethoven's moonlight sonata rang out around the hall, and he asked everyone to sit. The order of service was short; whatever was going to be said wouldn't take long, and Ralph would be the one saying it. Then the casket would be driven to the Wildflower Wood, and Sarah would be laid to rest.

It was quiet then, apart from Beethoven's piano music. Ralph and his fellow pallbearers went outside to meet the hearse, which was waiting for them. There was an awkward moment when Lucien usurped the place of one of Mr Stansfield's hired pallbearers without warning, and then they were carrying the casket inside. They put it down on the raised platform provided, and everyone but Ralph found their places in the gathering. He walked up to the lectern, and the music faded away. He thought he'd be nervous about speaking, but he looked at the wreath of red roses resting on the casket, and just forgot about it.

'Thank you all for being here today.' He stopped. Someone had come in, and the opening of the door at the back of the hall had distracted him. It was a man, and for a moment Ralph couldn't quite believe his eyes. It was Fabian Kingsley. He slipped quietly into a back row seat, and Ralph continued.

'This isn't a religious ceremony. Sarah believed in something greater than herself, but she didn't need to label it with a name, or subscribe to a faith. She saw it reflected in the better aspects of the world around her, but mostly she found it in her love of the natural world. So, although I was surprised when she started living in a tree house, I wasn't at all surprised at the reason why. Unlike a lot of us, she knew that protecting our natural heritage matters.

'I loved and admired her for that. We're twins, and we had this unwritten pact between us from an early age that we'd always look out for each other. It pains me to say it, but I failed her in that respect. Sarah was free-spirited, open-minded, and she cared for others. She took up a healing vocation, and she loved helping people. She was also stubborn, strong-willed, and had a crazy sense of humour. Her taste in music was questionable, too … We didn't always see eye to eye, but we always knew we had this special link between us, and that creates a bond that can't be broken by death. Because of that, to me she's still here. Not physically, but emotionally and spiritually. It's a real presence. I hope that those of you who knew her personally can feel that presence, and I hope that all of you here today will join with me in celebrating the life of my beautiful sister. I also hope that you'll keep the memory of her in your hearts for a long time to come.'

A short, sweet and altogether inadequate tribute, thought Ralph, stepping down from the lectern and joining the others in the front row. There followed an interval, in which Aretha Franklin belted out 'I say a little prayer' and people stepped forward to lay flowers on the casket; and then Sarah was borne out of the hall to the sound of Eva Cassidy singing 'Over the Rainbow'. Ralph looked at Kingsley in the back row as he helped carry her out, and Kingsley looked back at him with what was obviously an attempt at a neutral expression. But Ralph could see pain in his eyes. The pain of grief? Or something else?

He didn't dwell on it. Sarah was driven a short distance to the Wildflower Wood, where just Ralph and his immediate party joined her to witness the casket being lowered into the earth. Derek, the facilitator, read out a short statement committing her body to rest and twenty minutes later, it was all over. There would be no gravestone to mark her resting place. Instead, an oak tree was to be planted there.

Some people had followed them out to the burial site. They were standing back at a respectful distance, and congregating in small groups around the nearby trees. Someone standing alone some thirty feet away, who was obviously focused on the burial party, caught Ralph's eye.

'You know that guy?' he asked Chloe, indicating the man in question with a nod of his head.

Chloe looked. 'No, don't think so. Should I?'

Ralph shook his head. The man in question was tall, with shoulder-length black hair and a heavy stubble. Around 40 years of age, with an intensity about his expression that the stubble couldn't hide. He picked up on their interest and turned abruptly away. Then he walked off.

'Looks like he doesn't want to be known,' said Chloe.

They forgot about him for now. The next thing to do was to drive to the Flying Stag pub for the wake. Ralph was worried.

'If all these people come, there won't be enough money to cover the tab behind the bar,' he said.

'We can cover it,' said Chloe. 'Don't worry about that.'

In the end, about eighty people came along. They packed themselves into an upstairs room, where a buffet had been laid out and bottles of wine stood open. Those who wanted beer or spirits could order them from the bar. A lot of people who Ralph didn't know came up to him and offered their condolences. There were people there from Greenpeace and Friends of the Earth, along with a few other environmental pressure groups he'd never heard of. He accepted their wishes with as much equanimity as he could muster, and decided not to drink too much. He hadn't shed a tear as yet, but he knew it was coming. The booze might act as a catalyst for that, or it might also release the bitterness and anger he'd felt stirring when he saw his parents again for the first time after so many years. This wasn't the place to have a shouting match. He saw DC Ainsworth approaching.

'My condolences, Mr de Malmanche. I thought the natural burial was a nice thing to do. Very appropriate.'

'Call me Ralph. How's your investigation panning out?'

'Well, I can tell you that Mr Kingsley had an alibi for that evening. He was having dinner with friends. There's nothing in the burnt out house that's proving useful as a lead, and the four men that allegedly took Sarah away haven't been traced yet, either. We're continuing with our enquiries.'

'I see. Is that it?'

'At present, yes. It was interesting that Mr Kingsley turned up today. I don't see him anywhere around here, though.'

'You wouldn't. He knows he isn't welcome.'

Ainsworth nodded. 'Thought that might be the case. Well, he's set a date for clearing the wood now, 14 September. Two weeks away. And he's busy fencing it off so nobody can take up where the tree-sitters left off. It's all eating into his operating costs.'

'Must be. Especially when people blow up and burn down his houses.'

'Exactly. I'll leave you in peace, Ralph. We'll catch up later.'

Ralph watched him depart. Ainsworth had gone before he remembered he was supposed to ask about Roz Kingsley, and how she died. Time enough for that, he decided.

It was getting hot with so many people clustered in this small space. After a while, they spilled out into the garden at the rear of the pub. The clouds were overhead now and they looked black and threatening, but they didn't deter anyone from sitting outside.

Ralph went down into the garden with Chloe, where he noticed Brett deep in conversation with Ben Ramsey. They were drinking beer and seemed absorbed in whatever they were saying to each other. Lucien and Daisy had stayed upstairs, ensconced on a sofa in the corner, and Ralph had kept his distance. He could see they weren't inhibited where the booze was concerned. They had two bottles of wine on the table in front of them, one of which was empty already. He was standing with Chloe, who as the designated driver was sticking to mineral water, when Daisy appeared at his side.

'Before I forget, I have something for you,' she said. She gave him an envelope. 'And there's the matter of Sarah's will. I made her draw one up when I bought the flat for her. She had no children, so we decided that if she should die first, the flat would revert to me. When I die, it goes to you. As I'm not dead yet, you can live there until I am. Just so you know.'

'Oh, right.' He didn't know quite what to say.

'Can I get you a drink?' said Chloe, stepping in to fill the void. 'Come on, let's find the bar.'

Daisy allowed herself to be led away. Ralph opened the envelope, and was a little stunned to find a cheque inside for £20,000. His mother's way of making amends for her abandonment of them at boarding school as children? Whatever it was, he wasn't going to be proud about it. He'd take the money. He needed it.

At that moment, there was a flash of lightning overhead, swiftly followed by a crack of thunder. Then the heavens opened. Everyone fled inside. Upstairs again, Ralph saw that Chloe had steered Daisy back to the corner with Lucien, and actually appeared to be having a civil conversation with them. He looked at the rain pouring down outside and smelled the earthy scent rising up from the dry, scorched grass. Fuck it, he thought. It's a wake, I'm getting drunk. He found an as yet unplundered bottle of white wine and a glass, and then proceeded to do just that.

Kingsley hadn't appeared for the wake, and neither had the man Ralph had noticed near the grave. He was pretty sure who it was, though. Dominic, had to be. If Eileen had been there, he'd have known for sure, but she'd changed her mind about coming to the funeral. She'd told him she didn't like funerals, they only served to remind her of her own mortality.

Ralph sat on a stool at the bar and observed the gathering as clearly as he could, given his increasing intoxication. He noticed that the place was gradually emptying of people, some of whom had stopped to say goodbye on their way out. The parents were still in the corner with Chloe, and Lucien was actually smiling occasionally. It could only be the presence of a young, attractive woman eliciting such *bonhomie*, he thought. He didn't know where Brett had got to until he suddenly appeared, as if summoned by that thought.

'You alright?' asked Brett. 'Not overdoing it?'

'Alcohol was invented for funerals. You can't overdo it.'

Brett looked unconvinced by this argument. Not that he was entirely sober, either.

'I've been talking to Ben Ramsey,' he said. 'He was telling me about Fabian Kingsley, and what a jerk he is.'

Ralph wasn't really listening. 'You know, we're no closer to knowing what happened to Sarah. Did you see Kingsley? He was in the hall. What the hell was he doing at Sarah's funeral?'

'Yes, I saw him. He didn't hang around, though. Listen, Ralph. I'm talking about Ramsey.'

'What about him?'

'He gave me his business card. Look.'

Brett slapped it down on the bar, so Ralph could see. Ralph picked it up and focused as best he could.

'Ramsey Real Estate and Developments,' he read. 'Specialists in Norfolk and Suffolk. So …?' Then it hit him. 'Shit, you're kidding me.'

'Nope. Another property developer. And then there were two. They're business rivals, and not friendly ones, either.'

'Do we assume from this that he was just a client of Sarah's, which is what he told me, or that there was more to it?'

'Just a client, he told me. But he was very fond of her, he said. Very fond, Ralph.'

'Could he have been the one she dumped?'

They sat there contemplating that prospect. Brett suggested another drink, to help them think.

'I've had enough, mate,' replied Ralph. 'Come on, let's grab Chloe and the parents and get out of here. There's still a lot of work to do before we get to unravel this mess.'

They dragged Lucien and Daisy away from their third bottle of wine, and said goodbye to those few people that remained. Chloe nipped out to find the bar manager so she could settle the bill, and then they braved the rain to make their way back to the car. Sarah's funeral was over.

Chapter 14

Ralph had only managed a few words with Gerald and Sandra at the funeral before turning his attention to getting seriously drunk. He'd only partially succeeded in that endeavour when Gerald collared him at the bar, and said they were staying in Norwich overnight. If it wasn't too much of an intrusion, they'd like to drop in at the flat tomorrow morning on their way back to London.

The next day, in spite of his hangover, he remembered they were coming. He wasn't sure what time they'd turn up and in the meantime, he'd had a brainwave. Or thought he had. He'd woken up with a nagging feeling that he'd seen the guy he thought was Dominic before. So, after some orange juice and two large mugs of coffee, he was seated in front of his laptop, looking through the photos he'd taken on the day of the demo at Foxdown Wood. They were mostly of the crowds of people nearby at the time, and he'd got a few of the site behind the police cordon, just after the bomb went off. He'd also snapped a few of Ben delivering his speech prior to the explosion. Karl and Bettina were in one of them, and a little way behind them stood a man with the same long hair and stubble Ralph had seen at the funeral. It was him, Ralph was sure of it. It was a high resolution photo, so he was able to zoom in on it without losing too much clarity. Yes, definitely the same man. He checked his watch; 10.15 a.m.

'Just going downstairs,' he said to Brett, who was stretched out on the sofa nursing a hangover of his own. He muttered something in reply.

Ralph took the laptop and went down to the next floor, where he rang Eileen's doorbell.

'Sorry to bother you,' he said, when she opened the door. 'I wonder if you'd do something for me. I've got a photo of Dominic, at least I think it's him. I want you to confirm it for me.'

'Oh, really? Well, I'll do my best. Where is it?'

He held up the laptop so she could see the screen.

'I'll just get my glasses,' she said. She was only gone for half a minute. 'Right, show me.'

He did. She looked for a full ten seconds and then nodded.

'Yes, that's him. More unshaven than the last time I saw him, but it's Dominic. Is there a problem?'

'No, no. He turned up at the funeral, but he didn't stay. I thought it might be him, that's all. Just wanted to be sure of it.'

He left her after she'd obtained a promise from him that he'd come back soon and tell her all about the funeral. He raced back upstairs and told Brett.

'So if it's him, why didn't he stick around?' said Brett.

'When we find him, we'll ask him.'

'If we find him, you mean.' Brett groaned. 'More coffee?'

'Sure.'

Gerald and Sandra arrived half an hour later. Brett dragged himself off the sofa so they had somewhere comfortable to sit and busied himself with making even more coffee.

'I know it isn't the best of times for you at the moment,' said Gerald, showing uncharacteristic consideration. 'Good send off, though. Lot of people there, too. I just wanted to drop by and find out where you're at with your investigation.'

'And see if there's anything we can do to help,' added Sandra.

'Ah, thanks,' said Ralph. 'Well, we've found out a few things. But in terms of how they relate to Sarah's death …'

He spent the next hour bringing them up to date. He wasn't sure about revealing Brett's hacking activities, but Brett had no qualms about it. He came right out with how he'd installed the virus on Kingsley's computer network. Gerald seemed unperturbed about it.

'Brett's done it for me once or twice,' he confessed. 'You can get useful stuff from people's emails, but because it's obtained that way, it's inadmissible in a court of law. And it's not exactly legal either, which is why I'm very selective about using that method. Be careful if you volunteer something you learned that way to the police later on. You might drop yourself in it. Keep your sources confidential as much as possible.'

At the end of their summary of the situation, Sandra played it back to them.

'So, Fabian Kingsley may have been Sarah's lover. Or maybe it was Benedict Ramsey. Or maybe it was someone else entirely. Dominic was definitely in a relationship with her around the time of her disappearance. But do those relationships have anything to do with what happened? The question you need to ask is, why would someone send thugs out to the wood at short notice looking for Sarah? They couldn't wait. Which suggests to me that Sarah was about to do something they didn't want her to do.'

'And that person sending the thugs out doesn't have to be one of the people we just mentioned,' said Gerald.

'What about the burglary?' cut in Ralph. 'That wasn't a random event. They wanted Sarah's laptop. She had something incriminating on it, or they thought she did. We need to track that laptop down.'

'Agreed,' said Gerald. 'And given there's nobody else to work with yet, you also need to establish a motive for either Kingsley, Ramsey, or Dominic to want to harm Sarah, if that was their intention. Your witnesses said the fall wasn't in the script, didn't they?'

'That's right,' said Brett. 'Then there's this Hermes guy … What do we do about him?'

'He made accusations. Get your friend Chloe to message him back and ask for evidence. You'll soon find out if he's for real or not.'

'Those two witnesses,' said Sandra. 'Have they had any more thoughts about that night? How reliable are they? You said the detective on the case has doubts about their story.'

'Karl and Bettina have gone back to Germany,' said Ralph. 'DC Ainsworth hasn't found any evidence to support their story, but he hasn't found anything to say it's a fantasy, either. It seems like he isn't getting any further along than we are.'

Sandra sighed. 'Well, just like a good cop, you'll have to eliminate people from your enquiry. Start with Kingsley, I'd say he has the most to lose on the face of it. Sarah was in his wood, and she was opposed to his development. Look for something she might have known that would stop him clearing the wood. Keep reading his emails, you never know what might fall out.'

Gerald had a carrier bag with him, which he handed to Brett. 'Brought something for you. It's a tiny web camera. Set it up somewhere with a view of this room and install the software. You can control the whole thing from an internet browser. So, if you have a return visit, you'll get it all digitally recorded. OK?'

'Cheers, Gerald. We'll definitely do that.'

Sandra hadn't quite finished with her suggestions. 'Go back and see this Clarissa woman. If Kingsley was a regular at her parties, she might remember something useful.'

'And go and take a look at the house where Sarah's ring was found,' said Gerald. 'Ask around the neighbours. I'm sure the police have done it, but explain who you are and see what they say. Right, we'd better get going.'

That was that. The nearest thing they'd had to a council of war was over. Gerald told them to keep in touch, and then he and Sandra left.

'Want to go and see Clarissa later?' said Ralph to Brett. 'Do we have a phone number for her?'

'I don't. There might be one on her website, want me to look?'

'No. On second thoughts, let's just drop in. It will be easier if I explain who we really are in person.'

'OK, but she might be at work. Or just out somewhere. Long way to drive for nothing.'

'We'll go this evening. I promised to drive the parents to the airport this afternoon. They could have got a taxi, but my mother insisted. Picking them up at 1 p.m. In the meantime, there was an article online about Kingsley, with a photo. Can you find it and print it out? We'll show it to Clarissa.'

They had brunch; a fry-up of sausages, bacon, eggs and beans on toast. Ralph had always found the traditional English all day breakfast to be a good cure for a hangover, and as they'd had nothing but orange juice and coffee so far today, they were ready for it. Afterwards, he left Brett to his own devices and drove to the hotel to collect his parents. They were in reception, waiting for him just like before, except this time they were more casually dressed.

Suitcases were wheeled out to the car and packed away, and then there followed a minor disagreement between Lucien and Daisy about who would sit in the front seat, which was resolved in Daisy's favour. Then they were off. The airport wasn't far away.

'Thanks for the cheque, *Maman*,' said Ralph. 'I'll pay you back.'

'No need. What would be nice is if you would condescend to visit us in Bergerac in the not too distant future. Just a weekend. Bring Chloe.'

Daisy seemed bright and breezy today, no hangover blues for her. Not surprising, thought Ralph. She's an accomplished drinker.

'Chloe and I aren't an item. And I don't know when I'll be able to come to France again …'

A snort from Lucien in the back seat broke Ralph's train of thought. He felt the irritation rising up in his chest, an effect his father produced in him so effortlessly, it seemed. He pushed it down again.

'She likes you, Ralph,' said his mother, ignoring her husband. 'And she's very attractive. You really could do a lot worse, you know.'

He didn't know whether to laugh or tell her to mind her own business. Then to his horror, he realised she might have a point. But he wasn't about to concede it.

'Thank you, *Maman*. I'll tell her you said so.'

'You haven't asked me about my latest book,' said Lucien, determined to make some sort of impression on his son. As Ralph was about to be rid of the old man in a few minutes, he thought he'd be diplomatic.

'I'm told it's very good, *Papa*. Send me a copy.'

That seemed to hit the spot. Lucien didn't make any further comment, and when Ralph checked in the mirror, his father looked about as content as he ever did. With those sullen, fierce features, you never really knew.

He dropped them off outside the terminal; he wasn't going to go inside and hang around. When he watched them walk away, he suddenly realised how old they were getting. He wondered what Sarah had thought of them when they all met up again after such a long interval. She'd obviously managed to make some sort of peace with them, considering the fact she'd been back to Bergerac a few times recently. He wasn't at all sure he could follow her example, though. He sighed, put the car into gear, and drove away.

That evening, armed with the article printed from the internet, he and Brett drove out to see Clarissa. It was a pleasant journey. The big sky in the flat Norfolk landscape was cloudless again and the heat was back, but the air felt cleaner and fresher after yesterday's storm. They arrived a little after 8 p.m., just as the sun began to set. Ralph had the sudden, belated realisation that their blistering summer was slipping away. Soon, the leaves on the trees would turn all shades of red and gold, and then they'd fall, harbingers of the bare winter to follow. He was a fan of autumn, not so much of the cold and darkness that came afterwards. It could get a bit tiresome by February. Could always go to France, he thought, and laughed.

'What's so funny?' demanded Brett, as they pulled up outside Clarissa's house. There was a car outside, so someone was in.

'Nothing. Right, let's see what your friend Clarissa has to say.'

Clarissa was home. She answered the door wearing a more conservative outfit this time; jeans and a short-sleeved blouse.

'Hello, I remember you two. To what do I owe the pleasure?' She looked a little surprised. The smile was there, but the extrovert party persona of Saturday night was missing.

'We wondered if we could talk to you about something,' said Ralph. 'Can we come in?'

'Yes, please do.'

She led them through to the room that had been reserved for spanking on the last occasion they'd been there. The glass tables and assorted upright chairs had gone, and now the room was furnished like any other living room, with a three-piece suite and a couple of low wooden tables. A big TV screen and a hi-fi system took up most of one wall.

'Have a seat. Want a drink?' They shook their heads. 'So, what did you want to talk about?'

Ralph did the talking. 'We came to you a little bit under false pretences the other night. My …'

Clarissa laughed. 'Everyone does that, darling. They don't tend to use their real names. In fact, I don't remember yours. I remember Bert, of course.'

She flashed a smile in Brett's direction. He grinned back.

'Well, actually, my name's Ralph. You might remember my sister, Sarah. She used to work here, doing the tantric massage. Using the name Antoinette.'

That had quite an effect. Clarissa's smile vanished, and there was a trace of anxiety in her expression. She tensed up.

'She was your sister? The girl who died at Foxdown Wood?'

Ralph nodded. 'You remember her, don't you?'

'Yes, yes. Antoinette, Sarah. She told me her real name. But she stopped working here ages ago. Serena took over.'

'Do you know why?'

'Why she stopped working? No, I didn't ask. As long as two masseuses turn up on the night, I don't mind who they are. Grace organises everything, and I trust her judgement. Nobody's ever complained. Look, I'm sorry about your loss, but what did you expect to find out about your sister by coming to one of my parties?'

'I'm just trying to figure out a few things, that's all. I thought Grace might be able to help. And we thought you might be able to help, too.'

That was Brett's cue. He produced the folded up sheet of paper he'd printed out and handed it to Ralph, who unfolded it and gave it to Clarissa.

'Did this man ever come here? And if he did, did he meet Sarah here?'

Clarissa stared at Kingsley's photo. It was a clear likeness; if you'd ever met Kingsley, you'd know who you were looking at. Clarissa took a good, long look, and then her eyes narrowed. She withdrew into herself a little.

'No, I don't recognise him. Who is he?'

'Fabian Kingsley. As I understand it, he's a regular at your parties.'

She looked again. 'Well, if he is, I don't remember him. The name means nothing to me, either. But as I said, people don't tend to use their own names at my parties. I like to respect that confidentiality. Which is why you shouldn't really be asking me.'

'He came here with his wife, Roz,' said Brett. 'Blonde, about 35. Ring any bells?'

Clarissa almost snapped at him. 'No, it doesn't.' She recovered herself. 'Sorry. I wish I could be more helpful, but you're actually making me uncomfortable. The whole ethos of my gatherings is built on confidentiality. You come along as whoever you want to be on the night. So, unless there's something else I can do for you …'

'Sorry to make you uncomfortable,' said Ralph. 'Sarah disappeared. I don't know if you read about it, but she had a fall, and then just disappeared. I'm trying to reconstruct what happened leading up to it. That's why I'm asking.'

'I did read about it. And I'm sorry, I thought she was very nice on the few occasions we spoke. But shouldn't the police be doing the reconstruction?'

Ralph realised that they'd got as far as they were going to get with this line of enquiry. Time to back off. He didn't answer Clarissa's question. Instead, he stood up.

'Sorry to have bothered you,' he said. 'We'll go now.'

She saw them to the door. 'Nice to see you again,' she said. She smiled at Brett, but it was a lacklustre effort. They said goodbye and returned to the car.

'Think she's gone off me after that,' said Brett.

'Gone off both of us. Why did she lie?'

'I don't know, mate. She must remember him. We've got an email between her and Kingsley, and Kingsley's using his real name. Maybe it's just the confidentiality thing, like she said.'

They drove along the winding driveway and turned onto the main road.

'She's protecting him,' said Ralph. 'The question is; from what?'

'Good question. Looks like it's back to trawling through his emails.'

It was close to 10 p.m. when they got back to the flat, so they decided that tomorrow would be devoted to that task. The last thing Ralph wanted to do before calling it a night was to ring Chloe, and ask if she'd message the mysterious Hermes. He knew she'd been working all day after rearranging her appointments so she would be free for Sarah's funeral, so he hesitated. She might not be in the mood for a chat right now. He sent her a text instead. He got a reply ten minutes later, saying it was a good idea, but as she was tired, she'd do it in the morning.

After yesterday, he wasn't exactly bursting with energy either. Today's activities had served as a distraction from the emotional turmoil that burying his twin sister had wrought on him, not to mention the conflicting emotions he'd endured on seeing his parents again. Those emotions weren't about to be repressed any longer. A wave of sadness and exhaustion hit him, like a physical blow to the chest.

'Think I'll have an early night,' he said to Brett.

'Yeah, you look pretty knackered, actually. You OK?'

'Just tired.'

'I'm going to set up that web camera Gerald gave us. Then I'm right behind you.'

Ralph left his friend to it. There were a myriad of thoughts competing for space in his head as he lay in bed, trying to sleep. Here he was in Sarah's bed, in Sarah's flat, which had suddenly become his flat. It had all happened so fast and he was no closer to knowing why. It was senseless and frustrating.

And he missed Sarah. Her presence in his life had been replaced by a void. Even when they hadn't connected in months it wasn't an issue, because she was alive and real, and at the end of a phone. He'd even been convinced; no, he knew, that there were occasions when they thought the same thoughts at the same time. It was weird and uncanny, and when it happened he used to call her up if she didn't call him first, and they'd ask each other about it. Nine times out of ten they'd be right. And now that connection had been severed, like cutting off a telephone line.

Given what's been happening and what I've found out recently, he thought, maybe that line was cut off a while ago. He lay there on his back contemplating the ceiling until finally, the tears came. When they'd run their course, he turned on his side and fell into a dreamless sleep.

Chapter 15

The following morning, Brett and Ralph drew up the day's action plan.

'We're looking for something that Kingsley didn't want anyone else to know about,' said Ralph. 'Something that could stop the Foxdown Wood development if it got out.'

'Like bribing the planning committee,' said Brett. 'Or murdering his wife.'

'Could be anything, it just has to be incriminating. Keep checking those emails.'

'You're not helping?'

'No, not right now. I want to concentrate on Clarissa's Place. That's where the link is between Kingsley and Sarah. Why is Clarissa covering up for him? Did something dodgy happen at Clarissa's, and did Sarah know about it? I'm going to call Grace and ask her some more questions.'

Brett began the tedious task of reading emails again. Ralph, meanwhile, parked himself on the sofa and extracted Grace's card from his wallet. He called the number, which was answered straight away.

'Yes, of course I remember you,' she said, when he'd explained who he was. 'It was only last Saturday. Are you wanting another massage already?'

'No, it's not that. There's something I forgot to ask you. When did Sarah stop working with you?'

'Ahh ... I'm not sure. Wait a second and I'll get my diary.' She wasn't away long. 'OK. Yes, here it is. She did her last party in March.'

'Why did she stop?'

'Well, because ... Look, I wasn't supposed to talk about this, but it was because of something that happened around the time of the party in February. The day after, I think.'

'What happened?'

'A woman who came to that party committed suicide. Sarah knew her. She was a client and a friend, she said. I didn't know anything about it until Sarah turned up as usual in March and told me. She was pretty upset about it. She said she thought she'd be able to keep on working at Clarissa's, but now she was there, she realised she couldn't. It just reminded her of her friend too much.'

'I see. You never told me any of this when I saw you.'

'I was told not to mention it. But actually, I don't remember you asking the question.'

'Who told you not to mention it?'

'Clarissa. I asked her about it, and she said it was best not to say anything. She didn't want everyone to know that one of her guests had committed suicide the day after attending one of her parties. It would send out the wrong message, she said.'

'Do you remember Sarah's friend's name?'

'Oh god ... She told me. It was ... Roz. Yes, that was it.'

'And when was the date of the February party?'

'Let me look. Yes, here it is. The 24th. A Saturday.'

So, thought Ralph. Food for thought. 'Thanks, Grace. Can I call you again if I think of anything else?'

'If you want to. You don't want to book another massage while you're on the phone?'

'I'll get back to you on that. Thanks for the help.'

He disconnected, to see Brett staring at him from his seat at the dining table. 'What did she say? I only got bits of it.'

Ralph told him. 'And Sarah's last appointment with Roz was also in February. I don't remember the day, though. Where's her appointment book?'

'Chloe's got it.'

'Damn. I'll call her later and ask her to look. What if it's like Hermes said, and it wasn't suicide at all? Is that why Clarissa's covering it up?'

Brett was sceptical. 'It's too early to make that kind of leap, mate. Clarissa might not want people to know because it's bad for business, so to speak. Like Grace said.'

'Well, what we do know now is that Roz and Sarah were at the same party. I bet Fabian Kingsley was there, too. Even if it wasn't him she had an affair with earlier on, they must have met that night.'

'Maybe. I thought you said that the masseuses kept to themselves. And even if they met, it still doesn't give us a motive for Kingsley to go after her in the wood.'

Brett was right. Ralph's gut was telling him that he was on to something, he just didn't know what. And unless they tied Clarissa to a chair and started ripping out her fingernails, that was probably the way it would stay. He phoned Chloe.

'That appointment was on the 27th, three days after the party,' Chloe said, once he'd filled her in on the conversation with Grace, and she'd fetched the appointment book. 'And there's something else. Benedict Ramsey is in here as seeing Sarah right up till August. If he was the property developer she was having an affair with, would he still be coming to her after she dumped him?'

'Seems unlikely. Looks like Fabian's still the favourite, then.'

'Yes. Oh, and I sent the message to Hermes. No reply yet. Listen, do you guys want to go out for a drink, tonight? I'll bring one of my flatmates along. She's nice.'

'For Brett? Very thoughtful of you, Chloe.'

Chloe laughed. 'What makes you think she's lined up for anyone? Typical man, making assumptions on the basis of no evidence whatsoever. Well, are you up for it?'

Maybe letting off some steam wouldn't be a bad idea, thought Ralph. 'Yes, I think we're up for it. Brett won't say no. We'll pick you up in a taxi, say around 7.30?'

Chloe was fine with that. He hung up, and after telling Brett about their social arrangements, sat on the sofa with his laptop open. It was time to do his share of the email trawling. But Brett interrupted him.

'Breaking news, there's been another fire,' he said. 'Just saw it on the local news site.'

'Another fire where?'

'At Kingsley's development in Aylsham. Last night. Listen: "*A second house on the new Aylsham estate recently completed by Kingsley Developments was burnt down last night in what police describe as an arson attack. Initial investigation points towards an incendiary device being used. This is the second house on the Aylsham site to be destroyed this way in the past two weeks. A group calling itself the Global Green Garrison contacted the news desk of the Eastern Daily Press this morning to claim responsibility, saying that further attacks are imminent if the company doesn't halt its plans to clear Foxdown Wood, part of a controversial new housing build also being undertaken by Kingsley Developments. The company has so far declined to comment*".'

Ralph got up and looked at Brett's screen. There was a photo of what remained of the house in question, still smouldering.

'Global Green Garrison,' he muttered. 'Triple G. They didn't claim the first house. Still … Let's go take a look.'

Brett was happy to leave the emails till later. They found the address on the Kingsley Developments website and drove out there. When they arrived, it was to find a police tape around the perimeter of the burnt out house, along with two police cars and a fire engine. Several people who Ralph thought must be locals were standing close by. There were two faces they knew; DC Ainsworth, who was getting into a police vehicle; and Benedict Ramsey, who stood alone some distance away. As they approached the scene, Ramsey recognised them and came over.

'What brings you here?' said Ralph.

'Professional curiosity. I have a couple of developments of my own in the Norfolk area. I don't want these Triple G people turning their attention on me.'

'That's unlikely. It's all about stopping the Foxdown Wood clearance. You're not involved with that.'

'No. But it's still a little unnerving.'

Ramsey didn't look like a man who was unnerved. His tanned, handsome face seemed quietly amused. Ralph thought Ramsey was probably enjoying Fabian Kingsley's misfortune. Perhaps the real reason he'd come here was just to gloat.

'What is it with you and Kingsley?' he said. 'You don't like the guy. Why's that?'

'That's a very direct question,' said Ramsey. 'But since you've asked, no, I don't. Partly because of his business practices, and partly for personal reasons.'

'Can you elaborate on that?'

'Yes,' added Brett. 'You told me at the funeral that Kingsley was a bit unorthodox. That's the word you used.'

Ramsey laughed, but it was clear that his composure was giving away to annoyance.

'See this site?' he said. 'The land was up for auction. It had outline planning permission for thirty houses, so there were no hoops to jump through if you wanted to develop it. A great proposition. On the day of the auction, I was bidding against Fabian and I won the bid, only to be told a day later by the auctioneer that there'd been a mistake with the reserve price. I hadn't reached it. Then he said not to worry, they'd put the site up again in the next sale. In the meantime, Fabian sneaked in with a direct bid to the seller. Took it out from under me. Wholly unethical, and not a thing I could do about it. That's what I meant by unorthodox. That's the polite term for it, anyway.'

He was definitely annoyed. Ralph tried to capitalise.

'That's the business reason. What about the personal one?'

Ramsey gave a bitter-sounding laugh. 'That incident *was* personal.'

'Alright. Tell me, how was Sarah's state of mind when you last saw her?'

'Sarah? She was perfectly fine. She wasn't depressed, if that's what you're driving at.'

'I wasn't. She could be sad at times, but never really depressed. By the way, do you know a Clarissa?'

'No. Should I?'

Ralph shook his head. 'Not at all. Well, excuse us. I want to take a look around.'

'Sure. I should be going anyway.'

They left Ramsey, and walked to where they could get a better view of the post-fire ruins.

'Think he's for real?' asked Brett. 'About Clarissa?'

'Don't see why not.'

The police car that Ainsworth had got into had driven off. Ralph and Brett joined the small crowd of people milling around the taped-off area. There was a police constable in attendance, and two firemen were sitting in the cab of the fire engine, eating sandwiches.

What had been a house was still recognisable as such; the exterior construction was brick, which was singed but mostly still standing. There was fresh air where there'd once been windows, and the roof had collapsed. The inner structure was a mass of ashes and blackened timber.

'Wonder where the first house that got this treatment is,' said Brett.

Someone heard him. A woman, young and with a child on her hip.

'Further down the road,' she said. 'You can't see it from here.'

'You live here?' asked Ralph.

She nodded. She was a solidly-built brunette in her twenties.

'Unfortunately.'

'Why, don't you like it here? These houses look pleasant enough to me.'

The houses he could see were a mixture of terrace and semi-detached. All brand new and compact. The development had a main entrance road, and avenues leading off to left and right. It was a typical new build site, for young people with families. Bland, energy efficient houses, but Ralph had never been keen on them. The rooms were too small; for him it would feel like living in a doll's house. The unfortunate doll's house they were looking at now was on the corner of the first avenue you came to after driving in.

'Yes, well they look alright from the outside,' said the woman. 'But they're not up to standard. Five families living here, and we've all got problems.'

'What kind of problems?'

'Piping that leaks, windows that don't open, doors that aren't fitted properly. And the mortar between the bricks is crumbling. All these houses are sub-standard.'

'But you'll have a ten-year warranty,' said Brett. 'It can all be fixed, can't it?'

She guffawed. 'When someone is available. We've been waiting months for a builder to turn up. And these Kingsley Development people are no help. They just tell us it's an insurance matter. Bastards. Anyway, we tell anyone we see coming to view that they shouldn't touch the place with a barge pole. Best thing you can do in my opinion, is burn these houses down. I don't know how they passed the building regulations.'

She clutched her child to her and stalked off, looking suitably indignant. The child, whose sex they were uncertain of, looked pretty indignant as well.

'What's all this doing to Fabian's bottom line?' asked Brett. 'If I was him, I'd be a worried man.'

'Fabian's bottom line is his problem. Come on, guess there's nothing more to see here. Let's go.'

They spent the rest of the day reading emails and by 5 p.m. they were up to the end of November, 2017. There'd been no further emails to Clarissa. It was all pretty dreary stuff about magazine subscriptions, more wine orders, money Kingsley owed people in a personal capacity, and the occasional message to Roz, without the saucy suggestions. The tone between husband and wife seemed quite neutral, but as the subject matter mostly concerned curtains and colour schemes, perhaps that was only to be expected.

'It will be nice to get away from this lot and have a few beers,' said Brett, when he closed his laptop for the day.

'Let's get ready. I'll have a quick shower, then it's all yours.'

The taxi picked them up just before 7.30 and when they drove on to Chloe's place, the two women were ready and waiting. Ralph had got out of the taxi and was walking up the path when the front door opened, and out they came.

'This is Angela,' said Chloe.

Angela was a tall, thin redhead with a pale complexion and an intelligent face. She smiled and said hello.

'Angie's doing creative writing at UEA,' continued Chloe. 'She's writing the next bestselling novel.'

'Take no notice of her,' said Angela, making a face. 'I haven't even started it yet.'

Angela sat up front, while Chloe squeezed herself in between Ralph and Brett in the back seat.

'You hungry?' said Ralph. 'Fancy some tapas?'

The taxi dropped them off near the Forum, and they walked from there to the tapas bar Ralph had in mind. Now that they were out on the town, he felt ambivalent about it. When Chloe suggested this outing it had seemed like a good idea, the reasoning being that meeting up with friends, and going out for a few drinks, would bring some respite to what had been a difficult emotional time for him. But he knew that one night out wasn't going to purge those emotions. There was still a way to go on that score. So, he resolved not to drink too much tonight.

He started well enough. The bar did food, so they had gazpacho soup to start, and followed that with bruschetta and a selection of small dishes featuring chorizo, potatoes, and salted sardines. That was accompanied by cold white Rioja, and a few bottles of beer. Later in the evening, Angela, who became increasingly uninhibited as she got more intoxicated, insisted on drinking tequila shots. After several of those they'd crossed the Rubicon of sobriety and were now well on the way to getting hammered. They decided to leave the tapas bar to try a few more watering holes, which is when Brett got paranoid.

'We're being followed,' he announced, as they made their way towards Prince of Wales Road, where all the clubs and several bars were situated.

'Don't be stupid,' said Angela. She was arm in arm with Brett by now, more as a gesture of mutual support than anything else. 'Who would do that?'

Chloe and Ralph were a few paces ahead. They walked a foot apart and it seemed to Ralph that Chloe had chosen tonight to set a boundary. He knew that the potential for something more than friendship existed between them, and he was pretty sure Chloe knew it, too. But her eyes and her whole demeanour said she wouldn't be responsible for the consequences if he crossed that boundary. That seemed to be the message she was sending, or perhaps he was just over dramatising things after too much tequila. She was uncharacteristically quiet tonight, he knew that much. She stopped, so Angela and Brett could catch up.

'What did you say?' she asked Brett.

'Two guys in the tapas bar. They're following us.'

They all turned to look behind them. There were plenty of people to look at, none of whom seemed interested in them.

'They've disappeared,' said Brett.

'You're imagining things, Brett,' said Ralph. 'Come on, let's try this place.'

They went in. It was a big open space inside. Parts of it were furnished with arrangements of sofas and low tables, and other areas had bar stools and high tables. The centre piece was a huge revolving silver disco ball hanging from the ceiling. The place was low-lit, noisy, and packed.

'Too many people,' said Chloe. 'Can we go somewhere else?'

'I'll just use the men's room,' said Brett. 'Give me a minute.'

The rest rooms were in a corner, right over the other side from where they were standing. They waited while Brett threaded his way through the crowd and then disappeared. Five minutes later, and he still hadn't reappeared.

'What the hell is he doing?' muttered Ralph. 'I'll go get him.'

He began to follow in Brett's footsteps through the groups of people between him and his objective. He saw two large men with beards barging through the crowd in his direction, which prompted some abuse when they spilled people's drinks in the process, but they bypassed him and disappeared. Then he heard a woman scream.

'Help! Help me!'

He broke out of the crowd on the far side of the room and raced into the corridor leading to the rest rooms. A young woman was there, bent over the body of a man. He was face down on the floor, and there was blood pooling around his head. The woman, a young, distressed brunette wearing too much make up, stared up at Ralph.

'They were just attacking him,' she said, her eyes wide with fright. 'They kept punching him in the head. Oh, My God …'

'Let me see,' said Ralph. He already knew who it was; Brett's stocky figure and the clothes he was wearing were enough for that, it didn't matter if he was face down or face up. He kneeled down next to his friend, who at least appeared to be breathing.

'Brett? Can you hear me? Brett!'

There was no reply. 'You got a mobile?' he asked the shocked woman. She nodded. 'Call an ambulance. I'm going to turn him over and get him in the recovery position.'

She took out her phone and made the call. The corridor was heaving with spectators by now. Ralph managed to manoeuvre Brett onto his side and adjust his leg into the recovery position. There was blood coming from his nose, which looked broken, and his mouth. Ralph took out a handkerchief, and did his best to mop it up.

'Give us some air here, will you?' he shouted at the gawking faces. Most of them withdrew after a few seconds.

'They're on their way,' said the girl. 'Do you know him?'

'Yes, I know him. I'll wait.'

She got up and walked unsteadily away.

Chapter 16

Brett was still unconscious when the ambulance crew arrived and by that time, Chloe and Angela had found Ralph. They were all suddenly much more sober than they'd been when they walked into the bar. Chloe had persuaded the bar manager to make them some coffee, and now they sat on the floor in the corridor next to Brett, hot mugs in hand, in a state of semi-shock. Then two green-uniformed paramedics were there; a man and a woman.

'What happened?' said the woman, bending down to examine her patient.

'We don't exactly know,' said Ralph. 'He was assaulted. Hit in the head, according to a girl who was here when it happened.'

The woman, a dark-haired Afro-Caribbean, was busy checking Brett's pulse and respiration.

'Has he had much to drink?' she asked. 'Has he been unconscious the whole time?'

That was a yes to both questions. The paramedic consulted with her colleague, who nodded.

'He needs to be taken to hospital for further assessment,' she said to Ralph. 'One of you can come along with him.'

'You go, Ralph,' said Chloe. 'We'll get a taxi home.'

Brett was lifted onto a stretcher and wheeled out of the bar, no easy task considering the number of people in it. There were some concerned glances as the stretcher passed by, but most of the patrons weren't particularly curious. Ralph clambered in the back of the ambulance with Brett and they drove off. Five minutes later, Brett regained consciousness.

'What happened?' he croaked, trying to sit up.

Ralph gently guided him back to a lying position. 'Don't you remember?'

For Brett, it was a complete blank. Ralph told him what had just transpired, but it didn't seem to jog his friend's memory. When they got to the hospital, they wheeled Brett into triage in the accident and emergency department, where they had to wait an hour before being seen by a doctor. After questioning Brett and inspecting his face, the doctor, a young, tired-looking man, pronounced his diagnosis.

'A mild concussion. And your nose is broken. The fact you can't remember anything might be indicative of more than a mild concussion, of course. I'll ask the nurse to book a CT scan, just to be sure, and we'll keep you overnight for observation.'

A nurse and a porter appeared fifteen minutes later, and Brett was admitted. Ralph accompanied him to the ward, but there was little point in him hanging around. They gave Brett a painkiller and shortly afterwards, he fell asleep. Ralph rang a taxi, and when it arrived, he went home.

First thing the next day, he rang DC Ainsworth and reported the assault.

'We've been burgled, and now Brett's been assaulted,' he told Ainsworth. 'I'm pretty sure I saw the guys who did it, too.'

'We'll get the CCTV footage from the bar and on the street,' said Ainsworth. 'What provoked the assault?'

'I don't know. Last night, Brett couldn't remember anything about it. Have you made any progress on the burglary?'

'I'm afraid not.'

'What about Sarah?'

'We're in the process of contacting and interviewing all the protestors again.'

'The German couple were the last people to see her alive, but they're back in Germany. Will you be questioning them, too?'

'They gave me a full description at the time,' said Ainsworth. 'If anything emerges that necessitates me questioning them again, I will.'

We're getting nowhere, thought Ralph. He changed the subject.

'Can you tell me anything about Roz Kingsley? Her suicide?'

'Why are you interested in that?'

Ralph hesitated. Then he realised that if Ainsworth leaned on Clarissa in his capacity as a detective, she might say more than she'd been willing to divulge when he and Brett were asking the questions.

'Sarah worked as a masseuse at a party that Roz attended on the night before she died. I think there might be a link between that and Sarah's disappearance.'

That piqued Ainsworth's interest. 'And you found this out how?' Shit, thought Ralph. Can't mention Kingsley's emails. He thought fast. 'Roz Kingsley was a client of Sarah's. I've been doing some investigation of my own, and it turns out that they were both at this party. The next day, Roz is found dead in her car at the beach.'

'That's a rather vague explanation, Mr de Malmanche. You're doing your own investigation?'

'Yes, and I'm not obliged to reveal my sources.'

'Christ, that's all I need,' muttered Ainsworth. 'In that case, tell me about this party. If it doesn't compromise your sources, that is.'

Ralph told him. 'We tried to ask Clarissa about it,' he concluded. 'But she said she didn't know Roz or Fabian Kingsley. We don't believe her. If you were to ask her the same question, I think she might respond differently.'

'Perhaps she might. So, is there anything else you can tell me that might assist my own investigation into your sister's death?'

'I don't think so. I saw you at the scene of the latest fire. Any update on that?'

Ainsworth's annoyed tone was unmissable. 'I think that's a completely separate issue. We're following up some leads on this Triple G organisation, and that's about all I can tell you. When the footage comes in from the bar, I'd like you to come in to the station and take a look. In the meantime, email me a summary of what you've just told me about the party, plus an address for this Clarissa woman. Does she have a last name?'

Ralph was sure she did, but he didn't know what it was. He said he'd do as Ainsworth suggested, and hung up. He typed up the email straight away, including a link to Clarissa's website. After that, he got in the car and drove to the hospital to visit Brett. Brett was in much better shape this morning, although on first glance, you might have doubts about that. His face was badly bruised and his nose was swollen, but otherwise, he seemed fine. Ralph found him in the patients' lounge, dressed and ready to go.

'I've been discharged,' he told Ralph. 'I was just about to phone you, actually.'

'Do you remember what happened now?'

'Yep. I was coming out of the men's room and these two guys just laid into me. I didn't see it coming. Two big, bearded bastards.'

'What, and they didn't say anything?'

'All I remember was one of them saying, "stay out of what doesn't concern you or you'll get more of this". Then I must have passed out.'

'They said that? Well, it's not hard to guess what they were referring to; Clarissa's Place.'

'Exactly. Looks like we touched a nerve there, don't you think?'

They left the hospital building and walked to the car park. Brett told Ralph that his nose would heal in around three weeks, and that all his teeth were intact.

'Could have been worse,' he said. 'I'm just pissed off that I didn't get in a few punches of my own.'

'I saw them coming through the bar on their way out. I told Ainsworth about it, and we might pick them up on CCTV. Who knows, you might get a rematch if we identify them.'

Brett didn't want to do much when they got home. Ralph started on Kingsley's emails again, while Brett amused himself by watching Netflix. Around lunchtime, Chloe called, wanting to know how Brett was.

'He's much better,' said Ralph. 'Back here with me, now. Did you and Angela get home OK?'

'No problems. There's something I want to ask you. I've been talking to Greenpeace. The petition they started to save the wood got nearly 100,000 signatures, but they've just heard that it won't be debated in parliament. Even if it was, we've only got till September 14. So, that looks like a dead end. But they're sending a guy up from London today, some kind of wildlife expert. Apparently, there may be some bats in the wood and if there are, then they're protected. If we can establish that there's a protected species in the wood, then we can try for a court order to halt the clearance. We want to go out to Foxdown about 7 p.m. and see if we can spot these bats. Will you drive us?'

'Yes, sure. I'll pick you up from your place. Anything from our friend Hermes yet?'

'No. Looks like he's all style and no substance. But if that changes, I'll let you know.'

They finished on that note, and Ralph went back to his reading. He was well into December's emails when he found something that gave him pause for thought.

'This is interesting,' he remarked to Brett, who had his earplugs in and was concentrating on 'House of Cards' on his laptop. Ralph waved.

'What?' said Brett, once he'd realise something was expected of him, and he'd removed the earplugs.

'This email. It's from a Mr Renshaw. "*Just to let you know that the outstanding amount in addition to my invoice, for services rendered at Aylsham, needs to be paid in cash. If you can bring it to my house one evening this week, that would be appreciated.*"'

'So? I've found a couple of emails like that. He's got a gardener he owes money to, and a cleaner. Nothing suspicious about them.'

'Yes, but this guy's a building inspector. His logo and his qualifications are listed at the foot of the email. He's an approved, independent operator.'

Brett got up from the sofa to take a look. 'That *is* interesting. Well, we've got all his details. Phone number, address, the lot. Looks like it was Mr Renshaw who approved the Aylsham houses, which that woman we met thought were sub-standard.'

'And it looks like Kingsley bribed him to do it. If he did it at Aylsham, he might do it again for Foxdown. Can we use this?'

'Not officially. We obtained this information illegally. But that doesn't mean we can't leak it to the press. Did Kingsley send a reply? Check the "Sent" folder.'

They found it without too much hassle. Kingsley had been brief in his reply, merely stating that he'd call at Mr Renshaw's house on the Friday evening, and bring cash as agreed.

'I'll set up a temporary email address and use it to send this information to the *Eastern Daily Press*,' said Brett. 'Maybe they'll do something with it.'

Brett paused Netflix in order to do that. When he had everything ready, he sent their discovery to the paper's crime correspondent. 'It's an anonymous tip-off, but that doesn't mean they won't check it out,' he said. 'We'll need to keep an eye on their website.'

Ralph figured that if Kingsley had to deal with accusations of bribery, then it might compromise the Foxdown development. It would certainly slow him down. But it didn't help as far as finding Sarah's attackers was concerned. It was more important now than ever to lean on Clarissa and find out whatever it was she didn't want them to know. He phoned Ainsworth, intending to share what Brett had told him earlier about the men who'd assaulted him. Surely that would spur the detective into action. But Ainsworth wasn't answering, so Ralph had no choice but to leave a message. Ainsworth still hadn't come back to him when they went to collect Chloe that evening. She had a middle-aged man with her, who introduced himself as Richard. He was tall and whippet thin, with sparse, greying hair. It was still warm out, but Richard had come prepared for any climatic condition; the waterproof walking boots and the lined, zip-up jacket were testament to that.

'Best if we can take a look in the wood when there's still some daylight,' he said. 'Though bats do a pretty good job of concealment. If they're around, we should see some at dusk.'

He had a pack with him, which he said contained cameras and binoculars. He got in the back of the BMW with Chloe, and they set off. It wasn't until they reached the Foxdown Wood car park that Ralph remembered about the fence. The one that Ainsworth had told him Kingsley intended to erect around the wood. He'd certainly fenced off the car park and the area nearby, which made it difficult to stop the car, so they kept on going along the perimeter road.

The fence was constructed of wire mesh panels, and rose to a height of about 10 feet. It looked quite secure from the car. The road they were on was narrow, with occasional passing places. After perhaps half a mile, the fencing stopped.

'This is as far as he's got, by the look of it,' said Brett.

'Right, we can go into the wood from here,' said Richard.

'I can't park here,' said Ralph. 'We'll turn around and drive to the village. How long do you need?'

'An hour should do it.'

Chloe got out with Richard, and the two men left in the car watched as they vanished into the trees.

'We'll go to the pub for an hour,' said Ralph.

He turned the car around with an eight-point version of a three-point turn on this narrow road, and they headed for the Foxdown Village pub. It was a typical Norfolk pub; whitewashed walls and a tiled roof on the outside, with high-backed chairs and wooden, varnished tables on the inside. There was a fireplace, too, but it wasn't in use. They walked up to the bar, and ordered one of the Norfolk real ales on tap. There were about a dozen other patrons there already, all hard at work appreciating their beer and quietly conversing. And on a barstool, just a few feet away, sat someone they recognised. It was Byron, the irascible tree dweller with a penchant for laying animal traps. He saw them and raised his glass.

'What are you doing out here?' he said.

'I could ask you the same question,' replied Ralph. 'The protest's over, you can go home now.'

'I often come here for a drink. Not my local, exactly. But not too far away.' He looked at Brett. 'What happened to you?'

'I walked into a door.'

'Some door.'

Byron seemed less hostile than usual. Ralph thought he might have had a few beers already.

'We're out here looking for bats, in the wood. Well, not us, friends of ours. They're out there now.'

'Bats?' Byron was lost for a moment, and then he understood. 'You mean protected bats. There aren't any bats.'

'You sure?'

Byron nodded. 'Yes. Don't think that didn't cross our minds when we were living out there. But wait, I'll get you a second opinion.'

He beckoned to the barman, a grey-haired man in his fifties.

'Jason, this is Sarah's brother. Tell him if we've got bats around here.'

Jason came over. 'Here, or in the wood? Never seen one in either place. I very much doubt it.'

So much for the bats then, thought Ralph. He realised that Jason was looking at him with a curious expression.

'You're Sarah's brother?'

'That's right.'

'I've got something here that belonged to her. Wait a minute and I'll get it.'

What on earth? wondered Ralph. Jason was only gone a minute. He came back and put the something in question on the bar.

'This was hers.'

'Holy shit,' said Brett.

It was a laptop computer. Ralph and Brett just stared at it.

'How did you end up with it?' said Ralph, a few seconds later.

'She came in nearly every day,' said Jason. 'Plugged it in and used our wi-fi to set up appointments and stuff. She asked if she could leave it here. There was no point in keeping it out in the wood, because there was no internet out there and the battery only ran down. So, she left it with me until she wanted it the next time. Guess it belongs to you now.'

Ralph opened the lid. 'Where did she plug it in?'

'She sat at the bar. There's a plug over there; look.'

There was a socket in the wall by the bar, just beyond where Byron was sitting. The lead was attached to the laptop, so they moved across and plugged it in. It was a Windows machine and it took a while to boot up, and that was as far as they got. The machine wanted a password.

'I knew it was too good to be true,' muttered Ralph. 'We could be here forever.'

'Maybe, maybe not,' said Brett. 'I'll run a password crack on it.'

'I'm sorry about Sarah,' said Jason. 'She was a great girl. We miss her around here.'

'Thanks. I miss her, too. Didn't the police come and ask you questions?'

Jason shook his head. 'No. Haven't seen anyone from the police. Do they know what happened yet?'

'Not yet. Well, thanks for this. We'll take it home. We might find something useful on it.' He turned to Byron. 'What about you? Have the police spoken to you again?'

'I'm going into Norwich police station on Monday. That Ainsworth bloke that came out when it happened wants a word. But there's no point in talking to me, I wasn't there. It's Karl and Bettina who saw the whole thing.'

'Yes,' said Ralph. 'And they're back in Berlin. Still, he'll get around to talking to them.'

Byron laughed. 'What? No, mate, they're not in Berlin. They never went back to Germany. They're still here in Norfolk. They rented a caravan, or some holiday home or something. Out at Hemsby. They never went anywhere.'

Hemsby was a town out on the coast. A holiday town with caravan parks, amusement arcades, and a long stretch of beach.

'You're kidding me,' Ralph said. But Byron looked deadly serious. 'OK. When you see DC Ainsworth, tell him that. I don't think he knows.'

They stayed for another beer and bought one for Byron, but Jason insisted that these were on the house. When they left the pub an hour later, Ralph had the laptop clutched tightly under his arm. Brett was buzzing with excitement.

'This is it, mate,' he said. 'The reason the flat was burgled, the key to Sarah's disappearance. The thing someone doesn't want us to have. We might just be on the verge of cracking this investigation.'

'I know. But right now, we have to tell Chloe there are no bats in Foxdown Wood. She's going to be disappointed. Come on.'

We really are on the verge of cracking it, thought Ralph, as they drove back to the wood. But first, Brett has to crack that password. Without that, we've got nothing.

Chapter 17

It turned out to be ridiculously easy to crack Sarah's password; Brett simply bypassed it. He set the machine to boot up from the USB drive. Then he inserted a USB stick and started the machine up again. The software on the USB stick interrupted the boot up process to display the users of the laptop. Sarah was the sole user, so he selected her and the program overrode the existing password, setting it to blank. Then after booting up again normally, he logged in.

'Nice one,' said Ralph, who had witnessed this procedure.

It was Sunday morning. They were back home after taking Richard back to the station the night before, and then dropping off a disappointed Chloe at her place. Brett had been pretty confident about being able to get into Sarah's laptop, and it was late when they got back to the flat, so he'd performed the task while munching cereal and toast for breakfast.

'Didn't think it would be a problem,' he said to Ralph. 'Now, what are we looking for?'

'Good question. Just go through her folders and see what's there.'

Several of the folders were related to a course that Sarah had done at Middlesex University in London years ago in Ayurveda, which was traditional Indian medicine. Others were repositories of massage techniques and other types of bodywork. She'd spent time in India doing postgraduate work, too, which had resulted in lots of documents and photos. They were all sorted under various headings. Then there were more folders devoted to things like 'Legal' and 'The Flat'. But Brett ignored all of that.

'Let's have a look in "Sarah's Stuff",' he said. He opened it up. 'There's an electronic diary in here. Password protected, I bet.' Ralph was sitting next to him. Brett opened the application, but no password was required.

'I guess she thought hiding it away in this folder was good enough,' said Brett. 'So, how far back does it go?'

The diary had been started six years earlier. Around the time she moved to Norwich, thought Ralph. But it was only this year and 2017 that interested him.

'We need to go back a year,' he said. 'That's about the time she started working with Grace. Let's see if there's anything in there about our mysterious property developer.'

'And February of this year,' said Brett. 'She might have written about what happened to Roz then.' He stood up. 'You can do the reading. After all, she was your sister.'

He moved away, so Ralph could have the laptop all to himself. Yes, she was my sister, thought Ralph, but that's not an excuse to invade her privacy. I'm going to do it just the same. 'Make some more coffee,' he said. 'This could take a while.'

He clicked back through the calendar and started at the entry for August 1, 2017. He tried to speed read everything in order to get through it all as fast as he could, but it still took several hours to separate what was significant from what could be ignored. He made notes of the relevant dates, and once he'd finished, he just sat back in the chair and stared into space for a while.

While all this was going on, Brett had been out to the supermarket with a shopping list. He'd returned and made a salad for lunch, and now he'd gone out again, to find the nearest takeaway bar. The evening meal was going to be haddock and chips, with lots of salt and vinegar. Ralph thought about that prospect, and his stomach rumbled in anticipation, but he knew Brett wouldn't be back for a while yet. So, he returned his attention to what he'd discovered, and re-read the first entry of significance in 2017.

'Saturday, September 9. My second stint as tantric masseuse at Clarissa's Place. Had two clients tonight, a man and a woman. It's nice giving sensual massage, as long as the clients aren't jerks. Nobody has been a jerk as yet. And it's certainly more lucrative than regular massage. I went downstairs between clients to get a drink, and got chatted up by a good-looking man. He told me his name was Fabian, and that it was his real name. No last name though, it's a house rule. You can call yourself what you like, but no surnames. Clarissa is paranoid about it, according to Grace. He's married, too. I saw the wedding ring, and when I asked him about it he said he had an open marriage, otherwise he wouldn't be here. His wife wasn't with him; apparently she'd made other

arrangements. Made me wonder if he was there without her knowledge, or if she just isn't into casual liaisons. Not that it's any of my business. He wanted my number, but I told him I was here on business, not pleasure.'

Fabian popped up again in October.

'Saturday, October 14. Guess who booked a tantric massage? Fabian, of course. And he insisted on me doing it. Although it's an intimate treatment, I always manage to retain my objectivity with a client. It's not a sexual service. But with him tonight, I found it difficult. He's attractive, and he has a nice body. He asked me for my business card afterwards. So, now he's got my phone number.'

By the end of the month they were seeing each other outside the confines of Clarissa's Place, and it was a full-on sexual relationship. Sarah had broached the subject of Kingsley's wife again and had been told that her name was Roz. If Sarah had misgivings about sleeping with another woman's husband, she didn't commit them to her diary. She seemed happy enough in her new relationship. Kingsley appeared to be nothing but charm itself. But a month later, it all changed.

'Tuesday, November 14. Fabian is jealous! At Clarissa's on Saturday night I had two young male clients, and I don't know if they said anything to him afterwards, but yesterday he was furious. He said, and I quote, "you don't do sex work when you're screwing me, is that understood?" I couldn't believe it! I tried to

tell him that it's not sex work and that tantric massage and screwing him are mutually exclusive anyway, but it took him ages to calm down. He doesn't want me to carry on at Clarissa's, said he'll make up the lost income himself. Then, just to complicate things, a woman came into the practice rooms to book a consultation. She introduced herself as Roz Kingsley! We talked for a while and she's really lovely. She's suffering from depression, and wants to know if I can suggest some natural remedies. I felt a bit awkward, seeing as I'm screwing her husband. But I made an appointment for her.'

Sarah realised that doing what Fabian wanted by quitting at Clarissa's meant putting Grace in a tight spot. Serena wasn't around to step in at that time. She told Fabian that she couldn't put Grace in that position, and that she was going to carry on as normal. He didn't take it well.

'Wednesday, November 29. I saw another side to Fabian tonight. I told him I couldn't let Grace down, and I thought he understood. Then in bed, he got rough with me and called me a whore. It really upset me, but he seemed to enjoy that. I actually thought he might hit me when I asked him to leave. Then he just transformed, as though nothing had happened! I was glad when he left. Maybe this is a blessing in disguise, I've seen through the facade to the ugly man lurking underneath. Don't know if I want to go on with this relationship.'

By the next party in December, it was over. Sarah kept working at Clarissa's and Kingsley kept attending, but they stayed away from each other. Or to be more precise, Sarah made sure she didn't leave the massage room. Roz Kingsley had been to see Sarah at her clinic on two occasions now, and the two women liked each other. Sarah gave her conventional massage treatment, and prescribed herbs and teas that were known to improve depression, without the side effects that pharmaceutical drugs produced. She told Roz that herbs and teas might work in a week or two, but in most cases they took up to three months before a noticeable improvement manifested. Roz was OK with that. The pills she was taking had given her insomnia, which she then had to counteract with sleeping pills. She wanted to come off that regime as soon as possible. She never said what she was depressed about. The next entry of significance was in January, 2018. The party went on as usual at Clarissa's, but this time, Fabian Kingsley turned up with his wife.

'Saturday, January 20. I ran into Roz at Clarissa's tonight! She'd booked a massage with Grace and we met as I came out into the hall after finishing up with my client. She was a bit shocked to see me there, but she said it sort of made sense that I combined tantra with my other treatments. Apparently, the guy I'd just massaged had been paired up with her by Fabian, but you could see her heart wasn't in it. She used her meeting with me to fob him off and then we had a bit of a chat. She told me she'd been having an

affair, and when Fabian found out, he went apeshit. Then he made her dump the guy. Christ, he is so controlling. And he's supposed to be an advocate of extra-marital relationships ... Go figure.'

The finish of the affair didn't do much to improve Roz's depression. She didn't come to see Sarah again in January, but she did make an appointment for February 27, so Sarah thought that maybe things were looking up. Then at the party on the 24th, disaster struck.

'Sunday, February 25. An awful, awful time last night. I don't know what happened between Fabian and Roz at Clarissa's, but apparently Roz locked herself in one of the bedrooms and took a bottle of sleeping pills, and then washed those down with a bottle of vodka. It must have been around 3 a.m. when I finished. Grace had already gone and so had everyone else. I was getting ready to go when there was a loud crashing sound from down the hall, where all the bedrooms are. I looked out, and Fabian was shoulder charging the door. Clarissa had keys, but Roz must have locked it from the inside. I didn't know what the hell was going on, until the door finally gave way and Fabian went inside. He called out Roz's name, and he was obviously upset. I rushed down the hall and went in. Roz was on her back on the bed, fully clothed. The empty bottles were next to her. Fabian was there, slapping her face and calling her name. Clarissa was in tears. I told Fabian to stop slapping her like that and he actually took notice. Then I checked Roz's pulse

and respiration, but it was too late. Her body was cool to the touch as well. She must have been dead for a couple of hours at least. Then I think I must have shouted at Fabian, can't remember what I said, but it must have been bad, because he looked pretty shocked. She was so lovely! What did she do to end up with a prick like him? In the end I just told him that his wife was dead, and that he should call the ambulance service. He just nodded. Clarissa took over then. She said they'd take care of it and practically pushed me out of the room. I drove home, but although it was late, I couldn't sleep. Then, when I did get to sleep I wake up this afternoon to find that Roz was found out at Brancaster this morning, behind the wheel of her car! But that's impossible! Except it isn't. Fabian must have moved the body. But why on earth would he do that?'

She didn't get an answer for that. She fretted about the fact the body had been moved, but she figured that Roz was dead, and did it really matter if they found her at the beach or at Clarissa's? She wanted to go to the funeral, but she couldn't bear the thought of laying eyes on Fabian there. But she went to the March party, where she told Grace that she didn't want to work there anymore. Grace said that she had someone else to call on if that was how Sarah felt. What Sarah didn't tell Grace was what Clarissa told her when she finished that night.

'Saturday, March 17. Clarissa corners me after my last client. I tell her this is my last party and that a girl called Serena will be

replacing me. She says that's a shame. Then she goes on to say that last time, when I pronounced Roz dead in the bedroom, I was wrong! Because an hour later, Roz got up, sobered herself up with lots of coffee, and drove off! Are you kidding me? So, now I get it. Clarissa didn't want the scandal of a dead woman at a sex party to be laid at her door! That's why they moved Roz. Fabian must have been worried about the impact of the publicity on his professional life, too. That's surely the only reason he went along with it. Then Clarissa said the whole thing was a tragedy and she hoped she could rely on my discretion about the events leading up to it. I didn't say anything, I just got out of there.'

That was the end of that particular story. Spring arrived and Sarah became an environmental protestor. The irony of the wood belonging to her former lover wasn't lost on her, either. Her diary entries reflected that, and if Kingsley knew she was out there opposing his development, it wasn't mentioned. And then things changed, because in May, Dominic came into her life.

'Thursday, May 17. This rather gorgeous guy turned up at the wood today. He's been here once before, but it's the first time we've really spoken. He said his name was Dominic, and he'd come to support the protest in whatever way he could. For some reason he singled me out and gave me £500 to help with expenses for all of us! Said it came from a well-wisher, but wouldn't say who that person is. Then he disappeared! Very intriguing ...'

Dominic came back the following week, with more money. He resisted Sarah's attempts to find out where the money was coming from, which only made her more curious. By the middle of June he'd asked her out, and they started seeing each other regularly. Then Sarah's diary entries became shorter and more mundane; about life in the wood and the pros and cons of living in a tree house. She flitted between the wood and the flat in July. Reading between the lines, Ralph thought that was no doubt due to her desire to be with Dominic in the privacy and comfort of her own bed. She was in love with him by now. But in late July, dark clouds gathered.

'Friday, July 27. What a mess. I've fallen for another man who isn't all he seems to be. I should know better. I believe that he does love me, but I still know so little about him. Today, I came out to the wood early after a cancelled appointment, and I found Dominic with Karl and Bettina. I walked in on them at the pub and they immediately all looked guilty about something. There was a diagram on the table, and before I had a chance to look at it, Dominic folded it up and stuffed it in his pocket. I asked them what was going on, and it wasn't until I hassled Dominic on the walk back from the pub, that it came out. He wants to use a fire bomb on some of the houses that are already partially built! Karl and Bettina didn't seem to be doing much to dissuade him, either. I told him that was a bad idea, but Dominic is all for "totally direct

action" as he puts it. We had our first real fight then, and Dominic wouldn't back down.'

Maybe things soured after that, because Dominic wasn't mentioned again. Whether Sarah had resigned herself to Dominic's intentions or not wasn't clear, but she did decide there was one thing she might be able to do to stop the wood clearance, and it didn't involve blowing things up. She contacted Fabian Kingsley.

'Wednesday, August 8. I phoned Fabian today. He knew I was part of the protest, I guess he must have seen me on the Facebook page or something. He was a bit off with me, but he didn't hang up. I basically told him that he should accept the offer he'd been made for the wood. It was £2 million, after all. He said it wasn't going to happen, so I said that if it didn't happen by the 15th I would go to the police and the press, with my version of what happened at Clarissa's Place the night Roz died. And it didn't matter if the police didn't believe me, they would still investigate it. And the publicity alone would damage his reputation. His choice. He thought about that for a bit and then he said he wouldn't advise me to entertain the idea. Because it might prove harmful to me. I got the message, but I told him I wasn't prepared to be intimidated. He hung up. I hope I've done the right thing.'

That was the last entry. Just as Ralph finished re-reading it, Brett came in with the fish and chips. The smell of vinegar wafted through the room.

'Tear yourself away from that and get some of this inside you,' he said. He proceeded to put the meal on plates and brought one over.

'Cheers,' said Ralph. 'You can read it for yourself if you like. I've written down all the relevant dates.'

They swapped places. Brett munched his food and went through the diary entries. The meal was over and the plates were cleared away before he finished.

'If this isn't a motive for Kingsley to go after Sarah, then I don't know what is,' he pronounced.

'Yes. DC Ainsworth needs to see it. Why the hell hasn't he returned my call yet?'

'It's Sunday. Even detectives must take a day off.'

It could wait till tomorrow. Then, thought Ralph, we might at last see some action. Fabian Kingsley had a lot of explaining to do. He was about to be dropped in it, big time.

Chapter 18

Chloe dropped in on her way to work the next day. She didn't have time to sit down and read Sarah's diary, so they gave her the short version. She was amazed.

'I had no idea she was seeing Fabian Kingsley,' she said. 'But then I had no idea about Clarissa's Place till recently, either. Sarah was a dark horse, no question. And you think he wanted to harm her?'

'Looks that way,' said Ralph. 'Anyway, I'm taking all this to DC Ainsworth. We'll see if he agrees.'

'It's a criminal offence to move a body like that,' replied Chloe. 'Assuming that's what happened. But I almost forgot – Hermes came back to me. Says we should check out someone on the Norfolk Council Planning Committee. "Ask him how he's paying for the new extension on his house", was the suggestion.'

'We already found something that links Kingsley with bribing a building inspector, never mind planning committee members,' said Brett. 'It's all very interesting, but I'm not sure I trust this Hermes character.'

'Me neither,' said Ralph. 'Roz wasn't murdered, which is what he's implying. Hermes has got an axe to grind, but I don't think we can take him seriously. Best if you just don't reply, Chloe.'

'OK, I won't. Let me know how you get on with DC Ainsworth.'

She left, and twenty minutes later, Ainsworth called. He listened to Ralph's latest revelations without comment, and then invited them into the station.

'We've got the CCTV footage from the evening of the assault,' he said. 'And bring the laptop with you. I'll take a look at this diary.'

Ralph and Brett duly arrived at the station an hour later. After announcing themselves, they sat on a bench in the reception area and waited. Ten minutes passed, and then Ainsworth appeared from an elevator at the far end of the room.

'We're in a room upstairs,' he said. 'Follow me.'

They stood with him in the elevator, which slowly rose to the second floor. When the doors opened, they emerged into one end of an open office space, which extended the length of the building. It was populated by plain-clothes men, most of whom were seated at their desks behind a series of partitions, with phones to their ears. The rest were walking around the place with cups of tea or coffee and looking purposeful. They walked past at least a dozen desks and several photocopiers, until they reached a room at the far end with a sign on the door proclaiming it as the 'Viewing Suite'. Ainsworth opened the door and ushered them inside.

'Over there,' he said.

There were six big flat screen monitors on the wall and several computer terminals on desks opposite them. They sat at the desk Ainsworth had indicated, and waited while he logged in. He eventually found what he was looking for, and clicked on a file. The screen directly opposite came to life, and an image appeared. It was a street view at night time, but it wasn't exactly dark; the lighting on this particular street was clear and bright. Ralph recognised the entrance to the pub they'd been in on Friday.

'We've got nothing from inside the pub,' said Ainsworth. 'This is around the time you said the assault took place. Tell me if you see anyone you recognise.'

The camera was recording from across the road, which gave it a perfect view of the footpath outside the pub, as well as the entrance door. Lots of people passed by that door; either alone or in company. Some of them went in and others came out. It wasn't until what looked like a hen party of women in identical red skirts and white blouses emerged fifteen minutes later, that they saw something significant.

'There,' said Brett. 'That's them.'

Two big, bearded men wearing tight-fitting T-shirts had come out directly after the hen party. Ainsworth stopped the recording. He zoomed in.

'You're sure?'

Ralph and Brett nodded together.

'OK,' said Ainsworth. 'I'll see if we can match them to our records. Now, show me Sarah's diary.'

Ralph had the laptop open and ready. He also had his list of relevant dates with him. They waited patiently while the detective worked his way through it all. When he'd finished, he looked thoughtful.

'Sheds a lot of light, doesn't it?' he said. 'Not just on what possibly happened to Sarah, but also on Roz Kingsley, and Sarah's friend Dominic, who appears to be the one behind the bombings. The only problem is the fact that it's electronic evidence and as such, needs to pass an authentication test before any of it can be used in a court of law. Otherwise, it's just hearsay.'

'Does that mean *you* think it's hearsay?' demanded Ralph, who wasn't entirely surprised by Ainsworth's statement. He already knew through working with Gerald and Brett that electronic media was considered easy to manipulate. For all Ainsworth knew right now, it could have been Ralph who'd made the diary entries.

'I don't think that. I hope it's not, Mr de Malmanche. If it is, you could go down for conspiring to pervert the course of justice, which is what Fabian Kingsley could be charged with if he did indeed move his wife's body.'

'We didn't invent this, I can promise you that,' said Ralph.

'Well, there is a way to test some of it. Your friend Clarissa …' Ainsworth produced a notebook and flipped through it. 'Yes, here she is. Clarissa Price, 51 years of age. Divorced, no children. Interesting website, too.' He looked up at their enquiring faces, and allowed himself a smile. 'I did some checking on her after the email you sent me. She has a fascinating social life. I'll go and talk to Ms Price and run the allegations Sarah made past her. See how she reacts.'

'And what about Kingsley?' asked Brett. 'He threatened Sarah. Don't you think there's a motive there?'

'Well, that depends. He said if she went to the police it would be harmful to her. If she had come to us, and what she told us turned out to be true, she could have been charged with withholding information. That might have been what he was referring to. But if he meant hurting her personally, then the fact is, he has an alibi for that night.'

'So, you're saying we've wasted our time with this diary evidence, is that it?' said Ralph. He felt that perennial feeling of frustration creeping up on him.

'Not necessarily. I was talking to Byron Foster before you arrived. He told me about meeting you in the pub at Foxdown, and that the German couple are still in Norfolk. If we find them and this Dominic, they might provide a piece of the puzzle. Combine that with more interviews with Ms Price and Mr Kingsley, and we should make progress. Leave it with me. Can I print the relevant entries from this diary before you go?'

They waited while Ainsworth connected Sarah's laptop to a printer and did that. When he'd finished, he walked them back to the elevator.

'I'll go and talk to both Ms Price and Mr Kingsley this evening,' he said. 'I'll let you know what they say.'

When Ralph and Brett came out of the police station a minute later, the sky overhead had darkened. The end of the heatwave had announced itself in the last day or two with a five degree drop in temperature, a cool wind, and lots of billowy white cumulus clouds. But today, those clouds were black and heavy with moisture. The two friends were halfway to the car park when the weight of all that moisture became too much, and the rain poured down. After a spontaneous outbreak of cursing, they managed to find shelter in a shop doorway.

'You know, I don't think Clarissa will just wilt and tell Ainsworth what really happened,' said Brett, as he ran a hand through his soaked hair. 'Or Kingsley, for that matter.'

'If you mean what happened with Roz, then I agree. And Kingsley's got his alibi for the time Sarah was attacked, so he's clear on that, too. But what about those two guys at the pub? Maybe they're part of the gang who went out to the wood that night. Find them, and we might get some answers.'

'We'll just have to wait and see if they're on record. There's still one person left that might know something about that night, though.'

Ralph looked out at the shiny, wet street they'd just crossed. There was a fast-running river pouring into the storm drains. He sighed. 'Dominic. But how the hell do we find him?'

'Maybe Ainsworth will do it for us.'

They couldn't help but feel deflated. They stood in silence and watched the rain come down. Five minutes later, it stopped.

'Let's trust in the forces of law and order, and see what happens,' said Ralph. 'We'll just have to wait. In the meantime, it's back to reading emails.'

They set off. The air felt light, washed clean by the rain. They walked back to the car and drove home.

Over the course of the next twenty-four hours, they tried to be patient. They applied themselves to the rest of Kingsley's emails in the hope they'd find something to link him directly with Sarah's death, knowing all the time that anything they found would be inadmissible. Or maybe there was an email in there somewhere substantiating Hermes's claim about the corrupt planning committee member. Also inadmissible, but it could still be leaked to the press.

They found nothing. They were disappointed about that, but also glad to be done with it all. There was, however, one cause for celebration. The *Eastern Daily Press* had published an article about Kingsley's Aylsham development, with its sub-standard houses. Brett found it on the EDP website and read the relevant bits out loud.

'"*When residents complained to Kingsley Developments about a number of structural defects, they were reportedly fobbed off and told to use their ten-year warranties as given by the National House Building Council. The fact that these defects were approved by a Building Regulations inspector begs the question: how was this possible? Acting on anonymously leaked emails between Kingsley Developments and the inspector who approved the houses on the Aylsham Estate, we contacted both parties to determine if money changed hands to facilitate that approval. Neither would comment. The emails are now with the head of Building Control at Norfolk County Council, who has promised to take a further look at the matter, and ascertain if the houses do in fact meet Building Regulations.*" Ha! One up to us, mate!'

Brett was grinning. Ralph laughed.

'That could be embarrassing for Fabian,' he said. 'Couldn't happen to a nicer guy.'

But their jubilation was short lived. Ainsworth came back to them on the evening following their visit to the station, by phone. The news wasn't good. He'd spoken to both Clarissa and Kingsley, and neither had deviated from their story about Roz's suicide at the beach. They flatly denied moving the body on the Saturday night. When Ainsworth had asked Kingsley about his alleged threat against Sarah, that too had been denied. Kingsley had wanted to know where the allegations for all of this had come from, but Ainsworth assured Ralph that he hadn't mentioned Sarah's diary. As things stood, until some more concrete evidence of Kingsley's involvement in both incidents came to light, he couldn't be arrested. Or Clarissa. As for the two men at the pub, enquiries were ongoing. Ralph thanked the detective and hung up. He told Brett what Ainsworth had just told him.

'As we thought,' Ralph concluded. 'They denied the lot and there's nothing to prove otherwise. Hopeless.'

Later that night, around 10 p.m., there was another phone call. It confused them at first, because they could hear a phone ringing somewhere in the flat, but it didn't belong to either of them.

'Shit, it's Sarah's,' said Ralph. He rushed into what was Brett's bedroom, where he'd left Sarah's phone plugged in on her consulting desk. He answered it, and put it on speaker.

'Hello?'

'You found it, then.' Kingsley's voice.

'Found what?'

'Sarah's computer. Listen, de Malmanche, I advise you to stop trying to incriminate me in what happened to your sister. If you persist, you'll be sorry. Do you understand me?'

'Is this what you did to Sarah when she said she'd expose you? Threatened to kill her? I know you're responsible for what happened to her.' Ralph was trying to keep his voice calm, but his temper was rising.

Kingsley, by contrast, sounded icy cool. 'You don't know what you're talking about,' he said. 'I'm sorry about what happened to Sarah, but there's nothing to be gained by trying to pin it on me. Back off.'

'Or what?'

'You'll regret it. Watch your back, Ralph.'

He rang off before Ralph had a chance to reply.

'Prick,' mouthed Ralph at the unresponsive phone. Brett was standing next to him by now. 'You heard all that?'

'He's a cocky bastard,' said Brett. 'He put it together. He knows those allegations about Roz could only have come from Sarah, and he doesn't mind us knowing that he knows.'

Ralph was quietly seething. 'He thinks he can get away with it. We should just go to his house and beat the shit out of him. Arrogant bastard.'

'Not a good idea, mate. We need to calm down. That's just the kind of thing he'd like us to try. I bet we'd turn up to find those two guys from the pub waiting for us. Not that I wouldn't mind having a crack at them with a baseball bat. But no, we take Kingsley's advice.'

'What are you talking about?'

'We watch our backs. This place has been burgled, and I've been attacked. I wouldn't put anything past Kingsley when it comes to intimidating people. So, we take precautions. Starting now. OK?'

Ralph knew sense when he heard it. 'OK, fine. We'll be careful. But I'm not going to be intimidated. Let's give Fabian some publicity; I'm going to post a link to that article the EDP published, on the Save Foxdown Wood Facebook page.'

He did that straight away. He noticed that the page hadn't been so busy since the protestors were removed from the wood, there were fewer posts and comments. But there were still close to 25,000 followers who could potentially be reached, so posting the link wasn't a futile exercise. Anything that might dent Kingsley's reputation was worth putting out there.

'Tomorrow, we'll go out to Hemsby,' said Ralph, closing his laptop for the night. 'See if we can find Karl and Bettina. They might be able to point us at Dominic.'

'Won't Ainsworth be doing that?' said Brett.

'Why wait?'

Brett could see that Kingsley's phone call, instead of intimidating Ralph, had only served to fire him up. He didn't demur.

'Right, we'll go to Hemsby.'

With that decided, they turned in for the night.

It wasn't until they arrived at Hemsby late the following morning that they realised how difficult it was going to be to find Karl and Bettina. The place was a holiday resort, and the season went on until late October. It was now early September, and although the weather had cooled off in the last week, there were still plenty of holidaymakers around.

There were also plenty of caravan parks in and around this area of Norfolk. The two Germans could be living in any one of them, or they might have chosen to rent one of the many holiday chalets and cottages close to the beach. Ralph had tried Bettina's number before they left home, but it was switched off.

'Where do we start?' said Brett, as they drove up the main road to the beach. There were caravan parks on both sides of them. Large ones.

'We'll have to look everywhere,' said Ralph. 'Look for the Kombi. It's orange, with German plates. And a D for *Deutschland* sticker on the back.'

There was a car park further along the road, where the shops and amusement arcades began. They left the car there and walked back. They spent the next two hours traipsing around the caravan sites on the beach road, without success. Then they drove to three other sites nearby, with the same result. That left the streets bordering the beach front, where many of the cottages and chalets were. And Hemsby was a long beach.

'This is hopeless, Ralph,' said an exasperated Brett. 'They could be anywhere within a ten-mile radius. Best chance of finding them is if they drive right by us.'

It was late afternoon by now. They sat in the BMW, drinking from bottles of mineral water. They'd skipped lunch, which wasn't improving Brett's mood.

'You're right,' said Ralph. 'It's a needle in a haystack job. If we drive around, we might get lucky. Thing is, the switched off phone makes me think they don't want to be found. Which kind of begs the question; why are they still in Norfolk?'

Brett shrugged. Before he could answer, Ralph's phone rang.

'It's Chloe,' said Ralph. 'Hold that thought.'

He answered it, but it wasn't Chloe. It was Angela, and she sounded upset.

'Chloe's been hurt,' she said. 'An hour ago, at the house.'

'Whose house? You mean your place? Is she OK?'

'She's in bed, with an ice pack on her stomach. She's going to be alright, I think. She asked me to call you.'

'What happened?'

Angela had come home to find Chloe slumped on the couch, holding her stomach and vomiting into a bucket. Once she could talk, she told Angela that half an hour earlier two men had come to the front door, and when Chloe opened it, had forced their way inside. One of them grabbed her from behind and held her still, with one hand covering her mouth. Then the other one told her why they were there.

He said he knew she was the administrator of the Save Foxdown Wood Facebook page. He wanted it removed from the web within twenty-four hours. If that didn't happen, or if it did and then it reappeared for any reason, she would be in big trouble. And just in case she didn't believe him, he wanted to give her a taste of what that meant. He said he'd do it where it didn't show and this time around, he'd spare her pretty face. Then he took his fists to her breasts and stomach for a short while. After that, they left her retching and crying on the floor and walked out.

Ralph had the phone on speaker. He and Brett listened in growing horror as Angela told the story. When she finished, they were stunned into silence.

'Ralph? Are you there?'

'Take Chloe to a doctor, Angela. Go to Accident and Emergency if you have to. Can I speak to her?'

'She's finding it hard to speak at the moment. But she doesn't understand.'

'Understand what?'

'Why this should happen now. The page has been up for months. What triggered it?'

Brett and Ralph looked at each other. They didn't have to think too hard to answer that one.

'I think I know what might have done it,' said Ralph. 'What did these guys look like? Does Chloe remember?'

'They were the same guys you saw leaving the pub. You know, the night Brett was attacked.'

'OK. Take Chloe to the doctor. We'll be around to see you both later on.'

Ralph disconnected. Both men sat staring out the windscreen. Ralph took some deep breaths, but they did little to quell the cold rage bubbling up inside him. He looked at Brett's face, and saw that same rage reflected back at him.

'It's 4.30,' said Brett.

'Kingsley's office closes at 5.30,' said Ralph.

Brett nodded. Ralph started up the BMW. If he put his foot down, they could be back in the city in half an hour. He drove as fast as he dared on the single lane road back to the motorway. His overtaking manoeuvres earned him a few irate horn blasts, and then they were on the A47, with its dual carriageway. He touched 100 mph in a few places, and in twenty-five minutes they were back in the city.

Ralph drove right into Tombland and managed to find a parking space down one of the cobbled side streets. He and Brett had hardly exchanged a word on the drive in. They had an unspoken agreement concerning what would happen next.

They marched into the office building that housed Kingsley Developments and climbed the stairs to the second floor. The officious receptionist on Kingsley's front desk wasn't around when they entered the office, so they walked straight into the main work area. There were two women and a man seated behind desks, staring at computer screens. They all looked up at once when Brett and Ralph appeared.

'Can I help?' said one of the women. She was a chunky, middle-aged blonde, and she looked justifiably alarmed by the grim-faced visitors in front of her.

'Where can I find Fabian Kingsley?' said Ralph.

'I ... He just went out for some coffee. Do you have an appointment?'

Ralph ignored the question. 'Where did he go for this coffee?'

The woman got up from behind the desk, and so did her two colleagues. The male colleague, who was slightly-built and in his mid-twenties, decided to be assertive.

'If you don't have an appointment you'll have to make one with our receptionist, and she's gone for the day. Please leave and call her tomorrow.'

All he got in reply were two blank stares.

'I'm phoning the police,' said the blonde.

At that moment, Fabian Kingsley walked in. He had a takeout tray in his hand, with four cups of coffee on it. He saw Ralph and Brett, and after a brief moment of alarm his eyes narrowed, and his face got a little ugly.

'What the bloody hell do you think …?'

He didn't finish the sentence. Ralph covered the distance between them in two quick strides and planted a fist in Kingsley's face. The tray flew out of his hands and when it hit the floor, coffee sprayed in all directions.

'Shit,' said Kingsley. He fingered his bleeding mouth. 'You've done it now, de Malmanche. And I have witnesses to back it up. I'm going to …'

Again, he was cut off in mid-flow by a fist to the cheek. He staggered back. The blonde was dialling a number on her desk phone, while the two other Kingsley employees watched in fascinated horror. Brett calmly took the phone receiver out of her hand.

'Step away from the desk,' he said.

She didn't argue with him. Meanwhile, Kingsley had decided to retaliate. He had only suffered minor damage up to this point, and as Ralph came at him again, he stepped to one side and weighed in with a punch of his own. Ralph managed to block it, but he was forced back a step or two. Kingsley looked encouraged by that. He was the shorter man and more solidly built. Even if Ralph was running on adrenaline, a neutral observer would probably put their money on Kingsley to win this particular fight. Brett must have come to a similar conclusion.

'Allow me,' he said. He pushed Ralph out of the way, and then he went to work.

It had only been a few days since Brett had been on the receiving end of a beating, and his face still had the bruising to prove it. Kingsley looked into that bruised, angry face, and what he saw there wasn't pretty. He took an involuntary step backwards. He opened his mouth to speak but Brett, who was a big man, smashed it closed with an equally big fist. And then he took out his anger on Kingsley. He methodically battered the man around the head and the body until Kingsley fell to his knees and tried ineffectually to cover up his face with his raised arms. There was a lot of blood coming from his mouth and nose by now. Brett was beyond mad, and showed no sign of letting up.

'Stop it!' screamed the blonde woman, who was in tears. 'Just stop!'

That brought Brett to his senses. He stepped away, breathing heavily. Ralph shook his shoulder.

'Let's go,' he said. He looked down at Fabian Kingsley, who was now lying on the floor, staring back at him through puffy, semi-closed eyes. 'Touch Chloe again and we'll kill you,' he said. There was no reply. With one last glance at Kingsley's prostrate figure, they walked out.

Chapter 19

When Ralph and Brett got back to the car and drove away, they knew what an incredibly stupid thing they'd just done. It was only a matter of time before Kingsley reported the incident, and the police turned up. But there was a part in each of them that didn't really care.

'Let's see how Chloe is,' said Ralph.

The traffic was slow coming out of the city; everyone was on their way home. It gave them time to calm down after what had just happened. When they got to Chloe's house, it was to find her in the lounge with Angela and another woman they'd not met before. Chloe was on the sofa, with a dressing gown wrapped around her, and a towel with an ice pack in it pressed to her stomach. Ralph sat down beside her.

'Are you OK? Have you seen a doctor?'

Chloe shook her head. Her face was drawn with pain, but when she spoke, her tone was pure outrage.

'How dare those bastards come into our house like that. Who do they think they are? And why haven't they been caught? They were the same guys we saw leaving the pub, Ralph. Is your detective friend just going to let them walk around and beat up anyone they like?' That short outburst cost her a lot of effort. She gasped for a second, and then gently massaged her abdomen.

'Damn it,' she almost whispered.

Ralph tried to put a comforting hand on her shoulder, but she shrugged him off. 'You need to see a doctor,' he said.

'She's got an appointment first thing tomorrow,' said Angela, who was now hovering over Chloe with a replacement ice pack.

'Why did they come here?' asked the third woman. Ralph and Brett gave her curious looks.

'This is Zoe,' said Angela. 'She lives here, too.'

Zoe was not much more than twenty. She had close-cropped, short ginger hair and a pale, freckled face. She stood in the doorway to the kitchen looking angry, with her thumbs through the shoulder straps of a pair of pale-blue dungarees. One Doc Marten shod foot tapped the floor impatiently as she waited for an answer.

'I put a link on the Facebook page about Kingsley Developments,' said Ralph. 'About how he may have bribed a building inspector. I don't think he liked it too much.'

'Yes, we checked it out,' said Angela. 'Seems like a massive over-reaction if you ask me.'

'More like confirmation that we hit the nail on the head,' said Brett. 'You sure you're alright, Chloe?'

Chloe gave him a weak smile. 'Yes, I think so. What happened to your hands?'

Brett held them up. He had dried blood on his knuckles. 'Shit,' he said. 'Can I use your bathroom?'

The three women just stared.

'We visited Kingsley,' said Ralph. 'Did to him what was done to you.'

Chloe's eyes widened. 'Oh, Ralph. Wasn't that a bit stupid? Did you injure him? Did anyone see?'

'Yes to all of that,' said Ralph. 'When we heard what happened to you, we lost it a bit. He went too far.'

'Maybe you did, too,' said Chloe.

'I'll show you where the bathroom is,' said Angela. She led Brett out of the room.

Ralph leaned back on the sofa, with a great exhalation. All the adrenaline had drained out of him. He felt exhausted.

'You need to report what happened to the police,' he said. Then his phone rang. It was DC Ainsworth. 'Speaking of which …' He answered it.

Ainsworth didn't sound friendly. 'Where are you Mr de Malmanche? I'm getting no answer from your doorbell.'

'I'm at a friend's place. She was attacked earlier today, by the same two men who attacked Brett. Perhaps you should come around.'

Ainsworth thought about that. 'I see. Where does she live?'

Ralph gave him the address and Ainsworth said he was on his way. He hadn't mentioned his reason for visiting Ralph, but you didn't need to be a mind reader to figure it out. Brett reappeared with Angela a few minutes later, with freshly washed hands.

'Ainsworth's on his way here,' said Ralph. 'Prepare for the worst.'
Brett looked grim. 'We're going to need legal advice,' he said. 'Soon as possible.'

'You can get free legal advice at the station if you're arrested,' said Chloe. 'I know this. Protestors get arrested.'

It didn't take long before Ainsworth and two uniformed officers arrived. The lounge was getting overcrowded. Ainsworth looked at Chloe on the sofa, and then cast a quizzical eye over Brett and Ralph. 'We'll start with the assault you mentioned on the phone,' he said. He looked again at Chloe. 'Are you the victim?'

He had the details explained to him. Chloe opened enough of her dressing gown to display a mass of angry bruising on her stomach. 'And my breasts,' she said. 'I'm not showing you those.'

'I'd like you to come into the station,' said Ainsworth. 'I'll get a female constable to take some photos and also a statement from you. Are you up to it?'

Chloe nodded. Then Ainsworth turned his attention to Brett and Ralph.

'I've come directly from Mr Kingsley,' he said. 'He looks a lot worse than Ms Miller here, at least his face does. I'm arresting you both on suspicion of assaulting Mr Kingsley. You're coming to the station with me.'

'We want to consult a solicitor,' said Ralph.

'There's a duty solicitor at the end of a phone. You can talk to him and then you'll talk to me. Let's go. Ms Miller?'

'Let me get dressed. Five minutes.'

There were two police cars parked outside. Brett and Ralph were split up; Brett went with Chloe and one of the uniformed officers, and Ralph got Ainsworth and the other uniform. When they got to the station, Ralph and Brett were deprived of their possessions and then locked in separate cells until a duty solicitor arrived. It took less than an hour for that to happen. They met with her in a private room.

'I'm Helen Strauss,' she said. She was a thirty-something, serious-faced brunette, dressed in a dark trouser suit. 'I understand you're both suspects in a common assault case. Did you do it?'

They were sat around a circular wooden table. Brett and Ralph looked at each other. Brett shrugged.

'We did,' said Ralph.

'Do you have any defence to offer?'

'We were provoked. Our friend Chloe was attacked earlier today by Mr Kingsley's thugs. We retaliated.'

Ms Strauss wasn't impressed. 'You can't use provocation as a defence. Not in assault cases. You're about to be interviewed, so you can either say nothing, or admit to the assault. If there's no defence and clear evidence to convict you, I would recommend admitting it. Staying silent could backfire once you get to court.'

They decided to take her advice. The upshot was that they were cautioned and then interviewed by Ainsworth and another detective. They admitted to what they had done, and why. Ainsworth wasn't impressed with their retaliation argument either.
'You don't even know if those thugs work for Mr Kingsley,' he said. 'And as your solicitor no doubt told you, provocation doesn't count.'
At the end of it all, Ainsworth said they'd be charged with common assault, and a trial date would be set.
'In no more than fifty-six days from now,' he added.
'What happens now?' asked Ralph.
'I'm releasing you on conditional police bail. You're to report here once a fortnight until the trial starts. And I'll want your passports within the next forty-eight hours. You're free to go.'
'What about Chloe?' said Brett. 'It would be useful if you got the two guys who beat her up. Before they do it again.'
Ainsworth glared at him. 'Don't try my patience. On your way, both of you.'
Chloe was waiting for them in the reception area. She looked a little more cheerful than a couple of hours ago.
'The constable who took my statement thinks they've identified the two men who attacked me,' she said. 'From the CCTV footage of the pub that night.'

'Ainsworth didn't mention that,' said Ralph. 'How are you feeling?'

'Sore. And tired. Will you take me home?'

They got a taxi. On the way, Ralph filled in Chloe on their situation.

'So, you're going to court,' she said. 'You'd better get a lawyer for that.'

'We will. Don't you forget about going to the doctor tomorrow, OK?'

Chloe promised not to forget. When they reached her place she invited them in, but given that she was tired, they declined. They promised to check in with her the next day, and told her to lock the doors and windows.

'I will,' she said. 'I'm not taking the Facebook page down, either.'

Ralph admired her courage, but it worried him.

'What time is the doctor's appointment? We'll take you there. And if you're working tomorrow, I'll drive you there, too. We have to go to London after that and pick up Brett's passport. But we'll be back to drive you home.'

'Ralph, you don't have to ...'

'No arguments, please. What time should we pick you up?'

They agreed on 8.30 a.m. With that decided, the two men got in the BMW and drove home. They hadn't eaten since breakfast, and neither of them felt like cooking. So, they ordered a pizza, which arrived twenty minutes later. Now that the rage of earlier had passed, they were reflective.

'Now we're criminals,' said Ralph, picking up another slice of pepperoni and pineapple. 'We could actually go inside for this.'

'He deserved it,' said Brett. 'I've got no regrets about thumping the bastard. Apart from the going to jail bit.'

'Exactly. Helen Strauss gave me her card, so I'll see if she'll take our case. I tell you what; you take the car tomorrow and pick up your passport, and I'll stay here. If you don't make it back in time, I'll take Chloe home in a taxi. How does that sound?'

'Works for me. I'll call you when I leave London.'

The next day unfolded as scheduled. Chloe was taken to the doctor's surgery at 8.30 a.m., and Ralph went in with her. It felt a bit like overkill to be shadowing her this way, but given that she was ignoring a twenty-four hour deadline to remove the Facebook page, he was a little bit paranoid about her safety. Chloe wasn't with the doctor for long and when she came out, it was with a prescription for some painkillers.

'He doesn't think there's any internal damage,' she told Ralph. 'I ache, but otherwise I feel fine.'

Brett dropped them in the city, close to the practice rooms. Then he was off to London. Ralph watched the back of the BMW as it moved away from him and down the side road bordering the

Norwich market. It turned a corner and was gone. Chloe noticed his anxious expression.

'What is it?' she said.'

'Nothing. He's not insured to drive it, that's all. As long as he doesn't crash the bloody thing …'

'What are you doing now?'

'Well, I'll ring a solicitor, then I'll go to the library for a bit, and then I'll take you to lunch. OK?'

'OK. You don't have to stick around like this, you know.'

'I want to. Those two madmen who attacked Brett and now you … They worry me. They don't seem to give a damn about whether they're seen in the act or not.' Now it was Chloe who had the anxious expression. 'Not that I think they'd do anything in the middle of town. Just humour me, Chloe.'

She smiled. 'No, you're right.' Then, to his surprise, she kissed him. 'Thank you. Walk me to work.'

'Yes ma'am.'

The day progressed without incident. Ralph made an appointment to see Helen Strauss next week, and visited the library. After lunch with Chloe, he wandered around town for a bit. Brett called to give him an update.

'Got the passport,' he said. 'But I'm going to be held up. While I've been away, there was a leak into my flat from the washing machine upstairs. I've got some water damage to sort out.'

'That's nasty. But it's not a problem for us if you have to stay down there for a while. We'll get a taxi.'

Which is what they did when Chloe finished for the day. They got back to her place to find that Angela and Zoe had been busy barricading the house against unwelcome visitors. There was a bookcase in the hall by the front door, which was going to be leaned up against it overnight, according to Angela.

'And we're going to bring in the freezer from the garage and put it up against the back door,' she told Ralph. 'There's somewhere to plug it in overnight.'

Zoe appeared. She had a heavy-duty hammer looped around her wrist. 'If those two muppets dare to come back, I'll use it,' she said, in reply to Ralph's quizzical look. 'Will you help us get the freezer in?'

The women had gone into warrior mode. He stayed with them for a few hours and shared a meal, after which they sat around drinking wine and watching a movie. Around 11 p.m., Ralph thought it was about time he left.

'Thanks for the meal,' he said. 'I better get going.'

'Is Brett coming to pick you up?' asked Chloe. She looked much more like her usual chirpy self now, and because the marks left by her attackers weren't visible, you'd never know she'd been the victim of an assault just twenty-four hours ago.

'He hasn't called. I won't bother calling him now. I can walk home from here.'

'You sure?'

'Yes. Those guys won't be bothering you tonight. But don't forget to barricade the door behind me.'

Chloe saw him to the door, and gave him a long hug.

'Ouch,' she said. 'It hurts to do that.' She let him go.

'Call me in the morning and we'll pick you up for work,' said Ralph. 'Bye, ladies.'

He stepped outside. It was a pleasant night for walking; a bit breezy, but not cold. The residential area containing Chloe's house was situated virtually opposite the university, but after turning left out of her place and walking a few hundred yards, it gave way to a more rural setting. To get back home, Ralph had to walk down Bluebell Road, which at the university end was bordered by farmland on one side, and woodland on the other. It was quiet and deserted at this time of night, with very little traffic. He'd been walking for ten minutes without meeting anyone, and only two cars had passed him. A third was approaching now from behind; a van. It passed him, pulled over, and stopped. Two men got out. He recognised them.

'Shit,' he murmured.

He thought about making a run for it. Until he saw that one of the bearded duo was pointing a gun at him.

'In the van,' said the gunman. 'Someone wants to talk to you.'
Ralph looked around, but there were no vehicles coming his way.
'Move it,' said the other one. He came up to Ralph and grabbed his arm. 'In the back.'
He had no choice. The one with the gun opened up the back door, and then once Ralph was inside, joined him. The other guy jumped in the driver's seat, and the van pulled away. In less than thirty seconds, Ralph had been snatched off the street. To make matters worse, once he was sitting on the floor in the empty space behind the front seats, the man with the gun slipped a hood over his head.
'Just sit there, stay quiet, and don't make a move,' he said.
'What the hell do you two clowns think …?' His sentence was interrupted by a punch to the side of his head. He slumped to one side, dazed.
'What part of "stay quiet" don't you understand?'
Ralph pulled himself into an upright, cross-legged position, raised an exploratory hand to his sore head, and said nothing. Were these two men crazy enough to kill him? Is that what was happening here – they were driving him to some secluded spot so they could put a bullet in him? But no, the gunslinger had said that someone wanted to talk to him. If that was true, it must be Fabian Kingsley. Or maybe instead of talking, he just wanted to reciprocate the beating Brett had given him. There was nothing else to do but wait and see.

They drove for almost an hour, Ralph figured. He was pretty sure they were on a motorway for most of that time and then they slowed a bit, which meant they had probably turned off somewhere. It was another twenty minutes before they got to where they were going. He felt himself lurching to the right as the van made a left turn and then they were passing over gravel, if the tone of the tyres was anything to go by. A minute later, there was a sudden deceleration and a squeal of brakes, which almost toppled him over. The van shuddered to a halt.

'What the hell?' said the gunman, who was in the back with Ralph. 'What's going on?'

There was silence from the driver, but the gunman must have seen for himself by then.

'Holy shit,' he said. 'Go take a look. I'll stay with our friend here.'

Ralph was curious as hell by now, but he decided not to ask any questions. He heard the driver's door open and shut, and then there was nothing but silence for the next five minutes. Then the driver was back, breathing hard.

'Not good,' was all he said. 'Not good at all.'

'Now what?' said the gunman. He thought for a few seconds. 'Open the back door.'

Ralph was manhandled outside. The hood was still in place, so he had no idea where he was.

'Start walking.'

The ground was soft underfoot, like a lawn perhaps. He heard the crashing of gears as the driver reversed the van and presumably turned it around. The gunman had him by one arm, and the barrel of the gun was pressed into his ribs. Then he let go of Ralph and stepped away.

'We're leaving you,' he said.

For one horrible second, Ralph thought it was all over. Then he felt an explosion of pain just above his left temple. His knees buckled and he crashed to the ground, semi-conscious. He vaguely registered the sound of the van as it drove away, before rising groggily to his knees and pulling off the hood.

He'd been right about the lawn. It was a big lawn, too. It might be close to midnight, but there was enough light being cast to make out a good deal of the surroundings. There was a large tree directly in front of him and beyond that, some twenty or thirty yards away, was a house. It was a big, two-storey affair, and it was easy to see right now because the rooms on the second floor were on fire. Flickering yellow and blue flames were visible through shattered upstairs windows.

'What the hell is this?' Ralph muttered.

He got to his feet and looked around. The house was in a private spot in the middle of nowhere, as far as he could make out. There was a Range Rover parked out front, and nobody to be seen anywhere. He staggered towards the front door, which stood wide open. It was hot out here, but not unbearable. He went inside. There was no one in the hall or the kitchen. Maybe they were asleep upstairs, he thought. But can I go up there? There was a door through from the kitchen to the dining room; a big room with a long mahogany dining table and a couple of oak sideboards. He stepped in, and only got one foot through the doorway before he was brought up short. There was a body stretched out on the carpet beside the table. A man, on his back.

Ralph took another tentative step. He could hear the crackle of flames above him, and he felt the heat. The fire must have started upstairs, because there was no sign of it down here. Not yet. The floorboards above might burn through at any moment, though, and if that happened, they would fall right on top of him. Was the man on the floor unconscious? Ralph had to get him out of here.

But the man on the floor didn't need Ralph's help. He didn't need anyone's help. Ralph found himself standing over the body of Fabian Kingsley, whose bruised and battered face, with one puffy, closed eye, was twisted in a sneer. His shirt was stained with blood. Not enough blood to disguise the gaping wound in his chest, though. He'd been shot at close range and he was dead, there was no doubt about that.

'Oh my god,' breathed Ralph. There was nothing for it, he had to ring the emergency services. Then he realised what it would look like when they got here.

He hesitated. Then he heard the sirens.

Chapter 20

The fire engines were the first to arrive. Ralph was standing outside several yards away from the blaze when they tore down the driveway with their blue lights flashing. They didn't waste any time unrolling the hoses. Thirty seconds later, high pressure jets of water were being directed at the top floor of Kingsley's house. One of the firemen ran up to Ralph.

'Who else is in there?' he said.

'There's a body inside,' said Ralph. 'Ground floor, in the dining room. I don't know if there's anyone else in the house.'

The fireman ran off to tell his colleagues and a minute later, three of them were entering the house. Ralph watched it all in a semi-daze, his head still humming from the blow he'd received earlier. Then a police car pulled up. Two uniformed officers got out, and, seeing Ralph staring forlornly at the conflagration, walked up to him.

'Is this your property, sir?' one of them asked.

'No.'

'Do you know who it belongs to? And what are you doing here?'

'I was brought here. Against my will.'

That got an interested stare. 'Would you mind elaborating, sir?'

He told them what had happened. The firemen emerged from the house while he was doing that, carrying Kingsley's body. They laid it on the lawn a safe distance away and then, apparently having satisfied themselves that he was the only occupant of the house, returned to hose duty.

'You say you think this is a Mr Fabian Kingsley's house,' said the policeman. 'Is that him?'

'Yes. Someone shot him.'

The two policemen looked at each other. 'I'll call it in,' said the second one. He walked off.

'You're bleeding,' said his remaining colleague. 'How did that happen?'

Ralph wasn't aware of that fact. The blow above the temple must have been done with the butt of the gun, he suddenly realised. He put his hand up again to feel the damage and sure enough, it came away coated with sticky, half-coagulated blood.

'One of the men who brought me here did it,' he said. 'Before they left.' He held up the hood that he'd unconsciously been holding on to all this time. 'Where are we? They put this over my head on the way here, so I don't have a clue.'

The policeman looked at the hood and then at Ralph. 'We're just outside Martham,' he said.

Ralph wasn't sure where Martham was. He noticed that the policeman was now studying him with a rather dubious expression. If I was in his position, Ralph thought, I'd probably be doing the same thing.

'There's an ambulance on its way,' said the cop. 'They'll take a look at that cut and then you can come into the station with us and give us a statement. In the meantime, take a seat in our vehicle.'

He made sure Ralph was comfortable in the back seat and then, with his colleague standing guard, he walked over to take a look at Kingsley's body. He stood back far enough to ensure he didn't contaminate it any more than it already was after being removed from the house. Then he came back.

'You're right,' he said. 'Someone shot him.'

When the ambulance turned up, Ralph was treated by a paramedic. After answering a few questions and having his head bandaged, he was delivered back into the care of the Norfolk Constabulary.

'You feeling OK?' said the second policeman.

'Not concussed, if that's what you mean.'

'Good. Get in then. We're going to the station.'

As they turned the police car around, Ralph could see that the blaze was being brought under control. Parts of the top floor had collapsed while he was being treated, but it seemed as though half of the house remained intact. A police forensics van had turned up during his head injury assessment, too. The two men who'd arrived in it were in the process of putting on their white overalls. That was the last thing he saw before the police car began moving down the driveway, and the scene disappeared from view.

It was close to 2 a.m. when they arrived at Norwich police station. Ralph was shown into the same interview room he'd occupied with Brett and Helen Strauss, so very recently. One of the officers who'd brought him in asked for his jacket.

'What for?' said a slightly indignant Ralph.

'We want to run some tests. You'll get it back.'

Ralph emptied his pockets and took the jacket off. The officer held it carefully by the collar while transferring it into a large plastic bag.

'Right, done. Don't go anywhere.' He walked out of the room.

Ralph was given a cup of coffee by a woman constable, and then he kicked his heels for half an hour before someone came in to talk to him in an official capacity. It was a man in plain clothes, not much older than Ralph. He sat down opposite.

'Detective Constable Williams,' he said. 'And you are Ralph de Malmanche. Correct?'

'That's right.'

'You were here just two days ago on an assault charge. On the same man who is now lying dead out at Martham. Is there anything you want to tell me about that?'

'Not without a solicitor present.'

DC Williams couldn't quite stifle a yawn. Ralph wondered if he'd been woken up to do this interview. Williams rubbed a bristly chin.

'Yes, fair enough.' He took some papers out of a manila file and read for a minute. 'Mr Fabian Kingsley,' he muttered. He read on for a bit and then returned the papers to the file. 'This is DC Ainsworth's case. Given the circumstances, we're detaining you for what's left of the night. DC Ainsworth will be notified first thing. You might want to get some sleep in the meantime. Is your head OK?'

Ralph told Williams that his head would survive.

'OK. Just tell me exactly what happened from your perspective. I'm recording it, and it will be typed up later. You can review it with DC Ainsworth later this morning.'

Ralph made his statement. After that, one of the two policemen he'd come in with took him to a cell for the sleep Williams had mentioned. Ralph wasn't entirely sure if he could be detained this way, but he wasn't about to argue. Ainsworth would want to speak to him in any case. When that interview took place, he wanted Helen Strauss to be there. He lay down on the bunk in his new, spartan accommodation, and pulled the blanket over him. But he couldn't sleep. Images of the burning house and Kingsley's lifeless body kept whirling around in his head, interspersed with thoughts of how easy it would be for Ralph de Malmanche to be held responsible for Kingsley's death.

He must have dozed off at some point, because at 7 a.m. he was woken up by a policeman rapping on the door and offering him toast and cornflakes for breakfast. But he had to wait until 9 a.m. before he was let out to call Helen Strauss. Fortunately, she said she could attend the interview, which was scheduled for 10 a.m. They let him wait in the interview room after that. Helen appeared on time, but Ainsworth didn't show up till twenty minutes later.

'Sorry I'm late,' he said, casting a quizzical eye over Ralph's bandaged head. 'I was just reviewing the statement you gave my colleague last night.'

'Is my client under arrest?' demanded Helen.

Ainsworth, who looked slightly worried about these new developments, shook his head. 'Too early to arrest anyone. Just let me confirm a couple of things. First, you say you were with Chloe Miller until 11 p.m., and then on your way home you were abducted. Yes?'

'Yes,' said Ralph.

'You were walking at the time. Why weren't you driving home?'

'Brett's got the car. He went to London to get his passport, and got held up. I hadn't heard from him and I didn't think there was any need to call him, so I decided to walk. He could be back by now, or still in London, I don't know.'

'And these two men you allege abducted you; they were the same men who attacked Mr Saunders and Ms Miller, correct?'

'Yes, that's right.'

'What vehicle were they driving?'

'A white Transit van.'

'Did you get the registration?'

'I got a look at it before they shoved me inside, but I can only remember the first part of it. They whacked me on the head, so maybe I'll remember the rest of it later. This is all in the statement I made last night.'

Ainsworth nodded. He had the typed up statement in his hand.

'Alright. Here's your statement. Read it and if you're happy, sign it. Then you can go.'

There was silence for ten minutes while Ralph did that. It was an accurate reflection of what happened, so he signed it.

'I'm going to corroborate your story with Ms Miller and Mr Saunders,' said Ainsworth. 'Email me as soon as he arrives back in Norwich. And you're still on conditional bail, so don't forget to report in on Tuesday as scheduled. It might also be a good idea to see a doctor about that head wound. Right, you can pick up your possessions from the desk sergeant.'

Ainsworth walked them to the desk and then, rather grim-faced, left them there without saying goodbye. When Ralph got his phone back and turned it, on he saw two missed calls from Brett, who must be wondering where the hell he was. There was a missed call from Chloe, too. Helen Strauss was itching to leave by now.

'If you're arrested or you need any legal advice at all, just call,' she said. 'I have another appointment, so excuse me.'

She rushed off. Ralph left the police station, and was practically at the nearest taxi rank when he remembered he was supposed to be taking Chloe to work. He rang her.

'I'm not working until this afternoon,' she said, when he apologised for not getting back to her. 'Is Brett back with the car yet?'

'I don't know, I'm about to call him.'

'What? Aren't you at home?'

'No. Something happened after I left you last night.'

He told her the story of the fire and Kingsley's demise. 'I'm just about to get a taxi home,' he ended.

Chloe was lost for words, but not for long. 'I'm coming around,' she said.

'That's exactly what you're not supposed to do. Go out alone, I mean.'

'What, you think they're going to snatch me after what happened to you last night? Anyway, I'll walk down the Newmarket Road, which is always busy. And it's the middle of the day, Ralph. So, expect me soon. OK?'

She was right. 'Sure,' he said. 'Soon as you like.'

He waited until the taxi dropped him off at home before returning Brett's call. His friend was actually driving as they spoke. He had to tell Brett what he'd just told Chloe and listen to a lot of Brett's expletives, which were firmly directed at the two bearded bastards, before Brett finally calmed down.

'Should be back in an hour,' he said. 'Had to make an insurance claim about my leaking ceiling. The girl upstairs fixed the washing machine, too. So, it's all good. Oh, and after all that, I got the passport.'

It seemed like some sort of normality was reasserting itself. Ralph had a shower, and then made some strong coffee. He settled down to wait. Chloe arrived twenty minutes later. He'd taken the bandage off his head when he'd showered, so when he opened the door to Chloe, the first thing she saw was the angry gash above his temple. She came in and insisted on looking at it. She ran a gentle, tentative finger over it.

'A bit lower and he could have killed you,' she said. 'You should have told me over the phone. I've got some really good cream for that.' She began to cry. 'Dammit, Ralph. What's going on?'

'I don't know.' He put his arms around her and then, without thinking, he kissed her on the lips. 'It's fine,' he said. 'It's going to be OK.'

She sighed. 'I hope so. Do that again, please.'

He did. It was clear to both of them that they wanted to do more than just kiss, but Chloe decided that wasn't going to happen right now. She gently removed his arms from around her waist and wiped her eyes.

'I look like a patchwork quilt under these clothes,' she said, smiling. 'It still hurts, too.'

'And Brett will be here in a minute,' he replied.

They both laughed.

'To be continued,' said Chloe.

'Definitely before I go to jail. Or maybe you can visit me; conjugal visit, or whatever.'

She got serious. 'That's not funny. You're not going to jail. Get that out of your head.'

He didn't share her confidence and decided to change the subject. 'Want some coffee?'

When Brett got back, Ralph emailed Ainsworth, who replied almost immediately to say he'd be around shortly. He was as good as his word. It was a flying visit, and he killed several birds with one stone in the course of it. First of all, he brought back Ralph's jacket. But he offered no explanation for wanting it in the first place. So Ralph asked the question.

'We tested it for gunshot residue,' said Ainsworth. 'We didn't find any.'

Then he got Brett's neighbour's details so he could contact her and confirm that Brett had indeed been in London. He asked Chloe to back up Ralph's story, and said he'd be calling around at her place later to talk to Angela and Zoe, to ensure they were in agreement. And finally, he took the passports. He had a parting shot for them.

'Those two men who attacked you, Ms Miller. They've both got records. They're local men, but neither of them are at their last known addresses. However, we may be able to trace them with that partial registration number you gave us, Mr de Malmanche. Let me know if you remember all of it. I'll keep you posted.'

'What about Mr Kingsley?' said Chloe.

'I can't comment on that just yet. I'm waiting for forensics and the autopsy. Right, I'm off. I know my way out.'

He left. Brett looked at Chloe.

'Ralph tells me you're not working till this afternoon. Can I buy you guys lunch?'

'We accept,' said Chloe.

They adjourned to the pub.

The next day was Saturday and with the arrival of the weekend, everything seemed to quieten down. There were no visits from policemen or bearded thugs. It gave Ralph a chance to sit back and reflect on what to do next. Now that Kingsley was dead, it looked like his link to Sarah's death might never be established. The only people left who might be able to confirm that link were the two men who'd abducted Ralph the other night. He had no doubt at all now that they worked, or had worked, for Kingsley, and it was highly likely that they were part of the gang of four who'd caused Sarah's fall. He ran all this past Brett.

'Arrest those two guys and we'll finally get to the truth of what happened,' he said.

Brett wasn't quite so upbeat about it.

'I don't think they would confess everything just like that,' he said. 'And what evidence is there? None, unless Ainsworth picked up something from the scene that night that we don't know about. Didn't you say he was pretty sceptical about Bettina's story?'

Ralph had to concede the point. When it came down to it, maybe they'd never know what happened between the time of Sarah's fall, and the discovery of her body six days later. He couldn't even be sure she'd actually fallen; he only had Karl and Bettina's word for that.

'Whatever happened, someone took Sarah's body out to Blickling and buried her there. Who was it? Then there's the business of her ring turning up in that burnt out house. How did it get there? I know it won't bring her back, but I still want answers.'

'Ainsworth will find those two guys. Then you might get some answers.'

Ralph could only agree. Which meant that there was nothing he could do next other than wait. And now, Brett had come to the conclusion that he'd done all he could to assist. He said it was time for him to go back to London.

'Will you drive me back next week?' he asked Ralph. 'People will be coming to repair my ceiling, and I should really be thinking about getting my next freelance gig.'

'Sure. Gerald will want you back on the job as well.'

'I'll have to come back for our fortnightly report to the cop shop. And our court appearance, whenever that's going to be.'

'I'm sure you'll get a letter about it. I'll let you know what Helen Strauss is going to say in our defence before then. If there is anything she *can* say, that is.'

They were both silent for a bit while they considered what might come out of the trial. It wasn't an attractive prospect. Brett changed the subject.

'What about you, mate? Isn't it time you got yourself a job?'

Ralph laughed. 'You sound just like Holly. But you're right, that money my mother gave me won't last forever. I'll get around to it soon.'

This sudden facing up to reality needed an antidote, in Brett's opinion. He made a suggestion.

'Let's go into town and get hammered tonight. You up for it?'

'What, so you can get the shit kicked out of you again? Great idea.'

'You can't let them intimidate you, Ralph. OK, we'll only get a bit hammered. Deal?'

'Sure. I'll see if Chloe is as crazy as you are. I'll call her and find out.'

Chloe wasn't enthusiastic about the idea, even if she did say booze was a good anaesthetic when it came to physical aches and pains. And besides which, she was going to the movies with her flatmates.

'Will I see you next week?' she asked him.

'Yes. We'll sort something out. Go for dinner or something. I'll call you.'

In the end, Ralph and Brett decided it wasn't necessary to go all the way into town. They went to the Unthank Arms instead, which was only a fifteen-minute walk away, and a very pleasant place to drink alcoholic beverages. But when they got there, they found they weren't really in the mood to drink vast quantities of beer. They did manage a few pints though, and in doing so found time to discuss what had happened to Fabian Kingsley.

'So, who shot him, Ralph? Assuming it wasn't you, I mean.'

'Very funny. How do I know? Perhaps he had enemies we know nothing about. Could be business related. Your guess is as good as mine.'

'Maybe Clarissa knows something about it. I hope Ainsworth has got sense enough to ask her. Last thing you need is …'

'A murder charge? Yes, it had crossed my mind.'

It was all far too sobering. They gave up their attempt to forget about it with booze, and went home. It wasn't until Sunday night that there was any update on the situation, and it didn't come from Ainsworth. They found out about it when they watched the news that night. The Look East local TV bulletin had the story. According to that, Fabian Kingsley had been killed with a shotgun and as yet, no arrests had been made. The fire at his house had been started with incendiary devices that bore a strong resemblance to those used in the earlier fires at his Aylsham development. Norfolk police were now looking for the radical environmental group Triple G in connection with the incident, and Kingsley's death was being treated as a murder investigation. This was all relayed in a short video report, by someone named Detective Inspector Martin. Ainsworth was standing next to him, but said nothing to the interviewer.

'Who the hell is this guy?' said Brett.

Martin was a tall, barrel-chested man, with broad shoulders and a reddish, jowly face. He stayed impassive throughout the interview. Not surprising, given the subject matter. Then the programme switched to other news.

'Of course, it's a murder investigation now,' continued Brett. 'Ainsworth is a detective constable and this Martin guy is a detective inspector. He must have taken the case over.'

'Just a question of time before we meet him, then.'

Brett decided not to wait for that. On Monday, they drove to London so Brett could return to his apartment. They didn't start the journey until mid-afternoon, and by the time Ralph got back to Norwich, it was close to 10 p.m. When he pulled into the forecourt, he noticed a Triumph motorbike parked there. He didn't think too much about it until he got out of the car and walked up to the main door of the house. There was an enclosed porch leading to the door, which meant he didn't see the person standing in it until he nearly bumped into him. The visitor was holding a crash helmet, and seemed to be there for no apparent reason. He was tall, with shoulder-length black hair. For a moment, Ralph wondered if he was about to be attacked again. He took a step back.

'Something I can help you with?' he said.

The man extended his hand. 'Ralph. I'm Dominic. I knew Sarah. Mind if we have a word?'

Ralph stared. Yes, it was the man from the funeral, no question. He didn't shake his hand.

'I know who you are.'

'Sarah mentioned me?'

'In a manner of speaking. Have you seen Fabian Kingsley recently?'

Dominic didn't blink. 'No, I haven't. That's what I wanted to talk to you about, actually.'

Ralph thought about it for a second or two. Then he made up his mind.

'Why don't you come in?'

He opened the front door and they went inside.

Chapter 21

No words passed between them as Ralph led Dominic up the two flights of stairs to the flat. It wasn't until they were inside and Dominic had accepted Ralph's offer of a seat on the sofa, that the questions began. Ralph was doing the asking.

'You could have let yourself in through the house door. You've still got a key, haven't you?'

'That's true. I've got a key to the flat as well, but there's no reason to use it anymore.'

Dominic reached a hand into his jeans pocket and extracted the keys. He put them on the coffee table. Ralph didn't bother explaining that he'd changed the locks since Dominic's last visit.

'Was it your guitar?' Ralph asked.

'Yes. I dropped in to get it back. Sorry if that spooked you. I would have said something, but you weren't around and I wanted to stay out of the limelight.'

Ralph had been standing by the front window. Now he took a seat on a chair, facing Dominic.

'What did you want to tell me?'

Dominic wasn't about to be hurried. 'What did Sarah tell you about me?'

'She didn't tell me anything, she wrote it down. You're part of this Triple G group. You've been planting bombs and burning down houses, and now it looks like you've shot someone as well. Any comment on that?'

Dominic sighed. 'I didn't shoot anyone. Mind if I explain?'

'Go right ahead.'

'It's a long story. You got some water or something before I start?'

'There's some beer in the fridge, will that do?'

Ralph opened two bottles, and Dominic started talking.

Dominic Fischer had been in and around protest movements since he was a teenager in the mid-90s. He was 18 when he first took to the trees in the West Country, where he joined forty other people to protest the building of a bypass through pristine green countryside containing an ancient hill fort. That particular battle was lost to government transport policy; the bypass got built. He'd dropped out of school early to do an apprenticeship as a mechanic. He finished it, and then hardly had time to find work before joining the bypass protest. When that ended in the violent removal of the protestors by private security men, he was politicised. He'd seen government policy in action, and for him it was nothing more than a process serving corporate interests, implemented by force. It made him cynical. Especially when in the following years, that pattern repeated itself.

Some of the protests might be strengthening the environmental lobby and moderating policy decisions, but it wasn't changing things fast enough. Governments, especially western governments, preferred to ignore global warming and climate disaster in favour of maintaining the status quo. Almost twenty years after his first protest, Dominic knew that non-violent resistance wasn't going to change anything. So, he made a political choice of his own. He became a Green radical environmentalist. Which committed him to a more active form of resistance. The kind that couldn't be ignored.

The Global Green Garrison, or Triple G, was the organisation with which he decided to affiliate himself. Its structure was decentralised, and built on the model of leaderless resistance. Anyone could carry out an act of sabotage and claim it on behalf of Triple G. People worked alone or in small independent cells, and nobody communicated with anyone else. Triple G was more like an independent press office than a formal organisation. It publicised environmental acts of sabotage through its website, and released the details to the media. There was never any open encouragement towards acts of sabotage, but there were plenty of links on the site pointing to literature that would help you put your plans of sabotage into action, if you were that way inclined.

Dominic had been on their mailing list for years. During that time, he'd sent in anonymous articles on protests he'd attended, and essays outlining his thoughts on the subject of violent versus non-violent protest. They were all published on the website. He'd even informed the 'press office' about a fire he'd set at a Sports Utility Vehicle showroom in France ten years ago, along with photos of the event. All done through encrypted emails on virtual private networks, to preserve his anonymity. That particular story got plenty of exposure online, and in the media, too. The only thing the press office knew about him was that he was based in Norfolk, in the United Kingdom. Which is why, in his opinion, he was contacted by the website administrator.

It came in the form of an email, just two months after the start of the Save Foxdown Wood protest. It said that someone had been in touch using the 'Contact Us' option on the website. That person was offering financial support to the tree sitters, but wanted to remain anonymous. He wanted to know if the website administrator could put him in touch with a local person sympathetic to the aims of Triple G, because he wanted that person to distribute the money. Any conditions attached would be discussed with the individual in question and the anonymous benefactor's representative, if and when they met.

Dominic was wary; after all, this could be an attempt by some law enforcement agency to get a Triple G sympathiser out into the open. But to what end? It wasn't a crime to support the radical environmental group. And if this person wanted to distribute money in order to support the protest, that wasn't a crime, either. Nor could it be connected with anything Dominic had done in the past. If that was the case, they'd already know about him, and where to find him. On top of which, he already knew some of the protestors out at Foxdown Wood. He thought about it for a while and then replied, saying he would meet this representative. He then supplied the website admin with another email address he used, to facilitate the first contact between them.

Which is how on one breezy morning in May, after an initial exchange of emails, he met a man who simply identified himself as David. He was in his mid-thirties; tall and thickset, with a tough, unsmiling face. They met at a pub in Cromer, a town on the Norfolk coast. David was pleasant enough at that first meeting. He bought Dominic a beer, and they sat down to discuss the arrangement.

'My client is prepared to donate £500 a week,' he said. 'Towards living costs for the protestors out at Foxdown. All you have to do is deliver the money. You can tell them it comes from a well-wisher. Which it does.'

'And how will I receive this money?'

'We'll meet here every Monday, same time. I'll give you an envelope full of cash. That's it.'

'That's it? I thought there were conditions attached.'

David took a long drink of beer. He cleared his throat. 'You're a Triple G supporter, aren't you?' He registered the look on Dominic's face. 'Let me put it another way; you're sympathetic to the idea of direct action in order to achieve the aims of the protest. Would that be more accurate?'

'I may be able to help, depending on what you have in mind, that is.'

'In that case, we may ask you to take some direct action against the building work currently underway. Damaging action.'

Dominic had half expected it to be something along those lines.

'I'm not in a position to promise you anything. For all I know, you're an undercover police officer. Who's your client?'

David laughed. 'No names.'

'Fine. So, if you want to do some damage, why not do it yourself?'

'To be brutally honest, if it all goes tits up, I don't want it coming back on me or my client. We want it attributed to environmental extremism.'

Dominic thought about it for a while. 'Alright. Give me the money regularly for a month. Call it goodwill. I'll think about the options and if I can help you, I'll let you know. How does that sound?'

David seemed happy enough. 'We'll go with that. Here's your first instalment. We meet again here on Monday. You can buy the beer next time.'

With that, David pushed a fat envelope across the table, stood up, and walked out. Dominic sat there, staring after him. Then he took a surreptitious look at the ten-pound notes padding out the envelope, and quietly finished his pint. He knew that if David was really a police officer, then he was encouraging Dominic to commit a crime, which was entrapment. Even if they got him to court on that, it would never stick. Still, he was in no hurry to burn down or blow up anything just yet. He'd distribute the money for a while and then see if it was realistic, or even desirable, to do what David wanted.

He rode the bike out to Foxdown Wood the following day. He had been there last week, just to visit. He knew Karl and Bettina from Germany, and he'd spent time with them and others at the protest in the forest over there. Not long, maybe three weeks or so. A lot of the time spent at protests was idle time; sitting around waiting for something to happen. At that particular time, nothing was happening. They were totally committed to passive protest, too, and he'd seen enough of that to know it didn't end well. He thought it best to leave them to it. And then they'd turned up here in Norfolk.

He was considering giving the money to Bettina so she could use it as she saw fit, until he remembered the rather gorgeous woman he'd met on his previous visit. Just fleetingly, but she was a bit older, and she'd struck him as more mature, more organised. She might be a better custodian of the cash. He couldn't remember her name at first, and then, as he parked the bike in the wood car park, it came back to him. Sarah.

But Sarah wasn't around when he got out to the tree houses. He asked after her, trying to sound as though it had just occurred to him in passing, and learned that she was an alternative medicine practitioner who usually turned up late afternoon, after her clinic. He spent some time with Karl and Bettina, catching up on the news from Germany and asking them how long they were prepared to sit this one out, but he didn't mention the money. When Sarah hadn't arrived by 4 p.m., he thought he'd try again tomorrow. He said goodbye and walked back to the car park, where he saw her getting out of her Peugeot. She seemed to remember him. She smiled.

'Hi,' she said. 'Back again?'

'Just leaving, actually. But I'm glad I caught you. I want to talk to you.'

'Oh? What about?' She walked across to him, and he could see that she was inspecting the motorbike. 'Don't see many Triumphs on the road, anymore,' she said. 'I always loved the sound of these bikes.'

'You ride?' She shook her head. 'I'm Dominic, by the way.'

'Sarah de Malmanche.'

'Interesting name. Are you French?'

She laughed. 'My father's French. Mum's English. I'm a half-breed.'

There was something about this woman. Tall and slim, dark-haired and dark-eyed. A slightly sad look in those eyes, until she smiled and they sparkled. He struggled for a moment to remember what he wanted to talk to her about.

'Look, I thought, as you seem like a responsible sort of person …'

'On such short acquaintance – really?'

She was flirting with him now. Not that he minded.

'I'm a fine judge of character. Trust me. Are you willing to take money and use it to keep you and the others in food and drink for the foreseeable future? Because if you are, I have some.'

She studied him with an intense curiosity then. 'Are you rich?' she said at last.

'No. But I have been promised money to help with this protest, on a weekly basis. I want somebody responsible to take care of it. And I don't want anyone to know that it came from me. Will you do that for me?'

'How much are we talking about?'

He fished the envelope out of his leather jacket and handed it over. 'Count it. £500.'

Sarah's eyes opened wide. She said nothing, just opened the envelope a fraction and looked.

'Where do I say this came from, if not from you?'

'Just say it came from a well-wisher.'

Sarah considered that for a second before replying. 'Alright, then. That's very generous, Dominic. I accept.'

He said he'd be back again next week with more of the same, and then he got on the bike and rode away. He thought about her on and off over the course of the next week, and he also thought about what he might do to disrupt the building work, when the time came. There were about ten houses currently under construction on the site, but they weren't much more than brick shells. A fire on its own might not do much damage, but an explosion caused by a fire bomb certainly would. It was easy to get access from the wood, too. The site as it was at the moment had been fenced off where roads adjoined it on three sides, but the wood side was still wide open. The developers were doubtless not expecting the kind of thing Dominic had in mind, but they did have a portakabin on site, with a night watchman in attendance. Dominic thought it would be easy enough to get past him. If he planned it right. If he decided to do it.

Then when he met Sarah again the following week, it occurred to him that his regular visits, followed shortly afterwards by Sarah waving money around, would soon lead the other protestors to conclude that he must be the source of it. Her car wasn't there when he arrived, so he waited for her in the car park. She drove in twenty minutes later. She got out and walked over to him.

'Hello,' she said. 'I wondered when you'd turn up again.'

It was only May, but it was already getting warm. She had on a blue cotton dress and her hair was loose, flowing around her shoulders with the breeze. He thought she looked great.

'How did the first contribution go down with everyone?' he wanted to know.

'Well, they interrogated me, but I didn't break. Your secret is still safe.'

'I've been thinking about that. Is there any way we can meet somewhere else? Then no one will ever know about my secret.'

'Well, I …' She thought about it for a bit. 'I'm not here every day. Actually, I do a long day on Wednesdays, and after that I usually go back to my flat. You could come around in the evening.'

'Will your boyfriend or your husband be there? I don't want anyone to get the wrong idea …'

She laughed. 'I'm not married, and you don't have to worry about boyfriends. I'm a bit off them at the moment.'

That was a setback. Maybe she doesn't like men, thought Dominic. Prefers girls or whatever. But he didn't really believe that. There was a mutual attraction unfolding here, he was certain of it.

'Oh, OK. Well, let me know where you live and I'll drop around a week on Wednesday. About 7 p.m.?'

She said that was fine. He gave her the second envelope that he'd just collected from David in Cromer, and then said he wasn't going to hang around. When he rode out of the car park, he could see her in the bike's mirror, looking after him. Then she was out of sight. Gone for another week.

The first time he met up with her at her flat in Newmarket Road, she asked him in. She wanted to talk. Wanted to know about him and his connection to the protest movement. She had opened a bottle of wine, and even had some snacks laid out.

'Didn't Karl and Bettina tell you about me?' he asked her.

'They said they knew you from Germany. Said you'd been involved in environmental protest for years. Why aren't you out with us more often?'

'I'm not involved in the way I used to be. And when I am, I'm a fan of more direct methods. Bettina doesn't always agree with me about that.'

'Yes, she said you're a Triple G supporter. Is that where the money's coming from?'

He drank some wine. 'No. It doesn't work like that. I left some pamphlets and booklets with Steve and Diana. You know, the Earth First! guys. Have a look at those.'

She was taking a serious view of this. 'I will,' she said. 'So, you're not an extremist, I hope. I don't think damaging property or whatever will help save Foxdown Wood. It will just get us bad publicity and lose us supporters.'

He grinned. 'Sarah, don't worry. I'm not an extremist.'

She seemed happy enough with that reassurance. He didn't think of himself as an extremist, so he wasn't lying to her about it. They spent a pleasant evening together drinking wine, and she told him about her travels and her work as an Ayurvedic lifestyle consultant. He, by contrast, managed to say as little as possible about himself. Then they arranged to meet again the next week, and he went home to his little house in a village near Attleborough, some twenty minutes' motorcycle ride away. He hadn't even told her where he lived.

On the third visit, they drank more wine and ended up in bed. And they were good together. There were no nerves like two people often experience the first time they make love. It was like they already knew each other's bodies. He didn't go home that night. By the end of June, when the long, hot summer was already burning up the lawns of Norfolk, they had fallen in love.

Dominic had realised by then that Sarah was nearly as secretive as he was. He hadn't met any of her friends. In fact, she'd told him that for now, she wanted to keep him totally to herself. Even when he went out to the wood, which he did more often now, they tried to keep it a secret. But he was pretty sure most of the other people out there weren't fooled by their subterfuge.

He had been riding out to Cromer regularly on Monday mornings to meet David, who was now hassling him about his intentions. It was mid-July, and there had already been two demonstration days at Foxdown Wood. Hundreds of people had attended, and so had the TV cameras. There was a third demo lined up for the first week of August. David thought it was time for some action.

'We need a result,' he told Dominic, over the customary beer in the usual pub. 'Just before or just after this next demonstration. You've had plenty of time to think about it, so what have you got lined up?'

Dominic had been expecting some pressure. After all, he'd been taking this man's money for two months or more. But he wasn't going to promise anything.

'When I do something, you'll know after the event. But you're right about the timing. Something will happen in the month of August. Does that satisfy you?'

'It better happen, mate. My client wants some bang for his buck. Understood?'

Dominic got the message, and it wasn't as though he hadn't been thinking about it. He already knew how to build an explosive device that worked with an electrical timer. All he needed were the necessary chemicals and other ingredients, which were readily available, and he could put one together. But he thought he owed it to Karl and Bettina to at least let them know what he had in mind. They probably wouldn't agree with it, but they wouldn't stop him, either.

Which is how he and Sarah had their first real fight, when she walked in on him in the Foxdown Arms with Karl and Bettina. He was showing them a diagram of the device at the time, and when she got there, he hurriedly hid it away. She wasn't fooled, though. She saw the looks on the German couple's faces, and she knew something wasn't right. On the walk back to the wood, she wouldn't let it go. So he told her. She didn't yell at him, Sarah wasn't the yelling type. But she made her feelings clear in her quiet, intense way.

'I told you before, it will work against us if you damage property. And you might kill someone. Did that ever cross your mind?'

'I don't harm humans or animals. I'll make sure neither species is in danger. And this kind of action forces change, Sarah. I've seen it.'

Sarah wasn't convinced. 'Look, I know the guy who's developing this site. His name is Fabian Kingsley. He's not very nice, Dominic. He won't take it well if you blow up his buildings. He'll do something.'

'You know him?' came three voices at once.

Sarah was only momentarily embarrassed. 'Shit,' she said. 'Yes, we … Never mind. I know him, OK? Dominic, let's talk about this.'

In the end, she talked him out of it. And when he met David again the following week, he communicated that decision.

'I had to discuss my planned action with some of the other protestors, including my girlfriend. We've decided not to go ahead. We thank your client for his support, but we won't be taking any more of his money.'

David's face set in a mask of angry disappointment, but he kept his voice level.

'Your girlfriend. Sarah, you mean.'

That rocked Dominic, as David no doubt intended it to. But Dominic wasn't going to satisfy the guy by admitting to the relationship.

'Look,' he said. 'I'm sure it suits your client to make sure the protestors stay where they are, otherwise you'd never have given me this money in the first place. Let's leave it at that.'

David wasn't buying it. 'I suggest you talk to Sarah and whoever else you need to talk to, and get them to change their minds. In fact, I strongly recommend it.'

Dominic stood up. 'I'll see what I can do. Don't hold your breath.'

He walked out. As he rode back to Norwich, his mind was working overtime. David's veiled threat hadn't been lost on him, but what exactly would the guy do if Dominic refused to back down? He decided to keep quiet about this conversation. He'd told nobody that the money had been conditional upon the action he'd admitted planning on the walk back from the pub. He would just tell Sarah that the well-wisher had donated as much as he was able to, and there was no more available. As far as Dominic was concerned, the subject was closed.

And it *was* closed. Until the night Sarah fell from a tree, courtesy of four men. One of whom was addressed by the others as 'Dave'. He emailed David after her disappearance and demanded a meeting, but he never got a reply.

Dominic was devastated. Sarah hadn't arrived at the hospital, and that meant if she was still alive, she'd been abducted. It was all his fault. If he wanted to remedy the situation, there was only one course of action open to him. He went out shopping. When he returned from that expedition with everything he needed, he started assembling a fire bomb.

Chapter 22

Dominic and Ralph had consumed several bottles of beer during the course of Dominic's story. It was after midnight when he finished.

'You planted the bomb at the last demo, then?' said Ralph.

'That was me. I made sure it was well away from everyone.'

'I don't get it. Did you think Fabian Kingsley was responsible for Sarah?'

'No. It had nothing to do with Kingsley. Why would he want me to bomb his own development?'

'He might have had a reason. Insurance claim, perhaps. His company might have been in financial trouble.'

Dominic shook his head. 'If that was the case, he could have accepted the £2 million he'd been offered for the wood. No, David was working for someone else.'

'Yes, and you held up your end of the deal with that someone else when you planted the bomb.'

'I had to. Sarah was only missing at that point. Abducted, I thought. I was hoping whoever took her might let her go.'

'And you didn't stop there. You started burning down houses.'

'That's just the thing, Ralph. I didn't.'

'What? You mean you didn't burn down two houses in Aylsham, and then Kingsley's place?'

'Of course not. It was made to look like I did. Or not me, specifically. Someone claimed one of those houses on behalf of Triple G, but it wasn't me.'

Ralph made another trip to the fridge for the last two beers. He handed one to Dominic and sat back down.

'So, you weren't at Kingsley's house then. You didn't shoot him. Assuming I believe that, who did? You know, it might have been useful if you'd told me about you and Sarah earlier.'

'I wanted to, at the funeral. But I decided it wasn't the time or the place to say anything. And it might have stayed that way, until Fabian Kingsley got shot. That's not something a committed Triple G supporter would do. We don't harm humans or animals.'

Ralph didn't say anything for a long time after that. He sat back in his chair and thought about everything Dominic had told him. Then he made a few observations.

'OK, Kingsley was telling the truth when he said he had nothing to do with Sarah's disappearance. We have to look elsewhere. The only lead we've got for that is this David character. But you get no reply from him. Got a phone number?'

'No, we did all our communicating away from the pub by email.'

'Write down his email for me. I'll get a post-it.'

He went into the second bedroom and grabbed a stack of post-it notes from Sarah's desk, along with a pen. Dominic took them and did as he'd been asked.

'You're not about to come forward and repeat this for the police, are you?' said Ralph.

'What do you think? No, this is overdue, but it's for your ears only. Will you be mentioning me to the police?'

Ralph sighed. 'I see no point in that. But they might figure it out for themselves. If they do knock on your door though, it won't be down to me.'

'They can knock. I won't be home. I'm going away for a bit. Off the grid.'

'Going where?'

'I'm not going to tell you that. Bloody miles away, that's all you need to know.'

Ralph felt tired now, and just a little bit drunk. 'Fair enough. I'll give you my phone number and email. If anything comes to you that might help identify David, let me know.'

He took the post-it notes from Dominic and wrote down his details. Dominic stood up and stuffed the note in a pocket.

'Time I went,' he said. 'I'm sorry about Sarah, Ralph. I loved her to bits. If there's anything I can do to help you track down whoever killed her, send an email to this address.' He paused long enough to write it down. 'And don't try to trace it. It goes through loads of proxy servers and VPNs, which makes it impossible.'

'Sure. Thanks for coming.'

He saw Dominic to the door of the flat. He could find his own way downstairs. Ralph saw the pain on that handsome face and realised that Dominic still felt guilty about Sarah. Perhaps he should, after all that had happened. He watched as Dominic descended the first flight of stairs, until he was out of sight. Then he shut the door, collapsed onto the sofa, and tried to marshal his thoughts. But they weren't playing ball. After ten minutes he gave the whole thing up and went to bed.

When he woke up late the following morning, he remembered that he wanted to phone Chloe, so they could arrange to go out somewhere. He wanted to tell her about last night, too. But when she answered the phone, he had to wait. She had news to share.

'Guess what?' she said. 'Bettina sent me a private message on Facebook yesterday. She heard about Kingsley being shot. Now she and Karl and a couple of others are back out at Foxdown Wood. It's a last ditch effort to raise awareness before the clearance starts on Friday.'

'That's only three days from now,' said Ralph. 'Where's she been, anyway? Did she say?'

'No, she just asked me to go out there and take some photos. Then I'll post them, and see if I can get some people to attend a last demo. I know it's short notice …'

'It's all fenced off, Chloe. Nobody will even get close to the wood.'

'No it's not. We drove out there, remember? They'd only done some of the fencing, then. Bettina said they're back in the tree houses, so they definitely got in OK.'

Ralph wondered what Bettina thought they could possibly achieve in three days, but there was some publicity value in their last ditch stand, he supposed.

'Shall I drive you?' he said. 'I want to speak to Bettina anyway.'

Chloe laughed. 'That was my next question. Come and get me when you're ready.'

He picked her up an hour later. As they drove, he told her about Dominic.

'So, that's where the money came from,' said Chloe. 'And when Dominic wouldn't do what they wanted, this David person went after Sarah. Is that what you're telling me?'

'That's my theory. OK, it could have been another Dave that night. It's a common enough name. But I think they're the same person.'

'Could it be one of the men who attacked me and Brett?'

'That wouldn't make sense. When they grabbed me, they were taking me to see Kingsley. I can't believe Kingsley gave Dominic money to sabotage his own development. No, I've got to find David, or Dave, or whatever his name is. He's the only lead I've got. Maybe he knows who shot Kingsley. Maybe he did it …'

Chloe registered the anxiety in his voice. She put a hand on the back of his neck and slowly massaged it. 'Ralph, the police will solve it.'

He grunted dismissively. 'You think so? What if they decide to charge the bloke they found at the scene? After all, wasn't it that same bloke who just twenty-four hours previously, assaulted the murdered man? Wouldn't you arrest me?'

'And what about the weapon? What did you do with it? You didn't fire it. They tested your jacket for gunshot residue and didn't find any.'

'Just because ...' he began. And sighed. 'Yes, you're right. I still feel like the prime suspect. I still *am* the bloody prime suspect.'

Chloe changed the subject. 'Are we going out for dinner soon?'

That distracted Ralph for a while. They discussed it and decided to go out tomorrow night. Chloe wanted tonight to organise whatever needed organising for the last demo at Foxdown Wood. Shortly afterwards, they arrived there.

Or more precisely, at the Foxdown Arms car park. The wood car park was inaccessible, so they'd have to walk to where the fencing ended to get among the trees. After parking the car, they began to walk up the road alongside the wood. There was a stiff breeze blowing in from the coast, with a cold nip to it that the bright sun overhead did nothing to dispel. Chloe had a camera with her, with its strap wrapped around her wrist. She put her free arm through

Ralph's and huddled up close. They marched up the road that way, until the fence ended some twenty minutes later.

Coming in that way got them a bit lost at first, until Chloe seemed to recognise a landmark that Ralph was totally oblivious to. She took the lead, and they found a track through the silent oaks and rustling beeches till they came to a clearing that Ralph recognised. They walked through it to the tree houses.

'Bettina?' called out Chloe.

From what Ralph could see, nothing had changed since the protestors had been evicted. The tree houses were still intact. A head appeared, just visible through the branches above.

'Chloe?'

Bettina descended via a harness, and once it had been pulled up again, Karl did the same. When he got down to ground level and stood next to his girlfriend, Ralph had a crazy sense of déjà vu. Like meeting them for the first time, all over again. They both looked at him rather blankly, and he couldn't figure out if they were happy to see him, or annoyed. Or just plain indifferent.

'I tried to call you,' he said to Bettina. 'Your phone was dead. I thought you were going back to Berlin.'

'We were,' she said. 'We changed our minds.'

No explanation about the dead phone, he noticed. 'I met Dominic.'

They couldn't hide their surprise at that. 'You know about him, then,' said Karl.

'He and Sarah were in a relationship. You told me Sarah wasn't seeing anyone, Bettina.'

Bettina's serious brown eyes didn't waver. 'I said I didn't think so. They liked each other, I could see that. But he wasn't here that much. What did he tell you?'

'Everything. He's gone, now. Somewhere miles away, he said.'

'Well, whatever he did, he did it on his own. Don't involve us in it.'

'I won't. There are some things he told me that you don't know about. I'd like to have a chat about that.'

Two other people had appeared. Byron, and a young woman he hadn't seen before.

'Where's your mate with the broken nose?' said Byron, grinning.

'Find anything on Sarah's computer?'

'Why don't I buy everyone a drink and I'll tell you all about it? You might be able to fill in some of the blanks for me.'

Byron was up for it. 'Sure. This is Ellie.'

Ellie was a shy-looking girl, no more than 16. A pretty, pubescent, brown-eyed brunette. Ralph noticed the satchel on her shoulder and wondered if Byron had kidnapped her from the local secondary school. She smiled and said hello.

'Yes, OK,' said Karl. 'Let's hear it.'

'Let me take some photos first,' said Chloe. 'Some in the tree house and some down here, alright?'

Ralph got out of the way while they did that. Karl ascended via the harness, followed by Chloe. After five minutes up there they both reappeared, and then Chloe arranged her subjects and took some shots of the last four tree-sitters in Foxdown Wood. They managed to smile. Then they all set off for the pub.

When they arrived, it was lunchtime. The Foxdown Arms was somewhat off the beaten track, so it wasn't too busy. There were two white-haired old gentlemen at a table in one corner of the lounge bar, hunched in silent concentration over a chessboard. In the corner diagonally opposite and about as far away as you could get, four younger men were busy eating and drinking. That was it. The diners had on bright yellow, high-visibility vests, so Ralph assumed they must be doing roadworks somewhere nearby. They looked up as the new arrivals came in, and then returned their attention to their hamburgers and chips. Ralph's party took the table by the fireplace, halfway between the two groups.

Jason the bar manager remembered Ralph from his previous visit. He asked after Brett while he poured a white wine for Chloe, and a pint of Norfolk Ale for Ralph.

'He's back in London,' said Ralph. 'Looking much better than when you last saw him.'

Byron had been conferring with the other tree-sitters, and now he joined Ralph at the bar.

'Wine for the ladies and …' he began, but Jason cut him off.

'Nice try, mate. But if you think I'm serving that schoolgirl of yours alcohol, you're sadly mistaken. Soft drink?'

Ellie had to settle for a Coke. Once everyone had a drink in front of them, Ralph told them about Dominic's visit.

'You knew he was going to do something extreme,' he said to Karl and Bettina. 'He showed you what he had in mind right here in this pub.'

'Yes, but Sarah talked him out of it,' replied Bettina. 'After she disappeared, it was different. We didn't agree with it, but we understood it.'

'Interesting about the money,' said Byron. 'We didn't realise it was coming from Dominic, he fooled us pretty good about that. Then Sarah said not to expect any more cash.'

'But that wasn't the last time we got money,' said Karl. 'We received an envelope full of cash just before the last demo, remember?'

Byron remembered. 'Yeah, but so what? That came by bike courier. The guy walked all the way out from the car park to find us, it really pissed him off. And we never did find out who sent it.'

'No, but the courier said he'd ridden all the way from Cromer to deliver it. Same place as Dominic met David.'

Ralph's antennae were twitching now. 'Is that all he said? No sender details?'

'I asked him where it came from,' said Bettina. 'All he said was that he'd collected it from an office in Cromer. Estate agent's office, I think. Yes, that was it.'

'That's it?' said Ralph. 'No note with the cash? No return address on the envelope?'

Bettina shook her head. 'Nothing.'

Ellie made her first contribution to the debate. She whipped out her phone. 'I'll do a search for estate agents in Cromer,' she said.

It didn't take her long. She looked at the results, and scrolled up and down a few times. 'Only twelve of them,' she said. 'Want to see?'

Ralph held out his hand for the phone. He scrolled through the onscreen data a bit slower than Ellie had done.

'Suppose it could be any of them,' he muttered. His finger stopped moving. 'Hang on …'

'What is it?' said Chloe.

'Ramsey Real Estate and Developments. My god. I've even got his business card at home. He was talking to Brett at the funeral …'

'What are you on about?' insisted Chloe.

'Ben Ramsey. He and Kingsley were business rivals. He didn't like Kingsley. That's what he told Brett at Sarah's funeral. Said Kingsley was a jerk. He also said that Kingsley had ruined a business deal for him. It must be him.'

'The Ben Ramsey who spoke about Sarah at the demo?' said Chloe. 'Is that who you mean?'

'I do. Bettina, how did he get to speak like that in the first place?'

'He found us the day before, and said he was a friend of Sarah's. He wanted to say a few words in her memory. I told him to find us on the day, and we'd have some PA equipment and a microphone for him.'

'That can't be coincidence,' said Ralph. 'The cash arrives, and Ben Ramsey turns up right behind it.' He gave the phone back to Ellie. 'He was a client of Sarah's,' he said, more to himself than anyone else. 'Surely he wouldn't have hurt her …'

Chloe was following his train of thought. 'Maybe not deliberately, Ralph. It was an accident, after all.'

'Well, accident or not, I think I should speak to him. Soon. We should go, Chloe.'

'Finish your drink, first. I want to talk to Bettina.'

Ralph drank and half-listened as Chloe made arrangements with Bettina. She had decided to organise a candlelit vigil for Thursday night.

'Maybe we can find twenty local people,' she said. 'We'll stay up all night and greet whoever they send to cut down the trees on Friday morning. I'll see if I can get some TV coverage for that, as well. Keep your phone on, I'll let you know.'

He and Chloe left shortly afterwards. Ralph was grim-faced on the way back to Norwich, his hands tense on the steering wheel, eyes straight ahead. He didn't say a word. Chloe let this state of affairs continue for the best part of half an hour before breaking the silence. She spoke softly.

'We don't know for sure, Ralph. Don't jump to conclusions.'

He turned his face to her and she saw the rage in his eyes.

'It's just bloody logic, Chloe! It's him. *Must* be him.'

The venom in his voice made her flinch. And it scared her, too.

'Don't take it out on me,' she almost whispered. 'I'm not responsible.'

He was eyes straight ahead again, until he glanced back at her and saw the damage he'd done. He slowed down then and pulled the BMW over to the side of the road, bringing it to a halt across someone's driveway.

'I'm sorry, Chloe. Come here …'

They had to undo their seatbelts before he could get his arms around her in a decent hug.

'Sorry,' he repeated, his anger gone. 'I just can't believe Sarah was the victim of a business war. Such a waste …'

Chloe stopped him with a kiss. 'You'll sort it out,' she said. 'Just don't shut me out while you're doing it.'

A sudden horn blast interrupted their intimacy. Ralph looked across Chloe to see a woman gesticulating at him from behind the wheel of her blocked-in Audi.

'Whoops, gotta move,' he said. 'Buckle up.' He laughed, and got them moving again.

Chloe wanted to get started on organising Thursday night, so he dropped her off at her place.

'I'm working tomorrow,' she said, as she opened the door to get out. 'But we're still on for dinner, aren't we?'

'Sure. I'll pick you up, at say, seven?'

It was a date. He drove back to Newmarket Road, to contemplate his next move. How would he go about getting Ramsey to confess to his part in Sarah's death? Should he just confront the man with his suspicions and see what response it produced? What if he was wrong and the Cromer connection was nothing more than a coincidence? He didn't believe that for a second, but it couldn't be discounted.

The real problem was proving it. Proving that Ben Ramsey had sent men, David among them, out to Foxdown Wood on the night of August 14. And then presenting that proof to the police. He couldn't use Dominic's story to demonstrate the link between David and Ramsey, unless he broke his promise to keep Dominic out of it. If he broke that promise by going to the police, the first thing Ainsworth and this new detective inspector would want to know was why he hadn't reported it sooner. He didn't need that kind of grief; he was already on an assault charge, and might even be arrested for murder soon. No point in making things worse.

It was a dilemma. He sat in the lounge with a cup of coffee, and stared out the front window at the red beech tree. Its leaves were changing with the season, from deep red to rusty copper. When the sun hit them at certain times of day, they turned to gold. It wouldn't be long now until they started falling, carpeting the forecourt and blowing in all directions, including into the house. Not that Ralph minded. For him, the tree had become a kind of security blanket. It had a reassuring presence about it – big and solid, like a mountain. It was at least a hundred years old, and had every chance of still being there in another hundred. Unlike the mere humans who drove past it in their cars every day.

He realised he was daydreaming, and brought his mind back to the problem at hand. Whatever he decided to do next meant keeping the cops out of it, for now, at least. He would conduct his own enquiry. He had the surveillance equipment still here, courtesy of Catford Investigations. Why not put it to use? Brett would be up in Norwich again next week, so he could help out, too. All Ralph had to do was draw up a plan of action and follow through on it. What could possibly go wrong with that?

Chapter 23

Ralph had only done simple surveillance work for Catford Investigations. Simple, in that he'd been restricted to following ostensibly unsuspecting people on foot around the City of London. He blended in by wearing the uniform so common in that location; a suit and tie. He might take a discreet photo or video of the target, depending on where they went and if they met anyone when they got there, otherwise it was all about recording their movements and reporting back. Nothing too demanding about any of that.

But with Ben Ramsey, it was going to be different. For a start, they knew each other. If Ralph started following him around town, his cover would soon be blown. He'd have to do the surveillance part of the job from a distance. With the tools in Gerald's surveillance kit, that shouldn't be a problem. But before he got into that, he needed to run a background check. Which meant asking Gerald for help. Just for the check. This investigation, as amateurish as it might turn out to be, was his baby, and he wanted to involve as few people in at as possible. With that thought in mind, on Wednesday morning he called the Catford office when he thought it most likely that neither Sandra nor Gerald would answer the phone. They lived on the premises, but it was usually Vivian on the desk first thing. And at 8.30 a.m., she was. She was surprised to hear his voice and they exchanged a few bits of small talk, and then he got down to it.

'Can you do a background check on someone for me, Viv? I'll pay the going rate.'

'I don't see why not. You on to something, Ralph? Shall I ask Gerald to call you back?'

'No, just tell him I'll call him if I need advice. You can do it, can't you?'

'Sure, no problem. Might take up to forty-eight hours. Is that OK?'

'Yes, that's fine. But the sooner the better. Let me give you the details.'

He gave her Ben Ramsey's name and the name of his company, with the address in Cromer.

'All the usual stuff, please Viv. Home address, phone number, business history. Debts and so on.'

'I know how it works,' said Vivian, sounding a little miffed.

'Don't fret. If it's legally available, you'll get it. I'll email you.'

He left it with her. There was not a lot he could do until he had more information on Ramsey. The more he knew, the more opportunities he might spot to dig into the man's life, and start asking questions in the right places. Until then, he'd have to wait. That left him with time on his hands, which meant he should do the one thing he'd been putting off; disposing of some of Sarah's possessions. Living in the flat was a constant reminder of her absence, both in the world and the place she'd called home. The colours she'd chosen for the bedrooms kept triggering memories of his first visit, not long after she moved in. They'd had a discussion about how she should decorate the place, which was predominantly white at the time. Sarah wanted to keep the lounge that way, and repaint the bedrooms in multiple shades of blue, her favourite colour. Ralph preferred stronger colours, like red and orange. They both knew the other's preference, but it didn't stop them from making a game out of him trying to talk her out of it. The next time he visited, the bedrooms were kingfisher blue and green azure. Then there were the photos of India and other places she'd been to, all framed and hanging on the walls. A selection of candleholders and other ornaments were scattered around the place. He knew exactly where most of them came from, because she'd told him. The green Buddha figure sitting in meditation on top of the bookcase, for instance. Six inches high and carved from stone, it had emerged from a canvas bag borne on the back of a young Indian man, who appeared out of the heat haze while Sarah lay sunbathing on a deserted beach in Goa. The sack had lots of Buddhas and Indian deities in it, and must have weighed a tonne. She remembered being impressed by how easily the slightly built young man carried this cripplingly heavy load. They chatted for a while, and she bought one. Ralph just had to look at that, and any number of other objects, to remember his sister holding them up and telling him their story. He wasn't about to throw them away.

There were the books she read, the CDs she listened to, the DVDs she liked watching. They could all stay as far as Ralph was concerned, but her clothes and shoes needed a new home. He cleared out the wardrobes and drawers, and put everything in black plastic bags. There were three women he knew who lived close by who might like some of Sarah's things. Or they might have friends who wanted them. But as he filled the bags, he felt like a traitor. As if by throwing away Sarah's things like this, he was betraying her. It was ridiculous, of course, it wasn't like she needed them anymore. But the guilty feeling persisted, oblivious to the appeal of logic. He finished the job in spite of it.

Then in the afternoon, his phone rang. It was DC Ainsworth. Ralph couldn't help wondering if he was about to be arrested by phone, and almost didn't answer it. When he finally did pick up, Ainsworth had news for him.

'We've arrested the two men who allegedly attacked you and Ms Miller,' he said. 'Just wanted you to know.'

'When did that happen?'

'Last night. They were picked up in Liverpool, trying to board a ferry to Ireland. They used their driving licences as ID, and as we already have them on record, they gave themselves away. Not the sharpest tools in the box, those two.'

'So, what happens now?'

'They'll be transferred to us here in Norwich. That should happen tomorrow. I want you and Ms Miller to come in and identify them as your assailants. Till then, we'll remand them in custody. They're a flight risk, as they've already demonstrated.'

That was a relief for Ralph; no more bearded bastards to worry about. 'I'll tell Chloe you've arrested them, I'm seeing her later. Thanks for letting me know. Anything more on Fabian Kingsley?'

'Nothing I can discuss,' said Ainsworth. 'You'll be notified about the identification by post.'

He rang off. Ralph hoped that the two men arrested would be talkative enough to confirm that their employer had been Kingsley. Not that it would help him too much. As far as he knew, they'd come after him and Chloe because he'd been prying into Roz's death and the bribing of building inspectors, which was wholly incidental to what happened to Sarah. But if they knew who might have a reason to shoot Kingsley, then that was another story. That could help him a great deal. He'd just have to wait and see.

When he picked Chloe up that evening, he took a couple of black bags along. Chloe was all dressed up and ready to go, but they stopped long enough for Ralph to deposit the bags in her lounge with Zoe and Angela.

'You can take the barricades off the doors,' said Ralph. 'The two men who came here have been arrested.'

That was greeted with relief. 'What will happen to them?' asked Zoe, whose eyes still seemed to harbour thoughts of personal retribution.

'They will probably spend time in jail. We have to go into the station and identify them at some point.'

Angela changed the subject. 'What's all this?' she said, pointing to the bags.

'Sarah's clothes. I thought you might like to look through them. There's more, too. I've no idea if they'll fit or not, I think she was a size 10. But you know … I had to do something with them …'

Chloe read the situation. 'We'll sort them out later. Come on, let's go eat.'

They went to an Italian restaurant in the city. Over tagliatelle and a bottle of Barolo, Chloe told him what she'd been up to.

'The vigil will start around 7 p.m. tomorrow night,' she said. 'I don't know how many people will turn up. I've put it out on Facebook, and I phoned the BBC earlier. They're sending out a camera crew at 8 p.m. Are you coming?'

'Yes, I'll come. I think Sarah would want me to be there. For the end of it all.'

'Great. Zoe and Angela are coming, too. You can drive us.'

Sorting through Sarah's stuff had made Ralph feel a bit despondent. And his mood wasn't improved by thinking about the bulldozers and chainsaws arriving in Foxdown Wood on Friday.

They were about to consign the forest she had died defending to the dustbin of lost causes. It had all meant nothing. He said something to that effect to Chloe, who was more philosophical about it.

'No, it wasn't all for nothing,' she said. 'Every time someone stands up for the natural world, we raise awareness. We just need the courage to do it again and again, until people wake up.'

'You may well be right. I could have done without Sarah becoming a martyr for the cause, though.'

'She won't be forgotten, that's for sure. What are you doing about Ben Ramsey?'

He was caught off guard. 'What? Oh, nothing at the moment.'

Chloe wasn't buying it. 'Nothing? You were in a hell of a mood about him yesterday. Are you going to speak to him? Or involve the police?'

'No police. I'm thinking about it, Chloe. The best way to approach it, I mean. I want to keep it all low key. Let's just say I'm working on it, OK?'

Chloe sighed. 'You're as secretive as your sister was. Fine. I won't mention it again.'

He made an effort to perk up after that and Chloe helped by being her naturally ebullient self. She told him a few funny stories about the misunderstandings some of her massage clients had about the treatments she offered.

'I tell them I don't do happy endings,' she said. 'Most of them take it well. Nobody's walked out on me yet.'

'Are you going to do the tantric training with Serena? That could easily result in happy endings, intended or otherwise.'

Chloe laughed. 'Yes, I want to. But I don't think I'll offer it to everybody. And I may need someone to practise on while I'm learning. Know anyone?'

He smiled. 'I'll ask around.'

They were both a little high when they left the restaurant, and it wasn't just down to the wine. There was a sense of anticipation between them that heightened their senses, and made their pulses race just that little bit faster. They walked to the car, arms around each other.

'Can we go to your place?' said Chloe.

When they got there, he offered her more wine. She declined. She said she wanted to use the bathroom for a bit.

'Then I want to go to bed,' she said. 'What about you?'

He didn't need persuading. He got undressed while she was in the bathroom and got under the covers. When Chloe joined him, she was already naked.

'What about your aches and pains?' he asked her. 'Still sore?'

She kissed him. 'Not so much, now. I'll cope.'

'We're going to do this in Sarah's bed. I guess she won't mind.'

She pressed her body up against him. 'It's your bed, now. And no, I don't think she will.'

He put his hands on her and felt the sudden excitement flooding through his body. He had this urgent need to be inside her right away, but she slowed him down, making him wait while she drove him slightly mad with her mouth and her hands. She took him when she was good and ready. After which, they fell into the sated depths of sleep.

When he woke the next morning, he could hear water running. When he reached out for Chloe and found she wasn't there, he realised she must be in the shower. He reached for his watch on the nightstand; it was 8.15 a.m. He'd slept later than he'd intended.

The water stopped running, and a minute later Chloe appeared, wrapped in one of his towels. She was drying her hair with another one.

'Got to rush,' she said, grinning at him. 'I've got an appointment at nine. I'm only just going to make it.'

'I can drive you,' he said, voice still thick with sleep. 'Have some breakfast.'

He got up and made her some toast and coffee, while she got herself together. They were out of the house and on the road twenty minutes later, but as it was rush hour, so was everyone else. After ten minutes of crawling up Newmarket Road, Chloe decided to walk the rest of the way.

'Come and pick up the girls and me at 6 p.m., please,' she said. She gave him a quick kiss, opened the door, and was gone.

He turned down a side road and found a way home through less congested back streets. In the rush to get Chloe to work there'd been no time for his own breakfast, so once he'd had a shower and eaten something, he opened up his laptop. There was an email from Viv, who'd managed to come up with the results of the background check in just twenty-four hours. He downloaded the attached report and began reading.

He learned that Benedict Ramsey was 45 years old and lived in Overstrand, a village on the coast not far away from Cromer. He had a wife named Fiona, who was five years younger. She was in the process of divorcing him, in an action she'd started back in October of 2017. The divorce wasn't final yet. She'd obviously moved out, because there was an address for her in Holt, another town in north Norfolk. Ben drove a Toyota Rav4 SUV, registration number provided, and worked as a company director. The head office address in Cromer was in the report, but no breakdown on the company's financial health. If Ralph wanted that he would have to go online to Companies House. But there was plenty of other information that might prove useful, including Ben's previous addresses, his phone number, and details of his nearest relatives.

The parents were still alive; Edith and Jacob Ramsey. Ben had a brother named Stephen, who worked as an architect and lived in Leeds, in Yorkshire. There were no other siblings, but there were details of Fiona's brothers, one of whom was called David Stone. He had an address in the city of Norwich, and like his brother-in-law Ben, he was a company director. He ran a private security firm called 'Stone Security Services'.

The name 'David' caught Ralph's attention. Just a coincidence? Stone Security had a website, so he visited it. The home page was a summary of their expertise in personal security, event security, and commercial property protection. There was a testimonials page, too. Ralph checked it out and found that one of their clients was Ramsey Real Estate and Developments. Ben Ramsey had left a recommendation, saying he was delighted with the friendly and well trained members of Stone Security, who had patrolled and protected his sites under construction for the last five years or more.

That can't be coincidence, thought Ralph. He clicked on the 'Our team' option. There was a photo of David Stone on that page. He was shown sitting behind an office desk, with his arms loosely folded across his broad chest and smiling for the camera in a no-nonsense, 'trust me' kind of way, no doubt designed to inspire confidence in prospective clients. Dominic had described the David he'd met at Cromer, but Ralph had no idea if this was the same man or not. He copied the image and fired it off in an email to the address Dominic had given him, with a short message; 'recognise this guy?'

A plan was taking shape in Ralph's mind. He retrieved the surveillance kit from the wardrobe in the bedroom, and took a look through it. Apart from the hi-spec, handheld digital camera he'd already used, it contained a few other items. There was a voice recorder in the shape of a pen, a key fob camera that attached to your car keys and looked like the remote control for the doors, and two GPS trackers. The trackers were the magnetic kind that attached under the chassis of the vehicle you wanted to track. Then you could monitor its progress from your laptop. That was where he intended to start, later on tonight.

He collected Chloe and her two flatmates on time that evening. They'd come prepared for the vigil with a portable gas heater, torches, a box full of candles of all shapes and sizes, and several blankets. They had thick jackets with them as well. Ralph had also wrapped up warm for the occasion; he had on two T-shirts and a jersey.

'Ready for an all-night sit-in?' asked Zoe, who installed herself in the back seat with Angela.

'Can't wait,' said Ralph. 'I hope it doesn't rain.'

They got out to the wood just after 7 p.m. Ralph drove to the end of the fence line to let the women out, before turning around and returning to the Foxdown Arms car park. He locked the car and walked back. He needed a torch to guide him through the trees to the site of the wood's last stand, which was taking place at the fence that now separated it from Kingsley's building site.

'We'll have to go back and meet the camera crew in an hour,' said Chloe.

They settled in for the night. Blankets were spread out, and the gas heater fired up. Thermos flasks full of soup and coffee were opened. The four tree sitters appeared shortly afterwards, and brought some cold chicken and salad with them. Bettina had a banner with her, which she attached to the fence with duct tape. It bore the words *Remember Foxdown Wood, September 14, 2018*.

Ralph went with Chloe to meet the BBC crew at 8 p.m. It was just the two of them, a man for the camera and a woman for the interview. The man had his portable camera perched on his shoulder and the woman, who looked like the same one who'd interviewed Ralph at the demo, carried the microphone.

'I have to disappear for a while,' Ralph told Chloe. 'I'll be back in a few hours. I'll take the torch.'

'What?' She was startled. 'Where are you going?'

'Overstrand. Field trip.'

'Ralph ... I hope you're not doing anything stupid. Are you?'

'Don't worry, Chloe. Kiss me.'

She did, and when she stopped and opened her mouth to ask more questions, he put his finger to her lips.

'See you soon,' he said.

She was annoyed about that. 'Whatever.' Then she relented. 'Be careful, OK?'

The two BBC people looked intrigued, but didn't interrupt. Ralph strode off back to the pub and when he looked back, Chloe and the reporters had vanished.

It took him almost an hour to drive to Overstrand, and when he arrived it was quiet and very dark. The street lights seemed few and far between, but as Ralph had programmed Ben Ramsey's address into the satnav, that wasn't an issue. Overstrand wasn't a big place, either. He reached his destination, drove past the entrance to the house, and parked fifty yards away. There was nobody around when he walked back, and all he could hear was the soft whistle of the wind blowing in from the sea. He had the tracker in his hand, so now all he needed to do was get in undetected. Assuming Ramsey was at home, of course.

There was a brick wall out front of the property, bisected by a gravel driveway without gates. The outline of the house was visible some fifty yards down the drive, and there was a light on down there. There were trees and shrubs on the approach to the house, all conveniently situated for trespassers needing cover. Ralph kept close to them on his walk down the driveway. He didn't see the Toyota until he'd practically reached the front door. It was parked off to one side, and there was enough light spilling out of the windows to illuminate it for anyone inside looking out. The house was a modern red brick affair, on two levels. Ralph figured it must be four or five bedrooms at least. Expensive, too. Property development must be a profitable occupation. He wondered if there were any outside lights that would be triggered by his movement, or worse than that, if Ramsey had a dog. He crouched down, and just listened for a while. The Toyota was about twenty feet away from the house, and if he got his approach right he could keep the vehicle between him and the sight of anyone inside.

He made his move, coming out of the cover of darkness and running to the side of the Toyota facing away from the house. No lights came on. Nobody barked. He let out a breath he didn't know he'd been holding, and stuck his head out just long enough to confirm the registration number. Then, crouched on hands and knees, he placed the tracker on the metal underside of the chassis, directly beneath the passenger door. He'd only just made sure it was securely attached, when he heard a sound. To his horror, he realised it was the sound of someone closing a door. The house entrance door.

For a second, he couldn't move. Then he turned away from the Toyota and crawled as fast as he could on hands and knees for the nearest bush. The sound of footsteps on gravel made his exit even faster, and he hoped to god they were covering any sounds he was making in this mad scramble for safety.

He found cover just in time. The footsteps came to a halt, a car door opened and shut, and the engine started up. The Toyota reversed for a bit, and then turned in towards the house. The headlights were now lighting up the bush Ralph was hiding behind like a Christmas tree. For a moment, he thought he'd have to make a run for it. Then a second later, the SUV moved forward, and then off down the driveway.

Ralph's heart was beating like crazy, he could hear the pulse of it pounding in his ears. He stayed where he was for a full five minutes before daring to get up and make his way out. He kept an eye out for the tracker just in case it had fallen off, but he didn't find it on his walk down the driveway. When he got back to the BMW, he almost succumbed to a hysterical fit of laughing, out of sheer relief. He smiled stupidly instead, started up the car, and drove away.

Chapter 24

Trying to find his way back to Chloe and the others through the inky blackness of the wood was no fun. Ralph had the torch to guide his way, and there was a bit of a track forming after the number of people who'd used this route recently, but it was still hard going. The wood was spooky at night, too. The trees that looked so benign by day were now ghostly silhouettes against the sky. Their branches were twisted into ghoulish shapes that made him wonder if they might reach out any moment and skewer him. There was a forbidding, almost predatory atmosphere about the place.

That feeling left him when he got out into more open spaces and saw the lights he was looking for. A few minutes later, he was back at the boundary fence and in the company of human beings again. The gathering had increased by a dozen new faces in the time he'd been away; young people, mostly women. Someone had a guitar and was strumming it, picking out random chords. The others were either sitting around on blankets on the ground or walking back and forth in little groups; chatting and keeping warm. Chloe must have been looking out for him, because she detached herself from one of the groups and intercepted him as he approached.

'I could see your torchlight through the trees,' she said, wrapping her arms around him and squeezing him in a hug. 'Was your field trip a success?'

He squeezed her back. 'Yes, it was. At least I think so. Did the interview go alright?'

'Yes, but it won't go out till tomorrow night. By which time, we'll all be gone.'

They walked back to the fence line and sat down with Angela and Zoe. Ralph looked through the fence at the building site beyond. There was a light coming from the site office in the portakabin, about 100 yards away. He thought it must be the night watchman.

'You seen anyone in that portakabin?' he asked.

Zoe replied. 'Some guy came out a couple of times for a smoke,' she said. 'He waved to us.'

The rest of the site was pitch black. It was close to midnight now. The intention was to stay up all night, or sleep on a blanket if that was at all possible. The ground was wet with dew, and although some people had had the foresight to lay their blankets down over plastic sheets, the dampness in the air would eventually seep into their sleeping arrangements. It wasn't exactly cold, but it wasn't T-shirt weather either. Apart from the gas heater, some warmth had been created by the now hundreds of candles that were set up around the place. They ranged in size from giant red ones, the type you got at Christmas markets, all the way down to white house candles, and even tea lights. Their flames shimmered, swaying as one in whatever direction the breeze blew them. It was like watching a synchronised light show, hypnotic and rather beautiful. He lay down with Chloe for a couple of hours between 3 and 5 a.m., and managed to doze for a while. An hour after that they got up, and drank what was left of the coffee. The birds had started the dawn chorus by that time, and it wasn't even light yet. But by 6.30, the sun was up in a cloudless sky.

'What time do you think the demolition gang arrives?' said Ralph. There were a lot of bleary-eyed people staring through the fence at the building site next door and wondering the same thing.

'I don't know,' said Chloe, standing next to him, arm in arm. 'Nine o'clock?'

But nine o'clock came and went, with no sign of bulldozers or chainsaw wielding workmen. There was no building work going on either, the site was as quiet as a morgue. Then the night watchman appeared. He came out of his portakabin and headed their way. He was a grey-haired man in his sixties, wearing an orange vest and jeans. He came right up to the fence, and spoke to them.

'You can all go home,' he said. 'Nobody's coming today. All work on this site has been suspended.'

The recipients of this little speech stood there in uncomprehending silence. Ralph answered on their behalf.

'Why's that?'

'I just had a phone call. The managing director of this project died recently, and all current development is halted until they can appoint a replacement. If they can't find one, the company might go into administration. That's all I know, folks. But what I can tell you with certainty is that no trees are getting cut down here today. See you.'

He turned and walked off. There was silence in his wake for all of ten seconds. Then a spontaneous outbreak of hollering and cheering from twenty delighted protestors filled the air. They jumped up and down and hugged one another.

'We live to fight another day,' said Karl, who was grinning and pumping the air with a fist. He and Bettina looked happier than Ralph ever remembered seeing them. He couldn't help but be caught up in the euphoria of the moment, and grinned back.

'You never know,' he said. 'There's hope yet.' He turned to Chloe. 'Can we go home and catch up on some sleep?'

They gathered up their things, and got Angela and Zoe to do the same. They all started walking back to the pub. On the way, Ralph played through the ramifications of this new development in his mind. In all probability, a new director would just take up where Kingsley had left off, and the clearance would go ahead. But if the business went into administration, then the assets of the company might end up being sold off. If that happened, there was a chance that the wood could be saved after all.

There was a trail of people following them out now. They straggled behind his group all the way to the pub, and then they dispersed by whatever means they'd employed to arrive. Some had cars, others had bicycles, others simply walked to the nearest bus stop. When Ralph got back to Norwich with three tired but happy women, he dropped Angela and Zoe at their house. Chloe came home with him, where they had a shower together and then tumbled into bed. After a short but passionate distraction, they finally got some sleep.

It was mid-afternoon when they got up, and the first thing Ralph wanted to do was find out if the tracker was working. He had the tracking program already installed on the laptop, so he logged in and had a look.

The screen had a map of the area that any vehicle fitted with a tracker had covered. You could choose various timeframes, but as Ralph had only fixed the tracker to the SUV yesterday, the default period of the last twenty-four hours was fine. He could see that after he had watched Ramsey drive off last night, the man had been into Cromer, where he'd stayed for an hour before returning home. Then this morning, he'd gone there again. Presumably to his office. And the vehicle hadn't moved since. Chloe sat down next to him.

'What's that?' she asked.

He saw no reason not to tell her. 'It's a tracking program. I've got a tracker on Ben Ramsey's Rav4.'

Chloe raised her eyes. 'Is that what you were doing last night?'

'Yes. Keep that to yourself, please.'

'And what exactly do you hope to achieve by tracking Ben Ramsey?'

'Don't know yet. I just want to know where he goes. Then I can go there too.'

'Mmm. All sounds a bit vague, Ralph.'

He sighed. 'It is, at the moment. But as I've only just started …'

He minimized the tracking program and logged in to email. 'Ah,' he said. 'What's this?'

He had a reply from Dominic, short and to the point – '*It's David. Keep me updated.*'

'Not so vague anymore,' he said. 'I've just identified the guy who gave Dominic the money. Next thing to do is track him as well.'

Chloe stared at him. 'How did you manage to put a tracker on the Rav4 without being noticed?'

He decided not to go into too much detail about that. 'Well, I just did it. Under cover of darkness. It's easy enough to do.'

Chloe got up and wandered over to the front window. She looked out at the beech tree.

'Great view you've got,' she said. 'This all sounds a bit dangerous to me. I hope you know what you're doing.'

'I'll be careful.'

Chloe looked less than convinced by that statement, but she didn't say anymore on the subject. She told him that because she hadn't worked yesterday, she'd booked two massage appointments for later that evening.

'I'll go home until then,' she said. 'I want to update the Facebook page and find out when our news report goes out. I can tell them what happened this morning.'

She wanted to walk back, so Ralph kissed her goodbye and she left him alone. He thought he'd spend what was left of the day tracking down David Stone, and finding an opportunity to fit the second tracker to whatever vehicle he drove. The background check hadn't listed a vehicle, but he did have a home address for Stone.

There was no point in going there until it got dark, but in the meantime it might be useful to stake out the offices of Stone Security before they shut for the day. They were situated in a business park off Hall Road, which wasn't far away. Before leaving, he removed the remote control attached to his car keys and replaced it with the fob camera. He'd just have to open the car manually. He then picked up the bag containing what was left in the surveillance kit, and added a bottle of water from the fridge. He threw it all in the BMW and drove off to his first stake out.

The place was easy enough to find. It was on the end of a row of industrial units that included a building supplies outlet and a DIY superstore. The front of the building was nondescript, and the windows on the ground floor and the two floors above, were tinted. The entrance was through a big steel reinforced door that had a camera mounted above it. There was a keypad to gain entry, or you buzzed the door and waited for someone to let you in. There were a dozen cars parked out front and nobody to be seen when he drove past. He parked a few yards down the road, where he had a good view of the place without being directly in front of it. Then he waited.

Two people came outside in the next hour to have a cigarette, but neither of them was Stone. Then at 5 p.m., people began to leave. It was Friday night, so in all likelihood the staff would be getting away early unless they had something more urgent to do. Ralph pointed the big digital camera at them as they left, and took multiple shots of each one. Just for the record. Then he waited some more. An hour and nine cars later, he still hadn't seen Stone. It wasn't until there was only one car left at 6.30 p.m. that his patience was rewarded.

David Stone appeared, attired in a dark suit and lilac shirt. No tie. Ralph made sure he got some good pictures before Stone got into his Audi A6 saloon and pulled out of the car park. When he joined up with Hall Road a minute later, Ralph was two cars behind.

He knew where Stone was going, or thought he did. He lived in an apartment block that overlooked the river in the heart of town, but Stone didn't go there. Instead he drove to the Eagle pub, which was on the Newmarket Road but closer to town than Ralph's flat, and parked the car in the parking area out front. He went inside. That suited Ralph perfectly. The car park at the Eagle wasn't large, but it had a good number of vehicles in it, and Stone's Audi would be hard to see from inside. Ralph knew this because he'd been in the pub himself a few times. The Audi was parked between two other vehicles, which screened it from both the pub and the street. Ralph found a parking spot of his own and then, in contrast to what had happened out at Overstrand, had no issues with sneaking alongside the Audi and kneeling down to place the second tracker. He was in and out within a minute. Now that he had everything set up, all he had to do was keep tabs on the two vehicles and see if they went anywhere interesting. Not that he knew what interesting looked like.

Nothing much happened at first over the weekend. He had a letter from the Norfolk police, inviting him to a video identification parade next Thursday, which he made a note of. Chloe rang to say she'd had the same letter, and could she drop in later? He was more than happy for her to do that, but otherwise he had nothing planned.

He found himself checking on the tracking program on an hourly basis on Saturday. Ramsey's SUV was in Overstrand and didn't move all day, but Stone's Audi left Norwich and made its way to Ramsey's house that afternoon. Ralph watched it all in real time on the screen. The Audi didn't stay long in Overstrand, it left there and moved to a location near Holkham, further up the coast. It looked like the middle of nowhere to Ralph, but he made a note of the location anyway. Stone stayed for an hour and then went back to Overstrand, where he stayed for another hour before driving back to Norwich.

So, they see each other socially, thought Ralph. Nothing incriminating in that. Chloe came round on the Saturday evening, and they went into town to see a movie. She stayed the night and went home Sunday morning. Ralph was back on the tracking screen after that. And he noticed that Stone's vehicle didn't move an inch, but Ramsey's SUV made the same trip to Holkham that afternoon, to the same location. Only a flying visit, because it turned around after twenty minutes and went back the way it had come.

That got Ralph's interest. He had no idea what they might be doing out at Holkham, but he decided that it must be worth a look. But he wasn't going out there without telling someone about it. He rang Chloe.

'You busy?' he asked her.

'Umm, no. Not especially. Why?'

'I need you to be my wing woman.'

'Your what?'

'Can I come and see you? I'll explain it then.'

'Sure, come around.'

He took the laptop with him. Chloe was the only one at home when he got there. She opened the door, looking more than a little curious.

'What are you cooking up now?' she said.

They went inside. They sat side by side on the lounge sofa while he got her to connect the laptop to her wi-fi. Then he opened the tracking program and told her what he wanted.

'I'm going out to Holkham, to this place here,' he said, indicating it on the now open tracking screen. 'This blue dot here is Ramsey's SUV, and the red one is David Stone's Audi. If either of them moves, phone me and let me know. Will you do that for me?'

She thought about it. 'What's out at Holkham?'

'Don't know. Maybe nothing.'

'OK. If either of them moves, I'll be on the phone right away.'

'Thanks, you're amazing. Gotta rush.'

'Right now?'

'Uh-huh.' He kissed her and got up. 'I'll be back before you know it.'

He left her staring bemusedly at the screen. He jumped into the BMW and was off. He'd put the co-ordinates of the mysterious Holkham location into the satnav, but he wouldn't need to refer to them until he got to the coast. As it was Sunday, the drive took less time than usual, unlike summer Sundays when every man and his family choked up the roads. He got to the village of Holkham and passed the Queen Victoria pub in forty-five minutes. It was time to consult the satnav. But before he could do that, the phone rang. Damn it, he thought, must be Chloe. But it was Gerald, of all people.

'Ralph, got a moment?'

'Sure. I'm driving, but we're hands free. What's up?'

'You had Vivian do a background check on this Ramsey fellow. Just wanted a word about it.'

Should have known Viv couldn't keep it to herself, thought Ralph. 'I did,' he said. 'Not a problem, is it?'

'No, not at all. I was at a loose end yesterday, so I thought I'd dig into it a bit. I found out something interesting. Maybe you know about it already?'

'Know about what?'

'The wife, Fiona. She's divorcing him.'

'I know that much. Is it important?'

'She's divorcing him on the grounds of infidelity. Nothing unusual about that, but I did a search. She named the co-respondent in her petition. Guess who it was?'

'No idea.'

'Rosalind Kingsley. The deceased wife of Fabian, who I believe is also deceased. Interesting, don't you think?'

'What? Shit!' Ralph had involuntarily swerved the wheel and had nearly gone into a ditch.

'You OK?'

Ralph stopped the car. 'Yes. You shouldn't have mentioned that while I was driving. That changes everything.'

'It might well do that, Ralph. Didn't Brett say at Sarah's funeral that there was animosity between Kingsley and Ramsey? This might be the reason.'

Gerald was right on the money. 'Maybe it is,' said Ralph. 'Listen, I'm in the middle of something right now. Can I get back to you tomorrow?'

'Anytime. Just thought you should know. We'll talk tomorrow.'

He rang off. Ralph sat in his stationary car and joined up the pieces. Yes, hadn't Roz told Sarah she'd been having an affair, and hadn't Kingsley found out about it and forced her to end it? What had Ben thought about that? Would it have pissed him off to the point where he might take revenge by fire-bombing his rival's housing developments, or even picking up a shotgun?

There was a vehicle coming up behind him now, so he had to get moving. He filed his thoughts away, and concentrated on where he had to be next. He put the car into gear and sped off.

Half a mile on, he came up to a little side road on the left. The satnav told him to turn, so he did. The road was narrow; a one lane track leading to nowhere that was sign posted, with the occasional passing place. He drove along it for a minute until the satnav told him he'd reached his destination. But where was he?

He looked around. He could see a dirt track up on the right, just wide enough to get a car down. He turned onto it and drove for 100 yards until he ended up by a big wooden shed, surrounded by trees. There was just enough space in front of the shed to turn a car around to make the return trip.

He parked and got out. The shed looked like it had been there for years, it had red paint peeling off the weatherboards, and a roof missing a tile or two. But it was solid enough and there was a brand new, shiny padlock on the door. There were windows down one side, so he pressed his face up against one and tried to see what was inside. Through the cobwebs and grit coating the inside of the panes, he made out a couple of forty-gallon drums and some plastic containers. There was a table in there, too, with what looked like glass fish bowls resting on it. But there appeared to be no way to get in and find out more.

He went around the back, where he found another wooden door with another padlock. This one was old, though, and probably hadn't been opened in ages. He found a fallen branch nearby and used it as leverage on the hasp between the door and the padlock. The pressure told after five minutes, and the hasp separated itself from the door and fell on the ground, along with the padlock. He opened the door and went inside.

The first thing that struck him was the smell of petrol coming from the forty-gallon drums. He saw a plastic hose and a funnel on the floor nearby, and then he walked by the table to check out the plastic containers. They were clearly labelled. One had aluminium powder in it, and the other one contained iron oxide powder. What did that mean? He pulled out his phone, intending to do a search, before realising he couldn't. There was no signal out here. He cursed under his breath. Maybe if he went outside, he'd get a signal. He turned to go out, and then stopped.

The sound of engines filled his ears, and they were heading this way. He knew straight away what had happened. With no signal, Chloe had no chance of getting through. He peered out a window and saw that he was right. Coming right towards him was an Audi A6, and behind that was a Toyota Rav4.

And there was nowhere to run.

Chapter 25

Ralph heard car doors slamming as their occupants got out. When he heard the padlock rattling on the front door, he wondered if they thought the shed was secure and that whoever owned the BMW wasn't actually inside. Maybe they'd start looking around in the grove of trees, and he could slip out unnoticed. And then do what? Drive away? He was blocked in.

The padlock was being opened now. He decided to take his chances by going out the back way. But when he pushed open the back door, it was only to see David Stone blocking his exit.

'You're trespassing,' said Stone. He was a big man, and the scowl on his rugged face was intimidating. 'What are you doing here?'

Ralph didn't answer. He stepped back inside, where he came face to face with Ben Ramsey.

'Yes, just what are you …?' Recognition dawned on Ramsey's face. 'Ralph!'

There were a few seconds of silence, while the three of them stood in the shed in a state of suspended animation. Nobody moved a muscle. Stone was the first one to snap out of it.

'The brother?' he said to Ramsey.

Ramsey nodded. 'Perhaps you could answer my friend's question, Ralph. What are you doing here?'

His tone of voice wasn't friendly, even if he looked more worried than angry, and just a little bit lost as to what to do next.

'Research,' said Ralph. 'I should be asking you that question, actually. Just what is going on here?'

'Why don't you sit down and we'll have a chat,' said Stone. He placed an encouraging hand on Ralph's back and pushed him. Nothing too forceful, just letting Ralph know he was there. Ralph spun around to face Stone.

'Actually, I'll be leaving now,' he said.

Stone just stared at him, and Ralph stared back. This went on for a few seconds, until Ramsey broke the deadlock.

'I think you really should sit down,' he said.

When Ralph turned in Ramsey's direction, the man had a shotgun in his hands. It must have been in the shed the whole time, Ralph realised. The barrel was pointing at the ground right now, but the message was clear enough. Ramsey indicated a wooden chair next to the table. 'Over there,' he said.

Ralph looked at the chair, and briefly considered trying to get past Stone and out of there. But if Ramsey decided to use the shotgun, he wouldn't make it even as far as the back door. He walked over to the chair and sat down instead. He knew he couldn't bluff his way out of this and now he thought he had it all figured out, he was angry as well as scared. He decided to go on the offensive.

'You killed Sarah,' he said.

Stone and Ramsey exchanged looks. Ralph saw a flash of alarm on both their faces.

'What makes you think that?' said Stone.

The two men had remained standing. Stone was at one end of the table and Ramsey stood six feet away from Ralph, shotgun pointing down at the floor. Ralph answered the question.

'When Dominic wouldn't do what you wanted, you thought you could persuade him to change his mind. By intimidating Sarah. So, you went out to the wood and tried to get her to come down from the tree house. What were you going to do? Beat her up?'

'I'm sorry,' said Stone. 'Who is Dominic?'

'You know damn well who he is. He told me everything.'

Something passed between Ramsey and Stone then. A decision had been made. Ralph felt it more than saw it, and that was when he felt sure they weren't going to let him out of here alive. It seemed to liberate them in a weird way, he saw the tension leaving their postures and their faces.

'Beat her up?' said Stone. 'We thought we'd take her away for a few days. That was all. What we didn't intend to do was have her fall like she did.'

Ralph was a bit stunned to hear someone finally take responsibility. He felt a wave of grief welling up in his chest, which he fought hard to control.

'I thought you were Sarah's friend,' he said to Ramsey. 'You made that speech about her at the demo. You were her client. How the hell could you treat her that way?'

'I was her client, that's true,' replied Ramsey. 'I liked her, too. But she got in the way.'

He said it in a deadpan voice, like it was simply a business decision. Ralph wanted to know more.

'Was she dead when she left the forest? There was a doctor there, wasn't there?'

'Not a real doctor,' said Ramsey. 'Someone with medical training, let's just say.'

'Was she dead?' Ralph repeated.

'I wasn't there, Ralph.'

'She died a couple of hours later,' said Stone.

'You could have done what you said you were going to do and taken her to Accident and Emergency in those couple of hours. They might have been able to save her.'

'Don't think we didn't consider it,' said Stone. 'But it was too big a risk. There's CCTV all over the place. We couldn't do it.'

'So, you just took her out to Blickling and buried her instead. But not before you took the ring off her finger.'

'They found the ring?' said Ramsey. 'I wondered about that. We thought we might incriminate Fabian with it. I was hoping the police would think he burnt the place down because he wanted to erase all traces of Sarah being there. Not that she ever was. Didn't work.'

Ralph waved his hand at the petrol drums and plastic containers. 'You took over where Dominic left off. You burned down two houses in Aylsham and then you burned down Kingsley's house. You made the last two look like Triple G was responsible. This is where you made the bombs.'

Ramsey sighed. 'You seem to have it all worked out, Ralph. Aren't you going to ask why?'

'Why? Maybe it was about putting Fabian Kingsley out of business, so you could pick up the pieces. But I think it was more than that. I think it was really about Roz. You shot him because of Roz.'

Ramsey was shocked. 'How do you know about Roz?' The mention of Roz had upset him, and he didn't wait for an answer. His face twisted in an ugly scowl. 'Fabian deserved everything he got.' Then his shoulders slumped, and the scowl was replaced by a look of anguish. It all tumbled out of him then, like a river bursting its banks.

'I met Roz when I went out to one of Fabian's show homes. I thought I'd check out the competition. She was doing the interior decorating for his developments at the time, and I didn't even know she was his wife at first. I went back to see her again the next day and … Well, to cut a long story short, we fell in love. Real love, not some stupid infatuation that dies on its feet after six months.' He stopped and took a breath. 'I would have done anything for that woman. Then that fucking hypocrite found out about it. The man who prided himself on his sexually liberated lifestyle couldn't handle being cuckolded. And he was having an affair of his own at the time! It was unbelievable. I don't know what he threatened her with, but she told me it was over. We both knew she didn't want it to be over. Then months later, she killed herself. Or more to the point, Fabian Kingsley drove her to her death.'

'Were you sending us messages on Facebook? About the suicide not being a suicide?'

'That was me. It wasn't a suicide as far as I was concerned. Kingsley killed her. I couldn't let that rest. I wanted to ruin the bastard.'

'You didn't have to shoot him to ruin him. You were doing a pretty good job of it anyway,' said Ralph.

Ramsey had a wild intensity about him when he answered. 'You think I shot him? He had it coming.'

David Stone had stood by impassively while Ramsey expressed himself.

'Enough, Ben,' he said. He turned his attention on Ralph. 'How did you find this place?'

Ralph tried to deflect that. 'What's *your* problem with Fabian Kingsley?'

That annoyed Stone. He strode over and punched Ralph hard in the stomach. Ralph grunted and doubled over in pain.

'How the hell did you find this place?' repeated Stone. He waited for Ralph to recover enough to answer that question and while he was waiting, something occurred to him. 'Keep an eye on him, Ben.'

He went outside. Ramsey stood with the shotgun pointed at Ralph, and waited. Five minutes later and Stone was back, holding two trackers in his hands.

'Look what I found,' he said.

He pushed a fish bowl to one side and put them on the table. He opened both of them up, and extracted the batteries.

'GPS trackers,' he said, for Ramsey's benefit. 'No longer transmitting.'

There was a long silence while the implications of this discovery sunk in.

'Shit,' said Ramsey, finally.

'We need to clear out, Ben,' said Stone. 'There's nothing here that can be traced back to us. You need to get rid of that shotgun, too.'

'What about him?'

Stone considered that. 'First of all, Ralph, where are you tracking us from? Your phone? A computer? Give me your phone.'

Ralph handed it over. 'No signal out here,' he said.

Stone checked the phone to see if Ralph was telling the truth. 'You didn't follow us here, so you've been tracking us for a while. Who else knows about it?'

'Lots of people. You're both fucked.'

Stone glared at him. 'You've dropped yourself in it by coming out here. We can hardly let you drop us in it too, can we?'

'What are we going to do?' said Ramsey, who looked slightly panicked.

'Let me think,' said Stone. He did that for a minute. 'We put him in the boot of his BMW. Then we move our vehicles away from here. We come back and dispose of his vehicle after that. And we have to start doing it now.'

'Put him in the boot? You mean …?'

'I mean shoot him and then get rid of that gun. Which is what you should have done already.'

Ben Ramsey was having second thoughts. It might have been one thing to shoot Fabian Kingsley in a murderous rage, but this was cold blood.

'Is there no other way?'

'No, mate, there isn't. Look, give me the gun and go outside.'

Ramsey didn't say anything, just handed the gun over. He turned to go out the front door.

But it opened before he got there. Two uniformed policemen stood in the doorway.

'Sorry to disturb you sir,' said one of them. 'We had a report of a potential incident here and …' He saw the gun. Both policemen went tense.

'Put it down, sir,' said policeman number one.

Stone hesitated.

'I strongly advise you to put the gun down,' said the constable. 'No one needs to get hurt here.'

Stone considered that advice. Perhaps he decided that being armed only gave him a temporary advantage, and that if it meant shooting two policemen, that wasn't a smart move either. Whatever he thought, after several tense seconds he swore and then laid the gun down.

'Step away from it,' said the constable.

Stone did, and both policemen came inside. They looked at the petrol drums and the plastic containers. The GPS trackers didn't escape their notice, either.

'I'm calling for back up,' said policeman number two. He had a radio with him that wasn't subject to mobile phone signal glitches. He stepped back outside the door, but kept it open so he could see what was going on inside. He began talking into his radio. Meanwhile, the first policeman took control of the situation.

'Perhaps someone can tell me what's going on here,' he said.

Stone looked furious. Ramsey, crestfallen. Ralph was relieved beyond reason. But he got it together.

'I can,' he said. He extracted a pen from his pocket. 'And if I forget anything, it should all be on here. I recorded it.'

'Well then,' said the cop. 'Let's all calm down and talk about it, shall we? Which one of you is Ralph de Malmanche?'

Ralph raised a hand. 'I am. These men murdered my sister, and they were just about to murder me. They also murdered a man named Fabian Kingsley. With that gun.' Then Ralph nodded towards the petrol drums. 'They burn down houses as well.'

The police constable couldn't quite take that all in at once.

'Those are serious accusations,' he said. 'Do you two gentlemen have anything to say about them?'

'He's talking crap,' said Stone. 'This man is trespassing. We asked him to leave and he became violent.'

'So, this is your shed?'

Stone wasn't sure how to answer that, so he didn't. The policeman looked expectantly at Ramsey but he had nothing to say, either.

'Alright, let's go down the station and take it from there,' he said. Another police car arrived shortly afterwards, with two more police officers in it. They couldn't get down the drive because the first two policemen had parked their vehicle where it joined the road and then walked to the shed, which is why nobody heard them coming. Once all four cops were assembled, it was time to move out.

'How did you know where to find us?' asked Ralph, as he walked up the track with one of the constables, who had identified himself as PC Tarrant.

'A woman phoned us. Told us she was afraid for your safety. You were investigating a suspicious death, she said. Insisted that you were in a dangerous situation, and she couldn't reach you. She said the location wasn't far away, and she wanted someone to drive by and check. There was more about trackers on vehicles and Sarah de Malmanche, who I believe was your sister? Anyway, that name rang a bell with us. She was right about us not being too far away, and it's not busy today, so here we are.'

'Was her name Chloe? And where did you come from?'

'Chloe Miller,' said Tarrant. 'We're stationed at Wells. Not far.'

Wells-Next-the-Sea was, as the name suggested, a seaside town. Popular with tourists and holidaymakers, and close to Holkham.

'I should phone Chloe and tell her I'm OK,' said Ralph.

'Wait till we get to the station, sir,' said Tarrant.

One policeman had stayed behind to keep an eye on the scene. PC Tarrant had registered Ralph's comment about the gun being used in a murder and had left it untouched, presumably until a forensic person could remove it. The rest of the contents of the shed needed someone to keep an eye on them, too.

When they got to the station, Stone and Ramsey were put in an interview room and told to wait. PC Tarrant asked Ralph to accompany him to an office, where they sat down in front of a computer terminal.

'So, are you Ralph de Malmanche, and was Sarah de Malmanche your sister?'

'That's right.'

'Got some ID?'

Ralph produced his driving licence. Tarrant looked at it, and then hit a few keys on his keyboard. He looked at the screen for a while. 'The Sarah de Malmanche case is assigned to a DI Martin and a DC Ainsworth,' he said.

'Ainsworth knows me,' said Ralph.

'I'll see if I can contact him. You can phone Ms Miller now. Do it from this landline.'

Ralph assumed that Tarrant didn't want him phoning anyone other than Chloe at this juncture, hence the landline. He had to look up the number on his mobile first, while Tarrant watched. Then he made the call.

'I'm OK,' he told a relieved Chloe, when she answered three rings later.

'Thank god for that. It wasn't a false alarm, was it? Where are you calling from?'

He told her where he was and what had happened.

'Don't you ever ask me to be your wing woman again,' she said. 'When I couldn't reach you, I thought I was going to have a heart attack. When are you coming back?'

'Not sure. I'll let you know as soon as I can.'

'Alright. Come straight to my place.'

They finished on that note. Tarrant then asked Ralph to wait in another interview room while he raised Ainsworth. Ralph spent an hour or more in there, kicking his heels and wondering what was going to happen next. Then the door opened and DC Ainsworth appeared, dressed more casually than usual in jeans and a button-down shirt.

'Just what have you been up to now, Mr de Malmanche?' was his opening remark.

'I told …'

Ainsworth held up a restraining hand. 'You can show me yourself. We're going for a drive. PC Tarrant told me that you recorded something. Got it with you?'

Ralph dug the pen out of his pocket. 'The cable connecting it to a PC is in my car,' he said.

'A pen,' said Ainsworth. 'And GPS trackers. Becoming quite the private detective, aren't we?'

'I've done nothing illegal.'

Ainsworth's broad young face was a mixture of world-weary tolerance and amusement. 'Not that I'm aware of. I'll borrow a laptop and you can play this recording to me when we get out there.'

They returned to the shed in Ainsworth's unmarked vehicle. There was a forensics van there by this time, and the area around the shed was now taped off. Ainsworth went inside to have a look around while Ralph retrieved the cable he'd mentioned. They reconvened back in Ainsworth's car.

'Some interesting ingredients in there,' said Ainsworth. 'If you mix aluminium powder with iron oxide, you get thermite. Ignite the thermite with a magnesium strip and it burns at around 2,000 degrees Celsius. If you were to put a container of burning thermite over a fish bowl of petrol, then once the container burned through you'd get a nice big explosion and a fireball. Definitely a bomb making factory in there. Ties in with what was found in the ruins of the Aylsham houses, and Mr Kingsley's house.'

'What about the explosion at the demonstration?'

'That was more sophisticated. A timer device was used, and some other chemicals.'

'I think the shotgun in there was used to kill Fabian Kingsley,' said Ralph. 'What I recorded backs it up.'

'Play it for me then.'

They connected the pen up to the laptop and listened to it all.

'Is it admissible in court?' Ralph asked.

'Maybe. If the judge thinks it's in the interests of justice. We'll also run ballistics tests on the shotgun and see what that produces.'

'And if it's the weapon that killed Kingsley?'

Ainsworth smiled. 'If we can tie it to Mr Ramsey, then I'd say you're off the hook. But let's not get ahead of ourselves.'

'What about what David Stone said about Sarah? It's not just him, either. There were three other people there that night.'

'Yes, he says a lot on the recording about that night. I'll interview both those men when we get back to Wells. That's all I can tell you right now.'

'OK. Can I go now?'

'Follow me back to the station in your car. I'll take a statement from you, and then you can go.'

Once Stone's and Ramsey's vehicles had been shifted, Ralph was able to get out. He drove back to the police station, gave his statement, and was free to go. Ainsworth let him take the GPS trackers with him, but kept the pen as evidence. Once Ralph was out of Wells, he drove straight to Chloe's place as agreed. She opened the door and practically dragged him inside.

'Thank god you're OK,' she said. 'Come into the lounge.'

Angela and Zoe were home by now. He had to repeat everything that had happened out at Holkham for their benefit, while Chloe ordered a pizza for delivery and opened a bottle of wine.

'You solved it,' said Zoe, when he'd finished. 'You found out what happened with Sarah and you also know who killed this Kingsley guy. Maybe you should be doing this for a living.'

'It's one thing to know it and another to prove it,' said Ralph. 'As for doing it professionally …'

'What about the two men who attacked Chloe?' said Angela. 'Did the detective say anything about them?'

'I forgot all about them. We'll find out more next Thursday. Chloe and I have to identify them then.'

They drank wine until the pizza arrived, which meant opening a second bottle to accompany the meal. It had turned into a celebratory evening, and although Ralph felt some satisfaction about finally getting answers about Sarah's death, it was a bittersweet feeling. Knowing what had happened wasn't going to bring her back, and celebrating like this might just be a little premature as far as justice being done was concerned. He couldn't help wondering if Stone and Ramsey might somehow worm their way out of it.

He kept that all to himself, and instead allowed himself the pleasure of the company of two women he'd grown to like, and a third that he now knew he'd fallen head over heels for. They were all still a bit high after the suspension of work out at the wood, too, which added some boisterousness to the occasion. But around 11 p.m., Ralph thought he should be going.

'I should make a move,' he said.

'You can't go,' said Zoe. 'You can't drive, you're pissed.'

'I am not.'

Chloe stepped in. 'Stay here tonight.'

'You sure that's OK?'

Zoe laughed. 'Just don't make too much noise, OK?'

'Second that,' said Angela.

'Ignore these people,' said Chloe, snuggling up to him. 'Will you stay?'

'Of course I will.'

It was decided. On the strength of that a third bottle was opened, and they stayed up talking late into the night.

Chapter 26

In the course of their rapid enquiries, the police learned that the shed near Holkham, where Ralph had nearly met his end, had been rented to David Stone by a farmer. The farmer, who owned the shed and the land adjoining it, lived miles away in Suffolk. He had advertised the shed as a storage facility, but never visited the place, and had no idea what was being stored there.

David Stone was charged with possession of bomb-making material, and arson. They added manslaughter to those charges when the Crown Prosecution Service reviewed the evidence and advised the police that Ralph's recording was almost certainly admissible in a court of law. Given the seriousness of the charges, Stone was remanded in custody.

When the shotgun was tested positive by ballistics as the weapon that had killed Fabian Kingsley, and checks revealed that it was owned by one Benedict Ramsey, he was indicted for murder. He, too, was remanded in custody pending trial.

Stone had said nothing so far about the other men who'd gone out to Foxdown Wood with him on the night of Sarah's fall. But there was a good chance he'd reveal their identities when he realised the length of sentence he was looking at, and the prospect of having it reduced if he cooperated. What did come to light was the nature of Stone's grievance against Kingsley, which had fuelled his willingness to help Ben Ramsey. Stone Security had once had a contract with Kingsley Developments to protect his building sites, in just the same way as they now protected those belonging to Ramsey. The Kingsley contract had been deemed null and void on some legal technicality by Fabian, and Stone had been involved in expensive litigation about it ever since. Kingsley Developments owed him close to £200,000.

A week had passed since Ralph's visit to Holkham. In that time, Brett had arrived by train from London so he could report with Ralph to the police station in Norwich as part of their conditional bail requirement. He'd been amazed to learn about developments in his absence, and took Ralph out for celebratory drinks at the Unthank Arms. If he thought Ralph seemed a little underwhelmed by how things had turned out, he didn't comment on it. Brett had another contract job by now, which involved hacking a travel agent's website. That meant he needed to be back in London, because the hacking was being done on site. He took the train back on the Thursday morning.

Ralph and Chloe reported to the Norwich police station for their video identification parade appointment that Thursday afternoon. They did their identifications separately. Two policemen and a defence solicitor were present when first Chloe, and then Ralph, watched a video on a computer monitor. There were nine people on the video. They were shown one after the other, first looking straight at the camera, and then turning their heads to left and right.

It was like watching a moving mugshot show. The two bearded bastards, as Ralph couldn't stop thinking of them, were identified by both him and Chloe as the men who'd abducted him and assaulted her.

Ainsworth told Ralph that these two men had admitted to a business relationship with Fabian Kingsley, and had been working on his behalf. At one time, they'd been labourers on one of Kingsley's building sites. They'd been fired by the foreman for brawling on the job. They had records for similar offences, usually committed during drunken confrontations in local pubs. Fabian had bought them a drink in one of those pubs and asked them to work for him, as and when he needed them. As enforcers. Given the amount of money on offer, they were happy to accept. In all probability, they would spend up to five years in prison for what they'd done to Ralph and Chloe.

'Did you ever speak to Clarissa again about Roz Kingsley?' Ralph asked Ainsworth. 'About moving her body that night?'

'After the last time? No. She won't change her story. The man who did it is no longer with us, and the only evidence we have is Sarah's diary, which I'm 99.9% sure we'll never be able to use in court.'

Fabian Kingsley was buried on the Friday. Ralph had half-toyed with the idea of going to his funeral. He'd never liked the man, but he'd always had this niggling feeling in the back of his mind that he'd only ever seen the worst part of Fabian Kingsley. Once, not so long ago, Sarah had experienced the better side of his character, and had been seduced by it, if only for a short time. And Kingsley hadn't forgotten about their relationship, no matter how badly it had turned out in the end. He'd come to Sarah's funeral to pay his respects, which said to Ralph that the man wasn't entirely devoid of the better human emotions. But when he thought about how Kingsley was prepared to condone beating up women, and even driving one to suicide, he had to conclude that maybe Sarah had had a lapse of judgement. He stayed away from the funeral.

With Kingsley's death came the uncertainty surrounding his company. It was up to the shareholders to appoint a new director, and in the case of Kingsley Developments, there were only two shareholders; Kingsley and his accountant. A new director was appointed from among the former employees, some of whom had been with Fabian from the beginning. The new director was a woman by the name of Teresa Mullins. Ralph found out about the new appointment when he had a phone call from Chloe. Ms Mullins had contacted her via the Facebook page, on the Monday following Kingsley's funeral.

'You'll never guess what's happened,' said Chloe, who seemed to be bubbling over with excitement about it, whatever it was.

'Let's see ... I give up.'

'Kingsley Developments appointed a new director, a woman. She contacted me because she wants to talk to the company in London that made the offer for Foxdown Wood. If it's still on the table, she wants to accept it! Isn't that brilliant?'

Her tone was infectious and he laughed. 'That *is* brilliant. But what will the new owners do with it?'

'Well, they put a percentage of their profits into environmental projects and last time I heard, they wanted to turn it into a woodland for endangered species. They'll introduce butterflies and birds, maybe ...'

'And bats. Gotta have bats.'

'Yes! Bats! Anyway, I've given her the details, so now we'll just wait and see. But I think it's going to be a done deal.'

Which is what it proved to be, a few weeks later. Ralph wondered what would happen to Karl and Bettina now that this particular battle to save the world had been fought and won. He thought about phoning Bettina and asking her, assuming she had the phone turned on this time, but decided against it. They had probably left Norfolk already, hurrying on the way to their next battleground. When he thought about what tiny Foxdown Wood represented in the scheme of things, it seemed insignificant. He still believed that by the time people finally woke up to what they were doing to contribute to their own extinction, it would already be too late. Did that make him a fatalist? Then he remembered what Chloe had said about standing up again and again until people finally did wake up. Maybe people like Karl and Bettina were tilting at windmills, but that didn't mean the windmills shouldn't be tilted at. Were they crazy? A brilliant innovator of recent times had always maintained that it was the crazy ones who changed the world. Someone had to do it, that was for sure. And he respected them for trying.

He thought he ought to get a job, too. Daisy's money had a way to run, but it was time to get off his butt and do something. Preferably before he and Brett were convicted of assault, and it showed up when prospective employers ran background checks of their own. He would have to go back to coding, which was fine, he supposed. He could go online and find any number of jobsites that listed opportunities in that realm. He just had to get his curriculum vitae together and dream up something to tell employers about what he'd been doing since his last job. 'Solving the death of my sister' might be a great talking point at interviews, but it was unlikely to get him a job offer.

They had a trial date by now, in November. He'd spoken to Helen Strauss about it, and she thought that given the fact it was a first-time offence, they would probably get off with community service. She intended to mention the attacks that Kingsley had ordered on Brett, Ralph, and Chloe at the trial, even if provocation wasn't officially a defence for an assault charge. She rang him first week of October.

'Mr de Malmanche? I've received a letter from the police regarding your case.'

'Oh, what does it say?'

'They've dropped the charges.'

'What? Why?'

'Don't sound so offended. They don't give a reason. Both you and Mr Saunders have no charges to face. You should be getting a letter from them to that effect very soon.'

Ralph was a bit lost for words.

'Mr de Malmanche? You there?'

'Yes. That's great. I'm not offended. But why do you think they've dropped the charges?'

'Well, if I'm speculating, I'd say it was something to do with your efforts in solving the murder of Mr Kingsley, and the arson attacks. It doesn't justify what you did to him when you attacked him, by the way …'

'No, I get that. That's great news, I'll let Brett know. Send me your bill.'

He began settling into what was effectively his new life. He phoned his mother and told her what had happened since the funeral. She was pleased to know that the people responsible for Sarah's death had been apprehended, but like him, it was no substitute for the loss of her daughter. He said he'd join them in

France for Christmas, an offer that came out of his mouth before he knew what he was saying. When he heard how quietly delighted Daisy was to hear it, he was surprised to realise that he didn't regret making it.

Chloe spent a lot of time with him now, too. He had no idea how their relationship would turn out, just that he wanted to give it a shot. He'd once thought the same thing about Holly, and that hadn't ended well. But if he was brutally honest, a lot of that had been down to him. He wasn't going to make those same mistakes again.

And he thought about life without Sarah, his twin sister, who he'd assumed would always be there. Never more than a thought away, or a phone call, or a drive up the A11. The flat was full of reminders of her, she would always be around. It was Ralph's belief that the dead never really left you, unless you abandoned them by not thinking about them anymore. And with Sarah, that just wasn't going to happen. She wasn't going anywhere.

Printed in Great Britain
by Amazon